Close Encounters of the Urban Kind

CLOSE ENCOUNTERS OF THE URBAN KIND

Edited by Jennifer Brozek

AN APEX PUBLICATIONS BOOK
LEXINGTON, KENTUCKY

This collection is a work of fiction. All of the characters and events portrayed in these stories are either fictitious or are used fictitiously.

Close Encounters of the Urban Kind

Cover Art "Lights in the Sky" © 2010 by Alina Pete
Cover design by Justin Stewart

"Lollo," © 2010, 2010, Martin Livings; "Green Tears on Black Velvet," © 2010, Jeff Soesbe; "Racing Lights," © 2010, Erik Scott de Bie; "Waterheads," © 2010, Ivan Ewert; "The Fingernail Test," © 2010, Bev Vincent; "Headlights," © 2010, Jennifer Pelland; "Shiny Eyes," © 2010, Jonathan McKinney; "The Invitation," © 2010, Carole Johnstone; "Frames of Reference," © 2010, Nathan Crowder; "Late Night Snack," © 2010, Robert Farnsworth; "Two Out, Wendigo," © 2010, Rosemary Jones; "The Hippie Monster of Eel River," © 2010, Shannon Page; "Roadkill," © 2010, Rick Silva; "End of Life," © 2010, Richard Lee Byers; "Tea Cups & Saucers," © 2010, Ramsey Lundock; "Gloomy Sunday," © 2010, Eddy Webb; "Mastihooba," © 2010, Joshua Palmatier; "I Am Sorry for So Rarely Talking to Strangers," © 2010, Alma Alexander; "Dead Letter Drop," © 2010, Pete Kempshall; "It Came From the Backseat," © 2010, 2010, Eric R. Lowther

All rights reserved

Apex Publications, LLC
www.apexbookcompany.com

ISBN TPB: 978-0-9821596-9-9

TABLE OF CONTENTS

Foreword – *vii*
Jennifer Brozek

Lollo – 1
Martin Livings

Green Tears on Black Velvet – 19
Jeff Soesbe

Racing Lights – 35
Erik Scott de Bie

Waterheads – 48
Ivan Ewert

The Fingernail Test – 58
Bev Vincent

Headlights – 65
Jennifer Pelland

Shiny Eyes – 76
Jonathan McKinney

The Invitation – 82
Carole Johnstone

Frames of Reference – 93
Nathan Crowder

Late Night Snack – 107
Robert Farnsworth

Two Out, Wendigo – 120
Rosemary Jones

TABLE OF CONTENTS, CONT.

The Hippie Monster of Eel River – 132
Shannon Page

Roadkill – 144
Rick Silva

End of Life – 151
Richard Lee Byers

Tea Cups and Saucers – 159
Ramsey Lundock

Gloomy Sunday – 169
Eddy Webb

Mastihooba – 183
Joshua Palmatier

I Am Sorry for So Rarely Talking to Strangers – 202
Alma Alexander

Dead Letter Drop – 215
Pete Kempshall

It Came From the Backseat – 227
Eric R. Lowther

Author Biographies – 245

Foreword

Close Encounters of the Urban Kind is a journey of fear and discovery.

When I set out to create an anthology, I have a theme in mind but I must allow the stories themselves to help put the overall arcing storyline together. That way, the anthology becomes more than the sum of its parts. This is always my goal.

In *Close Encounters of the Urban Kind*, I decided I wanted the stories to tell a journey of discovery. In the beginning, the stories are nothing more than encounters with the unknown. They are where humans meet urban legends and aliens for the first time. There are no explanations given as to why anything happens. Alien encounter stories and urban legends are often filled with speculation but no concrete facts on why the monster (or the alien) is doing what it is doing.

However, as the audience of such tales grows and grows up, the encounter itself is not enough. The question of "why?" becomes as important as what happens. The further along the reader gets in this anthology, the more the stories hint at or explain why the encounter is happening. I know some readers will prefer the beginning part of the anthology where everything is a mystery, others the middle where only a hint of why what is happening is revealed and still others will prefer the ending where as much of the "why" is revealed as it can be without ruining the story itself.

When I set out to create *Close Encounters of the Urban Kind*, I knew I wanted stories that where specifically "encounters" and not an established relationship between the alien and the human who was encountering them. Though, I did allow for relationships to grow in the latter part of the anthology as more explanation of what was happening was revealed. In this case, it allowed the anthology to grow along with the reader's familiarity with the type of story I chose for the book.

At the end of every story, the author have an afterword to speak about which urban legend they chose and why. As an author myself, I appreciate understanding how another author comes into writing the story they wrote. It is a way of asking "Where do you get your ideas?" Instead of an off-the-cuff answer, we get to peek behind the curtain and to see a little bit of the methodology of each of the twenty different authors. There are twenty different answers and all of them are fascinating.

Close Encounters of the Urban Kind is my homage to the campfire stories of aliens and monsters and mysteries told in the dead of night to chill and thrill those who listen…and then look up into the night sky and wonder.

Jennifer Brozek
February 2010

Lollo

Martin Livings

"Okay, rugrats," Jenny said, as the credits of the animated film rolled up the television screen for about the eighth time that evening. "Time for bed."

Sofia was sitting up on the couch, lost in the movie. She was nearly six, as she'd told Jenny any number of times in the last few hours, and had her mother's straight, dark hair, currently tied in purple ribbons, and dark almond eyes. She was probably going to be a stunner in about ten years, when she was closer to Jenny's age. Domenic, who was watching the television upside down with his legs up on the couch, was the younger brother, just turned four; he had his father's pale blue eyes and a permanently curious expression. He didn't talk much. He didn't have to; Sofia talked enough for the both of them. They both looked over at Jenny with pleading eyes.

"Once more?" Sofia begged. "Just once more?"

Jenny laughed, "That's what you said three times ago, kiddo." She'd never babysat before, but the Rowes were nice people, good friends of her own parents, and needed her help. And they had a big plasma television, so that was definitely a bonus.

"*Pleeeeeeeeease?*" Sofia turned on the charm, cranked it up to eleven. It probably would have worked too, if Jenny hadn't already been subjected to it more than once that evening.

"I promised your mum I'd have you in bed by eight," she reminded them. "It's already past nine. If she finds out..."

"She won't," Sofia said. "We won't tell."

"Go on," Jenny insisted. "Go brush your teeth and get into bed, the pair of you."

The little girl sighed, as if the weight of the world had been laid on her tiny shoulders. She got up off the couch with the reluctance of a condemned man being led to his gallows. As she did, she pushed Domenic's legs, and the boy fell over sideways onto the floor. He bounced to his feet, still smiling. The two looked at Jenny one last time, as if hoping for clemency, a stay of execution.

"*Now*," she mock-growled, trying not to smile.

The children trudged from the lounge room. "Deafie," Sofia muttered as she passed.

"I heard that," Jenny shot back.

"Good!" Sofia stuck her tongue out at Jenny then ran out of the room. Domenic just stood there, looking up at Jenny with those curious eyes. No, she realized, not at her, not quite. At her left ear.

"That's my hearing aid, Domenic," she explained. "You've seen it before. It helps me hear properly."

"Her ears are broken!" Sofia declared from the hallway. Domenic frowned, and raised his hands to his own ears, eyebrows raised.

"No," Jenny told him, "my ears aren't broken, not really. It's my inner ears that don't work properly. You know, inside my head. But I can hear a little in this ear," she said, and pointed at her left ear. "Hence the hearing aid," she finished with a smile.

"*Deafie!*" Sofia yelled, still in the hallway.

"Bathroom," Jenny called back. "Teeth. Pajamas. Bed. Now."

Domenic grinned, then ran into the hallway after his sister.

Jenny stretched, and changed the television channel. There was some kind of nature documentary on, which she paid no attention to whatsoever. Really, this babysitting thing wasn't so hard. Especially when the kids were fairly good, like Sofia and Domenic were. They could most likely just about take care of themselves. She turned the volume of the TV down, turned her hearing aid up and listened.

"Guys," she called, "I can't hear you brushing your teeth!"

There was a long pause, then the sound of water running, toothbrushes being used. Jenny smiled, turned her hearing aid back down to normal, and decided to give them a few minutes, let them get into their pajamas and into bed, then she'd go and read them some stories. Just a few minutes. She turned her attention to the television, brought the volume back up.

"*...when studying the natural world, it is vital to obtain as many specimens* *as possible, particularly unusual ones. As important as the ordinary creatures of the world are, it's the exceptions that most often prove the rule..."*

"Jenny?" A small voice said near her ear.

Jenny almost yelped in surprise. She turned to find Sofia and Domenic standing next to the couch, almost identical worried expressions on their tiny faces. They'd never looked so much like brother and sister as they did at that moment.

"What is it, guys?" Jenny asked. Then she frowned. "Are you trying to get out of going to bed?"

Domenic nodded, but Sofia shook her head. "Dom is scared," she said. "He's scared of the clown doll. Can you cover it up please?"

Jenny sighed, "Can't you do it for him, Sofia?"

She shook her head.

"Why not?"

Sofia didn't answer that, not straight away. She looked down, at her feet. Then she mumbled something.

"Pardon?"

Sofia looked up, and there were tears in her eyes, "I'm scared, too," she murmured.

"Oh, honey," Jenny replied. She was an only child herself, and didn't have much experience with little kids. Sometimes she forgot how young Sofia was, how young they both were. She reached out and gave them both a quick hug, "I'm so sorry. I'll go and do it."

She got to her feet and walked towards the hallway. After a few steps, she turned. The children were still standing next to the sofa, watching her go, ignoring the chattering of the television behind them.

"Are you coming?" she asked them.

They both shook their heads in unison.

"Okay," she said, "I'll be right back."

The hallway wasn't long, but the light was turned off and Jenny didn't know where the switch was. She hadn't been in this house very often, and had found it embarrassingly difficult to find the toilet earlier in the evening. Luckily Domenic had shown her where it was. Now she was on her own. She passed the laundry door on her left and the master bedroom on the right, then the study and a cupboard, and finally came to the kids' bedroom, just opposite the family bathroom. The light was on in the room, and she stepped inside.

The room was a typical children's room. The wallpaper was bright pink; obviously Sofia had been the first to be in here. Her bed was on one side of the room, and Domenic's was on the other. Each had toys piled up on them, and more toys stuffed underneath. There was a single pine wardrobe, painted white, and a large padded box beneath the window, between the two beds.

Sitting on that box was the clown doll.

It was big, bigger than either of the kids, and dressed in a pure white unitard. Across its chest were letters, scrawled in feathery lower case writing:

Lollo

It had black boots and black gloves, both oversized for its body. Its hat was one of those old-fashioned jester's hats, three-pointed and white, with black pom-poms on the end. Its smile was wide and black as well, as were its eyes. In fact, the whole clown seemed to be black-and-white, like on old photograph.

Except for its round bulbous nose. No, that wasn't black or white. It was bright red, fire-truck red. Blood red.

Jenny had to admit, the doll was kind of creepy. She'd never had the fear of clowns that so many kids seemed to, and a lot of adults as well apparently, but this one was pretty horrible. She wondered why the Rowes had ever bought it. Maybe they won it at a carnival or something, throwing balls at milk bottles or the like.

She glared at the doll. "You, Lollo," she said, just to hear the sound of her voice, "are one ugly clown." She looked around the room for something to cover it up with. Bunched up at the end of one of the beds was a threadbare old blue blanket. She grabbed it and opened it up, then approached the doll. It gazed at her, impassive.

"Bedtime," she told it, and threw the blanket over it. It settled over its contours, hung on the points of its hat. Jenny looked at it for a moment longer, then nodded. Good enough.

She went back to the lounge room. The kids were on the couch now, but still not watching the television. They watched her approach, their eyes still skittish.

"All done," she declared, and clapped her hands. "No more scary doll. Now it's bedtime. Come on."

It took some coaxing to get the kids back into their bedroom. Their gazes kept flitting back to the shape on the toy box, all covered in the blue blanket now. Domenic still looked like he was going to cry.

"Okay, into your pajamas now," Jenny said in her most authoritative voice. "Then into bed, and I'll read you a story."

"Two stories?" Sofia asked. She seemed so different from before, less confident.

"Okay, two stories," she conceded.

"Jenny?" Again, Sofia's voice was tiny.

"Yes?"

"Will you sleep with us tonight? Please?"

Jenny didn't know how to answer that. She opened her mouth to respond, hoping that something would come to her.

In the kitchen, the telephone rang.

"Hold that thought, kidlet," she said, and bopped Sofia on the nose with her finger. "I'll be right back."

She left the bedroom and jogged down the hall, back to the lounge room and the kitchen beyond. The phone was mounted on the wall next to the fridge. She picked it up.

"Hello?"

"Hi, Jenny? It's Rachel."

"Hi, Mrs. Rowe," Jenny replied automatically. She wasn't used to calling adults by their first names, even though she was virtually an adult herself. It was hard to break the habit of a lifetime. "How's Tom?"

"Oh, Tom's much better today, thanks," Mrs. Rowe answered. "He's keeping some food down now, and the doctors say he should be out in a week or so."

"Thank goodness," Jenny said. "He looked terrible when we visited last week."

"I know," Mrs. Rowe said, and Jenny heard the quiver in her voice. There was a brief pause. "Anyway, I was just ringing to make sure the kids got to bed alright."

"Oh yes, they went to bed at eight on the dot, just as you said," Jenny lied. "They've been little angels."

"I'm sure that's an exaggeration," Mrs. Rowe laughed.

"No, really, they've been great," Jenny insisted. "There was a small drama, with Domenic being scared of that clown doll in their room, but I sorted that out."

There was a long silence. Jenny wondered if they'd been disconnected. She was about to speak again when Mrs. Rowe's voice returned to the line.

"What clown doll?"

"The one sitting on the toy box," Jenny replied. "You know. Lollo."

"Jenny," Mrs. Rowe said, her voice filled with confusion, "darling, we don't have a clown doll."

"What?" Jenny asked, her voice breaking a little. "What do you mean?"

There was no response. It took Jenny a few seconds to realize that the line was dead. She tried the phone a few times, but could not get a dial tone. A horrible feeling snaked down her spine to her stomach. She put the phone back on its cradle and turned to the lounge room, and to the hallway beyond. To the kids' bedroom at the far end.

"We don't have a clown doll."

As she hurried down through the lounge and into the hall, she heard the television still blathering away.

"…when Charles Darwin first visited the Galapagos Islands, he collected as many biological samples as he could, living and dead, despite the space restrictions he faced aboard the Beagle…"

Jenny paid no attention to it. All she could see was the long, dark hallway in front of her, and the rectangle of light at the end. All she could hear was her heart pounding in her chest, and echoes of the words on the phone, so simple, so awful.

"We don't have a…"

By the time she reached the door, she was actually running. She burst into the room, not sure of what she'd find, but sure it would be something horrible, something she should have prevented. Something.

The kids were still sitting patiently on their beds, waiting for her to come back. And, on the toy box, the blanket still covered the…

"…clown doll."

"Jenny?" Sofia asked, "What's wrong?"

Jenny looked at the kids, forced herself to smile. "Nothing," she said, "nothing at all. Just a little change of plans." She kept her gaze on Sofia and Domenic, away from the blue blanket, and what was underneath it. "I just talked to your mum, and she said we could have a sleep-over at my house."

"Really?" Sofia's face lit up. Domenic still looked worried. His eyes kept drifting to the lump underneath the blanket. To Lollo.

Jenny nodded, "So, c'mon, let's go." She started to lead them from the room.

"Buddy boo!" Domenic said suddenly.

Jenny looked at him. "What?"

"Buddy boo!" he repeated.

"He wants his Buddy boo," Sofia said. "His blanket."

"What blanket?" Jenny asked. But she already knew. She looked at Domenic, at his eyes. They were fixed on the blue blanket on the toy box. She sighed.

"Okay," she said, "I'll get the Buddy boo, and then we're out of here. Deal?"

The kids both nodded.

She turned and faced the toy box, watched it for a moment or two, keeping a close eye for any movement. *That's so stupid*, she chastised herself, but she could not shake the thought. There was nothing, though. It was as still as a statue. Or a doll, for that matter. She stepped forward, reached out, and grasped the top of the blanket. She pulled.

It came off easily, exposing the black and white clown doll. Jenny found it even creepier now, since the phone conversation with Mrs. Rowe. There had to be a rational explanation for it, though. The kids might have had it for a long time, and their mother had forgotten about it. Maybe they dragged it out especially to scare Jenny. But their faces… they were too young to pretend to be so frightened. No, this doll did not belong to them. Someone must have put it there.

Which meant someone else had been in the house. And maybe that someone was still there somewhere. So the doll was not the threat, not by a long shot, no matter how creepy it seemed.

Something about the clown caught her eye, though, another color within the monochrome. A glitter of blue on one of its puffy, black, three-fingered hands. She leant in to look closer. Between its finger and thumb was a wisp of thread, like a spider web with tiny beads of sapphire dew along its length. She reached out a finger to touch it.

Something plopped into the gloved palm of the clown, something small and round and pink. It rolled back and forth a little. On one side was a hard shell, which was metallic purple. The color seemed familiar to Jenny. It was the same purple as…

The same purple as Jenny's nail polish.

She looked from the object in the clown's palm to her own hand. Her fingertip had been sliced clean off.

Jenny just stared at her finger, her breath caught in her throat. Her head buzzed, like her hearing aid was picking up static. There was no blood, no pain. The tip was just…*gone*, leaving a circle of bright red flesh, and inside that, white bone, perfect white. It looked like a cut tree, as if she could tell her age by counting the rings. Her eyes moved from her finger to the black gloved palm of the clown doll, where her severed fingertip still lay, rocking back and forth a little. She watched it for what felt like a long time, mesmerized by the motion, unable to believe what she was seeing.

Then, slowly, the dolls bloated fingers curled shut around Jenny's shorn flesh.

Jenny shrieked and stumbled backwards, away from the clown doll, or whatever the hell it was. Away from Lollo. The kids cried out as well, startled by Jenny's sudden reaction. They had not seen what happened; Jenny had stood between them and the doll specifically, an attempt to be protective. She turned and faced them now, and the look on her pale face terrified them even more. Sofia burst into hysterical tears, and Domenic, Domenic just looked shell-shocked, moist eyes and mouth wide open, face white.

Jenny took a deep, shuddering breath. "Come on," she urged, trying to keep her voice calm. It was difficult, near impossible. She gathered the children up in her arms, one under each, and lifted them clear of the floor with a strength she never knew she possessed. She dashed from the room into the hallway, took a few more steps, then skidded to a halt and put the children down again. Sofia was still bawling; the high-pitched wails echoed in the confines of the hallway. Domenic was still silent, though, which was somehow worse.

Jenny turned back to the bedroom. She did not look inside, did not dare. Instead, she reached out and slammed the door shut. The hallway fell into gloom; the only light was coming from the other end, the lounge room. It looked a long, long way away.

"Okay," she whispered, feeling the tremor in her voice deep down in her chest. Sofia was still crying, but the tears were less now, the howls a little softer. Jenny tried again. "Shh, Sofia," she hushed, "it's okay, it's okay. It's okay."

Sofia went quiet all at once, like a button had been pressed. She looked at Jenny with big, traumatized eyes. A length of snot hung from her nose, swung to and fro like a translucent yellow pendulum.

"Okay," Jenny said again, "Sofia, Domenic, I need you guys to be brave for me now, okay? I need you to go to the lounge room…"

"No!" Sofia yelled. She clung to Jenny's leg desperately. Her tears started to flow again.

"Please, Sofia," Jenny begged, trying hard not to cry herself. "You have to go with Domenic, take him to the lounge room. He needs you now."

"What about you?" Sofia sobbed.

"I'll be right behind you," Jenny promised. "I just have to make sure…" She stopped, unable to finish the sentence, knowing how crazy it would sound. *I have to make sure the door stays shut until you're both safe. To make sure Lollo's not right behind us, reaching out with its spider web gloves that cut like a hot wire through butter.* Her fingertip throbbed with the thought, her missing fingertip. It hurt as if it was still attached, as if it was on the end of her finger, not in some horrible clown doll's closed hand. That image still hovered in her eyes, those fingers closing up, swallowing part of her. And the way they *moved*; curled, not bent, like a startled millipede making itself into a ball.

She pushed these thoughts from her head, forced herself out of the round-and-round of them. The kids were still looking up at her. "I'll be right behind you," she repeated. "Now go! Scoot!" She pushed them as gently as she dared, down the hall, away from her, away from their bedroom. Away from the clown doll. Away from Lollo. She held the bedroom door handle with one hand, certain that at any moment it would start to turn, slowly but forcefully. "Go!"

They went, scurried down the hallway with quick, scared little steps. It only took them a few seconds to get to the lounge room, but it felt like forever to Jenny. When they reached the lit doorway, they stopped and turned back to her. Sofia was holding Domenic's hand, tightly by the look of it. They both looked utterly terrified.

"Well done," she called to them, and tried to smile. She did not entirely succeed; it felt more like a grimace, tight and uncomfortable on her face, but it was the best she could manage. She turned back to the bedroom door, which she still held shut tightly. Her hand was cramping. There had not been any movement, which freaked her out even more. She could not shake the feeling that the doll was right on the other side of the door, white head pressed against the wood, listening closely to everything that was happening. She knew she had to let go of the handle, join the children in the lounge room, but her fingers simply refused to loosen their death grip.

"Come on," she muttered through clenched teeth. "Come on. Come on!"

She let go of the knob and staggered back a few steps away from the door. It stayed closed. She backed down the hallway, never taking her eyes off that door, ready for anything, any movement, a turn or rattle of the knob, a crack of light as the door opened. Ready to run like hell. The door did not open, though. The knob remained still. Slowly, as she retreated, the light around her brightened, until she was in the entrance to the lounge room, Sofia and Domenic by her side.

She looked down at them. "See?" she asked them as lightly as she could manage. "Piece of cake."

They both threw their arms around her legs, and she knelt down and hugged them both close to her. But her eyes, her eyes inevitably drifted back down the hallway, to the closed bedroom door.

Was that a noise? A rattle? A squeak?

"Come on," she said to the kids, and got to her feet. Her legs were shaking. "It's time to go."

"Buddy boo?" Domenic asked softly.

Jenny scarcely restrained herself from cursing out loud. She'd dropped the blanket when she'd lost her fingertip. The Buddy boo was in the bedroom. With Lollo. "I'm so sorry, Domenic," she told him, "you'll have to do without it, just this once."

Domenic's face crumbled, became a portrait of utter devastation. His bottom lip quivered, his eyes welled with tears.

"Don't be such a baby, Dom," Sofia chastised him, her voice haughty and mature beyond her years. It was as if she had not been crying her own eyes out just minutes earlier. "We don't need your Buddy boo. We have Jenny. She'll protect us."

The boy brightened at this. He gazed up at Jenny.

I wish I had their confidence in me, she thought, but she nodded anyway. "That's right. Now let's get out of here."

She led the kids through the lounge room, where the documentary continued to play on the television.

"*...when a cub is captured, to be raised in captivity for study, often the mother bear will be understandably protective. The zoologists will do their best not to hurt the creature, but sometimes, regrettably, it's a matter of kill or be killed...*"

They reached the front door, and Jenny turned the handle. The heavy door did not move. She tried to open it, but the deadbolt was in place, and locked with a key.

"The kitchen," she muttered. She'd been told that the keys were on a board in the kitchen, next to the refrigerator, near the phone. She remembered seeing them there, in fact, while she'd talked on the phone with Mrs. Rowe. Was that only minutes ago? It seemed like a lot longer.

They'd taken three steps towards the kitchen when the lights went out. Sofia screamed, and Jenny very nearly joined her. They froze in the darkness. No, not quite darkness; the television was still on, sending flickering colorful light across the room, so the power wasn't completely out, just the lights. Jenny bent over and grabbed Sofia's hand. She shrieked again.

"Shh," she told the girl, "it's only me. It's Jenny." She took a deep breath. "Sofia, can you hold Domenic's hand for a moment? I need to go to the kitchen and get the keys, so we can get out of here."

"Please don't leave," Sofia sniffled. She clung tight to Jenny's hand.

"I won't be out of sight, I promise," Jenny told her. "Just stay here, just for a minute. Then I'll be back, and we'll go to my house, okay?"

"Jenny?" Sofia asked.

"What?"

"Are there any clowns in your house?"

Jenny's reflexive laugh was more than a little hysterical. She regained control. "No, honey," she replied. "Not a single one."

Sofia grasped Jenny's hand for a moment longer, then let go. "Take my hand, Dom," she said to her brother, who nodded and took it.

Without hesitating, Jenny dashed for the kitchen. She knew exactly where she was going, despite the gloom, remembered it as clear as day. Straight in, to the right, around the cupboard. There was the fridge, humming to itself, oblivious to everything. Next to that, the phone, and then the pretty wooden board, painted with flowers. It had a row of little brass hooks on it, but Jenny knew that only one had anything on it, the left-most one, with its precious ring of keys. She reached out in the darkness and grabbed them.

All her fingers found was the cold metal of the hook. There were no keys.

"*Sometimes,*" the television said calmly from the next room, "*when tracking or capturing animals, it's necessary to construct a hide. This is designed* to blend in with its surroundings, to allow scientists to observe animals in their natural surroundings, to wait for the perfect moment…"

Panic rose up in her. Her hands shook as she tried the other hooks, but they were empty too. In desperation, she got to her hands and knees, in case the keys had somehow fallen to the floor, but there was nothing there. The keys were gone.

"Oh, Jesus," Jenny sobbed under her breath. She sat down on the kitchen floor, suddenly more exhausted than she'd ever been in her life. All she wanted to do was go to sleep. It would be so easy, just close her eyes and…

"Jenny?" Sofia's frightened voice from the next room brought Jenny back to herself. She shook her head to clear it, tried to think straight. There was a back door in the laundry, but knowing Mrs. Rowe, that would be locked and dead-bolted too. *Think!* Jenny ordered herself. *Think! Just…*

The darkness became total, as the television turned off. A sudden shocking silence filled the house.

Then, in the blackness, a little girl's scream.

"Sofia!" Jenny yelled. She scrambled to her feet in the dark, ran in the general direction of the lounge room. Her shoulder caught on a cupboard, spun her around a bit, and sharp pain lanced through her neck. She ignored it, kept running. "Sofia!"

A deep thrumming noise filled the air around her as she stumbled blind into the lounge room, soft at first, but quickly getting louder. It buzzed in her hearing aid painfully, made her whole body vibrate. Her hands and face became numb, her eyelids grew heavy. She fell to her knees, and something jabbed into the tender flesh there, something hard and square and plastic that cracked beneath her weight. The television came back on.

In the flickering light, Jenny saw Sofia slumped against the sofa. Her eyes were wide open and frightened, but she was not moving, not at all. Sitting next to her, cradling her head gently, was the clown doll.

It was running one of its black gloved hands over Sofia's head, stroking her hair. The movement seemed oddly affectionate, even intimate. Then Jenny saw the glitter of the web between its fingers. Great swaths of Sofia's hair fell away from her head into the thing's lap with each stroke. Pieces of purple ribbon fluttered to the floor, sliced neatly in two. Jenny watched, transfixed, the deep white noise rendering her unable to do much else. It looked up at her, its eyes dark and deep and dangerous, two old wells negligently left uncovered. Its head tilted to one side, a curious gesture, then it returned to its chore, harvesting Sofia's beautiful long straight hair, patient, meticulous.

With great effort, Jenny raised her left hand to her ear. It was like lifting a lead weight. Her numb fingers fumbled for a moment, then closed around her hearing aid. She pulled it off her ear.

It was as if she'd fallen into a freezing ocean. The deep noise was immediately swallowed by a familiar dull muffled roar, a soundless sound she was very familiar with. Some of it still penetrated, but not much. The feeling returned to her hands and face, and her strength with it. She tossed the earpiece aside, and looked down at her knee, at the object beneath it. It was the television remote control, and her knee was on the red power button.

She picked the remote up and hurled it at Lollo.

It struck the clown doll in the face and shattered. Batteries flew through the air, then fell to the floor and rolled away into the darkness. The doll looked up, distracted, watched as Jenny got to her feet. With a strange, sinuous movement, it pushed Sofia aside. The child fell over onto the couch, half-bald, eyes still open but motionless.

The doll slid down off the couch, landed on its feet. Its legs flexed beneath its weight like springs. It looked at Jenny, with that blank, expressionless painted face, the dead black eyes, the fixed toothless smile. It reached out its hand, the one with the shiny web between its fingers, and took a step towards her.

Without thinking, Jenny threw herself at the doll, bellowing as loudly as she could. She grasped its wrist with one hand, and clawed at its face with the other.

Something tore under her fingers, and the face came away from the doll's head. It did not feel like cloth, more like soft leather, warm and yielding. It fell to the floor from Jenny's hand, crumpled there like a discarded tissue. Where the face had been on the doll, there were no features, just a smooth flexible shell, translucent and milky, and within that, Jenny could see what looked like hundreds of gigantic grey earthworms, each one as long and thick as a rope, bodies segmented and writhing. It was always moving, the lithe strands flowing inside the shell like a solid bloodstream.

The doll struggled in her grasp, tried to move its webbed hand towards her again. She gritted her teeth, grabbed the thing's neck with her free hand, and lifted the whole thing off the floor. It was surprisingly heavy, and squirmed in her grip with a calm, silent desperation.

She spun around and hurled Lollo at the television.

The screen shattered and exploded as its head penetrated it. Sparks showered down onto the carpet like spent fireworks. It twisted and turned, jammed in the glass and circuitry. She turned to Sofia, barely visible on the couch. She was blinking, looking around in a daze as if awakening from a deep sleep.

"Sofia!" Jenny called, and scrambled over to her. She picked the child up, held her close for a moment. Then her stomach fell away, as she realized what was missing.

Domenic.

Sofia sobbed something into Jenny's chest, but she could not hear her, could not understand her.

"It's okay," Jenny told Sofia, "it's okay," but she knew it wasn't, it wasn't okay. She looked around the room desperately, but there was no sign of the little boy. Her eyes returned to the television. The clown doll's head was still stuck in the shattered screen, its feet kicking at the floor. Flames licked the sides and front of the television, and the carpet was also burning now, set alight by the sparks.

Lollo fell free of the television, onto its back. The milky shell of its head was blackened. It lay there for long seconds, perfectly still. Then it sat up.

Jenny pulled Sofia to her feet. "Run!" she yelled, and pushed her down the hallway. Sofia did not hesitate, she dashed off down the corridor. Jenny hesitated for a moment, grabbed the discarded face of the clown doll from the floor, then followed close behind her. She could just make out the doorway of the bedroom at the other end now, the door wide open. As they approached the end of the hall, just before the bedroom, Jenny spotted something across the doorway, about a foot off the ground.

A glittering blue thread.

"No!" she screamed. She leapt forward and grabbed Sofia off the floor, lifted her up and over as they tumbled into the bedroom. They rolled on the floor and crashed into the wardrobe with a painful thump. Jenny got unsteadily to her feet as quickly as she could manage, ignoring Sofia's silent cries. She looked down the hallway, but the clown was not there.

Lollo

Then she saw the object just inside the doorway, a street lamp outside the window providing illumination in the room. A rounded lump of brown leather, with some thick strings hanging loosely off it. This time Jenny knew what it was immediately. She glanced down at her feet and nearly fainted. Her left shoe was half gone, and a large chunk of her foot with it, sliced perfectly straight. She was deeply grateful she could not see the end of her foot, the flesh and tissue and bone. She wanted to cry, but there were no tears in her eyes, nothing to mercifully blur her vision.

She looked up again, and screamed. Lollo was in the hallway, approaching with a strange gait, like it was on a ship in a raging ocean, swaying from side to side on boneless legs. Its blank shell of a head stayed at the same level as it moved. Jenny could see the glimmer of blue spider webs between its black fingers.

She turned and picked Sofia up, held her close to her, felt the heaving sobs in her tiny body. She closed her eyes and said a short prayer. *God, please let this work!*

She ran at the window, leapt up onto the toy box, then twisted to shield Sofia as she hit the window with the shoulder and back as hard as she could.

The glass cracked and shattered beneath their weight, and they fell through into the garden outside. Broken shards sliced at Jenny's shoulder, back and legs, sending bright explosions of pain through her vision. They collapsed on the grass, and more pain shot through Jenny as pieces of glass were driven deeper into her. She did not make a noise, though, did not have the strength to spare.

She clambered back to her feet, and quickly checked to see if Sofia was alright. The child was saying something, tears and blood staining her cheeks. Only Jenny's blood, she was pretty sure. She picked Sofia up and limped away from the house, towards the front gate and the road outside. Towards safety.

A familiar car pulled up fast, a yellow station wagon, and right behind that, a police car, lights flashing. The door of the station wagon opened, and Mrs. Rowe leapt out, her face stricken. She ran up to Jenny and snatched her daughter from her, tears running down her face. Mrs. Rowe looked around with wide, frightened eyes, screamed something at Jenny. Jenny could not hear, but she did not need to. She knew exactly what Mrs. Rowe was saying.

Where is he? Where is he?

A policeman approached from the other side, gun drawn and aimed at Jenny. She must have looked like hell, bloodied and battered and cut. Smoke filled her nostrils, and the heat of silent flames from behind her made her torn back ache even worse.

But she did not care. She was safe now. She was safe.

Her vision browned and speckled, her knees folded beneath her, and she was unconscious before she hit the ground.

The hospital bed was hard and uncomfortable; they made the bandaged cuts in Jenny's back ache. The restraints were not helping either, wrists and ankles strapped to prevent her hurting herself, presumably, or maybe just to stop her escaping. She barely remembered getting there, just hallucinatory flashes; the bumpy ambulance ride, still with Mrs. Rowe and Sofia, the mother's traumatized, accusatory glare. Being treated, the glass fragments pulled from her flesh one by one. Confused expressions as the nurses saw her foot, her finger. Then here, the straps tightened, a hypodermic slid beneath the skin at the crook of her elbow.

Now she was alone. It was dark, just a dim light in the room and a sliver from the corridor outside. And quiet, of course. She'd left her hearing aid at the house, and nobody had given her another one. She had not seen her parents yet, but presumably, hopefully, they were on their way. And the police would have questions, so many questions, questions that she was not sure how she would answer.

What would she say? That a clown doll took Domenic and attacked her and Sofia? What evidence did she have?

She glanced over at the chair next to her bed. There were her clothes, torn and stained with blood. And, on top of them, the object she'd clung to all the way to the hospital, unable to let go. White with black patches, three conical points, a bright red sphere. The crumpled face of Lollo.

Jenny closed her eyes, felt the sedative coursing through her veins, calming her nerves one by one with a quiet but firm authority. She wondered if Sofia was okay, with her mum, safe, secure. She wished her own parents were there, to hold her and protect her and tell her everything would be fine.

She opened her eyes again, and did not quite understand what she saw for a second or two. When she did, a distant panic rose deep inside her, muffled by the drugs.

The face was gone.

She looked around, working hard to keep her eyes open. There was a tiny figure standing at the foot of her bed, face and clothes pale. Jenny was sure for a moment that it was Lollo, then realized that it wasn't.

"Domenic?" she murmured. "Are...are you...okay?" The boy did not look right; his face was pale, his eyes closed. In one tiny white hand, he held a familiar blue blanket, his Buddy boo. Jenny could not see his other hand. "Domenic?" she asked again.

Domenic's eyes opened. They were pitch black, like the clown's eyes. He opened his mouth, and a grey segmented tube snaked out, curled moist around his neck. Then he raised his other hand and opened it.

In his palm, charred and melted, was Jenny's hearing aid.

Movement to her left distracted her. She turned her heavy head. Sitting beside her on the bed was the clown doll, its face in place on its head once more. Its name scribbled across its chest:

Lollo

With drugged detachment, Jenny realized that the letters actually looked a lot like binary digits, ones and zeroes.

Lollo raised its black gloved hands and spun the glistening blue web between its fingers like a cat's cradle, twisted the threads together into a single strand between its palms. It leant over Jenny, and its puffy fingers brushed her ears.

Then the sedative finally took hold and carried her away against her will. Her eyelids fluttered one last time then closed forever, as the clown doll lowered its hands to her neck.

Martin Livings

AFTERWORD

This has probably been the hardest time I've ever had coming up with an idea for a themed anthology. I went through dozens of dead ends, and none of them worked. Then I stumbled across the story of a babysitter complaining to the parents about a clown statue, and being told they didn't own a clown statue. In the legend it's usually a psychopath, or sometimes a drunk circus midget. But my immediate, if odd, reaction was, how would an alien race infiltrate an ordinary house in order to examine the inhabitants or collect samples? And what would a clown doll look like, if it had been created by something that had never actually seen a clown?

Thus was Lollo born.

It creeped me out immediately, which was very encouraging. The two kids in the story are my niece and nephew, their names misspelled the way I always tend to do. The babysitter arrived full-formed in my mind, complete with a supposed disability that was actually an advantage in the extraordinary circumstances that she faced.

And from that point on, the story pretty much wrote itself. Or, more accurately, Lollo wrote it, and I just watched on in growing horror at what was happening.

I will never allow a clown doll into my house. *Never*.

Green Tears on Black Velvet
Jeff Soesbe

The smell of a burned body: the sick sweetness of charred human flesh; the musky sharpness of immolated hair; the chemical bite of synthetic fabrics melted into skin. All those smells are here, in this house fire, behind the burned wood of the house frame, the melted rubber of wiring insulation, the scorched metal of pipes and wires.

Yet it's the burned body smell that stays, that lingers in my nose and skin for days, no matter how much I try to scrub it out.

The smell of a burned body is one I always recognize, and I never forget. I know it far too well, and I've experienced it more times than I like. In my work as an investigator for the Sacramento Fire Department, the smell comes with the territory. I have to push my disgust aside, calm my seizing throat, and get on with the work.

The police report tells me the basic facts. Louisa and Eugene Chen, both in their seventies, died in the house where they lived together for forty-seven years and raised their family. 2504 B Street, a classic midtown house in an ordered row of classic midtown houses. Well-kept lawns, broad front porches, large flourishing oak and mulberry trees that arched shade over the street.

Now it's a shell of a house, a scar on the serenity of the block.

My job is to figure out what happened. One fact on the report gives me a major clue: Eugene Chen was diagnosed with advanced lung cancer four months ago. He and his wife both smoked.

It's one of the common causes of a fire involving the elderly. Smoking in bed. If not that, then space heaters, or faulty electric blankets, or pots left cooking and forgotten.

In fire investigation, we start from the least burned area and work to the most burned. Some of the kitchen remains; its location obvious from the charred husks of refrigerator, stove and sink. The blackened red brick of a collapsed fireplace, behind the kitchen, marks where the living room was. As I make my way towards the bedroom, the damage is more complete. Char patterns on floorboards show that the fire traveled hot and fast here, exploding out from the bedroom. The roof burned, buckled, collapsed, and burned some more.

The ash is thick, still damp from the water the firefighters poured on it, and it sticks to my boots, a warm heavy mass. It doesn't help that it's only two in the afternoon and already a hundred degrees. My hands sweat inside my plastic gloves. I just want to be done, to get back into the car, turn on the air conditioner, file the report and close this out.

I have to finish on time today, as I'm picking up Hugo from Sondra's house tonight. It's the second weekend of the month, one of the weekends I spend with my son. My time with Hugo is important to me. I don't want to be late.

The bedroom gives all the evidence I need. A warped lighter and cigarette butts in a pile of ash near the twisted metal of a bed frame. A solid tangle of wires and insulation near the thin stubs of what was a wall. An electric space heater, melted into slag.

It's everything at once. No wonder the place went up.

As I pick through the charred chunks of roof beams, stepping gingerly through the deep ash, confirming the final details, something catches my eye.

A small corner of wood, unburned, sticking out of the remnants of what once was a dresser next to the black stub of the frame of a closet door.

Curiosity gets the best of me. Carefully, I make my way to the corner of wood.

It's the edge of a picture frame. I ease the frame from under its grave of ash, cloth fragments, and metal knobs.

A small picture, about ten inches by twelve, reveals itself. I shake off the ash clinging to it, flip the frame around to see the picture; A pale grey alien, painted on black velvet, crying bright green tears.

And it's unburned. Untouched.

Back in my car I type up the report, including the evidence I found in the bedroom. Cigarettes. Electrical wiring. Space heater. Carelessness, forgetfulness, and now the Chens are gone. The flames claimed their lives, destroyed their home.

Except for the painting of the crying alien. It now sits on the passenger seat inside an evidence bag. It was in the heart of the fire, and yet it wasn't burned at all.

Why not?

I take the painting back out of the bag and prop it against the passenger door. The alien is hairless, grey like a cloudy sky, and the tears trailing from its large black eyes as green as an unripe pear. What a strange painting.

Why didn't it burn?

My rational mind says its survival is a fluke occurrence; a random coincidence of heat, flame and chance. Maybe it fell behind the dresser and was protected. Maybe. Already I feel my brain grabbing hold of this oddity and refusing to let go, and the pressure building at the base of my skull tells me a headache is coming. My subconscious will be gnawing and chewing at this the rest of the night as my obsessive mind takes hold, the same obsessive mind that drove Sondra crazy back when we were married.

I hold the painting in my lap as I lean back in the seat. A plain black velvet canvas, a simple wooden frame. It should have burned up. But it didn't. Why? What happened? My thoughts drift as I imagine a fire pattern that would spare the picture.

My phone vibrates in my pocket, and I jerk in reaction. I put down the painting and check the phone. Sondra.

I'm light-headed, and sweating. Why is it so hot in the car?

I forgot to turn on the air conditioning. How stupid of me. I start the car, crank up the fan, and answer the phone.

"Hello, Sondra."

"Ricardo, you were going to be here ten minutes ago."

I check my watch. It's 5:10. Where did the time go? I must have fallen asleep after finishing the report.

"Lo siento. I was working a fire. But I'm done now. I'll be there soon."

"Rapido, por favor. Marcos and I have a six PM dinner reservation at Supper Club, and the cab will be here at 5:40."

Supper Club. It's nice. It's expensive. How long have she and Marcos been going out? Almost a year. I bet it's their anniversary.

Sondra and I went to Supper Club, once. A long time ago, for an anniversary. Back when dinners were homemade burritos or spaghetti, back when we were junior firefighter and public defender. Back when we were a team, and our money went into fixing up the house.

Our house. Now, her house. Stop it, I tell myself, no more thoughts like that. "I'll be there in twenty minutes."

"Bueno. Adios, Ricardo."

Time to hurry. I shove the painting into my bag, between the laptop and a few folders, and pull out from the curb. Intruding into my thoughts of Hugo is the image of a small grey alien crying bright, green tears.

Nineteen minutes later, Hugo opens the door.

"Papa!" He throws his arms around my waist with a big hug and drives some air from my lungs. It was just Monday that I took him to the first day of school, but he looks taller, bigger, more mature. He's only eight, but he's changing so fast.

"Hey, hijo! How's my boy?" I bend over and hug him the best I can. I can't help but smile and laugh. He's the greatest kid, so full of energy, so enchanted with the world. He drives joy into me every time I see him.

"Papa, come see my new X-Wing fighter!" He yanks me into the house. "Mama, Papa's here!"

"Hola, Sondra."

"Hola." Her voice echoes down the hall from her room.

After the divorce, she kept the house in Rosemont and I moved into a cheap apartment on Howe near headquarters so now it is, indeed, her room. The house is decorated in her style: pictures of her family, candles and Oaxacan figurines on the mantle, Zapotec rugs, handwoven blankets draped on the leather furniture. Neat, classy, expensive. Her style. Corporate lawyer style. Not public defender style.

Hugo's room is chaos, toys and comic books and sci-fi posters and spaceships and planets. I love my boy's room. He grabs the X-Wing off the floor and holds it up. It's made out of Legos.

"Great spaceship, hijo."

"This is Gold Leader. Starting our run."

While he flies it over the bed, I reach up and press the test button on the smoke alarm. It squeals a high pitch and Hugo jumps.

"Papa!"

"You don't have to check that every time you come over, Ricardo." Sondra's voice, from the doorway.

I turn towards her. "Lo siento. Old habit. You know me...."

I see her and pause. She's wearing a summer dress, tan with big blue flowers. Her skin is the color of burnished gold, and the dress suits her perfectly. Her hair is up, the dress shows her shoulders. When she tilts her head to the side as she puts in an earring, I feel a tug somewhere deep inside me, an empty place with ragged edges that has never quite healed. It's been a year and a half now.

"Hi, Sondra. You look nice." I swallow a lump in my throat.

"Gracias."

She's hiding something. It's in the tone of her voice. Have things changed between her and Marcos? I sneak a glance at her hands. No ring that I can see.

"Papa, can we eat at Carlo's Pizza for dinner?"

"You bet. And I'm hungry, so let's go." I grab Hugo's suitcase, eager to get back outside the house and away from the feelings that fill my lungs like smoke.

At the car, Sondra hugs and kisses Hugo. "Be a good boy. Mind your Papa."

I put Hugo's bag in the trunk. "Sunday at six, right? You have Abuelo's birthday dinner?"

"Si." Her expression changes, her voice less certain. "You could come, if you want. My parents ask about you."

I wonder what they ask. I'm sure it can't be too favorable. I'm also sure Marcos would be there. He's a good guy, but I always suffer in comparison. "I should work. House fire in midtown last night. Old couple died."

"Oh. I'm sorry to hear that." She truly is. It's nice to hear her concern. "Well, the invitation is open."

"I'll think about it. Adios, Sondra."

"Adios, Ricardo."

When we're away from the house I ask Hugo. "So, hijo, Mommy and Mister Salazar have been dating a year, right?"

Hugo stops making spaceship noises. "I guess. Mama said it was their anniversary."

That explains it. Sondra and Marcos will go out to Supper Club, come back home, listen to music, dance in the flickering light of the candles. Sondra always liked lots of candles.

Good thing I'm eating pizza tonight. Pizza is good for filling up the hole I feel in my gut and the slow steady dull ache that crawls its way up to my heart.

The pizza at Carlo's is marvelous. Thick crust, rich tomato sauce, and fresh toppings. But what Hugo and I really love is Carlo's collection of old arcade machines. Pac Man. Centipede. Space Invaders. And the grand prize, an original Star Wars game. Hugo and I love to come here, fill up on pizza and root beer, and play Star Wars until we can barely see straight.

These are the good times, the times I live for. The times spent with my son. Video games, pizza, talking about school and friends and his soccer team and comic books and superheroes and science fiction movies.

As I'm going to the counter for more change, I notice a new picture hanging in the array of pictures on the wall next to the counter.

A crying alien, painted on black velvet.

This one is dressed in a cook's apron and hat, has very light red/orange skin, like cooked cheese, big wet eyes, and a single green tear running down its face.

"Giancarlo. Where did you get that picture?"

At the counter next to the oven, Giancarlo is spreading dark red sauce on pale dough. "Yasmin found it yesterday at the swap meet. The one under the freeway, Sixth near Broadway? She thought it would cheer me up. He's cooking, he's making pizza!"

"But why is he crying?"

"Probably cause business is so slow." Giancarlo laughs as he opens the register, then gestures to the nearly empty restaurant. "Not enough steady customers, like you."

Another painting. It's not exactly like the one in the Chens, but similar. I'm sure it's just a coincidence. But it nags at my mind as I walk back to the video games, and remains in the background of my thoughts as Hugo and I battle Tie Fighters and try to destroy the Death Star.

After dinner we're back at my apartment, sitting on the fold out couch, watching *The Empire Strikes Back*. Near the end, Hugo leans against me.

Green Tears on Black Velvet

Darth Vader has just told Luke that he is Luke's father, and Luke's response was to jump off the balcony inside Cloud City.

"Papa?"

"Si, Hugo?"

"Did Darth Vader love Luke?"

"I'm sure he did."

"Why did he leave him, then? Leave him on Tattooine with his tia and tio?"

Hugo hasn't seen the later movies, so he hasn't gotten the whole story yet. But, of course, this isn't really about Darth and Luke.

"Well, there were a lot of things happening to Darth Vader."

"Did he and Luke's mommy get divorced?"

"They split up, si. But he never knew about Luke and Leia."

"If he knew he had kids, would he still have gone away? Would he have joined the dark side?"

I put my arm around him and hold him close. He needed some reassurance.

"Maybe not. I don't know. But I do know that I love you, Hugo and I'd never leave you behind. Okay?"

"Okay." He's sleepy, his voice is trailing off. "I love you, Papa."

As the credits roll and my heart feels nearly full to bursting with love for my son, he drifts into sleep. Tears dot my eyes. What goes through his mind at times like this? What does he think happened? Sondra and I have been good about that. Any problems we had we never aired in front of him. We're always respectful to each other. I wonder what he thinks about the whole situation.

Hell, sometimes I wonder what I think myself.

The day is catching up to me and I'm getting tired. I unwind from Hugo, set him on the couch bed with his droid pillow and Star Wars blanket and tuck him in. He's so sweet, so young, so innocent and it breaks my heart to have him going through all this.

As I'm unpacking my work bag, the corner of the plastic bag holding the Chens' picture sticks out. It's been in the back of my mind since dinner, so I take it out, prop it up on the counter bar between the living room and the kitchen, hold it there with the salt shaker.

Did the Chens get their picture the same place as Giancarlo? The frames are different, but the style is similar. Crying aliens, black velvet.

Surely there's nothing to worry about, but my mind doesn't want to let it go.

A yawn overwhelms me. I'm beat. It's been a long day.

In the bedroom, I change into shorts and a t-shirt and settle into bed. Alien faces run through my mind. Aliens from *Star Wars*, aliens from pizza parlors, aliens from paintings that survived a house fire. So many aliens.

"Papa?" Hugo, sniffling.

I jerk out of sleep. He's standing next to the bed.

"Hugo? What's the matter?"

"I'm scared." He's half asleep, half-awake, and his voice has the tinge of tears in it.

I roll off the bed and go to him, kneeling down on the carpet, holding him close. "What's the matter?"

"I had a bad dream. There was a fire. Can I stay in your bed?"

"Sure, come on." He virtually collapses onto me, nearly knocking me over. He's getting so big. I remember the days when he was light and precious and so easy to carry. Now, he's all legs and arms, especially when he's sleepy like this and I'm holding all his weight.

By the time I set him into bed he's asleep again, his breathing slow and regular.

Dreams of fire. I don't think it's the movie. He had some nightmares after the divorce, but hasn't had any in a while. Why tonight?

Back in the living room, the painting still sits on the bar counter. It's easy to pick out, the green tears glow in the faint light coming through the sliding glass door and the black velvet has a luster all its own.

Could the picture have caused Hugo's dreams? I sit on a barstool and stare at it for a while, resting my chin on my arms. Black velvet, gray alien, green tears. It's not a pretty picture, ugly almost, but it pulls me in.

The counter is hard and warm beneath my hands. It's the end of August, the end of another day of hot temperatures, the end of another summer.

Another difficult summer. The second summer of being alone, of not having anyone in my life beyond my son, who I see every other weekend and when I'm not working. The second summer of being pathetic, dumpy, thinning hair, aching muscles, a constant coating of oil on my face from eating all the wrong foods, drinking all the wrong booze.

Goosebumps roll down my spine.

Thoughts spring forth in my head. *It's chilly in here, Hugo will get cold. I should turn up the heat. I'm hungry. I want to cook something on the stove. I haven't smoked in months, but I could use a cigarette.*

A high whistle, like a train, pulsing, beeping.

I snap to alertness. Where am I? I had a weird dream and now I'm, I'm what?

I'm standing in the kitchen. It's hot in the apartment. I'm sweating.

The smoke alarm is going off.

Beans are burning on the stove. The temperature is set on HIGH. I turn the burner off and try to move the pan but it's too hot. I yank a pot holder from the drawer and use it to hold the handle while I run cold water over the beans.

Smoke billows up and I grimace.

There's something in my mouth. I'm clenching a stale, unlit cigarette between my lips. Where in the world did I find this? I spit it into the sink.

I turn off the smoke alarm. Next, I check the thermostat. It's at eighty-five, as high as it will go. I flick it off and open the sliding glass door in the living room, open the front door of the apartment, go to the bedroom to open those windows too. A night breeze crawls through the apartment, clears out the smoke.

Hugo is still asleep, thank goodness, though he's sweating under his blanket. I pull it off him.

What's going on here? What happened? Last I remember I was looking at the picture on the counter.

It's still there, propped against the wall. The frame is warm in my hands. Weird. The heat from the apartment, maybe?

The alien eyes stare back at me, unmoving. I feel like there's an accusation in those eyes. Like I did something wrong.

I set the picture down, face down, on the counter.

Suddenly I feel cool. No need for the heat. No desire to cook. No urge to smoke.

I pick up the picture, keep it facing away from me, and go back into the kitchen. The electric burner where I was burning beans is still a dull red. I crank it back up to high and it quickly glows hot.

I touch the edge of the picture frame to the burner.

The picture frame doesn't burn. It doesn't smoke.

What it does instead is get incredibly hot, hotter than the pan handle. I flinch and toss the picture frame into the sink, where it hits the water in the pan then hisses and steams.

What is this thing?

I run the sink full of water to drown the picture. It doesn't float, but sits in the bottom, accusing me with its stare and its tears. A chill shivers down my spine and raises the hairs on my arms. Now I feel cold again, like I should warm everything up.

I reach into the sink and flip the picture around. The frame is still warm, even under a sink full of cold water.

I grab the ice cube trays from the freezer, crack out the cubes, and dump them into the water. They float, blocking my view of the picture.

The apartment feels normal again.

Is this what the Chens went through? Did they turn on electric blankets? Bring in heaters? Plug things into one outlet?

Did the picture tell them to?

This is crazy. I'm imagining things. I'm tired, sleepy. I'm making things up. I'm getting too obsessed with this. Time to go back to bed.

I close up the apartment, but leave the picture in the sink full of icy water. The bedroom windows remain cracked. Hugo is snoring lightly, and I lie down and curl up next to him. Quickly I'm asleep.

My dreams are of the *Star Wars* Cantina, lightsabers blazing with sparks, the gutted shell of a Sandcrawler burning in a hot desert wind.

"Papa! Papa!"

Hugo's voice, calling me. He's not in bed. I panic for a second, then realize he's in the living room.

I rush into the room. He's sitting on the couch, eating Raisin Bran, watching TV.

"Carlo's Pizza burned."

The reporter's voice carries over Hugo's. "*Firefighters have just finished putting out the fire at the local restaurant on Folsom Boulevard. No one was injured, but the business is believed to be a total loss. Firefighters suspect either an electrical problem or issues with the pizza ovens, but will investigate for possible arson. This has been a News Ten Action Bulletin.*"

Hugo looks at me, concerned. "Papa, do you think the *Star Wars* game is okay?"

"I don't know, Hugo. That fire looked bad."

Clone Wars comes back on, and the aliens remind me of the picture that is still in the sink.

I go pull it out of the water, set it on a towel to dry. It's not hot, just soaked with water. The fabric has sagged, the frame is a bit warped, some paint has flaked off. It looks like an ordinary painting, nothing special. If not for the pot of burned beans still in the water, I would think I imagined everything from last night.

What I need is some coffee. I'm so foggy-headed I can't really think straight. But one thing I know I will do. First thing Monday morning, I'm going to the swap meet and find the person selling these paintings.

Hugo wanders in with his bowl and goes to put it next to the sink. He stops and stares at the painting.

"Mama has one of those."

My heart stops a beat. "What?"

"A picture of an alien, crying. Marcos got it for her. It's in the office, next to my room."

"This same picture. An alien, crying?"

"Not exactly the same. Hers is wearing a jacket, like a suit. And the alien is brown. But it's still crying. Green tears."

Sondra. Fancy dinner with Marcos. Wine.

Candles. Candles everywhere.

The obsessive part of my mind is screaming inside my head. I should call. I might wake them up, and if nothing's wrong Sondra's will grumble. But I should call.

I quick dial the home number on my cell. There's no ring; just an immediate busy tone. Like the line is dead.

I try her cell phone. It rolls right over to voice mail. Is she on the phone?

I try again.

Come on, Sondra. Pick up the phone.

She usually puts her phone on silent. Could it be on silent? But then it would at least ring, not roll over to voice mail.

I try the house again. Busy.

Something is wrong. I need to go there.

"Hugo, we have to leave right now." I run into the bedroom, throw on clothes.

"What's happening, Papa?"

I grab his shoes, shove them in his hand, grab my keys and wallet from the counter, and yank open the front door. "We have to go to the house."

"Is something wrong?"

"I don't know. But we need to go."

On the road, dodging cars, hurrying to make the lights, we speed towards Rosemont. I'm hoping for the best but fearing the worst, and seeing in my mind a crying alien with tears that burn like flame.

The smoke is visible from Watt as I turn onto Keifer Street. It drifts up from the middle of the neighborhood, black and curling, as if there's a small volcano in the middle of Rosemont.

Left on Port, and when we hit the corner on Glenwood I see the smoke billowing up. The engines from Station 106, the closest one, are there pouring water on the shell of the house.

Standing in front of the house is a good-looking couple, in a pose I've seen before. Arms around each other, wife leaning her head on the shoulder of the husband. People staring at the physical remnants of their life going up in flames.

It takes me a second to realize its Sondra and Marcos.

They're both alive.

Relief washes over me. Behind it is a blow to the gut, a voice inside saying that they fit together.

When we park at the curb, Hugo jumps out of the car and runs to Sondra.

"Mama!" he calls.

Sondra, tears on her face, grabs Hugo and clutches him close.

As I walk to where they are, I scan the house. The fire obviously started in the living room then went into the bedrooms. I can see it in my mind, a candle catching a figurine, a figurine falling onto the rug, the rug under the couch. Once the couch caught fire, the house roof and walls wouldn't be far behind. Especially with the blankets helping the file along.

Both the office and Hugo's bedroom are completely gone. Once the fire grabbed the wall, it went through the office and all the books, then straight into his room. These older Rosemont houses go up fast. They used flammable material for insulation back then, sometimes even just piles of newspaper. Sondra did a remodel earlier this year, but she didn't touch the old walls or change Hugo's room.

If Hugo been there, it could have been bad. Very bad. I say a quiet prayer that he was with me last night.

Sondra is still clinging to Hugo. Marcos hovers next to them, one hand around her shoulders. Shock has frozen their stunned faces.

"Are you two okay? What happened?" I ask, though I already know.

Marcos's voice is shaky, "The alarm went off, and we smelled smoke. The bedroom door was too hot, so we went out the window. It must have been the candles."

Hugo's smoke alarm saved their lives. I say another silent prayer.

"Ricardo, could I borrow your phone?" Marcos asks. "I want to call Jorge from the office, let him know what happened."

I hand over my cell. "Sure."

He gives Sondra a quick kiss, protective, concerned. He's a good man.

Sondra sets Hugo down. "Hugo, go with Mister Marcos for a second. Let your papa and me talk."

"Okay, Mama."

We watch them walk off. Marcos, on the phone, pats Hugo on the back, like a good step-father should.

"How are you, Sondra?"

"Still a little scared. There was so much smoke, even with the door closed." She wipes tears from her face and brushes back her dark straight hair. She's wearing an engagement ring on her finger. A big ring. It wasn't there when I picked up Hugo last night.

She notices me staring and covers it with her hand.

"Marcos proposed last night. I said yes."

"Oh." What else can I say?

"I'm sorry. I was going to figure out how to tell you."

Things have changed. They will never go back to the way they were. Now, I know this. We move on. The life I was clinging to out of desperate hope, out of fear of what lies in front of me, is flying away like the ash on the wind.

I have a new life now, a new life that includes my son, my ex-wife, and what will be her new husband.

"I'm happy you're okay, Sondra. Both of you. And congratulations."

"Gracias, Ricardo."

Marcos comes back with Hugo, handing back my phone. "I got Jorge. He's happy to help get things filed." He puts an arm around Sondra, holds her close. "Sondra, we could head back to my house if you want, find some clothes."

She nods, the fear in her face transforming into action. "That would be good. Then I can call insurance, get going on claims." She gives Hugo a kiss and hug. "Hugo, you go back with Papa and I'll call you later."

Hugo sniffles, "I want to stay with Mama!" He sniffles, and then pops his thumb into his mouth, eyes wide.

"Hugo, it's Papa's weekend."

Hugo needs his Mama right now. It's in the way his eyes dart from the house to her to me. "It's okay with me, Sondra. I can stay here, help the Station 106 guys, then come by later."

"Candles." Marcos looks sheepish. "We left candles lit. Too much to drink."

"You were celebrating. As you should."

"Sorry."

"It's okay. Congratulations. I mean it."

There's silence. No one speaks. We all look at the house, what's left of it.

Someone has to get us moving, and it's me. "Go ahead, you three. Get some clothes, get going on insurance. I'll stay here and call you when I know more."

"Thanks, Ricardo."

"Hey, hijo." I offer Hugo my hand. "Let's get your stuff from the car."

After we get his blanket and shoes, Hugo grabs me around the waist, tight, and I pick him up and hold him.

"Papa. I'm sorry."

"Sorry about what?"

"Mama and Mister Marcos want to get married, Papa. She asked me yesterday if it was okay, but I couldn't tell you because it was a secret."

"It's okay, hijo. It's okay." It really is, too. I know the change will be tough for me, but I also know it's good. Everyone will be happy.

"I don't have any toys, Papa."

"But you do. I have your X-Wing, remember?" I carry him over to Marcos's car. "You go with Mama. I'll call you later and bring over your stuff." I'll make sure to stop by the store and get him a new *Star Wars* toy. Maybe a droid. We both love the droids.

"Okay, Papa."

"You be good, and I'll see you tonight." Marcos helps him get buckled as he gets into the car.

"Sondra?"

She turns, her face quizzical.

"I think I'll come to dinner Sunday night. If that's okay with you." I actually do want to get together with her family. It's time to start taking old connections and making new things from them.

Surprise and gratitude show brighten on her face. "Yes, that would be nice."

They drive away, Hugo waving at me from the back seat.

Once they're around the corner I walk slowly up the lawn towards the burned remnants of the house.

I don't really need to look through the wreckage. I know what I'll find. Molten piles of wax, twisted candleholders, a hot spot in the living room where the fire started, then jumped to the couch, the blankets, and then the walls.

But I know I'll also find something else.

A painting of a crying alien, dressed in a suit, green tears on its face. A painting undamaged by smoke or flame.

After I make sure the painting is here, my next stop is the swap meet. I'm not waiting until Monday. I'm finding those paintings, and I'm finding them now. The paintings have killed two innocent people, and destroyed a good man's restaurant. They almost got me, my boy, his mother and her fiancée.

I'll get every one of those paintings, from the swap meet or from the people who bought them. Then I'll dispose of them, in whatever way I have to in order to keep everyone safe.

No more smell of torched houses, no more stench of burned bodies.

No more pictures that take advantage of people and use their emotions against them.

No more, I vow. No more.

JEFF SOESBE

AFTERWORD

The "Crying Boy Painting" urban legend arose in Britain in the mid-1980s, when an article in the tabloid *The Sun* related how firefighters reported finding paintings of crying boys in the ruins of burned houses. As the paintings were very popular at the time, a small panic set in, one that eventually led to mass bonfires of the paintings (organized by *The Sun* as a publicity event).

After I read about the legend in *Fortean Times* (April 2008 issue), it stuck with me as a wonderful example of the power of the human mind to extract a malevolent conspiracy from a mere coincidence.

Also, the paintings themselves were truly touching. Scores of paintings, all featuring small boys with big eyes and tears rolling down their sad, accusatory faces.

For the anthology, I decided to use the "Crying Boy Painting" legend with some changes. The crying boys became teary aliens and the paintings affected people who were in heightened emotional states, somehow leading them into dangerous behavior.

The addition of a fire investigator still struggling with his feelings over his divorce and its effect on his son brought the story together.

Racing Lights
Erik Scott de Bie

There's a story about the lights—the two street lights on Gray Road—that makes everybody nervous. But right now, we're just waiting for the flicker: one of the two lights that buzzes on and off like a signal. Margery is our flagger, sure, but we know she's waiting for the light. She always does.

The engines rev and the cars shudder, pawing at the line like horses, their jockeys—we drivers—performing our own little rituals as the sun sets. Ruiz is crossing himself. Dickerson is puffing greedily on a cigarette. Juarez is cold and focused. Me, I crank up the Offspring. *Gotta keep 'em separated.*

Flicker. The flag comes down.

I lift the clutch, hit the gas, and we're off.

Wind whistles through the corn as I race past. Over the music, I hear my engine roar, not in protest but in desire...*need*. Clutch, shift through neutral, clutch, smooth shift into third, all within a split second. Six point two seconds in, and I'm doing sixty.

I'm around Ruiz, who waves the middle finger at me, but I just smile.

I jam past the gold Miata with the black flames, Dickerson, and swerve in front of him when I've cleared two feet. Dickerson slows down; typical. It doesn't matter, as long as I'm ahead of him by the turn, as his Miata kicks it in the corners. Not that he's as good as I am, anyway, but why take chances?

The race is all over before you cross the finish line. Before you hit the gas, before the flagger waves, before you even dig the line. It begins and ends before any of that, and it's all in your mind. It's like when Musashi psyched out Sasaki; the duel's over before it starts and the smarter fighter wins. I get this, and that's why I'm always set out three lengths back but I win anyway.

Dickerson's catching up, I realize, and wonder if he hasn't grown some balls today. I weave a little—not enough to hit him, but Dickerson panics as usual and over-corrects, swerving and braking. The shrieking chases me down the road. He spins and fish-tails off the shoulder. Everyone behind him honks and slows, trying not to crash.

It's just Juarez ahead of me now. We're streaking down Gray and he's three car lengths ahead.

We flash past the Racing Lights, and I can feel everyone's nerves fray. I can see it in their driving. Like I said, there's a story about the Gray Road lights: a story that makes everybody nervous. Everybody except me.

I make up half a second there because I don't hesitate. I punch the gas harder.

First turn is long and easy. I make up another half second. More on the second turn. Now it's two lengths between me and Juarez, and six seconds to go before the big turn.

Back in the day, we used this stretch for straight-up, quarter-mile drag racing—from the starting line to the first turn—but you can't just ignore a turn like Gray-Kobert, where Gray Road turns into Kobert Lane, which snakes back to town. It's tight and sloped and scares the hell out of drivers who don't know how to handle it. We do, and it still scares the hell out of us.

One way to take the turn is to drop the gas half a second, then just power through it. But that isn't the fastest way. Not *my* way.

The distance drops to one car length. Juarez backs off and starts the turn. I have to pass him in the turn; I knew it would come to that.

In my mirror, the lights—one flickering, one steady—disappear and I jam it.

The trick is to turn the instant you can't see the lights in the rearview anymore. There's the tiniest incline to the road, and it puts just enough of an angle in the road that the lights slide up out of the mirror. You think you're going to slide and spin out, but you aren't. Not if you stick it and don't waver. Fight it too hard, and you spin out. Too soft, and you spin out. You have to turn just right.

We turn. The world is our own, set at a steep angle and with its own rules of gravity. The pull is toward the outside and down and left.

Racing Lights

The force pushes me back in my seat. My heart is beating fast. Each of us moves like a ball in a spinning roulette, bound for either life or death: an exit onto hot blacktop or a bloody red crash in the trees. We're in the turn. We have to trust in the mercy of the universe now.

I see my chance and take it, turning a little sharper. My car shivers, but I reassure her silently. There isn't going to be anyone coming on the other side. We're going to be fine.

I'm passing Juarez inside by inches. My passenger door pulls level with his back door. I see him starting to waver; worried he's going to hit me. Now we're side by side. He glances at me, and his eyes are wide behind the driver's window. Scared.

It's over before it starts.

We come screaming out of the turn, Juarez just behind me. The home stretch is as wide open as the sky over the valley.

I relax my turn just a little, and swerve ahead of him as the stereo warns against talking back. Juarez can't get around me. He's done. He tries anyway, and I hear his tires squeal as he spins out. Dirt flies into the air as he skids into the ditch. Disrespecting me—now he's taken out.

I'm alone in a clear, midnight-blue world, infinite sky laid out before me. It's me all the way.

Crossing the finish line is as easy as breathing.

As the sun dips halfway below the horizon, we gather in the parking lot of the Christmas Tree Farm—empty in the off-season—surrounded by fields of growing crops. There's no one around and nothing else to do on a Friday night, but that's the way this town always is: about fifty of us hanging out in the country, acting like daredevils and wishing we had a keg.

In a town like this, if we didn't have racing, we'd all go nuts.

"2000 Acura Integra, Type R," I said when my parents asked me what kind of car I wanted for my sixteenth birthday. "A 1998 would work too, as long as it has the B18C5 engine. I prefer new, but used with less than twenty thousand on it would do fine."

"Oh," Mom said. "That's…that's a very specific answer."

"Don't you want something more…I don't know, sporty?" Dad asked.

I smiled. "Nope."

It may not look like much, but it's got it where it counts.

I do a victory lap and make my entrance. Music blares, the cars start honking, and there's even applause. I circle the lot once, then pull into my favorite space, spray-painted with my initials to mark my territory. I leave the engine idling and climb out.

"Puta madre!" Ruiz shouts at Dickerson. "What was that, cholo? You try to kill us?"

"Dude, he almost hit me!" Dickerson objects.

"What I tell you about tailgating?"

"Don't?"

"Don't, *Dick*." Ruiz smacks Dickerson upside the head.

I look around, but I don't see Juarez. For a second, I fear the worst, but then his ZX comes clanking into the parking lot, a long dent in the front end. Must have hit a log or something. Real tragedy...about the car, I mean, not his pride.

Juarez climbs out of the car, the door groaning as it opens. He looks OK, other than being pissed. "Bastard!" he growls at me. "You son of a mother...."

"Yep," I say, before he can finish the insult. People laugh.

Juarez sneers at me, then gestures to his car. People have gathered about, making "ooh" sounds and wincing. Juarez is coming closer, chest puffed out for a fight. I smooth my hair back from my face and think now would be a perfect time for a cigarette. Except that a year ago, I practiced smoking for three days before I finally gave up.

Juarez might have taken a swing at me, but someone stepped between us, and all my coolness evaporated in the face of a petite redhead crossing her arms and glaring.

"Hey, Hotshot." Margery's glasses are drooping on her nose and she's biting her lower lip and I *know* I'm going to get it. "Are you going to take me home, or what?"

The crowd goes "ooh!" and "oh yeah!" and "whipped!"

"Totally." I shake it off as best I can and put my arm around her. With my other hand, I click open the locks of my Integra. "Hop in."

She inclines her head and gives me a little smile that I recognize only too well.

"In front of all these people?" I murmur.

"Or not at all," she observes.

"That's a choice?"

She winks, "Totally." Her imitation is perfect.

Racing Lights

With an elaborate sigh, I bend down and kiss her, to the applause of all and a number of catcalls. Margery White, love of my life, queen of the world.

"Be seeing you, gringo," Juarez threatens as I turn the keys.

"Better wash your panties first," I say. "Think you wet them."

Then we're peeling out and driving off.

Two hours later, the engine purrs nice and smooth as I pull up in Margery's gravel driveway. To see her in her H&M halter and skinny jeans, her pink-tinted glasses and three hundred dollar purse, you'd never know she was a country girl except for the tan she gets working in the fields. You can't get a glow like that in a salon over in Sac-town. She's a collection of opposites, my Margery.

She lives out on Gray, a mile back from where we race. You can just see the racing lights from her house—the one constantly on, the other flickering. Off and on, off and on, every few seconds, like a sluggish hazard light. Both of them, lighting our race.

There's a story about those lights, like I said. When it's dark and empty, California's expanding flatness in every direction, the two lights are the only thing you can see for miles around, from any direction. And sometimes, when you're really tired, or worried, or distracted for some reason, the lights follow you. No matter which way you're going, or how fast, or how many turns you take, the lights never get smaller. Caused a few accidents over the years; somebody's cousin took his eyes off the road, or a friend of a friend pulled a wiggins.

Personally, I think it's all bullshit. But hey, it makes a good story.

The gravel rattles under my Integra's wheels as we take the turns on the long path nice and slow for her old man's benefit. The fewer reasons I give him to forbid his daughter to date that racing idiot the better. Around the last turn, I turn the key and shift to neutral to let us coast a few feet before the friction stops us. She hates it when I do this, but I can't resist the fun. Then we sit a while in the car, neither of us speaking, looking out at the sunset past her ranch. The blues and purples are perfect tonight, and I take some personal pride in that, thinking that maybe my fumes give it just that extra touch of color.

"You didn't do it on purpose, did you?" she asks, and I'm a million miles away and don't hear.

"Huh?"

"Made Juarez spin out like that."

"Tsch, right," I said. "It's not my fault wetback doesn't know his own...."

"Don't do that."

"What?"

"You know what I mean."

"Oh. Sorry."

She's sensitive about these things. A number of migrant workers come by every summer to work for her dad, and she's grown up in a place where Mexicans aren't the enemy. Helps that she was home-schooled, where she didn't have to see the fights on the playground every day—until of course she realized she was just too damn fine to stay home. Good for all of us. Especially me.

Now she's our flagger, and a finer ass there isn't to be seen on the Gray-Kobert track. Just seeing her gets us moving and makes us race our hardest on the tiny chance she might go for the winner.

I'm the winner.

"You're doing it again," she says. "Is racing all you think about?"

"Was not," I say. "I was thinking about you. Specifically, how hot you are."

"*And* about racing."

"OK."

Margery rolls her eyes. I don't even know why I bother lying to her. "Is this what you want to do the rest of your life? Racing?" she asks. "What about college?"

I shrug. "My grades suck too hard. I do OK in English, but math..." I wince.

"I could tutor you."

"Like *that* would do any good," I say. "Math is too, I don't know... too mathy."

"Mathy?"

"Exceptionally mathy." I nod wisely. "Algebra-y and calculus-y and trig...trigonom...*triggy*." I ease my arm around her shoulders. "Who uses math, anyway?"

"I got a seven-hundred seventy on the Math SAT."

"Who uses it besides *you*?"

Margery rolls her eyes. "I mean, you know more about cars than anything else," she says. "Don't tell me you want to work at the garage all day and race all night."

"Maybe," I said. "So long as no one brings in one of those cars that shall remain nameless."

"Jettas?"

I wince. "Dammit, woman, I said *nameless*."

She grins and shakes her head. "You and your irrational hatred of German cars."

Margery looks away into the sunset. The colors set her hair to glowing. Magical. I want to touch her but somehow I can't. We might be inches apart, but there is a distance between us that isn't measured in anything calculable, like degrees or integers or car lengths. She's not the same sort of person I am, and it's taken me two years to figure that out. What's going to happen next, I have no idea.

"You're smart," she says finally, her tone sad and serious. "Do you want to stay around here the rest of your life? Believing in stupid things like the Racing Lights?"

"Yeah, right." I look down the road at the lights. They come on before sunset this time of year, but they're easier to see as the night gets later, when darkness steals all the color from the world.

"Whatever," she says and opens the door.

"Hey." I pull her back in and put my arm around her neck, putting her face close to mine.

"What, with no one watching?" she asks.

"Or not at all."

She smiles and we kiss.

"Y'know." My hands creep where they really shouldn't go. "I could come in. Help you study."

"And be all *mathy* with me?" She pulls away and adjusts her shirt. "My dad's home, horndog."

"Well, that's the suck."

"*Mathy* and *the suck*...hmm," she says sarcastically. "I can just *tell* you're going to be a writer."

I make an obscene gesture to her.

"Some other night," she says. "Race on, cowboy."

She shuts the door.

After I drop Margery off, I drive for a while, thinking. Nowhere to go in the country, really, so I just kind of meander, at one with the California emptiness. I go as fast as I want: the country is so lonely you think you're just crawling along and don't realize you're driving a mile every forty-five seconds.

The clock ticks to 11:39 as I coast up to the starting line and put the Integra in neutral. I pop out Margery's Etheridge CD and put it back in its case. Her presence in my car is small, but there. It's not just CDs and lipsticks and things...but memories. I think of her every time I check over my shoulder, because once she decided flashing me at ninety mile an hour was a good idea. (Not that I minded.) Also the backseat is special—so special I don't let anyone sit back there.

The valley wind is cool through the window, and I turn off the engine so I can listen to it. I sit there in the quiet and the vast. The night sky stretches a long, long way before fading into dark invisibility against the foothills on the horizon. The lights on Gray road buzz; the one constant, the other winking. The light is hypnotic I'm floating, but I'm not asleep.

The night is perfect, and yet somehow cold.

It's the cold that jolts me up, as though the air dropped ten degrees in ten seconds. I'm watching my temperature gauge, and sure enough, it's dropping. One degree, two, three...from a cool fifty-five to a chilly forty-five. But it's supposed to be May. The temperature makes no sense.

And there's almost no sound. No traffic from I-80 a few miles away. Nothing from town. No wafting conversation from one of the farm houses within a mile. Just me and the Racing Lights on Gray Road. The broken one buzzes on and off—very loud in the otherwise total silence.

I'm not sure when I lost track of time, but when I look at the clock, it says 1:35. I remember seeing it was around 11:40 when I pulled up here. Where had two whole hours gone?

Need to go home, I think, which is weird. Here I am...alone, the night, the car, the road, perfect, and all I can think about is how I have class in six hours.

Maybe Margery's right. Maybe I should grow up while I have the chance.

I think about it.

Nah.

I open up the center console and pull out an unmarked jewel case with a burned CD inside. It's just got one word written on it in Sharpie: *Driving*. This CD goes into the player, and I flip to number six. As the intro plays, I turn the key, wondering how it's so cold my breath is steaming. My baby is purring; she wants to fly.

Then Zombie starts singing, and I peel out. Twenty. Thirty. Fifty. The engine roars as I double-shift like a pro.

I shoot past the Racing Lights, and dust swirls up to coat them in my wake. The broken one flickers, then snaps on. It glows permanently, as though I fixed it with my speed.

The cold air whipping in stings my eyes. I didn't close the window, and the wind resistance slows me down, but I don't care. I'm young, I'm free, and that's all that matters.

Lights in my rearview.

At first, I'm sure it's just the Racing Lights back along the road. I'm just not used to them both being lit up, and I keep waiting for the one on the left to start blinking. It doesn't.

Also, they don't seem to be getting any smaller.

"What the hell?"

A truck? Speed limit fifty-five, asshole. But hey, who cares? No way he can match my Integra.

I double-shift into top gear. I'm doing seventy. Eighty.

The lights are still there.

Maybe it's Juarez, looking for a little payback. Freak me out on the country roads so I spin out in a ditch like he did. But if it's Juarez, why would he wait while I just sat there for like two hours? Besides, the lights are too high off the ground for a Miata.

No. This is something else.

"Whatever," I say as we go around the soft turns. Six seconds before Gray-Kobert. "Eat it, loser."

The lights move a bit, then snap back into my rearview. No one corners that fast. No one.

Then one of them blinks.

I realize with a shock of revelation that drowns out the heavy metal on my stereo—realize it in the slow, creeping sweat at the back of my neck.

It isn't a truck. It's the lights on Gray Road.

And they're following me.

I shouldn't be able to see them like that. They're around every turn, never getting any smaller, always the same in my mirror. Maybe they're even getting bigger. No, that's not possible. Is it? How?

In my rearview, the blinking light twirls over and around the steady light. Circles it like a moon.

Panic rises in me. My foot slips on the gas and I press it back harder. My Integra whines and the wind howls. I've never gone this fast before—not here, on the country road. Ninety-five. One-hundred. One-hundred and ten. Streaking down what's left of Gray before it turns into Kobert…

It's only then that I realize. With the lights moving, I don't have my cue. I can't see them disappear in my mirror.

And that's when my headlights illumine the reflectors along the curving road. The turn is already on top of me. "Shit!" I cry, cranking the wheel and slamming the brake.

The force slams me to the side. My tires scream. I'm sliding, sliding, and for a second, I think I'm going to make it. I *know* it.

Then my left tires lifts clear of the road, the balance tips, and I flip over.

There's a weightless moment—my stomach sucks itself against my spine—and then the bumper of my Integra hits the ground with a scream. The seat belt cuts into my chest and stomach, sending spittle and a bit of my dinner flying. The wheel explodes like a cannon blast and we bounce off the front end like a rubber ball, flipping over and slamming down again and again.

Air bag, I'm shouting in my head. *Where's the f…?*

The airbag goes off into my face, punching me out.

The world comes back slowly, like excited kids called back in from recess one at a time.

First is sound, but not every sound. Only a few: the CD is still playing, which is funny. It's skipping on the word *beast*, over and over. *Beast–beast–beast.* I can hear a buzz, like one of the street lamps, but of course that isn't possible. There are no lights next to the turn.

Funny how I'm so concerned about what's possible and what isn't.

My Integra is upside down in a ditch thirty feet from the road. I can smell my own blood. It's in my nose and in my eyes. The reek of spilled oil mingles with it and I can also smell gasoline leaking out, surrounding my crashed car like a spreading red pool around a murder victim on a police procedural.

I'm trapped. Seatbelt, airbag, vehicle bending around me—all of it holds me jealously in place. Either that, or I'm paralyzed. I don't feel much of anything, except my right foot. It keeps hitting the gas, then the brake—gas and brake—as though somehow I can race my way out of this. As though I won't have to die.

There are three of them standing over me. I can't see them very well; can't see anything very well. It's too bright, as though floodlights are giving us illumination; high beams from three parked cars on the road. But the three of them aren't blocking the light. They look like they're *made out of* the light.

They throw around sounds—words?—in a clicking, whirring language that reminds me of the engines of racing cars. Their hands, if that's what those are, are flying around, making what I think are rude gestures. The CD keeps skipping: *beast – beast*.

One of them snaps off something at the one in the middle. He replies in a buzzing sort of whine, then slaps the first one upside the head.

My vision is dimming. It feels like falling asleep, or possibly like dying.

The light grows. Time stops.

I see *everything*.

I open my eyes and stare at my clock. The numbers are big and red: 6:44 a.m.

In a second, I'm going to wake up. In two seconds, I'm going to get up.

The numbers change to six four and five and my CD-alarm goes off. Rob Zombie plays—just the way to start a day. The same song as last night, actually.

I'm surrounded by pillows and music posters. The racing calendar says it's April. Dust dances in the light streaming through my window. I'm stripped down to my boxers. I inspect my arms and legs—no damage. Not even bruises. Aside from that particular feeling of not having showered the night before, I'm pristine.

It's like it never happened.

I reach over and hit snooze. There's another sound, I think—music playing somewhere else, a CD skipping—but I'm asleep in seconds.

Seven minutes later, the song picks up where it left off. I hit snooze again.

The clock says 6:58 when there's a knock on my bedroom door. "Aren't you getting up? It's not Saturday, you know."

Groan. "Yeah, Mom," I say, waking up a little more.

The shower feels good; warm water rolling down my face. The patina of grease you collect when you drive in the country with the window down flecks away and swirls into the drain. The water soothes me, washing away the night and the dream and all of it.

I really should think about the class starting in twenty minutes. I had homework yesterday, but of course I didn't do it. Racing is way more important...or at least, I thought that yesterday. Today, after Margery and I talked last night, I'm not so sure. Maybe I should try a little harder? You know, actually *do* something with my life?

Nah.

The clothes I wore yesterday are nowhere to be found, which sucks because those are my favorite jeans. I should probably wear shorts today anyway. The weather's getting hotter, though the mornings are always cold. Spring weather—can't make up its mind. Dressed and ready to go, I look for my backpack but it's also missing. "Mom?" I call. "Have you seen my bag? Mom?"

No response.

I look in the kitchen and living room, but she isn't there. The rest of the house is empty.

"Mom?"

I see her through one of the windows: she's standing on the front lawn, looking at something in the driveway. The screen door squeaks shut behind me as I walk out toward her. I hear something...a word repeating over and over...but I can't make it out.

"Hey Mom, have you seen...?"

That's as far as I get.

My car is sitting in the driveway—upside down. The front is smashed into the cabin and crumpled like balled up newspaper, the shattered engine spilling out like guts. The wheels are blown out and the torn rubber spirals off into the morning air like tassels. Spindly webs trace along every inch of the glass, and the driver and passenger doors have come loose and hang like broken wings. I see both airbags inside, collapsed like popped and half-deflated mattresses.

The CD is still skipping. *Beast–beast–beast*...it murmurs.

Mom is looking at me, her face completely open; shocked beyond understanding.

"I think," I said. "I think...I'm going to try harder in school." I reach into the destroyed car and turn the CD player off.

Racing Lights

AFTERWORD

While this story is indeed based on a true experience, the Racing Lights is a self-generated urban legend and not one in the classic lexicon.

I grew up in a small rural town in California, where (once I got my license) I drove out to visit a good friend who lived out in the country. I particularly enjoyed driving at great speeds on the dusty country roads, at one with the great open space that is unique to California. Usually, I would play loud rock music with the windows down as I drove (the songs featured in this story are "Come Out and Play" by the Offspring and "Superbeast," by Rob Zombie).

Driving back late one night, I passed the two operative street-lights on the road—one active, the other buzzing and winking on and off. The second light went on as I passed and glowed brightly. For the next two miles—for some reason—I could always see the lights in my rearview mirror, never growing smaller or moving.

I drove faster.

Waterheads

By Ivan Ewert

"You root for the Dawgs, you ask which Peachtree, and don't you ever, *ever* break down on the old covered bridge."

Those were Bethany's first words to me, on my first day at Campbell High. She was just the kind of Georgia peach dad had promised would be waiting after his transfer to Atlanta - ripe, firm and sweeter than sugar. I'm no kind of romantic, but I swear, she smelled like honeysuckle even from across the room.

I probably should have waited for her go-ahead, but looking like that, she was hard to resist. So I'd sat down at my desk, introduced myself, and asked what anyone new in town had to know. It was an interesting answer.

"I got the Peachtree thing three weeks ago: street, boulevard, avenue or battle," I told her, "and I'll see how the Dogs measure up. So, what's the deal with the bridge?"

She leaned over, smiling with a secret. I worked to keep my eyes above the cross at her neckline, leaning in and turning my ear toward her lips.

"Waterheads," she whispered. "They'll snatch you straight to Hell."

That was worth a grin. "Waterheads, huh? Why do I just know that we're not talking about a gang?"

"No sir," her smile stayed put. "Just the Waterheads. They live back in that old forest and the hills around Nickajack Creek; lived there since even before the War. You ever break down on that bridge at night—you ever turn off your lights, even for a moment—their little ones will swarm right over you and fetch you where nobody's ever like to find you."

"Nothing to worry about," I said airily. "My Corolla's all but new.

It's not going to break down, no matter where I go...or what time I get there."

"That's good," she said, "It's my pleasure to meet you, Tyler. My name's Bethany."

The teacher tapped on the chalkboard and that was that for our first conversation, but I'd made up my mind it wouldn't be the last. If she was serious about the straight-backed kid I saw her laughing with at lunch I'd be surprised.

Loved the story, too. That's a perfect way to pitch a quick lights-out after curfew; pull over to one side with your girl, kill the headlights and hold her tight, waiting for these Waterheads to come around. If she was laying a trap, I'd be the first to fall into it. That's half of the game, right?

I didn't catch her after school, and it was a little early in the game to start a real chase, so I decided to ride over to the bridge to see how much traffic I'd be competing with. Letting the Corolla's engine spin into life, I gunned it onto the street, getting both jeers and whistles from the kids in the lot. Dad always said that it doesn't matter what people say about you, so long as they're talking about you.

Once I was at the bridge, though, I realized she wasn't angling for a feel at all. There was hardly enough room for one car to fit through at a time, much less pull over in the dark.

It was a pretty enough place, though. More than anything I'd been having trouble getting used to the smells when we moved out from San Francisco, with peaches in place of patchouli and too many flowers wherever you might be. Here, though, it smelled of water and old cedars; like the docks back home, only scrubbed free of that fish stink. I got out of the car to take a closer look at the bridge.

The trees around it were draped in the weird Atlanta vines; kudzu, mud brown and sickness green, covering every single inch of the trees and blanketing the forest. There was a pair of streetlights at either entrance to the bridge, dim now but promising too much bright light when the sun went down.

The ground was deep green grass, red clay and grey stones, stretching away on either side and sloping down toward Nickajack Creek. A marker to one side had a bunch of historical information. I caught the year 1872 and quit reading. A history lesson wasn't part of my afternoon's plan.

Dull overall, compared to what I'd expected, until a quick breeze picked up out of the trees above that sent a shiver through my bones and held me in my place. It wasn't that it was cold, or unpleasant. It just felt...*wrong*, somehow.

I got back in the car and headed through the bridge proper, figuring I'd turn around once I was across. You had to drive slow, given how incredibly dark it was inside—despite the high windows along the tops of the walls—and you could hear the *click-clack-click* of the tires on the wood tapping against your teeth as you rolled slowly across. On the way back I turned the radio up nice and loud to tune that out, but I still had the vibration running up my spine, and the echoing music made the creepy feeling even worse.

So that was her game, I figured. Not to suggest a make-out point, but to see if the new guy got chased off by a make-believe boyfriend or creeped out by the local ghosts. I might not like that weird feeling the breeze and sounds gave me, but I'd be damned if I wasn't bringing Miss Bethany up to this bridge before the month was over.

"So how's Marshall?" I'd got the boyfriend's name in the class before, paying more attention than anyone else to roll call while I doodled across the notebook.

"Marshall's fine, thank you very much." The smile was back, her eyes closing sweetly. "He's such a *very* nice boy."

"Oh, well, if that's your type..."

She opened her eyes, looking more amused than offended. "It is," she said, "and it always has been."

"That's too bad," I shrugged, and watched her smile get a tiny slice wider. "Thanks for the sightseeing suggestion yesterday. That bridge is a weird little place."

"You went over?" Her eyes shone with amusement. "Did you see those rocks all over the place?"

"Yeah."

"Some of those aren't even rocks, you know that? They're sandbags, left over from the War. They've sat there so long they're petrified."

"Scared stiff by the Waterheads?"

That got a little laugh. "That must be it."

"That's something else. We've got petrified wood back home, but nothing like that." I paused, waiting for her to say something, and when she remained quiet I went for the opening. "I saw the Dogs opener is the first week in September."

She glanced over. "The bridge and the Dawgs. You paid good attention to my advice, huh?"

"I listen well, Miss Bethany. I always said it's the *nice* thing to do."

She blushed at that, sweet and pink. "They open on September fifth."

"Give me a call if your friends get bored. We've got a good setup in the television room."

"I'll bet," she smiled, "and we'll see."

I was in.

She came over with a few friends from the cheer squad and two guys to keep it even. We watched the Bulldogs stomp their way through Arkansas the entire afternoon, laughing and cheering and carrying on. Dad stayed out of the room after he'd met the group, and by the end of the afternoon we were shooting pool as the announcers wrapped up their commentary.

You don't learn that much about Georgia fans during a game except how loud they can get, so as the conversation lapsed I started on one of the few things I knew about.

"So who here can tell me more about these water babies?"

"Water babies?" Nicole, one of the cheerleaders, looked up from her shot. The look on her face told me to back away slow and leave it alone.

"No...not babies," I shook my head. "Sorry. I must have heard it wrong."

I'd have let it drop, but Justin was in too good a mood after the game. "He's talking about the Waterheads up Nickajack," he said, "you remember."

"*Duh.* Of course she does," Bethany said with a glare, and Justin's face got serious.

"Oh...hey, I forgot..."

"It's no big deal, Justin." Nicole forced a laugh, brushing away her dark bangs. "Forget about it."

Things got quieter after that, and Justin took off with his buddy just before Nicole and Haley made their excuses. "Bethany, you coming?"

"No," she said, "I'll have dad come pick me up in a bit. You go on ahead, I'll see you at practice."

When they'd closed the door, I turned to Bethany. "What was that all about?"

"Oh, it's…kind of awkward, is all. Nicole's brother, Chris, he crashed his car into Nickajack around Christmas last year."

"That's a hell of a drop off," I said. "Is he dead?"

"I don't know," she said quietly. "They never found him."

"What?"

"They never found his body, just…just the car, messed up real bad in the creek. All its electronics burned out, from the ignition to the GPS and radio. There was blood on the wheel where he must have hit his head, and the windows were all smashed up, but there was no body."

That same weird shiver from the bridge went through me again. "Hey, you don't mean you really think…"

"I'm not a baby, Tyler." She rolled her eyes, "I think he got pulled out by a current in the river and then caught in some weeds downstream. Maybe he was drunk, or high, and stumbled off into the woods trying to get away from the crash. Chris…he was a little wild.

"That's what everybody at school figures happened, but one of the clowns made a joke about the Waterheads stealing her brother's body and it just stuck. So she doesn't like talking about it. And if Justin weren't a complete idiot he'd have let it go."

"Yeah, I can understand that." I looked around. "Sorry about bringing it up."

"You didn't know. It's just so *weird*, that's all."

I didn't know what else to say after that, but she picked up the cue and we started another game. It was close to nine when I started getting hungry again.

"You been to the Varsity yet?" She asked.

"No, but I've heard about it."

She set the cue down. "It'll be quieter now. The game's been out long enough. Drive me down and I'll introduce you the best hot dogs you ever did eat."

We passed my dad in the living room on the way out the door, and he waved me on without looking up from his paperwork. "Back by midnight, Tyler. Nice to meet you, Bethany."

"Nice to meet you, Mister Rice. You do have a lovely home."

"Well, you're welcome in it anytime. Drive careful, Ty."

"Sure. C'mon, Bethany."

I hadn't had her in the Corolla before, so I hugged the curves a little quick and a little tight to see if I could get that sweet little catch in her breath.

It always worked like a charm in the hills back home, and sure enough, the second time I got her. I turned to her, keeping my eyes real gentle.

"Too fast?"

"No, no," she said, playing cool, but I made sure I slowed down from there. Hell, if she liked nice, considerate boys, then I'd give her one. She relaxed around the third curve and before long she was looking over at me more often than out the window.

The evening air was cooler than I expected, and the lines outside the Varsity were longer. "I thought you said it'd be quiet."

She grabbed my upper arm lightly and let her head go back a bit to laugh. "Tyler, this *is* quiet for the Varsity. Trust me, you don't want to be anywhere near it before the game."

"So am I taking you back home right away after we eat?"

"Do you want to?"

I shrugged with the arm she was holding and flashed her a smile. "Not so much."

"Then we'll see," she said, but she didn't let go of my arm until we'd been served. We went from there to Little Five Points for coffee, watching the locals pass by. The manager chased us off a little after nine, and we walked back to the car with her arm hooked in mine.

"Where to next?" I asked.

She tilted her head. "You tell me. You showed me your house, I showed you my hangouts, so it's your call what comes next. What do you want to see?"

"Well..." I thought it over for a second, weighing the possibilities. "I tell you what I'd really like to see is the ocean again. I don't think I've ever gone this long without listening to the water."

"You know we're nowhere near the Gulf, right?"

I took a playful swing at her, getting a little shriek of laughter as a reward. "Okay," she said, eyeing me. "I can't get you to the ocean, but come on. If you want to hear the water, maybe the river will do it for you."

The first lot near the Chattahoochee had a chain across it, but we got lucky at the second and parked at the edge of a light post's glow. Stepping out of the car I shook my head. No river was going to be a match for the ocean, but at least you could hear the water running over rocks, and the night breeze through the treetops added a nice counterpoint. Bethany took my hand and led me forward until we sat on a park bench looking over the river. It was wide enough that the casual light from the lot and surrounding areas barely illuminated it past the midpoint, but she pointed across the river anyway.

"There's launches on the other side, too. My dad comes out with his canoe sometimes."

"They do night rides?"

"I don't think so. I know I wouldn't."

"I'm kind of surprised it's not all lit up."

"People would just knock the lights out even if they did put them up."

"People? Or something else?" I leaned in closer with a smile and lowered my voice. "People, or the Waterheads?"

"Ahhhh! Stop it!" She squirmed in her seat, laughing. "There's no Waterheads on the 'Hooch, they're all up Nickajack."

"How do you know? Why would they stay in one place all the time?"

She shrugged. "Because that's where they always lived. They've got these caves and cabins built back in the woods, back where nobody will find them."

"They've got to come out if they're going to hunt people on the bridge, right?"

"I guess so, but they wouldn't come down this close to the city."

"Why not?"

"Because they don't want people to see them! They're crazy ugly, with big round heads that slosh around inside just like the creek." She looked behind her again. "They're a bunch of inbred retards. They're not going anywhere their dads or uncles didn't go and they're sure not going anywhere they might be seen."

"You can move around without being seen," I said. "I mean, I don't want the park rangers or police to find us, but here we are, right? We're in the dark." She gave a little shiver. "They might hide in the dark by the river, just like we are," I dropped my voice to a stage whisper and leaned in to sneak an arm around her. "Waiting for some dumb kids to stop off too close, and let down their guard, and then…BAM!"

She actually did jump a little at that, but in the wrong direction, leaning away from me. "Stop it, Tyler." She was still smiling, though, so I figured we were still playing, and kept leaning in with both hands out front now.

"Just like in a horror movie, right? A pair of hands reach out for you in the dark, big old heads staring out at you…no blinking. Just those great big empty eyes, black as that river at night."

"I said stop it," she emphasized the final words and the smile was gone from her face now. She looked around, nervous and suddenly unhappy. "God, I wish I'd never told you about that bridge. You're getting weird about it."

"It's just a joke," I said, "you don't believe in them, you said so yourself."

"That doesn't mean I want to be talking about them all the time!"

"This is only like the second…" I stopped myself and took a breath. She was pissed, and I wasn't about to get anywhere by pressing her. "Hey, I'm sorry, okay? I'm sorry. I was just having fun."

"Well, I'm not anymore." She crossed her arms. "Come on, it's way late. You better take me back home."

We walked back separately, no more hand-holding or half-hugs across the parking lot. I'd had a chance here at the riverside and I blew it, and knowing that made the silent trip back to her place longer than it should've been. When I dropped her off she didn't even say good night, just got out of the car and slammed the door before stalking to the wraparound porch. The silhouette of a man waiting in the front window said she'd get a lecture at least for staying out so long, another strike against me for the night.

Rolling to the stop sign at the intersection, I slammed my hands against the wheel in frustration. It had started out great, and this stupid story had screwed everything up. I wasn't in any mood to go home. Even if everything had gone well I sure as hell wasn't going to sleep so early on a Saturday.

It was a beautiful night, though; far enough outside the downtown that a few cold stars still turned overhead, fighting the ground light of the city. I hadn't learned the roads well enough to know many shortcuts, and it was a good night for learning. The hills rolled around me and got me to feeling homesick again for palm trees and sea air and less of this weird drape of kudzu, wound too tight to drift in the wind.

Before I realized it, I was on Concord, blinking into the guardian streetlights of the covered bridge, and I rolled to a stop in the middle of the road. I turned off the air conditioner and turned down the radio, brought my window down to feel the moist night air and listen to the creek and its crickets, but not a sound came to me as I approached, no insects, no traffic noise from the connector, nothing but the barely audible swishing of the breeze across my face.

Bethany had been right about a couple of things in the time I'd met her, including her opinion on the bridge. It was just *weird*, and I didn't like anything about it. I held the brakes and stepped on the gas a few times, just to hear a sound in that echoing gap between the hills, and then took my foot off the brake to jump forward, intending to get through that bridge quick as I could.

I didn't make it.

The minute my rear wheels struck the lip of the covered bridge, the streetlights sputtered and died, along with my engine, my headlights, and the slow grind of the automatic window. My mouth went slack as the car rolled forward regardless, lightless and lifeless, as if it were being *pulled* into the dark spaces before me.

I tried to reach for the door handle but my arm didn't move. I couldn't move. I couldn't even breathe. I was held tight as the car by something I couldn't even see as we rolled over those slats, *click-clack-click*.

Over that terrible vibration I could still hear it all too clearly, scraping noises against the wood like a dog scratching against a wooden door, waiting to get in, whining with hunger. I tried to scream, but my mouth and lungs just wouldn't do a thing they were told.

The bridge was dark except for that faint starlight. I could still see one of the stars through the high window in the bridge, hovering and fixed. It took all of my attention. It was all I could look at, all that seemed real in the middle of this bad dream.

The sounds came closer, and I saw them.

Two of them, shadowy and silent except for that terrible ticking, *click-clack-click*, of overlong nails on wood. Thin. Tall. Way too tall. Their heads, God, their heads were huge, misshapen almonds…

Waterheads.

The light exploded through the windows, blinding bright; with the roaring whine of heavy engines in the sky. I knew somehow that nobody heard it but us on the bridge, nobody saw it but me, as the spinning metal lip of the saucer blocked out that one real star I'd been holding onto.

Good-bye, dad. Good-bye, Bethany. If I see Nicole's brother, I'll give him your love.

WATERHEADS

AFTERWORD

Waterheads is based on an actual legend surrounding the Concord Bridge in Cobb County, Georgia, which I learned about from my in-laws from Smyrna and the surrounding countryside. They were kind enough to take me around Nickajack and the Cobb covered bridge after relating their own adolescent adventures with the Waterheads. Based on a small sampling of people between the ages of thirty and fifty, it seems to be a common enough story to qualify as a legend.

I haven't changed that much about the core concept—*don't be on the bridge after dark, or the Waterheads will snatch you away.* Some people say the Waterheads are a clan of malformed hillbillies hiding in caves back in the deep woods, others say they're the spirits of drowned babies. I found a single reference to the legend online, which revolved around leaving a Snickers bar on your car for the spirits of those drowned babies to eat. As contact with aliens sounds more appealing to me than contact with lawyers from the Mars Corporation, though, I've decided to use the version I already knew.

The Fingernail Test
Bev Vincent

The two men hole up in a crappy room in a rundown no-tell motel in one of the worst parts of town after the job goes south. The clerk at the front desk takes their money, cash in advance, without saying anything. He doesn't get paid to ask questions.

Their mug shots and a video surveillance tape run on the evening news. Crime Stoppers is offering a sizeable reward for information leading to their arrest.

"We'll stay until the heat dies down," Walter says.

Jeff says that sounds like a line from a TV show, but who's he to argue? He pulled the trigger, after all. Landed them in this mess. He thinks they should catch the next bus out of town, no matter where it's headed. Anywhere but here. Walter says the police are probably watching the Greyhound station. Jeff hasn't considered that possibility, but now that Walter mentions it he can imagine a guy sitting on a stiff chair in a dark room comparing passengers' faces to pictures on a handheld gadget like one of those Eye Phones, or whatever they're called.

So they stay put. Wait for the heat to die down. Find ways to pass the time. After five days in the tiny cell of a room, they start to get restless.

Walter is facing the toilet when Jeff enters the tiny bathroom to get a glass of water. The sound of urine splashing in the bowl stops abruptly.

"A little privacy, please," Walter says.

"Nothing I haven't seen before. Besides, don't you ever pee in a public restroom?"

"I got a bashful bladder." Despite this, his stream starts up again, sounding like rainwater draining from a gutter into a puddle.

THE FINGERNAIL TEST

After a few seconds, Jeff looks away and peers into the discolored mirror hanging over the bathroom's lone sink. Thinking about bashful bladders makes him wonder. Maybe they're being watched right now.

There's only one way to be sure. He extends his right index finger until it touches the mirror's surface. Then he leans to the side to examine the reflection. He exhales when he sees a gap between his fingertip and its mirror image. Safe.

"What're you doing?" Walter asks over the sound of the flushing toilet.

"Checking for two-way mirrors."

Walter pulls up his zipper, but doesn't say anything.

"I got this e-mail once that says they're everywhere," Jeff says. "Not just in interrogation rooms, like on *Law & Order*. People are always watching you. The only way to be sure a mirror is real is to check your fingernail's reflection. If there's no gap, it's a two-way mirror and there's probably someone on the other side watching. The e-mail says it's like visual rape."

"I got an e-mail, too," Walter says.

"Yeah?"

"Said some rich widow in Nigeria wanted to send me twenty three million dollars. She also wanted to sell me something that would make my dick two inches longer. All I had to do was give her my credit card number."

"You don't have a credit card," Jeff says.

"Don't need a bigger dick, either." Walter raises his eyebrows, as if challenging Jeff to dispute this statement. "Point is, don't believe everything they say in those e-mails."

"But what if someone's back there?"

"If the cops knew we were here, they'd break down the door and drag us off to jail instead of watching me take a whiz. It's impressive, but not *that* impressive."

"Come to think of it, I bet that's why the cops got there so fast," Jeff says. "They had someone behind a mirror."

Walter shrugs. They've been over the circumstances that led up to their present situation a dozen times. It's no big mystery. Jeff took his piece out before they went into the convenience store. A busybody in the parking lot probably noticed and called 911. That's why the cops got there so fast.

The bigger question is why Jeff ventilated the guy behind the counter. He says it was an accident, that he didn't realize the safety was off or that his finger was on the trigger, but that doesn't make the guy any less dead. All for two hundred and sixty lousy dollars. Now Jeff's getting paranoid about spies lurking behind two-way mirrors. It makes Walter wonder if his partner might be a little crazy. Maybe crazy enough to pull the trigger just for kicks.

Walter thinks it's time to get out of here. Take his chances out in the real world. They've already spent most of their money on the motel and on pizza and Chinese food deliveries. If he and Jeff split up, they won't be as noticeable since people will be looking for the two of them together.

"Here," Jeff says. "Put your finger on the mirror."

Walter knows better than to argue. He steps up to the sink and puts his finger next to Jeff's.

"See the gap?"

Walter admits that he does, indeed, see a small gap, the thickness of a pane of glass.

"Remember this slogan: 'No space, leave the place.' That's what they said in the e-mail."

"Got it," Walter says. "Leave this place." Sounds like a good idea. Jeff has been nothing but trouble since they met on the bus into town after being released from jail. Who plans his next robbery with a couple of armed guards a few seats away? That should have been Walter's first clue. There are advantages to hanging around with Jeff, but he can get that kind of action just about anywhere.

He pushes in front of Jeff to wash his hands, something he only does when someone else is present. He leans over the low sink and runs his hands under the tepid water for a few seconds. When he looks up, he thinks he sees something behind him in the mirror's reflection. Not wanting to freak Jeff out, he stands up straight and reaches for a towel, turning gradually as he wipes his hands. The only thing behind him is a wall covered with water-stained wallpaper.

He looks back at the mirror, but whatever he thought he saw is gone. Bugger's making me paranoid, too, Walter thinks. "What else did this e-mail say?" he asks, trying to sound casual.

"It says that people install two-way mirrors in changing rooms and public bathrooms so they can watch you get undressed. Hotel and motel rooms, too."

The Fingernail Test

"What people?"

"You know. People. The message came from some guy who knew a guy who heard a policeman talk about it at a seminar on personal safety."

Walter might not have a high school diploma, but that doesn't mean he's dumb. He reads newspapers and looks at things on the internet whenever he has access to a computer. He knows all about unnamed sources who are authorities on everything imaginable. Still, he can't shake the feeling that he saw something move behind the mirror. He doesn't want to get Jeff all riled up, though. It would be impossible to shut him up if he does.

"Interesting," he says, hoping to put an end to the discussion.

They stretch out on the king-sized bed and watch TV. Jeff has a thing for reality programs. They bore Walter silly. Being locked in a house for two months with a bunch of morons might seem like a challenge for a farm boy from Nebraska but another contestant isn't apt to stick a sharpened toothbrush under his rib cage or gang bang him in the shower until he bleeds. That's reality. Living on a remote tropical island for forty days, thousands of miles from here? Sounds like paradise to Walter, even if he had to eat bugs.

Still, Jeff is an okay guy when he isn't accidentally shooting convenience store clerks, so Walter doesn't complain when one of his programs comes on. They get along most of the time, which is more than he can say about those lunkheads on TV, yelling at each other over stupid, unimportant shit.

Walter's thoughts keep going back to the bathroom mirror. How often has he stood in front of it? Dozens of times. What would someone on the other side see? Not much, he decides. He and Jeff spend most of their time out here. They might have caught him in his underdrawers or picking his nose or squeezing a zit. Embarrassing, sure, but hardly visual rape. He knows about rape.

He looks around their stuffy motel room. The thick curtains are pulled tight. The only light comes from a low-wattage table lamp and the flickering glow of the television screen. The room smells musty, and the furniture looks abused and neglected. How many people have had sex in here? How many have been beaten or stabbed or died from drug overdoses? What would it be like to watch it all, like a reality TV show?

His eyes go to the mirror on the wall hanging over the battered chest of drawers. He hasn't paid any attention to it until now. Unless he's combing his hair or trimming his mustache, he isn't in the habit of looking at himself. Jeff is absorbed by his program, so Walter doesn't interrupt to ask if he's tested that one, too. Besides, it's probably nothing. Paranoia. Cabin fever.

He slides off the bed and reaches the other side of the room in two steps. He pushes around the pizza boxes on top of the bureau, pretending to straighten up. He turns far enough to monitor Jeff out of the corner of his eye. When he's sure he isn't being watched, he presses his finger against the grungy mirror and checks the reflection.

He's reminded of an old magic trick from a book he had as a kid. A book he bought with his own money at school. His father took one look at it and threw it in the trash, then walloped him for wasting good money on crap. That night he rescued the book from the garbage and read it with a flashlight under the bedcovers. One of the tricks was called the floating finger. You pressed your index fingers together and held them in front of your face. A third finger with two nails floated between them. It was hard to do while juggling a flashlight, but it worked.

His finger and its reflection meet at the mirror's surface, but there's no floating finger between them. No gap, either. What had Jeff said? *No space, leave this place.* Was there something to the crazy e-mail message after all?

A floor plan is taped to the back of the door. Someone lit a match to it at some point, but it's still mostly legible. It reveals that there's another guest room on the other side of the wall with the mirror. Is someone like that Norman Bates guy over there getting his jollies out of watching them? If so, the guy might eventually grow bored and decide to call Crime Stoppers to claim the reward. That would be a problem.

"I'm going to get some ice," he tells Jeff.

"Uh huh," Jeff says without looking away from the screen.

Walter takes his pistol with him, their one remaining weapon. The other gun, the one that accidentally propelled a bullet into the clerk's skull, is gathering rust at the bottom of the river.

The hallway is in worse condition than their room. It reeks of urine and burnt crystal meth. There's a gash in the wall that looks like someone took an axe to it, and stains that could be blood on the carpet. Walter tucks the pistol into his waistband, checks in both directions, and

The Fingernail Test

creeps down the corridor. He leans against the door of the room next to theirs. At the other end of the hall, someone is shouting, which makes it difficult to hear if anyone's inside the room. He puts his hand on the knob, but the door is locked.

A little thing like a lock, especially the kind used in shoddy joints like this, never stopped Walter before. It only takes a few seconds to pick it. He pulls the gun from his waistband and eases the door open.

The room is mostly dark, but a flickering light on the right attracts his attention. After he steps into the room and looks behind the door, he gasps. Damn it all, he thinks. The guy who sent Jeff the e-mail was right after all. Through the two-way mirror on the wall, he can see Jeff on the bed in their room, his eyes glued to the TV set.

Walter gropes along the wall for the light switch. When he detects motion on the other side of the mirror, he stops. Someone else is in their room. Two tall, thin figures clad in silvery garb emerge from the bathroom. Their heads are impossibly long. Each creature has four arms. Walter recoils in horror when they look his way. Nothing from this world could ever look as strange as they do. As alien.

"Jeff! Look out," he yells. He pounds on the mirror with his fists but this room, unlike all the others in the fleabag motel, is designed to keep its secrets. The creatures descend on Jeff, who doesn't notice them until it's too late. Walter bangs the mirror with the butt of his pistol, trying to smash through, but nothing happens. He steps back and raises the weapon, his hand trembling as his finger tightens on the trigger.

The aliens have Jeff in their clutches. He's screaming and thrashing.

Walter cringes in anticipation of the gunshot, but the safety's still on and the trigger doesn't budge.

Then there's a flash of light in the other room and the two creatures disappear with Jeff. The two-way mirror ripples and Walter is left staring at himself. At his gaping mouth and his empty, haunted eyes.

He slumps against the mirror. There is a small gap between his hand and its reflection, but he doesn't notice.

BEV VINCENT

AFTERWORD

I came to this anthology via a different path than the other contributors: I won the *Apex Digest* Halloween short fiction contest—for the second time in four years.

Since it was an open contest, I knew that the most common urban legends would be covered so I dug around for something relatively obscure. I'm not ashamed to say that I used a search engine to troll for an idea. Anything that sounded familiar, I ignored.

How things spark a writer's imagination is one of the great mysteries of life, but the moment I read about this e-mail people were receiving warning them about two-way mirrors in public places, I knew I had my story. Paranoia is great for driving plot, and it's a common element in alien abduction stories. The truth is out there—we're being watched, all the time.

Though I knew that there had to be an extraterrestrial element, I didn't want that to be the main focus of the story. I had recently written a noir vampire story that was well received, so my mind again turned to crime fiction, which I've been focusing on these days. Who is more likely to be paranoid about being watched than a criminal on the run? Almost every crime show has a scene with a perp sitting in the interrogation room while cops or lawyers watch from behind a two-way mirror.

I had all the elements I needed: the legend, the mirror, two men in a place not so different from an interrogation room and something watching from the other side. The rest of the story happened on its own. I swear. It was like I was possessed. By aliens.

HEADLIGHTS
Jennifer Pelland

Tim had known it was a mistake to get into the car with Colin and Brian that night. He'd known it before Colin had hit the highway and announced that they were leaving Worcester and driving out to Sturbridge to "smell some fucking trees." He'd known it even before Colin had informed them that he had not joined Brian, Tim and the graduating class of 2004 by passing math in summer school, because "algebra was for pussies."

But get in the car he did. He had no one to blame but himself.

God, college couldn't start fast enough. He was so sick of pretending that he still had anything in common with these two. Maybe at Dartmouth, he'd finally meet guys who didn't feel the need to use "fuck" every other word. In fact, if he never set foot in Worcester again, it would be too soon. He'd seen too many of his family and friends get stuck there, and he'd be damned if he'd join them.

He waited for Colin to pause in his rant against the latest 'fucking fascist convenience store Nazi who told me to apply again after getting my G.E.D.' to ask, "Hey, Brian, you're not still seriously thinking of enlisting, are you?"

"Fuck, yeah. I'm talking to a recruiter on Monday. That's all that got me through summer school."

"Maybe you should wait for the war to be over. Take some classes at QCC."

"Oh yeah," Colin deadpanned. "Because college changes everything. People who don't go to college might as well just shoot themselves in the head and get it over with." He hocked a loogie and spat it out the window.

"I'm gonna go eventually," Brian said. "The Army'll pay for it when I'm out."

"Well, yeah, if you live," Tim said.

"They're totally gonna send you to Iraq," Colin said. "You spent the summer learning history just so you could die and be a number in some kid's history book."

For once, Tim found himself in agreement with Colin. Which, of course, meant he had to defend Brian. "You know, I don't really get it, but good for you, Brian. Good for you for doing something with yourself."

Brian pumped his fist in the air and said, "Freedom isn't free."

God, he was a moron. But at least he was a well-meaning moron.

"Maybe you won't die," Colin said. "Maybe you'll be one of those guys who gets hit in the head with a bomb and comes home a total 'tard."

"Shut up," Brian mumbled, and slid down in his seat.

"Great," Tim said. "Let's just go home."

"I came here to smell some fucking trees, and I'm not leaving until I smell some fucking trees."

"Yeah, well Dartmouth is crawling with trees, so I'm good."

"I don't think there's trees in Iraq," Brian said.

"See? We're staying. For Brian." Colin pulled his old beater into the parking lot of Sturbridge Spirits and said, "Tim, you have your fake ID, right? You're buying."

"Hell, no. I'm not getting arrested two days before I leave for school."

"Tough shit. You're getting out of Worcester first, so you're buying."

"You dragged us out here. You buy."

"I'll buy," Brian said. "There's no beer in Iraq. I've gotta get my drinking in now."

"No one's buying," Tim said. He pointed at the dashboard clock, which was glowing "11:26." "No packie's open this late. The state was founded by Puritans, remember? Oh, wait, you only passed history because you cheated on every exam."

"So explain to me why it says 'OPEN' on the door, Einstein," Colin sneered.

Light flooded the car, white and hot, and Tim threw his arm over

HEADLIGHTS

his eyes to shield them from the blinding glare. "Where did that come from?"

He heard the sound of a pair of boots crunching towards them across the gravel parking lot, and out of the light came the unmistakable silhouette of a police officer. "Evening, boys," he said, resting his hand on the hood of the car and looking in through the open passenger-side window. "Why do I suspect that not a one of you is over twenty-one?"

Tim leaned between the front seats and gaped at the cop. He'd never seen a face so smooth and ashen. The man wore sunglasses, despite the fact that it was the middle of the night, and Tim got the feeling that he didn't want to see what was behind them. He could see Brian shrinking back from the window, and took an odd comfort in the fact that he wasn't the only one being weirded out.

Colin, on the other hand, was apparently too stupid to be scared. "Tim's got I.D. Show him, Tim."

"Uh…we were just here to buy some Red Bulls, officer," Tim said. Colin shot daggers at him from the corner of his eye.

"Well, unless you're twenty-one, you can't do that here. There's a convenience store just down the road."

"We…we're not from around here," Brian stammered. "We didn't know."

"I suspected as such. What brings you to our quiet little neck of the woods?"

"Trees," Colin said. "We're here for the trees, okay?"

"They're a lot nicer during the day when you can actually see them. Why don't you boys come back in the morning? There's not a lot of streetlights out in these parts, and strangers have a nasty habit of getting lost in the dark."

Tim nodded, "We're sorry, Officer. You're right, it's stupid to be out here so late. We'll be heading home, now."

"You do that." He stepped back into the light, becoming nothing more than a silhouette again.

"Why the fuck isn't he leaving?" Colin whispered. "Stupid fucking spotlight."

"He wants us to go first," Brian said. "Let's fucking go."

"I don't see his car," Tim said. "Does anyone else see a car?"

"It's behind the light, you retard," Colin said. "Good thing they didn't ask that on the SATs."

Tim peered into the light and saw nothing, just the ribbon-thin outline of the cop. "I don't think so."

"Retard." Colin backed out onto Route 20 with a clatter of gravel, heading back towards the entrance for the Mass Pike.

Tim heaved a sigh of relief. Good. The sooner this night was over, the better.

Then Colin drove right on past the on-ramp.

"What the hell?" Tim asked. "We told the cop we were going home."

"No, *you* told the cop you were going home. Which is tough shit, because *I'm* driving."

"That was a trap, you moron! That cop was waiting for us in the parking lot of a closed package store."

"I don't think he was a cop," Brian mumbled. "There's something not right about him."

"You two are such pussies," Colin said. "Scared of one small town cop."

"One really creepy small town cop," Brian said. "With a light and no car."

"Just turn around," Tim said. "Just take me home."

"So tell me, why the fuck did you even agree to come out with me tonight?" Colin asked. "Seriously. I wanna know."

Shit. He'd been hoping to get the hell out of Worcester without having this talk.

"Tell me, Tim. Just fucking tell me."

"Fine, you really wanna know?" Tim snapped. "Because I'm an idiot. You used to be fun, but now you're just pathetic, and I've been like that stupid frog sitting in a pot of water and wondering why it's getting so damned hot."

"Why are we talking about a frog?" Brian asked.

"What the hell happened to you, Colin? When we were kids, you were always talking about going to M.I.T., or playing for the Sox. And now you're, what, dreaming of living in your mom's basement for the rest of your life? God, you're pathetic."

Colin sat silently in the front seat for a long moment before saying, "Brian? What about you?"

"I don't think you're pathetic. I wish, you know, that you'd figure out something to do with your life and stuff, but…"

HEADLIGHTS

"He thinks you're pathetic, too," Tim said.

"I do not!"

"Seriously, don't you have any ambition? Be a man. Do something."

"Do something," Colin echoed. "Fine." He squealed across two lanes of traffic and ran a red light to turn onto Route 49. Pointing to the glove box, he said, "Brian, open that."

Brian popped the latch, let out a low whistle, and held up a pistol.

Tim's jaw dropped. "Whoa. What are you doing?"

"I'm doing *something*," Colin said. "Just like you asked. Oh, I'm sorry, is this not what you meant? Maybe you should learn to be more specific."

"When did you get a gun?" Tim asked.

"Found it in my dad's leftover shit in the basement." Colin turned around, still driving, and asked, "You know that Crips initiation ritual? The one where you drive with your headlights off, and then kill the first person who flashes their lights at you?"

"Okay, first of all, that's a total myth. And second, you think pretending to be a Crip is a good idea? On what planet?"

"Let me out," Brian said. "The Army doesn't take felons."

Colin whirled on Brian. "Pussy. You really think that sleepy-ass cop's gonna catch us? Besides, better to practice killing now before some fucking Iraqi puts you in his sights and you freeze up like a little girl."

"No way. Uh uh."

Colin switched off the headlights, plunging the road into near-darkness, illuminated only by the half moon hanging overhead. "We'll see who's pathetic."

"Seriously, Colin, cut it out," Tim said. "Turn the headlights back on before you hit a deer."

"Or before that cop finds us," Brian said. "Didn't he say people get lost out here? I don't wanna get lost out here."

Colin just cackled and hit the gas.

A pair of headlights approached from the left, and Tim grabbed the back of the passenger seat. "Look out!"

The car started to pull onto Route 49 before the driver caught sight of them, slammed on the brakes, and flashed their lights.

"Showtime," Colin said, and banged a U-turn in the middle of the road, tires squealing. "Brian, get ready to go."

"I'm not fucking shooting anyone!"

Tim looked around and said, "Uh, guys? The car's vanished."

Colin pulled the car over and thumped his hand against the steering wheel. "Fuck!"

"Good," Brian said. "Let's go home."

Tim peered up at the barely-readable street sign next to their car. "Podunk Road. Holy shit, there's actually a place called Podunk."

"I'll bet he turned around and went back down here," Colin said, and revved the engine a few times before taking off down the narrow street.

"He didn't turn down here, he vanished," Tim said. He stared at the houses as they flashed by the car window. They were far enough apart that they probably couldn't see into each other's bathrooms from their kitchens.

"This is creeping me out," Brian said. "I wanna go home."

"Fuck you both," Colin said. "We're doing this. You're gonna remember this night for the rest of your fucking lives. When you're both old and boring you're gonna look back on this night and say, 'That Colin, yeah, he couldn't get a high school diploma, but he had more balls than the two of us put together!'"

They crossed another street, and they were surrounded by nothing but farm land and trees.

A pair of headlights approached.

Colin let out another cackle. "There's our guy."

The headlights flashed, and then zoomed towards them at an impossible speed.

"Pull over!" Tim screamed. He lunged over the seat and dove for the wheel.

Colin shoved him back. "Fuck you! Brian—shoot!"

"No!"

The lights were nearly upon them.

"Shoot!"

Then they flew over the top of the car.

Tim snapped his head back, peering out the back window. "Holy shit, guys, it's gone."

"Cars can't do that," Brian said.

"That wasn't a car."

"Of course it was a car," Colin said.

Headlights

"A car that floated over our car?"

"It jumped or something."

"Jumped? Are you serious?"

The headlights dropped from the sky directly behind the car, flooding it with blistering light. And then they flashed.

"Shit! Drive! Go! Go! Go!" Tim screamed.

Colin floored it, and the car took off down the dark, twisty road, the lights riding their tail.

"We're gonna die…we're gonna die," Brian chanted.

Colin snatched the gun from Brian's hand and shot wildly out the driver's side window until it did nothing but click. The lights continued their silent pursuit.

"We're gonna die…"

"Shut up!"

Just as suddenly as they'd appeared, the lights vanished, and Tim let out a long, shuddering breath, all his muscles turning to jelly as the adrenaline wore off with a bang. It was over. Thank god, it was over. "Let's find a main road. Let's go home."

The car sputtered, clacked, and rolled to a stop.

No. Oh god, no.

Colin thumped the steering wheel. "Stupid fucking car! I filled it up this morning!"

"It's coming back for us," Tim breathed. "Shit, it's coming back."

"We're gonna die. We're gonna die…"

"Shut up! Both of you! What's the big deal?"

"What's the big deal?" Tim asked. "Excuse me for actually having a future that I want to live to see."

"You know what? I hope they *are* aliens. I hope they come back and probe your sorry asses and see what worthless sacks of shit the two of you really are, and then I hope they…."

The lights dropped in front of the car and flashed twice, and everything went black.

When the lights came back on, Tim tried to fling his arm over his eyes, but it wouldn't budge. He couldn't move anything, couldn't even blink, could only breathe as evenly as if a machine were breathing for him. He was naked, lying alone in the white light, his body spread-eagled over a cold curved surface of some kind, mouth agape. He struggled to scream, to call for help, to ask Brian or Colin if they were okay, but his body was completely out of his control.

Out of the white came the skinny outline of a person.

Tim felt his breath trying to hitch in his chest, but he was denied even that.

The outline wavered, lengthened, and then poured down his throat, a cold slime that coiled in his gut, pressing his stomach out in an obscene parody of pregnancy. Tim gagged inside his mind, but his body just lay there, obediently breathing in and out, in and out.

He felt icy tendrils in his brain, and his eyes rolled back as memories crashed over him.

...meeting Colin in kindergarten and laughing so hard at his poop jokes that he peed his pants...meeting Brian in little league and being amazed that a kid so young was so serious about his sport...boy scouts...birthday parties...pairing up with Colin for science fair after science fair until Colin suddenly lost interest and left Tim to do all the work...CCD...the summer Tim's dad left and Colin's dad was kicked out...Colin getting Tim and Brian drunk for the first time at Brian's bar mitzvah...Colin skipping school, dragging Brian along with him, taunting Tim for actually wanting to learn...the prom...Tim getting a full scholarship to Dartmouth and becoming the first person in his family to go to college...Colin egging Tim's house while his family was all off watching him graduate...

The memories spun through his brain like a tornado, so fast he could barely catch hold of them. He mentally begged his tormentors to stop, and the memories came to a dead halt with an image of Colin and Brian arguing in the front seat that night.

The worm in his gut coiled. "Choose."

He knew what his answer was supposed to be. He was supposed to be selfless and offer himself up for sacrifice. And the aliens, or whatever they were, would be touched by it and spare all of them, provided they all did the right thing.

Like hell Colin was going to do the right thing.

He wouldn't even be here if it weren't for him.

Oh god, he wanted to live. He wanted to go to college, meet people who didn't think that "study" was a four-letter-word, meet a smart girl, get his degree, move somewhere nice, with a house like the ones on Podunk Road, maybe get married, maybe have kids. He had a future. He wanted to see his future.

No, he was better than that. He'd do the right thing. He'd tell them....

Headlights

"Fuck Colin."

Oh god, he'd said it out loud. He'd....

"It is unanimous."

Unanimous?

He heard an inhuman scream—Colin?—and the light around him blinked twice.

Tim found himself on his hands and knees in the woods, naked, retching air and a thin trickle of bile into a pile of dead leaves as the earliest light of dawn filtered through the forest. He pulled into a squat, hugging his arms tightly around himself, and shivered.

Unanimous. How the hell had it been unanimous? Colin never would have....

There was a crashing sound to his left, and he choked back a shriek.

Brian stumbled into view, equally naked and freaked. "There you are! Oh god...I was afraid they'd kept you too. I...I can't believe Colin... That he..." He trailed off, looking off into the forest.

Tim shook his head. "I don't either."

"But he did."

"Yeah."

"And we didn't."

Tim ran his hands over his now-flat belly and choked back another retch.

Brian fell to his knees next to Tim. "I...I can't join the Army. I'm a fucking coward. I...."

They heard footsteps, and jerked their heads around to see a figure stepping out from behind a tree, silhouetted by the rising sun. The tall, wavering figure resolved into the familiar outline of a police officer. "I thought I told you boys to go home last night."

No. Not him. Tim scrabbled back, then froze as he finally got a good look at the officer's face. "Colin?"

The face behind the sunglasses was Colin's, but the voice...

It was the same voice from the officer last night.

It was the same voice from the ship.

Tim scrambled to his feet and took a tentative step forward, one hand raised before him. "C...Colin, are you in there?"

The officer said nothing.

"Why did you volunteer? I...I don't get it."

His face remained an impassive mask. "It sounds like that lost friend of yours wanted you to have a memorable night."

Tim felt the blood run from his face, and whispered, "You were right. You had more balls than the two of us put together."

The thing with Colin's face smiled, and his skin rippled for an instant before settling back into place. "Go home before someone else gets lost."

He pushed his glasses down his nose, revealing a pair gaping black pits that seemed to be peering at Tim from light-years away.

And then they flashed.

Tim and Brian scrambled out of the woods and nearly collided with Colin's car, which was sitting at the side of the road, all four doors open. Tim slid into the driver's seat, said a quick prayer, and turned the ignition.

Mercifully, the car started.

They spent the trip home concocting a story about getting drunk and lost in the woods. Tim immediately withdrew from Dartmouth, enrolling in QCC with Brian instead, claiming he was too distraught to think about leaving home with his friend missing.

It wasn't that.

It was the trees.

Dartmouth was crawling with them.

If he stayed in Worcester, at least, in the center of it, he'd be safe. He'd told himself he'd be damned if he'd stay here. Apparently, he was right.

He'd never leave the city again.

Because he knew how easy it was to get lost in the trees, in the dark.

Or in the light.

HEADLIGHTS

AFTERWORD

The urban legend in question is exactly what Colin says it is: a gang initiation ritual where aspiring gang members drive around after dark with their headlights off and kill the first person to flash their lights at them. I first remember seeing this on the internet in the late 90s, but according to Snopes.com, it's been around since the early 80s. In the U.S., it's been attributed to everyone from the Hell's Angels to the Crips, and has spread to Canada, Mexico, and even across the pond to the U.K.. To be honest, I think I chose it because it was the first urban legend that sprung to mind. Besides, I grew up in the 70s—the headlight-encrusted spaceships of *Close Encounters of the Third Kind* are my canonical flying saucers. So the two ideas seemed like a natural fit.

Shiny Eyes
Jonathan McKinney

Archie lugged the math book everywhere now. Preachers kept their bible at their side; Archie carried his *Calculus Edition 4* text book as if his soul depended on the further study behind its sacred pages. The lessons in the book mattered little. The numbers and formulas inside, though important to his school work, didn't match the list located in the pages just beyond the book's index.

Don't stare at the sun.

Written in hasty longhand, the rules penned by Jim Morrison encumbered most of Archie's time now. Doodles of pentagrams, and stick figures engaged in acts most never see them doing, decorated the list. Above the five rules sat the title "Shiny Eyes."

Shiny Eyes were used by parents to persuade their youth. "Better eat all your dinner or you might just see Shiny Eyes tonight." "Better get home before dark. Shiny Eyes wakes up about that time."

Archie became obsessed with the rules and soon started breaking the first rule. Don't stare at the sun. His classmates tapped their neighbor's shoulder and pointed at him as he stared upward. Soon his eyes hurt so badly at night he put cucumbers on them to keep the swelling down. His parents received letters from the councilor with concerns. Red swashes swam in front of his eyes constantly and finally one day….

Staring as always, walking home he tripped on the sidewalk and dropped his math book. A curse said to no one in particular issued from his mouth and he gathered the fallen grail. Looking again to the sky, for a mere moment, the sun shuttered. A small flick happened, like turning on a florescent bulb. It flashed for a moment, became less bright, and then came back with full power.

Don't question the stars.

Archie ran home, and his mom, Mabel stood slicing carrots. "Mom, the sun flickered."

She placed the knife on the cutting board, and rubbed her hands on the towel tucked into her waistband. "Son, do you want to go blind?"

Archie shook his head. "Don't you see? That's what Jim was talking about. He saw it, too."

Archie ran upstairs to fetch his Astrology book. Archie grew amazed reading up on the sun by the fact that it takes roughly eight minutes for the light to travel from the sun to the Earth. When he saw the flicker it must have happened eight minutes before he saw it. From thinking on this he soon had a headache.

Then he reached a fact that had to be wrong. Ninety-three million miles existed from the sun to the Earth. He called his friend Juniper. "Remember that quiz Hairy Sans gave us?"

Juniper laughed, "He'd kill you if he knew you called him that." Horatio Sans had a copious amount of body hair.

"I couldn't touch Mr. Sans, you know him being the missing link and all, but seriously when he declared that the sun was really one-hundred-forty million miles away from earth. Why do you think he said that?"

"Dude, no offense, but I don't really think anyone knows."

But Archie thought he did. Archie opened his math book, and stared at rule two. *Don't question the stars.* That night, telescope and his Astrology book in hand, he made a star chart. And gasped.

"Mr. Sans?"

"Yes Archie," Horatio Sans greeted after class.

"I made this star chart last night."

Sans nodded, "Not too bad. Looking for extra credit? You know your acing my class anyway?"

"Look again. It's May."

Sans laughed, and studied the chart once again as told. "I'm sorry...."

Archie grabbed the chart and pointed to random spot among the night sky. "This constellation here should be here. That one, over there. Listen, the weather outside is May, but the stars are loudly yelling it should be December."

Don't stop the medication.

Sans shook his head. "Have you had your little blue pill?"

Archie rubbed his head and chuckled. "We take them everyday don't we?"

"We have to."

"Why?"

Sans placed the star chart back on Archie's folder and helped gather up his books. "Archie that will be enough for today."

Archie, back outside, realized that, no, he had not taken his pill today, nor would he. Everyday since his mind had memory he had taken the little blue pill, just as his mother, and father, and his friends. He walked down the sidewalk and watched people going about their lives. Every one of them, no doubt, shook awake this morning and even before their teeth hit toothbrush, downed a glass of water, and the pill.

Why did they take them?

Archie found out at two the next morning. He wrapped himself tightly in the blanket, but this accomplished nothing. His heart ached. His fear increased when he suddenly felt his pulse slowing. Chattering teeth accompanied him to the bathroom and shaking all over from the utter chill surrounding him, suffocating him, he managed to shake out a blue pill and pop it in his mouth.

He shook all the water out of two glasses before the third finally made it to his mouth, and down his gullet. He fell shaking in front of the bathroom sink, shivering until he lost consciousness.

Don't venture to Elijah's Valley.

Archie woke up feeling warmer than he could ever remember. The cold fit he had the night before, still fresh in his mind, was unlike anything ever experienced. Why had he had it? What did the blue pill actually do?

He skipped school to bike ride to Elijah's Valley. Warning signs littered the route there. No one lived this far outside of town. Soon warning signs gave way to toxic waste signs, and radioactive symbols. Archie laughed. Some one seriously didn't want anyone to venture out here.

Soon the grass, too, decided it wanted no part of the valley, just soil and a few scattered weeds, littered the roadside. Twisted trees sparsely decorated the scenery, and all of these looked menacing, almost carnivorous.

Stopping on the cliff that crested the valley, Archie looked across the scenery. "This sucks," Archie declared. After the chill feast last night he expected something else life changing, but all he took in was a large valley. He placed his bike at the top and eased over the edge. Three steps later he couldn't breathe. He collapsed to the ground clawing at his throat. The ground moved...weirdly. He couldn't find purchase to manage his way back.

He sucked in air, finally, only for it to be taken away again. Archie discovered he was drowning in the open air and every now and then getting a breath. It took him ten minutes of fighting to regain the cliff and settle back into regular breathing.

Don't go to McCready's Mill at midnight.

His mom asked him why he hadn't attended school and he blew her off saying he didn't feel well, which wasn't a lie. He shambled up to bed, and lay there until his parents retired for the night. He popped the window open and crawled down the column on his porch, listening for anybody near. Shady Brooks had a very severe curfew.

McCready's Mill sat atop the hill above town. His bike would do him no good. As far as he knew, no road had been cut up to the mill since it closed, which wasn't in his lifetime, nor had he ever heard of anyone working there. He wondered on his walk up why no one had reopened it, or set it up for tourists. At least built a road up to it?

The windows were boarded up, and the long wooden blades of the mill looked like an unhealthily man's teeth. He reached the rear of the mill and looked at the door with shock. Everything about the mill sang loudly of disrepair, dilapidation, but the metal door, reflecting Archie clearly, looked more than modern. He moved his head forward, gazing at himself. When he leaned too far his head collided with the metal.

Steps issued from behind the door and, as the door swung open, he screamed. Shiny eyes stared upon him, and two more sets came out as well. The three things examined him, with their reflective chrome-like eyes. Archie felt their emotions: disappointment, and anger. He grasped a complete thought: We going to need more specimens.

The moon shown above and, as Archie went backwards, he noticed the graffiti painted in glow-in-the-dark paint on the back of the mill.

WE ARE THE ALIENS!

J. M.

Shiny Eyes

AFTERWORD

There are actually two urban legends at work in "Shiny Eyes." First, there is the urban legend the title applies to that is nothing less than a name given to any "bad thing" a parent may use to keep their child on the straight and narrow. They'll get you if you don't.... Their name in this story just happened to be Shiny Eyes.

The second legend had to do with something someone wrote in the back of Archie's math book (could it have been Jim Morrison himself?). Growing up in public school many times I had second hand books given to me for the year and often I saw different annotations. Some of these were helpful in my classes, but other scribbles and doodles had nothing to do with school work at all, and I sometimes spent more time considering what these mysterious quotes or questions could mean than focusing on school work.

What made these my choices? We all have a nice attraction to the unknown. You may see a weird symbol on a page of the book your reading. Sure, it may be a doodle, but what if it is the clue needed in finding a lost treasure, or the answer to why we are here? Or maybe Jim put it there and is waiting for you to open your eyes.

"Shiny Eyes" was the first runner up story in the *Apex Magazine* 2009 Halloween short fiction contest.

THE INVITATION
Carole Johnstone

"Just help me!"

Her last word came out in a nervous shriek as the first crack of lightning flashed across the dark carpet and walls. Dan glanced over at her, seeing the inside of her mouth lit briefly white, its walls trembling and smooth, tongue coated in white plaque. He closed his own, and looked away with a peculiar sense of sorrow that almost managed to eclipse his scorn. He wasn't too old yet to have forgotten how much fun his Nana Pat had once been; how much he had once looked forward to visiting this little house high in the hills above the North Sea or how much he had relished a favorite grandson status that had soured in recent years.

Anger returned in another flash and tremulous shriek. Lumbering across the carpet in her frayed tartan slippers, his gran thrust a bundle of tea towels into his hands. Dan accepted them with bad grace. He hoped Billy was midway through his sausage sizzle round about now. He hoped that he was being royally pissed upon.

While his gran shuffled over to the oval Chinoisorie mirror next to the cloakroom closet and began hanging a towel over its speckled face, Dan still stood in the centre of the room, cloths in hand, mentally counting.

"Help me, Danny!"

"It's Dan, Gran." Still he didn't move, not even when the rumble of distant thunder finally came. Fifteen seconds.

For a moment his gran lost the puffy vacancy of fear that made Dan want to lock himself in his room and leave her to her childish dread. Her lips became thin white lines that puckered. "Then it's Nan, Dan."

When that expression didn't immediately disappear—the same

pursed look that she had once reserved for only the most heinous of misdemeanors; a precursor to chasing him around the cottage with a broom or wire coat-hanger—he forgot his anger.

"Okay, Nan."

She reached around the mirror, and its chain rattled as she pulled the tea towel down behind the frame, anchoring it in place. Another lightning flash lit up the room as the first of the rain began to batter against the thin panes of its sash windows. The late afternoon sky had dulled to a sickly yellow that sneaked long fingers across the sheepskin rug and hearth, and into the scullery beyond. The Chinoisorie began suddenly to shake, its chain jangling as the frame banged twice against the wallpaper behind. His gran snatched her hands away from it as if it had burned her. Dan caught a glimpse of that doughy terror again.

"It's just the thunder, Gran, jeez." He glanced out of the window at the jaundiced sky. Anything was preferable to that puffy face and the expectation in it. The expectation that a twelve year old boy would be any protection for someone who had lived his life half a dozen times over. Another too-adult sorrow momentarily drowned his frustration. There was a good measure of fear in it. One day this would happen to his parents. One day they'd shuffle and shriek at shadows, their faces slow with slack fear and grasping need. Maybe he'd start forgetting what they were really like, too.

With loud reluctance, Dan pushed a footstool towards the hearth and climbed it, catching sight of his po-faced reflection before he hung the first towel over the mirror's face. The last one depicted St Mary's church and the cliff-top ruins of Whitby Abbey above white-topped surf. The eastern headland stretched out towards Kettleness at a frayed edge. Dan allowed himself a briefly rueful smile. Only one more night. One more night and one more morning and then his parents would arrive to take him home, and he wouldn't need to think about his Nana Pat again until at least Christmas.

A flare of lightning caught him suddenly unawares, and he wobbled on the footstool before climbing back down. He stumbled over the cat basket and almost lost his footing again. The Crab Apple's low branches scratched at the window panes in agitation. Dan's heart jumped a little too quick; quicker still when his gran let loose a reedy shriek at the following thunder.

"Danny! The storm's coming, it's coming!"

Were it not for Dan's furious pity, there might have been something almost comical in her panicked, labored shuffling in housecoat and slippers, her cauliflower head bobbing this way and that in directionless fright. He suddenly worried that she might have a heart attack. Panic, rather than concern, compelled him to cross the room, relieving her of her burden.

"It's all right, Gran. I'll get the rest of them."

She grasped his free wrist in surprisingly strong fingers. They were dry, their skin like crepe paper. Above pale, powdery cheeks, her eyes appeared beady and sunken. Dan tried not to shudder.

"They come down in the lightning, Danny."

"I know, Nan."

She didn't have many mirrors. His gran had few new obsessions, but those of old had been cultivated over years of absolute devotion, their ramparts continually embellished so as to be impervious to all attacks or persuasion.

"The storm's still two miles away, anyway."

She shot him a startled, almost suspicious look as he hung the last of the towels before turning three photo-frames face down on the sideboard without prompt. Henry padded down the stairs from the first floor, greeting Dan with a familiar strangled growl: a grey-haired tabby that had become as cantankerous and mistrustful as its owner. Dan barely glanced in his direction. Since her double hip replacement, his gran had no mirrors whatsoever upstairs, not even in the bathroom.

"You count the seconds between the lightning and thunder, Nan. Five seconds for every mile."

"So clever you young ones, so clever," she murmured, but there was still a measure of wariness in her eyes. It was abruptly drowned by fresh horror. "The curtains, Danny. Oh Jesus, Mary and Joseph, close the curtains!"

Dan slouched over to the living room windows. This was a new development. Last time she had been content with only covering the mirrors and pictures. Although last time the sky hadn't been quite so black and congested. He stared out at a low bank of clouds. The sun struggled behind them, casting an infected grey caul over the sodden hills beneath. He saw his own expression overlying the landscape in stark, linear relief. Two black, square holes, a thin slash of….

"Oh don't, Daniel. There are still reflections in the glass!"

The Invitation

His gran's expression crumpled into ugly relief as he stepped back and pulled the curtains to. He felt some amount of relief himself.

"You'll have me in an early grave, so you will."

Annoyed that he had momentarily caught her bug, Dan scowled and muttered under his breath: "Too late for that." Immediately, he snatched the thought back. She was still his Nana Pat.

They ate a subdued cold meat dinner by an unlit fire. His gran had calmed down enough to eat it in her armchair close to the obscured mantelpiece. Nervous jumps and shoulder hunches had taken the place of shrieks after every thunder clap. When the storm moved fully over the house, she went on stoically eating: a forkful of gammon, a forkful of cured ham, a forkful of potato salad. She cast only the occasional glance towards the covered mirrors.

Bizarrely, it was Dan who became afraid. The wind roared through old eaves and un-insulated gable ends. The Crab Apple cringed and convulsed, battering itself against the window in ever louder pleas. The attic dormers rattled and banged. Henry shrank back against his basket, a growl inside his throat, hackles raised in ugly spikes.

When the power went out, Dan was suddenly assailed by a sense of terrible and oppressive weight—as though every brick and beam was pressing down upon him—and he was forced to swallow a shriek of his own. His gran shuffled into the scullery and returned with a handful of candles, methodically lighting each one with too slow fingers.

After dinner, the gaps between lightning flashes and thunder slowly lengthened. Nana Pat let him have two fingers of dusty scotch, and afterwards his muscles felt heavier and his thoughts lighter.

"I know you think I've become a mad old fishwife, Daniel."

When he didn't answer, his gran sighed long and low and stared into the hearth as if flames were dancing up from its cold, rusty grate. "Your father thinks it. Your mother has *always* thought it." A whisper of a smile crossed her lips before she turned her gaze back to him. "But I never wanted you to think it."

Dan remembered overhearing his parents discuss his visit to Whitby. When his mum had protested, his dad had said something about treating the first child like glass and the second like rubber, and she had laughed a brittle laugh before giving in. "Nan...."

"You're so grown up, Danny, not like that older brother of yours and his endless dib-dib-dob-dobbing."

Despite himself, Dan felt a grin twitch at his lips. The wicked gleam was back in his gran's eyes. The whisky warmed in his full belly.

"Maybe I *am* old and mad. But I've come to think that old age is just a coming to know things. An *understanding* of things. Do you know what wisdom means?"

He nodded, wondering if she'd let him have another scotch.

His gran leaned closer. "They *do* come down in the lightning, Daniel. They always have. And God help you if you let them in."

"Nan, not the aliens again, please. Look, the storm is going away! It...."

"It always comes back. Always."

Dan let himself grow angry again. He suddenly felt very tired.

"Oh, I know you think it's nonsense...."

"That little green men beam down in lightning, and then teleport through mirrors into your front room? Yes, I do."

"The reflections *invite* them in," his gran admonished, jowls puffed and trembling with either fear or anger. "Everyone knows that north Yorkshire is the biggest UFO hotspot outside of Bonnybridge, Daniel. Everyone knows that the...."

The power came back on in fizzing protest and the telephone emitted a series of exultant beeps. Dan's heart squeezed tight and his belly gurgled; he bit down hard on his lower lip. Henry let escape his growl and skulked closer to the rain-battered back door.

"Nana, you believe that Dracula is buried in St Mary's cemetery."

His gran blinked in the sudden light. "He is."

"*And* you believe that Mrs. Thompson's neighbor's daughter's friend came back from Thailand without her kidneys."

"Don't talk to me in that tone of voice, Daniel."

Dan stalked over to the sideboard and helped himself to a quick slug of whisky. Lying alongside the turned down photo-frames, he glanced at a bunch of angelica stalks tied together with red thread. "It's all superstition, Gran. They're urb-"

"It's the truth! Everything comes from the truth." Her voice had become querulous and reedy again. "Don't you watch the *X-Files*? The truth...."

Dan rolled his eyes and risked another surreptitious swig. "*No one* watches the *X-Files* anymore."

The Invitation

She came up behind him without warning, plucking the whisky bottle from his hands. The fat-faced dread that he had imagined was completely absent. The pursed lips and narrowed eyes were firmly in its place. "And the Martians are very far from little green men, Danny. They look just like people. They look just like Dracula."

"For God's sake, Gran." The scotch no longer warmed just his muscles; his whole body felt hot with it. "Aliens are not bloody vampires! You're getting everything all mixed up!" He held up his fingers and began counting them down. "Vampires don't like mirrors 'cause they have no reflection." One. "People are scared of mirrors 'cause if they smash it's seven years bad luck, 'cause if you don't cover them up when someone dies then they drag your soul away forever, and 'cause it attracts lightning and burns your house down." Two. "Aliens can't come down in lightning 'cause it's just an electric current from the clouds, Nan, not Mars." Three. "And you don't invite vampires into your house, not into your bloody mirror!" Four.

The whisky was only a small part of it. Dan's anger truly stemmed from the fact that he and his once beloved Nana had had the same conversation every October break for three years. "You're old, Gran! You're old and you're stupid!"

Something changed in her face. Something *crumpled*. Dan instantly wished his words back, though he knew well enough that it was far too late for that.

"Everything comes from something, Daniel. Urban legends come from folklore and myths that were once born in truth." She stabbed at her floral flannelled chest, her expression pleading. "*I've* merely made the connections. Why can't it be everyone else who is wrong?"

When Dan wouldn't meet her eyes, she looked to the curtained windows with a sorrowful smile. "Your grandfather didn't believe me either. *He* invited them in without a second's thought."

"Grandpa died of a stroke while you were in hospital! How can...."

She leaned in close. Dan could smell rose water, and the remains of raw onion and mayonnaise on her breath. "You know what us old timers used to call a stroke, Daniel?"

He shook his head, feeling suddenly uncertain.

"A Shock. That's what your grandpa died of. The biggest Shock of his life." She blew out the nearest candle before drawing him into an uncomfortable embrace. "Bedtime."

"But...."

That familiar pursed look no longer comforted. "Bedtime, Daniel."

She shuffled around the living room, snuffing out every candle until the room was thick with soot. At the foot of the stairs, she stopped and tried to smile again. "'Night, 'night, Danny. 'Night, 'night Henry puss."

They heard a distant rumble that could just as easily have been a freight hauler on the A171 between Whitby and Middlesbrough.

"Put another blanket in Henry's basket before you come up, and shut the scullery door so he can't get upstairs." Her smile imperceptibly trembled. She tried and failed to meet his gaze. "I've always kept a sharpened stove length under both your bed and mine, Daniel. Indulge a mad old granny. Check that the mirrors are covered. Make sure we don't invite them in."

After she'd plodded upstairs and creaked shut her bedroom door, Dan crept back to the sideboard. The scotch was gone. He coughed at the enduring smoke. The Crab Apple tapped patiently at the window. Henry scratched and mewled at the scullery door. Snatching the angelica stalks into his fist, Dan stormed towards the scullery, muttering his dad's best curse words under his breath. In the dim, Henry flashed amber eyes at his approach and hissed.

Dan had pulled back the curtain, turned the key and opened the door before any other thought crossed his mind. His fingers shook as the whisky turned to acid in his belly. His anger was frighteningly unwieldy and too beyond his years to comprehend. The sudden wind battered against his T-shirt, his jeans. The rain wet his face.

"Fuck off then, Henry. You want to go out, go out."

Henry tossed him another withering look. He lifted a tentative paw towards the threshold before shrinking backward from it.

"It's only rain, idiot." Dan squinted out into the absolute darkness. The North Sea wind whistled in from the exposed headland, and he imagined that he could see the far off blink of the automated lighthouse on Ling Hill.

He loved his Nana Pat. His Nana Pat had once loved him. Now she thought that Martians dressed up as Vampires had killed his Grandpa. She thought that red skies at dawn and shoes on the table were the Devil at work. She thought that aliens were still called bloody Martians. Hurling the angelica into wet, dark space, Dan reached down with both hands, pushed a still-hissing Henry out of the door and then slammed it shut. She loved that stupid cat. It was the one thing that had never altered.

Dan drank the best part of two pints of water while standing by the scullery sink and listening to the plumbing's rattles and whines. Henry glowered in at him, pacing the windowsill, his fur matted, amber eyes wild. Sensing that there would be no swift reprieve, he returned to the back door, his claws scratching at the broken cat flap. Dan watched Henry's paw reach through the narrow plastic gap before getting stuck and then retreating out of sight. Seconds later it was back again, scrabbling for elusive purchase. His yowls were outraged.

"Fuck off, cat."

Henry would be okay. A soaking would serve him right. Show him who was still boss.

Dan had gotten as far as the fireplace when he heard the scratching change. The hackles that rose up against the nape of his neck were as alien as the sudden onset of a terror more physical than cognizant. His skin became cold and clammy, his breath fast and shallow, kidneys heavy. His neck cricked, throwing off shivers. His bladder swelled, biting into the waistband of his jeans. His mind was a very careful blank.

He crept back towards the scullery, breath held behind his tongue. The overhead fluorescent stuttered over the metal sink and tiled floor. Henry was still pawing through the cat flap. Dan steeled himself to let him back in. Those hackles grew suddenly higher.

His hand had already begun turning the key when he looked down at the brown coir doormat. It wasn't a cat's paw that swiped at his ankle any more than it was a cat's growl that suddenly shook the door inside its narrow timber frame. Dan caught a glimpse of long, pale-knuckled fingers before he wrenched his foot backward with a wheezed cry, slamming it against the skirting board behind. He let out a scream only long enough to let it go.

Retreating back into the smoky living room, he risked a craned glance into the scullery once he had muttered the first verse of the Lord's Prayer twice over. Those spindly fingers were still feeling their blind way around the mat, reminding Dan of *Thing* from the Addams Family only briefly. The association was too glib; instead of dampening his dread it only heightened it.

The nails were sharp and black, the hand that moved them lily white. When those fingers suddenly retracted back through the cat flap,

Dan felt little relief. When the tied stalks of angelica were spat onto the mat to the accompaniment of a low roll of returning thunder, Dan sprinted for the stairs at a wheezed shriek.

At their summit, he knocked on his Nan's door with a trembling fist. "Nana?"

Silence.

"Nana, I'm sorry." Dan's voice broke a little. His breath rushed loud inside his ears. He hunched his neck as if expecting a hand to fall upon it. When he glanced down the stairs he saw only static shadows. "I'm sorry for calling you old and stupid."

"It's okay, Daniel." Her muffled voice climbed louder out of sleep. "Tomorrow we'll go down to the harbor. We'll catch starfish and candy-striped flatworms."

Dan lay fully-clothed upon his bed as the storm bellowed closer. Its revived fury illuminated his stark room in brilliant white flashes. Ignoring the house's groans and bellows, Dan clasped his fingers tight and recited the first five lines of the Lord's Prayer twice again. It didn't feel like enough.

"I'm sorry, Nana. I'm sorry, Henry." Tomorrow he would make it up to them both. The unfamiliar beginnings of a hangover thudded at his temples and clutched at his already uneasy stomach. The floorboards creaked on the stairs, the landing. He screwed his eyes shut behind knuckles. *Tomorrow.*

A heavy thud shook him awake. He blinked once, twice. A jagged spike of white preceded a roll of closer thunder. Dan sat up. Ghosts danced in hidden corners. The solitary dresser squatted in ugly shadow. The knock came again.

"Dan?" His Nana's voice was thin and frightened. "Can I come in?"

"Yes." The door creaked open perhaps as much as two inches before his hackles rose again. "No!"

"Dan?" Her voice was confused. Confused, afraid, and familiarly crestfallen.

The floorboards were icy cold against the soles of Dan's feet. He patted down those shivers at his neck as he drew closer to the two inches of dark space. "Nana?"

"Daniel?"

The Invitation

A curious sob caught tight in his throat, forcing stinging tears into his eyes. The door conceded another couple of inches before Dan was able to reach it, stopping its too easy ingress with his foot. A roll of thunder followed so swiftly upon the heels of screamed white light that Dan felt momentarily disorientated. He touched the door with shaking palms, his voice a whisper. "Nan?"

Something crept inside his room. He felt it as a shiver down his spine; a subtle rearrangement of sound that transformed the small space into a horrifyingly smaller prison. He dropped to a crouch, scuttling backwards against the hinged jamb of the door.

"Who's there?"

"Daniel, let me in!" His Nan sounded petrified. "Is there something in there with you? *Did you let something in?*"

Another spike of lightning flooded the room with brief and terrible light. He saw his Nan's fingers wrapped around the door frame; he heard her frightened pleas. A monster touched him with a ravenous howl, its flesh cold and wet and grasping. He shrank further against the wall.

"Nana! Help me!"

Dan let go his foot mere seconds before another dance of lightning exposed those fingers at the door in long spindled shadow. Their knuckles were bleached white, their nails long and sharp and black. Dan screamed as he recoiled from the widening gap, blindly feeling his way back to the bed in a sudden return to darkness. Henry's amber eyes reproached from their hiding place under the dresser.

Horrible realization found Dan in the same instant that the door slammed open against the bedroom wall, admitting a breeze as cold as it was fetid. His Nana giggled, and it sounded like she was gargling mouthwash. Dan pictured her limping downstairs in the dark, one slow step after another, drawn to Henry's terrorized howls outside the scullery window. She had loved that stupid cat.

A sick dread that was as relieved as it was remorseful choked Dan's terrorized sobs dead. He crawled away from the lengthening silhouettes on the landing; in the doorway. He closed his ears to their chuckles.

Then he reached for the sharpened stove length that he hoped would be under the bed.

AFTERWORD

When I was a kid, we had a neighbor who always covered every mirror in her house whenever there was a thunder storm. She didn't know why she did it, she just did. Her mother and her grandmother had done it before her, and the very idea of not doing it terrified her.

I wanted to write a story that celebrated urban legends, but also questioned their source, their purpose, and above all their interpretation. Superstition, myth and legend are so often variations on the same theme. In terms of local urban legends, Whitby was of course a big inspiration for Bram Stoker's Dracula, and St. Mary's cemetery has long been rumored to be the count's final resting place. A recent report into UK UFO hotspots did rate North Yorkshire number one in England, second only to Bonnybridge in Central Scotland.

"The Invitation" is not intended as a pastiche or parody of urban legends, but rather a recognition that it is perhaps only our interpretation of them that is flawed. People need security in knowledge; the unknown is often too frightening a beast to confront.

Consequently, truths get mired in fiction and bias. Urban legends come into their own most often when we are in mortal danger and convention cannot help us. They offer explanation, even salvation. Under those circumstances, perhaps even the most cynical amongst us would be only too willing to believe in the impossible, and it was this above all else that I wanted to convey in "The Invitation."

FRAMES OF REFERENCE
Nathan Crowder

After viewing the footage, I sat there for the longest five minutes of my life, saying nothing as I got my thoughts in order. The smoke from Sol's cigar itched the back of my throat, brought an urge to blink more than usual, but I didn't wave it away or tell him to put it out. It was his office, after all. He could set his secretary on fire for all I cared. Sol Rubin might not have been the most powerful producer in this town, but he signed checks with a lot of zeros.

Eventually, Sol broke the silence with a sigh as he leaned forward and stubbed out his stogie. "So, kid, you've seen it. You understand why I can't trust my usual editors with this material."

Did I understand why Sol Rubin, maker of such films as *Vampire Showdown* and *Flesh Eating Cheerleaders* couldn't share the horror show I had just witnessed with his lowly paid hack editors? That was an unqualified yes. They might or might not be able to confirm its authenticity. But either way, they'd dupe and distribute their own copies in an effort to turn a quick buck in a heartbeat. And since the victim's head had been wrapped in a burlap bag, concealing his identity, they could make that money with a certain degree of anonymity. I considered the eight minutes and seventeen seconds I had sat through. Even if the video was a fake, the clinical torture and slow murder of an unknown man was a disturbing thing to watch. So disturbing that Sol had shown it to me without sound.

"And this just…showed up under your windshield wipers two days ago?" I watched Sol nod from across the burled maple desk. "No note, no name, nothing?"

"It's like I told you, Greg. I stopped off at location for the new flick and when I got back to my car, it there was waiting for me in a plain manila envelope. I'm just lucky that I'm the suspicious type and watched it by myself. If any of my staff had seen this…"

My heartbeat had returned to something approximating normal. This footage had to be fake…an incredibly accomplished fake…but a fake nonetheless. It just had to be. My career had been made with illusions just like this. I had practiced these deceptive arts for Sol's Rubicon Films and a handful of other discriminating studios for years. "You've been in this town for, what, two decades? You know as well as anyone that snuff films, real snuff films, are an urban legend."

Sol crossed his arms and scowled at me. "That film someone was showing around at private parties two years ago…"

"…was a fake. They've all been fake." I reminded him. "The girl they showed getting killed in that film you're remembering? She auditioned for *Angels of Mercy II* three months ago. A friend of mine was in the callbacks with her. Nice kid. Good set of lungs."

He pursed his lips and stared at me for a while. It must have been obvious to him that this video intrigued me, just as it was obvious to me that he wanted it to be real. God only knows why he wanted it to be real. It was bad enough that this nameless guy looked to have died horribly by inches. It was even more disturbing that the hand holding the blade hadn't looked human.

It was close: five fingers, and covered in pale blue latex. By that standard, it could have been my dentist. It wasn't until somewhere past the four minute mark, as my eyes began to search for something, anything on the screen that wasn't made of blood, muscle, and pain, that I noticed it. The hand was too long. I had to look down at my own hand to make sure. Each finger had an extra knuckle.

That, coupled with the realism of the vivisection shook me to the core. Why would someone go to such an effort to make the murder look real, but put in something so incredible as an inhuman hand?

"I know about the two movies you have on the slate now. This doesn't look like an audition piece for either one. What else do you have in production or pre-production?"

"Cop thriller and a slasher piece," he paused and thought it over. "You think he's trying to get my attention, maybe get a job out of this?"

"Maybe." I shrugged. Sol eyed me, waiting for the answer he knew was coming. Finally, I leaned forward with a sigh. "Ok, give me the disk and I'll look into it."

"This stays confidential," Sol cautioned me unnecessarily.

"Our secret, Mr. Rubin."

He put the disk back into the envelope he had retrieved it from at the beginning of our meeting. Sol slid it across the desk, but kept his fingers on the edge of the envelope, pinning it down for a long moment. "You find out if this is authentic and you can name your price."

I drove back to my bungalow, and parked my battered Vega. Shade from the palm trees out front was still hours from hitting the chipped paint of my front porch. It was hot outside and was going to be even muggier inside with only the single box fan stirring the dusty air. Naming my own price would allow me to get an air conditioner, or a newer car; something that didn't drip oil. I could get out from under the looming mortgage payments, at least for a while. There were a few ways to begin, some more discreet than others. Unfortunately, the more discreet routes were also the least palatable. I didn't own all the equipment to break down the images on the disk. Since most of my jobs were on other people's teams, I tended to use their equipment, allowing me to sell the more expensive and seldom used pieces of tech.

I thought again that it was certain to be sweltering in my bungalow, and there was only so much I could do on my own rig. I might as well get it over with quick, like tearing off a bandage. I fished out my cell phone while inventing a plausible cover. Dave Geller answered on the second ring. I barreled through his mumbled greeting, "Dave, this is Greg Watanabe. Long time no talk."

I waited a few seconds for recognition. I didn't care for Dave, but he had always liked me for reasons I just never understood. Most people around the industry didn't care much for Dave. He didn't have many friends, which is why I could trust him; there was no one for him to gossip to, and he had more to gain by his silence. Rare were the times that I initiated contact. "What can I do for you, Greg?"

"There's this eight-minute effects sequence I need to strip down and analyze. I wondered if you could give me a hand."

I listened to the unmistakable sound of Dave sucking on his teeth while I waited for him to make up his mind. "Stripping down a sequence, huh?"

"This is hush-hush stuff, Dave," I let the very natural hesitation over this call creep into my voice. "I shouldn't even be talking to you about it." I let his imagination fill in the gaps. Dave overflowed with conspiracy talk and wild speculation based on little information when someone was around to listen, which was rarely. Even if he did find a patient ear, they would discount what he told them as crazy talk.

Dave backpedaled, eager not to scare off a visitor. "Whoa, whoa, I'm not judging, man. Let me guess. You got someone else's effect and you're trying to reverse engineer and see how they did it?"

"Will you give me a hand breaking it down? I'll stop at Madam Li's for takeout."

"I'll put on some coffee. See you when you get here."

When I got there was almost an hour later, after slogging through the early evening traffic to Burbank and waiting in the air-conditioned bar of Madam Li's for takeout boxes of crispy salt and pepper tofu and chicken chow mein Hong Kong style. I found street parking in front of Dave's building beneath the lone functioning street light on the block. The digital effects journeyman buzzed me in not a second too soon. The alcove smelled like spilled malt liquor and piss. I picked my way down the half-flight of litter strewn stairs to the basement apartments, afraid of what I might step on beneath the discarded newspapers and sale flyers.

Dave waited with his door open. His slight hunchback and long, greasy hair was silhouetted in the flickering blue television light from his apartment. "You got me the chow mein?" I nodded and showed him the now-greasy paper bag. "Crispy?"

"Hong Kong style. I remembered."

He stepped aside and let me in. It looked like he had picked up a little for me, as there was a clear path through the clutter to the back hallway. TV Guides, worn sci-fi and horror paperbacks, stacks of porn magazines from the 80s, and weary cardboard boxes of old video tapes created a hedge maze at hip height in the living area. Dave didn't do much entertaining. The only seat not overtaken by nostalgia was a battered Lay-Z-Boy recliner at one end of a bottle-strewn coffee table. The place smelled of sweat, spunk, nacho cheese, and maple syrup. I did my best to block it out.

An antique CRT television squatted at the other end of the table, showing a frozen image of a naked woman holding a severed head in her lap. I recognized the image from the end of *Sleepaway Camp*. The fact that the film had been stopped at the moment before the big reveal unnerved me slightly. Another fifteen seconds and the reason people remembered that film at all would be in full display. But no, the image was frozen, the slight distortion of a paused VHS tape holding it in a state of horror-*interruptis*.

I let Dave lead me back to the editing suite in the spare second bedroom at the back of the apartment. He was rambling about how good it was to see me. The last time had been at a group dinner after the midnight screening of some cult film at an art house theatre in West Hollywood. I think it had been an early Giallo film, Bava's *Twitch of the Death Nerve*, possibly. Dave had gone on at length about how Mario Bava had been the grandfather to the slasher films that followed in America almost a decade later. No one disputed him. In fact, it was largely held as common knowledge. Among the horror film aficionados present, it was like he was saying over and over again that fire was hot and ice was cold. It had been almost ten months since that encounter, and I would have gladly waited another ten months given the chance. I felt dirty just being here.

The editing suite was more professionally maintained than the rest of the apartment. Heavy folding tables lined the edges of the small room, with two rolling desk chairs pushed up to the main workstation monitor. The door had been removed from the closet, and the interior fitted with shelves stacked floor to ceiling with videotapes and Criterion edition DVD's. Dave waved me in, allowing me to choose my seat first, though I didn't really see a difference. I handed over the disk.

"Any teaser on what this is?"

He was going to see it soon enough. I might as well start building the lie now. "It's a very well done torture murder with a twist. They managed to get it all in one continuous take but it's a little raw."

This got his attention, and even in the dimly lit room, I could see his eyebrows shoot up. "Raw? Like how raw?"

"Makes *Hostel* look like Mary fucking Poppins."

"Well, since we're looking for visual cues, do you want to run this through with no sound?" I was pretty sure I knew what answer he wanted.

Dave was a movie whore. There was no half-way for him. He wanted the full enchilada, the cinematic experience of picture and sound. After my first viewing, I was pretty sure that I didn't want to hear the screams, the whisper of razor slicing skin, the wet squelch of organs being lifted free that I had imagined during my lone, soundless viewing. The son of a bitch was practically salivating waiting for my answer.

"Put the sound on." I wasn't happy with it, but there could be clues in the sound track...a recognizable voice, machine sounds, airplanes or trains...I don't know. I was grasping at straws. At least I didn't have to watch the horror show the second time. When Dave hit play, I averted my eyes from the screen, and watched his reactions instead. His pupils dilated, his breathing became more excited. His noodles were forgotten on the table near his elbow, his hands clutching at his jeans in anticipation.

The sound was not as bad as I had imagined. The visual elements might have been polished, but the sound hadn't been enhanced. If I were to guess, they used a single omni-directional audio pickup with no professional finishing. It picked up the screams and cries, the desperate pleas. There was an irregular droning buzz in the background that set my teeth on edge. It could have been generators used to power the lights or any number of other sources in the location. And at least it covered the sounds of cutting.

Say what you will about Dave, he was true to his more repulsive qualities. If there was ever a market for legitimate snuff, I imagine he would have been on that very short mailing list. He also picked up on the twist immediately, freezing the frame less than a minute into the footage. "The hand is all wrong."

"It took me longer to notice, but yeah. Are you seeing what I saw?"

"Extra knuckles." He leaned in closer to the monitor and cranked the film back a few frames. "Wow, that's really well done. That's some good dexterity; too good to be a physical effect."

It wasn't what I wanted to hear. It too closely echoed my own thoughts. I felt the noose tightening. "So, finished CGI?"

"Yeah, probably." Though, he didn't sound convinced. He resumed the playback, hunched forward in his chair, staring with obsessive focus on the monitor. But as intently as Dave watched, it was now technical—dispassionate. As if he had unhooked one side of his brain to focus all his energy on decrypting the how while neglecting the why.

When his first viewing was over, Dave sat back and chewed on his lower lip for a few minutes. He grabbed a yellow legal pad from the table to his right and started jotting down notes. "Ok, right off the bat, I can tell you the body was done with physical effects. There are maybe one or two working studios doing that level of work in L.A. And who knows if there might be some wunderkind out there who developed a new technique as well. Either way, if it's local, the effects studio should be easy to trace."

The words on the tip of my tongue were, "So you're sure that's a model shot," but I squashed that idea quickly. It opened the door to all kinds of other thoughts, like "Maybe it's real." I waited a beat, looked at the now-dark screen, then back at Dave. "I don't know. Digital work is the way of the future. Why wouldn't they use CG?"

Dave puffed out his chest, arrogance dripping from him. "The shadows, the depth of field, the level of detail—you can do that with a computer but it takes more work than it's worth. Ultimately, you get more satisfying results with less work by using models."

It was simple economics. I knew how it worked as well as Dave, but it didn't answer my main concern. "Ok, so model work in the background. Then they use digital work on the hand in the foreground that adds the extra knuckles and masks out the actual hand holding the knife."

"That would be my guess, yeah." Dave cracked open his chow mein and started working at it with disposable chopsticks. He pointed to the controls, "You mind driving for a while so I can eat?"

Since I had been picking at my tofu for a while, I didn't mind taking the wheel. This was the grinding part, the grunt work. To spot digital doctoring, frame by frame viewing was a real basic option. With standard video, there are sixty interlaced frames per second of film. Going through even eight minutes of video could take all day. But thankfully, I only needed to analyze about twenty seconds or so of footage. I didn't need to know how it was doctored. I needed to know if it was doctored.

I wound the footage up to shortly after the hand first appeared, before the vivisection became too difficult to watch. I studied the chosen frame closely, paying particular attention to the knuckles and area surrounding them. Once I had contented myself with what I was seeing, I advanced to the next frame, searching for anything that didn't quite fit. I moved through thirty frames like this, not seeing anything technically out of place. Then I ran those thirty frames through at 1/10th speed. A half-second of footage, stretched out to five seconds. Nothing. Smooth as butter.

That hand, as wrong as it was, had to be either the best digital effect

I had ever seen or it was the real deal. Call me crazy. For my money, it was the real deal. Not that Dave could know. I played the footage back two more times for show, leaning closer, muttering under my breath. "Yeah…yeah, that's the goods." I waved vaguely towards screen.

Dave's eyes narrowed. He set aside his dinner and leaned in, straining to see what I claimed to have discovered. I played the loop back for him one more time, and raised a challenging eyebrow when it finished running. "You saw that, right? Along the lower edge of the hand near the wrist."

"I, um," he shifted uncomfortably, "I should see it one more time just to be sure."

I sighed and ran the footage again; certain he had already taken the bait. There was nothing to see, of course, but he trusted me. If I saw it, then it had to be there. Denying it would make it sound like he didn't have good enough eyes for this business. I felt a little bad about it, but it had to happen. Before the five seconds was up, Dave was nodding, convinced. "Yeah," he mumbled. "There's the seam. That's really well masked, though."

"Quality work for sure," I agreed. I stopped the editing suite and ejected the disk. I made sure to clean the file from the buffers in his computer. I couldn't leave any trace that I or the disk had been here. "I wouldn't have spotted it without your help, though. This rig you're using is sharp."

Slow realization crept into his features. "Wait, that's it? You're done?"

"That's it." I pointed at the open disk drive tray. He begrudgingly removed the disk and returned it to its envelope. "Knowing it's digital with model work in the background is a start. I need to think about how to progress next. I'll probably start calling around the physical effects workshops tomorrow."

He gave me doe-eyes, begged to burn a copy of the footage, promised to keep it "just between us," but it was a no-go. "Proprietary," I insisted. "I'd lose my job, and they'd sue both of us to oblivion."

Minutes later I was out in the parking lot in the urban nighttime glow of Burbank. The streetlight I had parked under had joined its dead brethren, but there was enough light from the surrounding buildings to see my car's bulk clearly. The block was all but abandoned, the only activity a small gang of toughs leaning against their car on the corner, smoking cigarettes. I kept an eye on the smokers and reached for my phone. The wind shifted and I caught the bum-stink in the doorway again. Before I dialed, I stepped upwind a bit, closer to my car. When I could breathe without gagging, I called Sol.

He answered a lot faster than I would have expected. It was like he was waiting for my call. "Greg? Tell me you still have that disk." He was trying to keep it together, but there was an edge to his voice. Something had spooked him.

"Yeah, Mr. Rubin. I have it. What's going on?"

There was an audible sigh of relief on the other end of the phone. "Have you shown it to anyone else?"

"No," I lied. I looked back at Dave's apartment building. "No one."

"Good, kid. That's good." His tone relaxed a bit. I could hear his desk chair squeak, indicating he was either leaning back in relief or leaning forward intently. The next sentence showed me it was the latter. "Now listen close. I want you to destroy it. That and any copy you might have made. Break it up, melt it down, whatever, just get rid of it."

I could sense my easy money flying away, and didn't much care for it. "Mr. Rubin, what's going on here? I already put in some time on this. I think this might be…"

"Don't tell me!" He shouted, cutting me off. He started panting, regaining his breath. "I'm sorry. You'll still get a check. Not as much, of course, but I recognize that your time is valuable. Come by tomorrow." He hung up without another word.

The street was suddenly too dark for my taste, the group of smokers too close for comfort. Whatever had spooked Sol was infectious. I hurried to my car. With the disk unharmed on the passenger seat, I keyed the old wreck to life. Sol will pay me. Right. Enough to buy me off…buy a bit of silence. It wasn't likely to be the kind of payday I had hoped for. There might be enough zeros to upgrade my car, maybe shovel my way out of a bit of debt, but likely not both.

What the hell had gotten to Sol Rubin? He had been unnerved by the footage before. Had he uncovered something on his own; something that pointed to the authenticity of the death, perhaps? Or had the unknown person who left the disk for him made a more formal introduction? The producer was unlikely to tell me. I was just an occasional contract employee. The puzzle consumed my mind all the way home.

The only certainty was that I would not destroy that disk; at least not until I had solved some of the mysteries for myself.

At home, I retreated to the relative cool of the workspace I had created in my former dining room. My computer was set up on a red Formica and chrome table my grandmother had salvaged from a diner decades ago, and I pulled up a seat, prepared for an hour or so of digging. I figured that if this had been a real murder, there might be missing person reports. I was wrong. It only took a few minutes. Particularly gruesome murders had a way of making front page news, even in Los Angeles. I recognized the name immediately, and it caught my attention long before the details of the methodically disassembled corpse were revealed later in the article. Brian Sark. I hadn't thought of that name for a year or two.

The video was real.

What was more, the victim's one claim to fame was a hoax: the creation and distribution of a fake alien autopsy video that sold for no small amount of money to the networks a few years back. In fact, the framing of the scene was so similar in retrospect that I was briefly embarrassed for not making the connection sooner. It couldn't be a coincidence. I put the disk into my computer and played it one more time. But this time I hid the gruesome images of what I now knew to be a very real murder behind the window of a suite of audio software. The program wasn't the best, but it was good enough for my purposes. I isolated the screams, the cries and whimpers, and I excised them from the soundtrack as cleanly as the killer had removed Brian's kidney. I lost track of time as I sliced and removed background noises, digging for the secret, up to my metaphorical elbows in the guts of the recording. Machine noises, slice. Passing cars, slice. Tools and instruments being picked up and put down on a metal tray, slice. I isolated and filtered the hum that had previously set my teeth on edge.

When I found the voice, I had to play it back three times just to convince myself it was real. It was a buzzing drone, like the sound of a hundred, giant wasps trained to specific pitches. My skin grew cold at the sound. "Brian Sark, you have been chosen to serve as a warning. Your crimes against visitors are well documented. The cruelty you have shown shall be visited upon you."

The same message repeated as if on a loop. Again, and again, and again, long after Brian would have been listening...long after he was dead.

Frames of Reference

It was unlikely that he would have understood, anyway. It wasn't like he had ever experienced a real encounter with an alien species. His autopsy video was well known in our industry as a fake. He had admitted it as much himself among my peers. What did it matter if a big segment of the population believed that it was real? What did it matter if its debunking as a hoax never got much publicity?

This is why it mattered.

Someone—something—might take casual disregard for a believably alien corpse as a sign of hostility.

I shut off the playback and sat with my face in my hands. I was exhausted to the core. New problems floated to the forefront of my mind. I could destroy the disk, as instructed. But shouldn't someone be told? I had no doubt that if Sol was having me destroy the disk, he wasn't about to notify any authorities. In fact, if not for his lurid alien encounter movies, he probably wouldn't have received this footage in the first place.

There was the possibility, however fleeting, that Sol Rubin was not the only recipient. There were a lot of producers in this town. Any number of copies could be in circulation. If I was able to filter out the message, others would be able to.

That buzz, that droning hum...listening to the sound intently as I tore it apart had gotten it stuck in my head. There at the back of my consciousness, I found I could still hear it. It was convincing enough that I had to check to make sure playback was off, not merely dampened. No. The computer was silent except for the incessant whir of the fan. Looking at the clock on the corner of my computer display, I realized it was past four in the morning. No wonder I was hearing things.

Except that I wasn't. The sound was louder now. There was no denying it. This wasn't some auditory phantom, some ingrained memory. The buzz came from outside, vibrating through window and wall, from the front of the house.

I turned and saw a bright light blazing through the small square of glass in my front door, a beacon highlighting floating dust motes like some improbable spotlight. Almost without thinking, I ejected the disk from my computer, blindly sliding it back into the envelope in which it had been first given to me. The drone was louder, the buzz of a pre-concert arena rock show crowd. My legs went numb, even as they lifted me from my seat, propelling me towards the door.

Of course the buzz wasn't exactly the same. It couldn't have been. I wasn't Brian Sark. The message was different, though the messenger was undoubtedly the same. Did he get the same strange visitation? Was Brian's last conscious act walking towards his doom; a bright light and an alien hum? Or was he snatched from his bed while he slept, or lifted in a beam of light on some lonely desert highway? I would never know. Even if I did, it wouldn't give me comfort.

The light was at eye level, so I had to skirt the edge of the hallway to avoid being blinded. Even so, my eyes rebelled against the brilliance. The buzz set the fillings in my teeth to vibrate. The hand that reached out to open the door was mine, though I only distantly felt any control over it. I might not understand exactly what was being said in the supraliminal messaging of the buzz, but their meaning was clear enough. I opened the door and stared into the vaguely humanoid silhouette on my porch.

As soon as I opened my mouth, the sound dropped from an ocean's roar to a whisper. I was relieved that whatever was waiting for me on the porch was at least giving the opportunity to speak. Not that I knew what I could tell them, not even as the words formed on my lips. "I understand," I said quietly, "and we're sorry. It was a tremendous misunderstanding. It will never happen again."

The figure didn't move. Lit brightly from behind as it was, I could only see that it had two arms and two legs, both pairs of limbs a little too large for its torso. The head was likewise oversized, bulkier on top, though not quite like a light bulb. Clearly, this visitor was not human. Brian might have faked the body he had autopsied in the video, but the design was a little too close for someone's comfort. The figure's head turned slightly to one side, giving me a too-clear view of a tiny, humorless mouth, and an enormous black eye with a red figure-eight pupil like an octopus. My visitor made no sign of retreat.

I held out the envelope with the disk. "I believe this belongs to you. Your warning has been heard, and it will be heeded."

The hand that took the envelope had an extra knuckle on each finger. I had spent too much of my day looking at that hand already. The skin was a pale blue and gray, and lacked pores. The hand retreated with the disk. A short burst of sound, the buzz roaring back to life for a few, terrifying seconds, caused me to yelp uncontrollably.

Frames of Reference

Then it was over. The light was gone and I was alone in my doorway with an empty porch. There were no lights on in my neighbors' houses, no signs that they had seen or heard anything.

I closed the door to a quiet street. Knowing that I wouldn't be able to sleep for some time, I made a pot of coffee and waited until I could drive over to Sol Rubin's office and pick up my check.

AFTERWORD

This was almost a story about sewer gators. Really. But fate intervened in a fabulous way and reminded me about the urban legend of "snuff films." In an era where it seems everything from the most mundane aspects of our lives to prisoner torture is televised entertainment, how far of a stretch is a human death captured on film? Not an act of war or tragic accident, but cold, deliberate murder as staged entertainment. It seems that for now at least, the real McCoy is as thankfully elusive as proof of extra-terrestrial intelligence.

This brings me to that alien autopsy footage from back in the X-Files heyday. Sure, most of us realized that it was a hoax right out of the gate. There were still people who thought it was real. What would an extra-terrestrial think if he were to watch that same footage? Would he be able to make that distinction?

As a life-long film geek, I find it strange that I had not really explored this disconnect between reality and filmed reality in my fiction. The idea of thematically combining an "it has to be FAKE" snuff film with an "it HAS to be fake" alien autopsy film was too rich of an oyster for me to ignore.

Late Night Snack

Robert Farnsworth

There were times when Tom really hated Los Angeles traffic. Only three hours ago, he had been driving north on the Harbor Freeway. Just as he crossed over the Santa Monica Freeway, traffic suddenly ground to a halt. While he waited for the traffic to clear, he called his girlfriend Danni and told her he would be running late and to eat dinner without him.

Tom and Danni had been so busy for the last few months that he was glad they could finally get away during Danni's Spring Break. With Tom working so much overtime and Danni busy with her last year of college, this trip to Las Vegas was their first chance to relax and have some fun since New Year's Eve. Just the thought of a whole week in a luxury suite with her and the chance to party, gamble and see some shows had helped to make the last few weeks of work bearable.

Using his car's hands-free remote, Tom spoke loudly toward his car's dashboard, "Call Danni."

After a few rings, a worried female voice answered, "Hi Tom, where are you now?"

Tom grinned at the sound of her voice, "Hey babe, it looks like traffic is finally clearing up. I need to pick up a burger on the way, but I should be there in about twenty minutes."

Relieved, she said, "Great. Give me a call before you get here and I'll meet you out front."

Tom pulled into a parking space around the corner from the entrance to Danni's apartment building. Stepping out of the car, he walked around to the front of the building and saw her standing there holding her garment bag. Tall and cute with the long legged, athletic build of a dancer, she was dressed in tight black pants, a dark red blouse and tall black boots with her long raven black hair tied up high on the back of her head.

When she saw Tom walk around the corner, Danni dropped her bag to run over to give him an enthusiastic hug and deep passionate kiss. "Hi, Tom," she said. "I'm so glad we finally have a chance to get away for a whole week. Things have been so chaotic with school and rehearsals for the big show that I can't remember when we last spent a night together."

"Yeah," Tom agreed, "Same here. I've been working so much overtime that if it wasn't for this trip, I don't know if I could have gotten through the last few weeks without going crazy. Let's get going; I can't wait to get to Las Vegas and show you how much I've missed you."

Picking up her bag and taking a hold of her hand as he led her to his car, he said, "Close your eyes and follow me, I have a surprise to show you."

"Ok," she said, curious. "What kind of surprise?"

"Well, it wouldn't be a surprise if I told you, now would it?"

Once he had positioned her in front of his car, he said, "Ok, now you can look."

Danni opened her eyes and saw a brand new, dark blue Dodge Charger. "Wow. Is that a new car," she asked, "or did you rent it?"

"Like it? It's all mine. Well, mostly. Right now, the bank and I own it. I just got it yesterday. Go ahead, climb in."

"Ooh," she said, as she inhaled the new car smell and wiggled around in her seat, "I like it, leather seats."

While he started the car, Danni asked, "So, what's that in the dashboard, a GPS?"

"Yep, but, it's more than just a GPS. Press the NAV button here and it's a GPS. The button shaped like a phone is for the hands-free remote for my cell. And this button is for the satellite radio and the last button is for the built-in MP3 player." Tom pressed the accelerator to rev the engine and shouted above the noise, "And, the best thing about the car is it that it comes with a five point seven liter V8 engine with a five-speed transmission. The speedometer tops out at one-hundred and eighty miles an hour, but I haven't even had a chance to open it up on the highway to see how fast it'll go."

Danni waited for the engine to quiet down, "Well, don't drive so fast we get a ticket on the way to Las Vegas. We don't need a speeding ticket to ruin our vacation."

Driving south on North Lake Avenue they passed under Route 210 and stopped before turning east onto the ramp leading up onto the highway. The traffic on Route 210 eastbound was heavy until they reached Interstate 15 and turned north. Driving northeast on Interstate 15, they climbed out of the Los Angeles basin through the mountains, leaving the smog and heavy traffic behind.

Once they reached the high desert country, Tom yawned and rubbed his face, "Danni, we're almost to Barstow. Is it all right if we stop? We need to get gas, and I really need something to wake me up. I didn't realize how tired I was from all of that overtime. Maybe if I can get an energy drink or something with caffeine, I'll be able to stay awake."

Danni stretched and began fidgeting in her seat, "Sure, besides, I really need to pee."

Tom exited the interstate onto Historic Route 66. Pulling into the *Gas and Go*, he parked next to the first free pump and climbed out to fill up the tank. While he was busy punching buttons to select premium gasoline, Danni jumped out of the car and dashed into the food mart in search of a restroom.

After he filled up the tank, Tom walked over and stepped inside the brightly lit Food Mart. Grabbing a green plastic shopping basket as he entered, he paused and glanced around the well-organized aisles until he spotted the snack section.

Strolling down the snack aisle, he grabbed an assortment of chips and pastries, throwing them into the basket. Reaching the end of the aisle, he swung open the glass door of the cooler and added two bottles of cola and three energy drinks.

Finished selecting his purchases, he looked around for his girlfriend. When he didn't see her, he started wandering the aisles, browsing the racks of merchandise killing time until she returned.

After few minutes, he gave up and walked over to the counter to set his purchases down. Bored, he scanned the display of cigarettes and skin magazines behind the counter while waiting for the red-headed teen in a Caltech t-shirt to finish ringing up items for a woman dressed in a leopard print dress with long bleached-blond hair.

While the blond woman in the leopard dress walked out the door, the attendant started ringing up his snacks and drinks. Tom looked closer at his t-shirt and his name tag and said, "Hey, I went to Caltech, too. Are you by any chance related to Mike Johnson? I graduated with him, two years ago."

"Yeah, Mike's my cousin. I'm Carl, by the way. I'm going to start at Caltech next fall. What was your major?"

Tom replied, "I was in Chemical Engineering with Mike. If you see him, tell him Tom Stewart says hi."

"Yeah, I will. Did you get gas, too?

"Yeah, I filled it up on pump two."

"Wow, that's your Charger?" Carl asked. "Some sweet ride you got there. Does she drive as good as she looks? Oh, and your total is fifty-four dollars and thirty-two cents."

At the mention of his car, Tom glanced out at the pumps and saw his car parked in front of a huge black SUV. From the large silver grille dominating the front of the vehicle, it was easy to recognize it as a HUMMER. After assuring himself that the HUMMER wasn't parked too close, he said, "Yep, that's my car. I just bought it yesterday. I haven't even had it long enough to open it up on the highway."

Carl replied, "You don't want to do it on I-15. Watch your speed if you're headed into Nevada. A guy that just came through there said that the Nevada state troopers are out at the border looking for speeders tonight."

"Ok, thanks for telling me; I'll have to keep that in mind."

From behind him, a familiar female voice teasingly asked, "Hey, are you going to talk about cars all night? We need to get back on the road."

As they drove back onto the highway, Tom slowed down to wait for the white hybrid Toyota in front of him to merge with traffic. As soon as he saw an opening, Tom sped up to enter traffic. Quickly switching over to the passing lane, he set the cruise control to eighty miles an hour and leaned back. "All right, next stop Las Vegas!"

Danni asked, "So, when do we get to the hotel?"

"Well," he replied, "The GPS says 2:30 AM. So I guess it'll be about two more hours. I wish I hadn't run into that traffic after work. If it wasn't for that, we'd be there by now. At least we can sleep in late tomorrow."

Bam! Thump, thump, thump, thump...

"What was that?" Danni asked.

"Damn," Tom cursed as he pulled off the road. "The tire display just lit up. It's saying that the back passenger tire is flat. We must have run over something back there. You'd think something like this wouldn't happen with a brand new car."

Once the car was safely off the road, Tom flipped on the emergency blinkers and parked the car on the shoulder. They both got out and walked around the car to look at the tire. Stooping to examine the tire more closely, Tom growled in frustration and said, "Well, it looks like we ran over a screw and it's still stuck in the tire."

Tom pressed the button on the remote to pop open the trunk. "Danni, can you get me the owner's manual? It should be up front in the glove compartment. There should also be a new flashlight there too."

While Danni was getting out the owner's manual, she heard Tom swear loudly from inside the trunk. "What the fuck? I just found the spare tire and it's one of those stupid little donuts!"

Trying to calm him down, Danni said, "Wait a minute. Let me look in the manual. Maybe there's something in it that can help us." After a few minutes of flipping through the pages, she said, "Ok, I think I found the section we need. Cool, it looks like there's something called a TIREFIT kit. Look in the trunk to the right of the spare tire. It looks like a pump with a big bottle of sealant attached to it. There's a mode knob on the side, switch it for Sealant mode."

"Ok, I found it, now what?"

"There's a note before the checklist warning you to be sure to leave the screw in the tire. Ok, first set the Mode Select knob to Sealant Mode. Then you can use it to pump the tire up with an air and sealant mix until the pressure reads nineteen pounds. After we drive the car slowly for ten minutes, the sealant should have coated the inside of tire. If the tire pressure is still checks out at nineteen pounds after driving it, we need to switch the select mode knob back to Air Mode before inflating the tire of the way. The manual also says that we shouldn't exceed fifty-five miles an hour until we can get the tire inspected."

"Well," Tom said, "at least we won't be driving all of the way to Vegas tilted over to one side."

Following the instructions in the owner's manual, they were able to seal the flat tire and get it inflated back to normal so they could get back on the road.

Frustrated by the delays to his trip, Tom said, "Yuck, now that we've slowed down to fifty-five, the GPS says 3:45 a.m. And, look at all of the other cars passing us."

Danni twisted around in her seat and looked backwards. "Not everyone is passing us, there's that delivery truck in front of us and there's a black SUV behind us. They're both going slow, too. So see, not everyone has to go fast to get where they are going."

An hour later, as they drove through the desert with the cruise control set to a safe fifty-five miles an hour, they were finally able to relax and enjoy the ride. Overhead, the half moon floating in an ocean of stars gave off just enough light to illuminate the desert as they drove through the night.

Traffic had lightened up to the point where besides their car, the only vehicles left on their stretch of road were the same delivery truck in front of them emblazoned with Mrs. Baker's Pies along its sides and a large black HUMMER with blue tinted headlights driving about a mile behind them.

Danni turned her head to look at Tom, "This is a really nice. Riding along in a brand new car, listening to music and watching the desert go by. You know we don't get to see stars like this in LA." Placing her feet up on the dashboard, she asked, "So, what does the GPS say about how much longer it will take to get to our hotel?"

"I'm sorry but it looks like we're even later than before. Now, the GPS is saying 4:00 a.m. Why don't we just sleep late tomorrow and spend the rest of the day relaxing by the pool?

"I have a better idea. Why don't we call for room service in the morning and then we stay in bed all day. Do you think we can find something to keep ourselves occupied?"

Leering at her, he nodded, "I think we might be able to find something to keep us busy."

They smiled at each other as Tom reached across the console to take her hand. When he turned his head back to the front, a puzzled look came over his face.

"What's the matter?" Danni asked.

"That's odd. The GPS just stopped working. It just says that it's acquiring satellites."

Suddenly, the music stopped playing over the radio. Instead they heard, *"Vree, squeal, beep, beep, pulse, pulse, pulse, pulse."*

"What's going on? First its traffic, then it's a flat tire. What's next?" Fiddling with the controls, Tom tried station after station, with each one repeating the same noise pattern. Frustrated, he turned off the radio and said, "The whole reason I wanted a car with satellite radio was so this wouldn't happen."

Bring, bring, bring, bring...

Annoyed, Tom asked, "Now what?" He reached over and activated the hands-free mode. Out of the speakers they heard, *"Vree, squeal, beep, beep, pulse, pulse, pulse, pulse."*

"Tom," Danni said, "turn it off. That noise scares me. Make it stop."

Tom stabbed his hand out to turn off the hands-free remote. Instead, his hand hit the wrong button and turned the satellite radio back on. The music they had been listening to earlier had returned. Still puzzled, he said, "Whatever was causing the noise just stopped. You don't see any big antennas around here, do you?" Then, speaking in a silly, odd voice, Tom stage-whispered, "I know, the truck in front of us is full of spies and we just overheard their secret transmission."

"Stop it. I hate it when you tease me like that." She looked out the window, "At least that bizarre noise stopped, whatever was causing it."

"I'm sorry. I didn't mean to upset you. Look, we're just tired. The GPS is working again and it says that we'll be at our hotel in only thirty minutes. After we've both had a good night's sleep, we'll be laughing about this over breakfast."

Danni unbuckled her seat belt and stretched over the console to give him a quick kiss on the cheek.

"What was that for?" Tom asked.

"It's because I'm sorry I snapped at you. I've been so stressed out lately. I think I just need to have some fun, maybe go out dancing and drinking. Can we do that?"

"Sure babe, I know a few clubs along the strip that we could go to. I think I need some rest and relaxation too..." he agreed as his eyes flicked to the review. "Damn it."

"What's the matter?

"Somebody's tailgating us."

Danni turned in her seat to look behind them. "It's that HUMMER behind us."

"I wonder what he wants. There's nobody in the passing lane. Why doesn't he just pass us?"

The lights of the HUMMER suddenly went out. Then the headlights started flashing on and off. When the light kept flashing, Tom glanced in the rear view mirror to see what the HUMMER was doing.

As he watched the HUMMER flash its lights, he suddenly realized that they weren't turning on and off so much as opening and closing like eye lids. Then he noticed that the HUMMER's headlights had multiple facets like the eyes of a giant insect.

Danni asked, "What's he doing? Can't we go any faster? Maybe we can run away from him."

"Sure. I'm sure the tire can take it. We won't know until we try it."

Tom pulled over into the left lane and passed the Mrs. Baker delivery truck. Carefully pressing on the accelerator, he sped up to seventy miles an hour. Following close behind their car, the black HUMMER quickly caught up. Increasing his speed up to eighty, Tom watched the HUMMER in the rearview mirror to see if the HUMMER kept pace. Seeing the HUMMER match speed again, he accelerated to one-hundred miles an hour.

"Well, the tire seems to be working okay. You want to try going faster?"

"I'm scared. Yes, go faster. I'll feel much safer if we can get away from him."

Silently agreeing with her comment, Tom was starting to worry there might be some sinister reason that the HUMMER was following them. He suddenly realized that they were being followed by the same black HUMMER that had been parked behind them at the *Gas and Go* way back in Barstow. Was the driver of the HUMMER stalking them? Was he going to try to run them off the road in some deserted area of desert and kill them? Were they going to be in tomorrow's news as victims of some serial killer?

Increasing his speed again, he got the car up to one-hundred and ten. Once he was sure that worked, he sped up through one-hundred and twenty, one-hundred and thirty, one-hundred and forty, and finally stopped accelerating when he reached one-hundred and fifty miles an hour.

"Danni, I'm going as fast as I dare, but he's still following us. What are we going to do?"

Late Night Snack

Danni said, "Tom look, there's a sign for an exit coming up. It says Sloan in ten miles. Should we take the exit, or should we try to make it to Vegas?"

"I don't know. If we pull off at the exit, he might try to follow us. I'd feel better going all of the way to Vegas. It's a big city, so maybe he'll stop following us when get near other people."

"Tom! The minivan!"

Up ahead, there was a green minivan and at their speed, an accident would be deadly. Tom nodded, his hands gripping the steering wheel tight. After they passed the minivan, he glanced up at the rearview mirror and was surprised when he saw the HUMMER suddenly slow down and pull over into the right hand lane. Remembering that the tire he fixed just a few hours ago might not be safe, he eased off on the accelerator and let the Charger slow down to a more normal eighty miles an hour.

"Look behind us. I think he stopped chasing us because of the minivan," Tom hoped he kept the fear out of his voice.

Danni spun around in her seat to look back at the black HUMMER. She could see that it was now in the right lane and had slowed down to the speed limit. As they pulled up beside the minivan, the black HUMMER continued to stay behind the minivan and stop following them.

Obviously relieved, Danni said, "Yeah, it looks like he's slowed down and is staying in the right lane. Does that mean that he's stopped following us?"

Tom looked back and saw the driver of the minivan turn his right turn signal on to get off at the Sloan exit. As they neared the exit, he watched the minivan slow down and exit off the highway. As the minivan turned off at the exit, Tom also saw the HUMMER slow down with its turn signals flashing and follow the minivan off the exit. "He's not chasing us anymore. It looks like he got off at the last exit with the minivan."

Tom watched the HUMMER follow the minivan as they both left the highway. Suddenly, he realized that the last time he had seen behavior like this; he was watching a lion stalking a water buffalo on a nature documentary. Was the HUMMER stalking the minivan now?

Without a word, he slowed the car down and pulled it over to stop on the shoulder. Puzzled, Danni turned to look at her boyfriend and saw the confused look on his face suddenly turn to horror. She had heard the saying *his face as white as a sheet*, but it was the first time she had ever seen anyone's face turn white in front of her.

"What's the matter?" She asked. "We're safe, right? He's not following us anymore, so what's wrong? "

Tom hesitated before replying softly, "I was watching that HUMMER as it followed the van off the exit, when I saw something."

"What did you see?"

At first, Tom didn't want to admit what he had seen. Maybe if he didn't tell her what he saw, it wouldn't be true. Finally, he replied. "I think I saw something odd as the HUMMER left the highway."

"What do you mean odd?"

"Well, I was watching as it followed the van off the highway. That's when the street light hit the driver's window just right…"

"Well," Danni asked, "what did you see? Were you able to see the driver? What'd he look like?"

"That's the problem, when I looked through the window, I didn't see anyone driving it. I didn't see anyone at all inside the HUMMER."

For minutes they sat on the side of the interstate, neither one wanting to say the first word. Finally, Tom broke the silence. "Danni, we have to go back and find out what happened."

Shocked, Danni shook her head, "No, don't go back! I'm afraid. What if something bad happens? What can we do about it?"

"Danni, I need to find out what that HUMMER is going to do. The only reason we're not being chased is because it took off after that minivan instead of us. I'm worried that something bad is going to happen and I don't think I could live with myself if I didn't try to do something about it."

She sat staring off at the lights of Las Vegas thinking about what he had said. After a few moments, she closed her eyes and sighed before replying, "Ok, I hate to admit it, but you have a point. But, at the first sign of any trouble we get out of there as fast as possible, all right?

"Sure, we'll get out of there as fast as possible. I promise."

Looking back, Tom double checked to be sure that no one was behind him and slowly backed the car up to the ramp off of the interstate. As soon as he was past the exit, he turned off and drove down to the end of the exit where he stopped and looked around for the minivan and HUMMER.

Tom asked, "Do you see them anywhere? They might have gone north toward Las Vegas, or they may have headed south."

To the north, the South Las Vegas Boulevard stretched off in the distance straight for Las Vegas. Just north of the exit ramp and across the way, they could see a well lit truck stop filled with trucks lined up and parked for the night. Past the truck stop, on the west side of the road, was a deserted truck depot filled with trailers. Off in the distance on the east side of the road, they could barely see the outline of a housing development under construction.

Suddenly, a column of intense white light speared up from the roadside and split the night sky, blinding them both.

"What the fuck was that!" Tom shouted.

Danni said, "I don't know, but I can't see."

While they waited for the eyes to clear, their car was rocked by a shock wave and they heard a loud, WHAM!

When they could see again, they saw a large column of smoke coming from a vehicle off to the side of the road just past the truck depot. Looking around for other cars, Tom pulled onto the boulevard and drove slowly north toward the smoke to see what was causing it.

Passing the truck depot, they saw people running out of the gas station and trucker drivers climbing out of their rigs to see what was going on. Pulling up to the burning wreck, they could barely make out the charred remains of a minivan. Still glowing red with intense heat, smoke was billowing out of the wreck blocked the view of anything inside.

Tom whispered, "What on earth did that?"

Danni shook her head, "I don't know. But, I don't think anyone survived that. Do you think it was that HUMMER that was chasing us?"

"I don't know, I don't see it around anywhere. If it was that HUMMER, where did it go?"

While Tom looked around for the HUMMER, Danni glanced and then stared north toward the construction site. "Tom."

"What's the matter?"

"Why is there a bright blue glow coming from that housing development?"

Something inside the construction site was glowing with a flickering blue light bright enough to be seen over the lights coming from Las Vegas. Curious and not waiting to ask Danni for permission, Tom pulled back on the road and drove toward the construction site.

As they drew closer to the construction site, they could see that something had torn off the large front gate for the chain link fence and thrown it over to one side. When Danni saw the gate lying on the ground, she said, "Tom, don't!"

"What? I was only trying to get closer to see what was making the light."

As they watched the blue glowing light flicker over the half completed homes, they saw a large glowing, cigar shaped object silently float up from behind the houses. As it rose above the houses, Tom saw two bright lights shining out of the front of the glowing object. He could barely make out that the lights on the front of the object looked just like the multifaceted headlights of the HUMMER that had been chasing them for miles. Turning slowly in mid air, the object darted off into the night sky and quickly disappeared from view.

"D-d-did you see that? Danni asked.

Tom nodded slowly, "I don't know what that was, but I don't think anyone would believe us if we told them."

"Tom," Danni's mouth was dry, "that could have been us on the side of the road back there."

"I know, babe, I know."

Late Night Snack

AFTERWORD

When Jennifer first told me about this collection of stories, I was excited to have a chance to write about Close Encounters and Urban Legends. With that in mind, I sat down and thought about the two crucial components for the story.

The first thing I did was to consider what I knew about Urban Legends, looking for something that they had in common. One of the things that I realized was that most of them seemed to involve young couples out for a romantic evening, parked somewhere in a car with some sort of murderer or mysterious stalker attacking them. So I had to have my young couple in a car somewhere.

Next, I needed a protagonist, someone or something to threaten the romantic couple. Now with the young couple in a car, I thought why not have them being chased by the alien? Then I thought, would the alien really need a car if it was the car? So I made my alien a machine life form. After that, it was easy to have the young couple driving down the road with a crazed machine chasing them into the night. I had fun writing this story and I hope that you had as much fun reading it.

Two Out, Wendigo

Rosemary Jones

Manitoba, 1907

It howled with hunger under the tall pines. The current body was dying, strangling itself, before it could consume enough to sustain the entire colony. Each century, more aspects of itself died, unable to live from jump to jump.

Once, when the world was hotter and the beasts greater, it tumbled from the stars, finding hosts of unimaginable size and appetite, drifting ever northward in the comfortable long hours of the night. It hated heat, it hated the sun, both caused the colony to decompose too quickly.

As the world froze and changed, and the great tusks died in the ice, it leaped into the hairless hunters, finding a grouping of intelligences not completely alien. But they had grown cunning in the many winters that it fed from them, learning how to drive it forth, separate it from itself, make it ever smaller, until it was reduced to mere ribbons of its former serpentine collective.

Now it was trapped inside this dying body, howling with hunger, seeking blindly for escape from the already cooling flesh that enveloped it.

Minnesota, 1928

Outside, the wind howled like a hungry wolf. Inside, a little girl crouched under the heavy wool blanket on her bed, watching the kerosene lantern cast smoky shadows across the wall. Ice crackled up the glass panes of the window partially hidden behind another blanket to stop the chill drafts.

"Wendigo, it stinks," her father said, repeating the lessons he had learned from his grandfather when he was still a little boy, back before the old man strangled himself to keep the creature contained. "You smell it before you see it. You smell it on their breath, on their skin."

"Have you smelled it?" Josephina whispered, although she knew the answer. But if she asked, he kept talking, the often silent father that she loved so much.

"Maybe, after the war, up north," he murmured. He oiled traps with quick, easy movements as he talked. When he was done to his satisfaction, he stacked them in a growing pile upon the big table that ate up the center of the cabin. Tomorrow, he would go walking along the lines, leaving her alone for a day or two in the little cabin. Rabbit skins and fox fur paid for their supplies in the winter. Once he caught a wolf, a heavy grey pelt that added Christmas candy and a doll to her stocking.

She was too small to walk all the way with him, even though she had her own snowshoes. But she was too big to stay inside the cabin while he was gone, playing with her Christmas doll. So he told her stories with warnings laced through them, bits and pieces learned from his namesake grandfather.

"What did you do when you smelled it?" she asked, sliding even deeper under the scratchy red blanket so only the tip of her nose and the top of her head remained bare to the room. It felt safer that way.

"I ran," said the man who had survived the trenches of France with only a bit of a cough and a long scar running down his tanned brown cheek. "I ran as far away as fast as I could. Wendigo will eat you, eat you all up. So, if you smell it, smell the breath of rotting meat, you run too. Promise me that you will run and you will hide. Promise me."

"But your grandfather didn't run," she did not know what foolish spirit made her say that. Even as his face flushed, she wished the words back.

"My grandfather went crazy when wendigo caught him," he slammed the flat of his palm on the table, making the traps rattle like iron teeth against each other. "Killed himself, got my father arrested too. No one believed us, no one listened. Now, girl, if you smell wendigo, what will you do?"

"I'll run, Papa, I'll run," Josephina promised.

With a sigh, he nodded. "Good girl. Be clever, be quick. And remember to run."

Roseau, 1939

Teddy drove her to the station in a rattling old Model T. Everything left of her father's farm was packed into two battered leather suitcases sitting on a baggage cart. Far off, she heard the train whistle howl.

"You don't have to go," Teddy said, even as the train appeared.

"Yes, I do," she answered. A ticket sat safe in her pocket and an acceptance letter to a nursing school in Chicago was tucked inside the handbag clutched between her two gloved hands. She spent an entire year boarding in town, finishing high school, and waiting for the ground over her father's grave to stop looking so raw, so recently dug. Now it was truly time to go.

Her mother died during childbirth and her father succumbed to influenza while still a young man. When she was a nurse, when she knew how to prevent such things, she would have the answers she craved. No one would die if she could prevent it.

"No, really, you could stay, we could..." But he could not quite finish that sentence.

"We couldn't," answered Josephina with a practicality far beyond her nineteen years. "Your mother would never allow it."

Teddy blanched. His mother, that formidable Scotch-Irish widow who ran the boarding house, had been more than happy to help Josephina collect the insurance owed to her and sort out the applications needed for nursing school. Anything to get a half-blood Cree girl away from her son and Teddy knew it. His mother had even packed Josephina a nice packet of sandwiches to take on the train.

"I'll write to you," Teddy called as Josephina hurried toward edge of the station platform, eager to board the train that would take her to a new life.

She did not hear him. There were two cattle cars behind the passenger cars. A terrible stench rolled off the cows, as if they had already arrived at the stockyards of Chicago. Josephina boarded the train clutching a handkerchief to her nose and hoping her stomach would settle down. She could not be squeamish and become a nurse, she told herself briskly.

In the last cattle car, one dried out Holstein mooed with hungry discontent, jostling against its tightly packed fellows. No one came to feed it. The maddened cow whipped its head around and sank its teeth into the throat of Jersey standing next to it. The other cow screamed even as the Holstein ripped a chunk of flesh from its neck and swallowed, barely chewing in its eagerness to fill its belly.

Chicago, 1945

Josephina Fiddler sat alone. Being by herself, that attracted glances from the reporters up at the bar, arguing about Philly's "Mack Attack" and the right-handed pitchers' domination of the mound. The boys in khaki flashed their tickets to today's game at Wrigley Field. These soldiers made the most of their leave at a table in the center of the room: yelling for more beer and making wild bets about the upcoming game. But even as they jostled one another, arguing about who deserved the pennant, a few slid shy looks at the dark-haired woman in a nurse's uniform.

Here in the happy noise of an excited crowd, Josephina felt safe. Outside, with the October wind rattling down Chicago's streets, she felt so vulnerable. So exposed. Even if she could reach her home before the wendigo found her, Josephina wasn't sure she would be safe behind the locked doors of her apartment.

Billy, the bar's owner, whistled through the room, slapping shoulders and making his own predictions of victory for his beloved baseball team. "It's the Cubs' year," he shouted. "I'll be there to cheer them on."

"How about your goat?" yelled one of the reporters.

"He's got his own ticket," Billy shouted back. "Wouldn't miss a game!"

"Bring it out! Bring it out!" yelled the soldiers at the bar. "Let's see Billy's famous old goat!"

Josephina slipped her hand into her purse. The cigarettes were there, the old-fashioned Bakelite case that belonged to her father, cool under the touch of her questing fingers. But if she took out one, somebody was sure to wander over to her table and offer her a light. And she didn't want company.

Then, again, maybe she was flattering herself. She slid her compact out of the purse instead of the smokes, flipping it open to confirm that the girl in the mirror was no Betty Grable.. Broad, flat features inherited from her Cree father, skin a little lighter than his but still tan enough to attract a few comments, even in Chicago. No amount of drugstore make-up was going to hide what she was.

She clicked the compact closed. The coffee in front of her was cold, but she decided not to ask the waitress for more. She would rather have had a beer or even a whiskey, but she did not dare. But alcohol made the stench worse, not better. When a shaman was drunk, he could smell the beast stalking through his nightmares, according to her father.

For so many years, the wind could scratch outside her window and cats could yowl in the alley below her room, and she slept easily through the night. Josephina never once remembered her father's stories until the mad woman arrived in her ward.

"The police found her in the butcher shop, stuffing raw meat into her mouth. She's the butcher's mother-in-law, and apparently did all the accounts for the business, worked alone there every night, no problems. Then he comes in last Friday morning to find her screaming and trying to eat everything in the shop! When he tried to pull her out of the case, she bit him! Bit both the cops and the ambulance driver too until they got her restrained," Madeleine Burke recounted with relish, when the pair were sharing coffee and a quick cigarette in the nurses' station. Josephina eased her feet out of her sensible pumps, more interested in rubbing the ache out of her toes than Madeleine's gossip.

Her busty blonde friend kept an eye out for an eligible doctor and an ear cocked for the latest story making the hospital rounds. A nurse for a year or two, Madeleine intended to remain in the profession as long as it took to find a good husband. But until then, Madeleine was determined to get as much entertainment out of the job as she could. She was always more than willing to share her best stories with Josephina.

"If she's crazy, what is she doing in our ward?" Josephina asked. Their beds were usually reserved for the very ill or the dying. It wasn't as nice or as cheerful as maternity, but it was never as bad as the psychiatric ward either. She worked that ward once or twice, back in her student days, and she hated the feeling of despair that haunted that hallway.

"She's sick, too," said Madeleine. "Fever, sweats, won't eat, keeps crying she's hungry. They had her upstairs." Madeleine meant with the other mad women. "But the women started screaming, they say, yelling she stank, until they moved her down here."

"Does she?" Josephina asked, sliding her pumps back onto her aching feet. She took a long pull on the cigarette, savoring the moment of calm before she had to go back onto the ward. She stubbed the cigarette out.

"Does she what?" Madeleine said.

Two Out, Wendigo

"Does she stink?"

"Not that I noticed. We're supposed to check on her every hour. That nice Dr. Allerson says she is an intriguing case. But I think she's just crazy." Dr. Anthony Allerson was nice because he was, as far as Madeleine knew, unattached. Josephina had found him politer and friendlier than most of the doctors; he always addressed her as Miss Fiddler. They also shared a mutual passion for the Cubs. Throughout the season, Dr. Allerson often snuck into the nurse's station to check the stats in the newspapers that Josephina bought on her way to work or switch on the radio if there was a game on.

When Dr. Allerson found Josephina reading the same scores, they spent more than a few pleasant minutes together praising the Cubs and despising their rivals. One night, when the ward was quiet and the Cubs had scored a satisfactory victory in the ninth inning, he even told her a few tales about his tour in the Pacific, halted by mine explosion and a return to the States with a limp that he tried to hide when he walked his rounds.

He was much like her father, Josephina decided, not quick with words but sincere in a way that she had not heard in a long time. And this doctor's passion for baseball and germs seemed far more interesting traits than the passion for dinner and dancing that Madeleine would have preferred.

"Can you start the rounds?" Madeleine asked, crushing her own cigarette in the ashtray. "I still have reams of charts to finish."

Josephina nodded. Better patients than paperwork as far as she was concerned. She picked up a surgical mask and stuffed it into her pocket. She hated covering her face, it always scared the patients, but there were a few infectious cases on their ward and the head nurse would have a fit if she saw Josephina in those rooms without a mask.

She decided to see their newest patient first. But, when she entered the room, she'd instantly regretted it. The room stank, a smell like rotten meat and sick dog that made her gag. The woman tied to the bed cried and giggled, thrashing from side to side, biting at nothing.

Josephina tried to stay calm, pulling out her watch and reaching for the patient's wrist to take her pulse. The woman flung herself so hard at Josephina that the bed shook and nearly toppled over.

"Hungry," howled the woman, snapping her teeth at Josephina's hands.

Josephina retreated across the room, inwardly chiding herself for the fear that drove her away from her patient. But the smell, the stink, it was the terror of black winter nights, the stench that her father warned her about, it was the smell of the wendigo.

"It's strange, isn't it?" said a voice from a dark corner of the room.

Josephina started.

Dr. Allerson rose up from the chair where he'd been sitting, watching the woman on the bed. His face was very pale, with a sheen of sweat dampening his forehead.

"Doctor?" Josephina said. He didn't spare her his usual shy smile. Instead he stared straight at her throat, at the pulse that trembled beneath her skin like doe hiding from the hunters in the dark forest shadows.

"Delirium, tremors, mild fever. Much the signs of an infection. But the hunger, it's so intense. Like an animal gnawing its way out. Perhaps a parasite." As Dr. Allerson advanced towards her, Josephina could see his hands clutching at the air, reaching toward her. "So hungry."

His breath billowed out his mouth like a black smoke, blowing the stench of the wendigo's madness toward her. "Get away from me!" he suddenly screamed even as he lurched forward.

"Doctor!"

He flung himself at her, teeth snapping at her shoulder. Josephina dodged around the bed. She grabbed the chair that he had abandoned and threw it across the room at him. The doctor tripped on the chair, landing heavily on the tiled floor. The stench of the wendigo made her gag and stumble as she whirled around him, heading toward the door. The infected woman on the bed giggled and cried, screaming to be fed.

Dr. Allerson pushed himself up on his hands and knees. He flung back his head and howled like a starving wolf.

To her shame, Josephina whirled and fled, out of the room, racing to her locker to grab her coat and purse, then down the hospital stairs and into the cool October streets. She started towards home, but she could hear Dr. Allerson's footsteps behind her, keeping pace with her, speeding up when she started to run, falling back when she paused in a doorway. She froze there, panting in terror as the beast stalked her in the body of the baseball-loving doctor.

Then she saw the open door of the bar, heard the noise of the crowd, and fled inside.

* * *

Two Out, Wendigo

Now she sat with a cold cup of coffee and a growing feeling of remorse. She should never have abandoned Dr. Allerson like that. The wendigo would eat him up from the inside out, driving him insane. That was what her father always told her. That the hunger grew worse and worse, until the person possessed did unspeakable things to feed the hunger inside.

But she couldn't do what her great-grandfather did to drive out the wendigo. She couldn't strangle Dr. Allerson. Killing the patient was no satisfactory cure.

Her father fled to the trenches of France and later to the deep woods of Minnesota to escape the expectation that he would take up his grandfather's and his father's work, that he'd keep the wendigo at bay by killing those it possessed.

"There has to be another way," Josephina told herself. "Come on, think. You're smart girl." It was something that her instructors always said in nursing school. "Think, Josephina, think, you're a clever girl. There's more than one solution to every problem."

But her father said the solution was to run away. That no one would ever believe her.

It moved from person to person, destroying them from within, and then leaving for a new host. "Like a parasite," Dr. Allerson had said in the infected woman's room.

"Like a flea," muttered Josephina to the cold coffee at the bottom of her cup, remembering the black cloud streaming out of Dr. Allerson's mouth. "Like a flea jumping from dog to dog."

Strangling someone, that was the method that worked best to keep it contained according to her father. Knotting a cord around their neck, killing the host, perhaps that did keep it trapped inside the lungs or wherever it infected a body, Josephina reasoned. But why not give it a new host? Lure it out before it could do much damage. But how? With what?

Then, in the middle of a crowded Chicago bar, Josephina heard a goat bleat. Billy was leading his pet through the room, boasting how he was going get the opposing team's "goat" by taking his own onto the field. The reporters crowded around him. The goat, annoyed by so many men stinking of cigars and beer, began to bleat and kick and butt its head against Chicago's muckrackers. There were yells and good-natured catcalls for Billy to get the goat out of the bar before it spilled too much beer or blood.

Josephina slipped into the crowd. "Poor thing," she said, grabbing the leash from the distracted bar owner. "Let me take it outside."

"Hey, Billy, have you hired a nanny for the goat?" laughed one of the reporters, catching the flash of Josephina's white uniform under her plain dark blue coat.

"Yeah, yeah, she keeps it healthy," Billy joked back. "Thanks, sweetheart," he said to Josephina, letting her lead the goat away. "Take him out front, there's taxi waiting."

Josephina gripped the leash tightly. Once, long ago, as the wind howled outside their door, her father had read her tales from an old book on hunting. About how men would trap tigers with a Judas goat. The creature trying to eat her skirt was supposed to be the luck of the Cubs. Would it be the luck of Dr. Allerson, too? Was this her chance to battle the wendigo?

She tugged the reluctant goat through the crowd and out into the cold street. A taxi sat idling just outside the door. Across the street, a shadow moved at the entrance of an alley, a rolling stench carrying across the street to where she stood.

"Damn garbage collectors," said Billy, bundling himself into a coat as he boiled out of the door with a crowd of soldiers and reporters. "Think a World Series is an excuse to take off and forget their job."

Josephina tried to move away from the crowd, keeping the goat with her, but Billy grabbed her shoulder and pushed her toward the taxi. "Come on," he said, "let's get to the stadium. The Cubs need us."

All through the rollicking ride with Billy, the goat, a couple of reporters and even a stray infantryman, Josephina smelled the scent of the wendigo following them.

They fell out of the cab and into the crowd churning into Wrigley Field. Somebody waved tickets over their heads while the taxi driver bawled in the background about his tip. More reporters joined their group and suddenly the yelling turned into questions being shouted back and forth about the probable number of runs, the lack of hitting power in Philadelphia, and the righteousness of a Cub win in their hometown. Today was the Cub's day; this year was their year, according to all the shouting ringing in Josephina's ears.

Then she saw it, a shadowy retreat under the bleachers, where a few garbage cans stood already overflowing with the garbage only an excited crowd could create. She darted out of the mob around Billy, dragging the goat with her, heading for the shadows where she could wait for the wendigo. This time, she would not run.

Long before she saw Dr. Allerson, she smelled the wendigo, the stench overpowering even the stink of the goat and the rotting debris inside the garbage can.

But this time she was ready. She pulled the surgical mask from her uniform pocket and tied it across her face.

Dr. Allerson lurched toward her, his face contorted with fear. "Get away!" he screamed even as he ran closer. "Can't help...myself...so hungry."

Josephina grabbed a garbage pan lid, swinging it in front of her like a shield to fend off Dr. Allerson and shoved the goat toward him.

Dr. Allerson grabbed at her, yelling and crying, trying to push her away even as he chewed the air, biting at her. The black cloud rose from his face but she didn't breathe it in. The mask protected her. She twisted in his arms, kicking his shins, shoving him down and across the angry bleating goat.

"The goat! The goat!" she yelled.

Some spark of comprehension lit his eye and the doctor clutched at the goat instead of her, pulling its mouth toward his.

The black cloud flowed out of his mouth, swarming around the goat's muzzle. The billy goat went nearly cross-eyed in anger, kicking over the garbage can behind it with a clang like a cathedral bell.

"Did that man just kiss my goat?" shouted an astounded Billy as he ducked under the bleachers to join them.

"Yes, for luck," Josephina said, dropping on her knees next to Dr. Allerson. He clung to the furious billy goat. The creature squealed and kicked in his embrace. The doctor kissed it on the top of its knobby head. His face was flushed but no rancid cloud of black smoke wreathed his features.

"How are you?" she asked. The doctor smelled like sweat, and garbage, and fear, and little like goat, but the stink of the wendigo was fading from him.

"Better," he panted. "Better." And then he fainted.

Billy just shook his head. "You should get him some black coffee," he advised her. "The game is about to start. I need my goat."

"Oh, man, does that brute stink," said one of the reporters as Billy paraded past him.

"Wait until Philadelphia smells this," responded Billy, "Then they'll know we mean business."

"Just glad I'm not sitting next to it," said another reporter. Then turning to Jospehina, he asked, "Do you need some help, sweetheart?"

She shook her head at the sea of friendly faces looking at them. Across her lap, Dr. Allerson seemed to be peacefully sleeping, his slight shy smile curling up the ends of his lips. Above her, the crowd howled as the Cubs took the field, hungry for the win.

Chicago 1948

She eyed the television with misgiving. Josephina saw no reason to spend money on such an item, but Anthony insisted that it would be good entertainment for her in the final months before the baby was born.

Watching him fuss with dials, she smiled. It was entertaining to have him home from the hospital and ready to watch the first ever broadcast from Wrigley Field.

Jack Brickhouse called the game, just an exhibition match with the White Sox, but a poor harbinger for the season. The Cubs quickly fell behind.

Anthony shook his head and sighed, "Sometimes I think Billy is right and we are cursed."

"He was just mad that they threw the goat out," she replied.

Anthony shrugged and rubbed his nose in embarrassment. Even three years later, sitting amid the thousands in the bleachers, it was not unusual for some overly excited fan to yell "Hey, there's the guy who kissed Billy's goat."

She stretched out a hand to him and he grasped it with a smile. "There was a wendigo," she said.

"There was a parasite," he answered. It was an old argument, made smooth by many months of discussion.

"There was a wendigo," she said again, beginning a story that she would tell in time to her own grandchildren. "But we did not run. We faced it, we fought it, and we won. Even if it left its mark on Wrigley Field, time will erase it."

On the television, the crowd howled louder, baying like a wolf, as the Cubs lost another game.

Two Out, Wendigo

AFTERWORD

The Wendigo and the Curse of the Billy Goat: Two Myths of the Midwest

In the north woods, cautionary tales were told about how the wendigo infected a person with extreme, insatiable hunger, driving them eventually to cannibalism and madness. Belief in the wendigo continued into the twentieth century and modern authors have turned it into America's own version of the werewolf.

In 1907, Cree Indian Jack Fiddler and his son Joseph Fiddler were tried in Manitoba for killing a woman possessed by a wendigo. During the trial, Jack, an elderly man, said that he had strangled fourteen wendigo-possessed people as part of his duties as a shaman to his tribe. He hanged himself prior to sentencing. Joseph died of consumption in prison and was posthumously pardoned of any crime.

Chicago tavern owner Billy Sianis did attend Cubs' games with his billy goat. He and the goat were tossed out of the 1945 World Series due to complaints about the goat's smell. According to Sianis, this act cursed the Cubs and prevented them from ever winning or even playing in a World Series. The curse has held for more than 60 years despite many Cubs fans' efforts to reverse it.

The Hippie Monster of Eel River
Shannon Page

Krystle leaned over the bathroom countertop, the fake-wood-grain surface pressing against her hipbone as she got as close to the mirror as possible. She paused, holding the liquid eyeliner a fraction of an inch from her eye, waiting for the tremor to stop. She probably should have done this first. Another example of *planning ahead*, as her mother loved to go on and on about.

Planning ahead. Krystle planned ahead *just fine*, thank you very much.

She willed her hand to be still, and it finally obeyed, at least long enough for her to draw thick black lines around both eyes. It quivered a bit at the end of the left eye, but the mascara would hide the raggedness.

"Christina? Are you almost done in there?" Her mother's voice was accompanied by a sharp rapping. The thin wood of the bathroom door bowed inward with the force of the old woman's fist.

"Krystle," the girl muttered, and then more loudly, "Jeeeezus! Can't I have some *privacy* in my own *bathroom*?"

"If you had your own bathroom, maybe you could!" After one final pound, her mother moved off down the shag-carpeted hallway.

"Jeeee-zus," Krystle said again, relishing the sound of it, and the feeling of the sibilants on her tongue. She put the eyeliner down and moved on to the blush, painting a reasonable approximation of a healthy glow into the hollows of her cheeks. Then three coats of mascara, some dark lip liner surrounding peach gloss lipstick, a spritz of White Diamonds, and she was good to go.

She scooped all the makeup into the top drawer and turned to leave, then spotted her hand mirror still resting on the closed seat of the toilet. "Right: clean up after yourself, Krystle," she said, bending down.

The Hippie Monster of Eel River

The sight of the scraps of dust at the corner of the mirror called to her. One more little snort, and then she'd be off. Trent wouldn't be here for another ten minutes at least.

Pulling the paper bindle from the coin pocket at the front of her Levi's, Krystle carefully unfolded it, measured out less than a quarter of what she had left, and nudged it onto the mirror with the razor blade. Then she squatted next to the toilet, tap-tap-tapping the powder ever finer before arranging it in two short lines. Next came the dollar bill, rolled tight to make a straw. She'd done it through a fifty one time. Her dream was to use a hundred-dollar bill, but nobody had ever managed to pull together that much cash at once.

Someday.

Leaning over the mirror, Krystle snorted the speed: right nostril first, then left. After scooting the dollar around to make sure no residue was wasted, she unrolled and folded it and shoved it back in her pocket, then went to the sink. She wet her fingertips, lifted them to her nose, and inhaled the drops of water with a sharp sniff. Then she stood there a moment, waiting for the drip.

Ahhh.

The tangy cash-scented stinging burn of the drug as it touched the back of her throat made her smile. *This is what it's all about.*

Sniffling, she stuck the mirror in the drawer with her makeup and unlocked the bathroom door.

Trent drove them out beyond the valley, over the hill to the Eel River, not far from Clayton's. He parked just below the bridge, next to Russ's battered red F150 pickup; another truck pulled in behind him, blocking them in.

Krystle did not care. It was the first weekend of summer: the biggest-ass party in a season of big-ass parties, and she and Trent would be here until dawn.

She could already hear the laughter and smell the cigarette smoke down by the river as she started to open her door and sidle out into the night. "Hang on," Trent said, pulling out a bindle of his own. He favored glossy dark magazine paper, usually *Sports Illustrated*. Krystle preferred snowy-white printer paper: pure and simple. Clayton would package it any way you liked; that was what was great about him. He understood his customers.

Anyway, Krystle would not turn down Trent's speed, no matter how it was packaged. She let go of the door handle and turned to face her boyfriend.

He measured a couple of generous lumps out onto the scrap of steel he used for a traveling mirror, then coaxed them into four lines with the side of his driver's license. Krystle almost offered him her razor blade, tucked behind her bindle in her jeans, but he was doing fine. He liked to be the big man, the man with the truck, the man with the drugs.

Her man.

It was all right with her. When he offered up the mirror and his own rolled-up bill (a five—big man indeed), she leaned in and snorted them up expertly. "Thanks, dude."

"My pleasure." He took his own lines, then stuck the mirror in the glove box without even wiping it down.

Everyone was different.

"Yow," Krystle said as the harsh powder sat on her nasal passages. She'd go dip her fingers in the river to get the drip she craved. Plus, you were supposed to rinse out your nose every time. If you didn't, you'd get a deviated septum, like all those coke users in the eighties.

Her heart racing, she got down from the truck and headed for the water, greeting friends and strangers as she went. Well, no one was a stranger really, not in this small town; she could name every kid on the rocky shore if she took the time. But they weren't *important*. Only her friends were *important*. And rinsing her nose, that was, too. Krystle felt nine feet tall and powerful and thin and strong and *rocking* solid hot as she strode to the river's edge, but her nose twitched and *damn* she needed to get some water in there right now, damn it.

"Careful of the Hippie Monster," Trent called out as he joined a few guys gathered around the keg: John, and Russ, and a big hairy dude everyone called the Ogre. The guys all laughed, and Krystle rolled her eyes.

"Yeah, right." They thought they were so funny. Get a little beer in them and they thought they were even funnier.

Besides, the Hippie Monster had been further down the river. And it was years ago. Everyone said it was just a wild animal, plus some kind of cult, with a bunch of idiots OD'ing on hallucinogens.

Which only went to prove what an urban legend it was. You couldn't OD on hallucinogens. You could have a bad trip, sure; but you only overdosed on heroin or PCP or stuff like that.

The river water had a muddy, green-algae-like scent to it, but it cleaned her nostrils and gave her the drip she needed just fine. Suddenly thirsty, Krystle went in search of a beer.

She did not have to look far.

Clayton was supposed to come down the hill about midnight and hang out, someone said. With his long greasy blonde hair and filthy blue jeans, Krystle always thought he didn't exactly fit in with the high school crowd. That, plus being super old, like forty or something. But she would be happy to see him. He was one of the few adults who treated the kids like equals.

And sold them speed, of course.

He cooked it up in a shed behind his cabin. It was totally reinforced and triple-insulated to keep the smell inside, and to not burn down the forest. His entire complex—shed, cabin, lean-to garage, and a whole collection of dead cars—was protected by a tall fence with razor-wire on top and a couple of big scary dogs.

Krystle remembered the first time she'd been included on a trip to Clayton's. That was when she was with Jeff; before Trent. She'd been so excited that she got to go, to see where it came from. To meet the guy himself—an outlaw! It felt dangerous and cool and important.

The reality was a bit bleaker than that, but she'd still felt special sitting on the countertop in his kitchen, sipping from the drink they'd given her—amaretto and milk. It was too sweet and kind of gross, and alcohol had never really been her thing anyway. Plus, the lights were too bright inside. She'd stared down into the drink as Jeff and Clayton did their business (this was before she'd started buying her own stash), watching the ice cubes melt into the milk, making little rivers of clear liquid.

Krystle sniffed again, the memory making her queasy. She took a sip of her beer, then set the plastic cup down on a rock. Not thirsty anymore.

What she was now was energized, totally, pure blasting focused WIRED energized oh-my-god. Her legs needed to *move*, her arms wanted to pump and bring air into her body, sweet fresh oxygen. She hadn't really needed that last line...oh well, it would wear off eventually. Faster, if she walked a bit.

She could go up to the road, but then she'd have to walk through the party again, all the laughing guys. And someone would want to *talk* to her, and she just fucking couldn't handle that right now, okay? She could walk up to Clayton's; but she didn't like his dogs, and if he wasn't expecting company, that could be bad. But she had to go somewhere, do something.

Her heart was racing, beating way too fast. She wasn't scared. This had totally happened before, she knew what to do. But it was super annoying, and if she had to *talk* to someone it would be even *more* annoying, and did there always have to be someone around asking questions, did you always have to *explain* shit to everyone?

Krystle started walking down the flat, rocky beach, away from the party. She picked her way slowly at first so that she would look like she was just strolling, so Trent wouldn't think she was mad and follow her, or want to fuck in the bushes or something. But her wired-up muscles strained and yearned against her pace. She was walking like a robot, she knew it, but couldn't stop. It was dark out, probably nobody noticed.

She got to the bend in the river, where the beach narrowed. Now she was out of sight of the party—of anyone who wasn't right down by the water's edge, anyway. She could walk faster here, and she did.

Damn, it felt good.

Krystle strode on, and the night air filled her lungs, and her legs burst with energy and speed. Well, ha-ha, speed as in going-fast, but speed as in the drug, too, of course. Which is why it was called that, she knew that, but it was funny, sometimes she forgot. It was speed because it made your heart go fast and your thoughts go fast and your muscles go fast. And your stomach, too: speed was the best thing for dieting, like, ever. Speed had taken Krystle's plump, curvy early-teen body and winnowed it down to the lean, strong, gorgeous thing she was today.

God, she loved speed.

The beach narrowed more as the sounds of the party faded behind her. Soon she'd have to turn back; the trees grew all the way down to the river's edge, dipping their branches into the water. But she didn't want to go back, she wasn't ready. The party seemed like a stupid thing. Why had she wanted to come, after all? She hated these people, everyone. Same old same old. Why did she have to live in this stupid town anyway? Why couldn't she ever get *out*?

She could walk back and forth on this part of the beach. But that seemed even stupider than the party. And someone would see.

Krystle got to the low branches on the water and peered around them. The beach picked up just past them in another long, open stretch. She pushed at the branches, but the trees were too thick and wouldn't move, wouldn't let her through. She'd have to go into the water.

She stood back, hands on her hips, and thought about it. Then she bent down and took off her high-heeled sandals.

The water was shallow here, and much colder than she'd expected. When she swam in the Eel River, it was usually later in the summer; this felt like snow-melt. She gasped as it touched her ankles, and slipped a little on the slimy algae that grew on the rocks. Reaching out with the hand that wasn't holding her sandals, she steadied herself on a thick branch, but it swayed at her touch.

"Fuck!" she yelled, only barely managing to keep her balance. If she fell in…she'd get her stash wet, and ruin it. It would dissolve in the river. It was only about fifteen bucks worth, but still. Not like she was a millionaire or anything.

With a colossal effort, Krystle kept from immersing herself. When she was certain she had her footing, she stepped forward, moving around the protruding branches.

The icy water lapped at her calves as it wicked up her jeans, approaching her knees. It felt like it was only about a foot deep at the deepest part, but damn, it was cold.

Then she'd gotten to the edge of the branches; now she was past, and there was the rest of the beach. Krystle picked up her pace and scrambled up towards the bank. Her foot slipped again on a big flat slick rock; she nearly tumbled up onto the shore, shivering and dripping.

"Fuck," she said again, softer this time.

Her heart was still pounding, but this time with anxiety. She had come *this close* to falling in and losing her stash, getting all wet and looking like a dork.

Not only that, but she would have to go back through the water to get back! Stupid, stupid!

"I'll go up to the road," she told herself. She realized she was on the crazy hippie beach now; they would have a path to the road, even if nobody had lived here for years. Then she could walk back to the party.

Right. Cool.

Satisfied, Krystle started walking down the beach, looking for the path. It was sandier on this side of the trees, and a bit steeper. And damn, it was dark. She wished she had a flashlight, but who took a flashlight to a party? Only dorks, she was sure.

But how hard could it be to find a path?

Once she got to the road, it would be fine. Of course there weren't any streetlights out here, twenty miles down a country dirt road, but her eyes would adjust to the starlight and the way would be open enough for her to find her way back. The noise of the party would guide her. There was only one road, anyway.

But damn, it was dark.

Suddenly, Krystle was very ready to get back. A crawling panic seized her and she half-ran up to the top of the beach, where the forest encroached hard and thick. Where was their stupid path? There had to be one. It would be overgrown, but it would have to be there, sort of, anyway. But she found nothing. She pushed and clawed at the branches and they clawed her back, scratching her face. "Fuck!"

Then one part of the forest seemed less thick than the rest, and she could see a bit of sandy ground under it, she thought. Or at least a lighter patch. Krystle pushed into it, shoving the branches aside and sliding her skinny body into the opening. But three steps in, it had closed up again. She turned all the way around: nowhere to go.

Whimpering, she slipped back out and stood on the beach once more. Her whole body was shaking, and her heart was slamming away, must be a hundred beats a minute.

Krystle turned around and looked at the water. She would have to go back through it.

After she rested. As much as her body was racing, she was also exhausted, she realized. She sat down on the cold sand and tried to catch her breath, to still her heart. *Just slow down*, she thought, soothing herself. *Slow down.*

That's when she noticed the bottom of the river glowing.

It was a low, steady green iridescence, pulsating slightly. The light made a sort of broken shimmering on the surface of the water, but it was also changing in its depths, she could see that.

"What the fuck?" Krystle leaned forward, too frightened to get up and have a closer look; too fascinated to leave it be.

THE HIPPIE MONSTER OF EEL RIVER

Besides, she couldn't run away. Where would she go?

Her heart rate doubled, it seemed, and ached in her chest.

What *was* it? "Algae," she whispered aloud. It had to be; some sort of weird glow-y green algae thing, reflecting the moon back or something. The rocks were slippery enough.

But there was no moon tonight, and the damn thing was getting brighter.

When the shape broke the surface of the water, Krystle fell backwards on the sand, her eyes rolling and her mouth gaping open.

Long have we waited, and far we have reached.

It was a dream. It had to be a dream. She was not seeing a total space alien thing coming out of the water. She was *not*.

Trust the words of your heart, and carry our message.

The only words of her heart were that it was going to fucking burst from beating so fast. She was lying on the freezing cold sand on a moonless night, staring up at the stars, but also seeing an *alien*. A monster. Coming out of the water. Impossible.

There is another way. Your path is faulty. The path of everyone on this planet is faulty. We have come to share our wisdom.

The Hippie Monster! That had to be it. Krystle struggled to move her limbs, to turn her head, to get up, but it was as though she was bound with a thousand tiny ropes. She could not budge. Also, she was still seeing the stars at the same time as she was seeing the long, narrow, big-headed, big-eyed alien, like right from a movie. In the water.

We choose the shape that makes sense to you. To make it clear, to make our origins clear. Do not fear. It is merely an image. Listen to the message.

Then it all became blurry, and still she could not move. Krystle felt cold, but her body would not shiver. Her mind roamed the stars, seeing visions that were not possible—extra dimensions, twisted shapes, creatures that bent and soared around others, a long line of bubbles that popped and soothed. And a strong sense of peace and joy grew in her. Slowly at first, and then more rapidly, as her mind and body opened up to the concept.

It was better than any drug ever. Better than mushrooms, more visual than acid, more euphoric than coke. It was true. It was real. The Hippie Monster wasn't a monster at all. It was an alien, a creature from another planet, and it was using her to take a message to the rest of humanity.

A message of peace, and harmony. A new way of being. Hope and love, and an end to faulty pleasure-seeking behaviors that only harmed. Instead, a pure, true joy: a promise of hope to humanity, from the stars.

All she had to do was carry this simple message.

Krystle started to laugh, there on the beach; joy sprung from her frozen lips, echoed through the trees, across the river. "Yes," she whispered. "Yes! I will."

When she came to herself again, she was lying on her side. Sand stuck to the corner of her mouth where she had drooled; she sat up and wiped it off.

"Holy fuck," she said, staring down at the water, heart still pounding. Now there was no more green glow, no more alien.

But it had happened. And now she understood everything. The thing—whatever it was—it had been here for decades. Trapped, moored to the land, to the river. It had tried to use the hippies to get the word out, to save humanity and its own self; but they had failed, for some reason.

Now the thing told her it was all up to her.

"No," she whispered. There was no way.

The very thought of it sent a sharp, acidic stab of fear through her chest. "No..." She scrambled to her feet, backing away from the water until she bumped into the trees, almost tripping over a tangled root. Turning, her breath escaped her as she saw the trail leading upwards, suddenly as clear as if it had landing lights. She ran up it with a gasp of relief as her wet sandals touched the groomed surface of the dirt road, still a bit washboarded from last winter's rains, but much easier than the beach.

Nearly running back to the party, Krystle noticed lights up the hill at Clayton's place. If what the alien said was true, he would have to go; drugs were forbidden. In fact, the whole party was no good, according to the monster. Teenagers shouldn't be drinking beer late at night down by the river. They should be spreading the word.

Anyone who wasn't already completely corrupted, that was.

But what was she supposed to do? She was only a girl. A skinny, weak girl.

It was much faster getting back; within a few minutes, she was picking her way through the parked cars, heading for the noise below.

THE HIPPIE MONSTER OF EEL RIVER

Russ's truck was rocking gently and the windows were fogged up. Krystle frowned.

That was bad, too.

So much to do! So much to solve. How could she carry this burden?

Her fingers went to her pocket, where the tiny razor blade rested behind the bindle. It was small, but it was sharp…

The bindle sang to her, though. The sweet, sweet call of speed. Such strength.

Krystle straightened her shoulders and walked towards the laughter.

"*There* you are," Trent said, slipping an arm around her and planting a beery kiss on the side of her face. "What happened to you?"

She stood trembling in his embrace, staring up at him even as he turned to talk to Trish. Exposing his neck, his jugular. Everyone was so fragile; she couldn't believe she'd never noticed this. Her fingers twitched on her pocket, rubbing, caressing. Trent's hand slipped casually to cup her ass.

It felt good. Right. Sexy, and solid. Safe.

Too bad it was all a lie.

"Nothing," she said, dropping her hand, then leaning up to return his kiss. "Nothing."

She shrunk away from him after a minute. Coming down was hard. She'd never hallucinated on speed before, but apparently there was a first time for everything. Krystle yearned for the comfortable familiarity of her own stuff. She didn't like Trent's. It tasted too much like magazine paper. And it was way too rushy. Clayton must have mixed the batch wrong.

That stuff was crazy.

It would all be okay later, after she got her head back together. It would. And then they'd fuck in the bushes, or on the front seat of his truck, like Russ and Lisa were doing. Because this was the biggest-ass party of a summer of big-ass parties, and it had to be done up right.

"I need a beer," she said, slipping out from under her boyfriend's arm and heading for the keg.

But she hadn't even gotten halfway to the river before she saw the glowing green, shimmering across the water. Almost like it was winking up at her.

"No," she whispered again, as she sank to her knees. "No, oh please no, don't make me…"

The glimmer of green caught the light of a distant star and echoed in Krystle's head as though that had been its purpose from the very start. From the beginning of it all, a million billion light years away across the universe.

And she whispered, "No."

The Hippie Monster of Eel River

AFTERWORD

The Hippie Monster of Eel River is an invented urban legend, based loosely on the terrible things that happen in my unpublished novel EEL RIVER, and taking place in the same setting, twenty or so years later. The place itself is real, all the way down to speed labs hidden in the woods and lost, cynical teenagers partying at the river.

It's hard to explain why I chose this legend. None of the "real" urban legends I knew about spoke to me, at least not enough to want to make them into a story of my own. And when I thought about adding aliens to the mix, my muse sort of shrugged and stared back at me.

I posed the question to my subconscious, and a few days later, Krystle popped up, bent over her mirror, her cheeks gaunt and ghostly as she snorted powdered death into her young body. And it all unfolded from there…

ROADKILL
Rick Silva

I covered fifty miles counting roadkill with a naturalist's attention to detail. Rabbit. Rabbit. Ground squirrel. Unknown. Unknown. Armadillo.

The unknowns were shapeless lumps, glimpses of raw hamburger streaking by at eighty, attended by ravens that were wholly nonchalant as they hopped aside.

I never got a good look at any of the unknowns, but I was pretty sure that there were no ravens among the fatalities. Ravens are too smart to get hit. This is their business, a highway symbiosis. *A commensalism*, to be more precise. The ravens gain some benefit from their close association with the automobile. For the cars, the interaction is of neutral value. I may have been trained in the archeology business, but I know my field ecology. Out in the desert, grad students cluster in quiet watering holes in Navajo towns and talk for hours about their work as they delicately maneuver the conversation to try and figure out if the grad student on the other side of the whiskey bottle wants to fuck. I paid attention to those conversations. I've got good attention to detail. Always have.

Coyote. Or dog. Then another unknown.

That particular glimpse of red meat called up the image of Cassie's face, and I slammed my hands down one the steering wheel hard enough that the pain took three mile-markers to fade. Not hard enough to banish the vision, though.

"Damn it!"

I thought about opening the window to scream it to the world. But by then the moment passed and I'm back in control. I need to be in control. I didn't touch Cassie. I didn't even raise my voice. I just walked out to my truck and started driving. Nice guys don't hit women; they don't yell and scream in the face of rejection.

Nice guys take it out on the road.

Under the tires, I felt the bump of something classified as woodchuck getting mashed into 'classification: unknown' for the next driver. In the rearview mirror, a raven touched down a few feet from the feast and approached in quick hops.

I'm remembering Cassie versus the fire ant researchers. Her point was that humans were the true invasive species. All that morning, Cassie sat close by under a tarp that kept off the sun, but not the heat, sweating close enough for me to smell her as we brushed dirt off of Ancestral Puebloan pottery shards that dated to the original invasion of North America. That night the entomologist made the point that all species were, by nature, invasive. Provide resources and territory, and they will take it. Hard to argue with that logic. The truck provides. The raven takes.

Walking back to camp, she was on my case for not backing her up. So the next morning I went out and squirted lighter fluid on a fire ant nest in her honor and tossed in a match. But I made sure it wasn't one of the nests in the invasive species study area, and I still kept my mouth shut during philosophical disagreements between the profs. Better for the career that way. You never know who you'll be working for.

I got two days of silent treatment from Cassie, and when I finally caught up to her at the dig, she gave me the bullshit about just wanting to be treated like a professional. I nodded and smiled while the pictures in my head showed Cassie's face where the burning ant nest had been.

"Damn it!"

I didn't want to think about any of this. I started fixating on the scene in the rear view mirror. The ravens and their meal were vanishing from sight now, and it occurred to me that you can drive a long way on a straight empty desert road while looking in your rear view mirror.

So when the cardboard box flopped into the road, I was almost on top of it, and I swerved toward it instead of away, picturing Cassie's face, picturing roadkill, picturing ants burning up.

On the second bump, the one that came when the truck's left rear wheel hit, my throat tightened and went dry. I forgot about Cassie for the first time all day.

I still drove a few hundred yards making the decision to stop.

The scene replayed in my mind, suddenly filling in details I hadn't realized I'd perceived.

A box, some trash. Something shiny. A box covered in strips of tinfoil.

I stepped down out of the truck, worried now, queasy in the stomach. I remembered the story, trying to figure out who I'd heard it from. Someone I knew freshman year at UMass? Someone drunk, sharing stupid stories in the stink of mostly-empty party remnants. Everyone hears about these things. In the version I heard, a guy swerves his SUV into the leaf pile and kills his own kid. Wasn't there a story about a cardboard box getting forwarded around in an email? Fuck this. I started rationalizing. Middle of nowhere. Flat land, barbed wire, sagebrush, and not even a cow from here to the mountains. But I couldn't convince myself that it was an empty box I jumped out of the cab and started toward it on foot.

The shiny streamer trailing from under the truck caught my eye, and I stopped suddenly. There was something about how the light played on it. I reached down and caught hold of the streamer and pulled. It didn't break. Aluminum foil should have torn. I pulled harder. I finally knelt and unhooked the stuff from where it was caught on the axle. I stood.

A raven landed a few paces from the crushed box and then took flight again.

The shiny smooth strip molded itself to my hand, a perfect second skin. I felt nothing, but when I held my hand up and the sunlight coming from behind me caught it, I found myself looking straight through my own hand to the road where another raven briefly alighted and then flew away.

I thought of two things at once. Discovery Channel UFO programs talked about strange materials left behind after the Roswell crash and other incidents. Materials that were thin and malleable and impossibly strong, that did strange things with light; that were passed off as polymer fabrics used for high-altitude spy balloons. No one could ever produce any samples of these substances for the TV shows. They dissolved into thin air, or were confiscated by nameless government agents dressed in black and armed with thinly veiled threats.

The second thing I remembered was the invisibility cloak, a topic that routinely made the top-ten lists on internet news sites around the time of the release of the final *Harry Potter* book. There would always be an interview with some scientist about how it was theoretically possible to bend electromagnetic radiation around a material with the right set of properties, followed by the usual disclaimers about how a real invisibility cloak was still decades away.

I peeled the stuff off my hand. It came off smoothly, like price tags of the better sort, and I poked at it with my pocket knife. It folded over the blade and the knife wouldn't cut it. It made the blade blink out of existence when held up against the background of the empty sky. Ever since I got into my PhD program in archaeology, I'd been involved in digging up bits and scraps of stone or flint or carved bone and trying to figure out what they might have been used for. I'm good at thinking up uses for bits and pieces of old tools, and this wasn't so different. The implications came fast. This stuff had endless uses. This stuff could make someone very rich.

I started walking, ignoring more scraps of reflective foil in the road as I watched the ravens arrive and depart. Something was sending them mixed signals.

There was liquid oozing out of one corner of the crushed box and I suddenly realized that I had gotten to the point where the brown red of blood flowing from the wreckage would come as a relief. What I saw was grey with flecks of gold, and it flowed in tendrils that crept out onto the highway, radiating from the crushed box.

Cassie once got into an argument with a SETI guy. He'd come out to the desert to use the empty, flat land to set up an array of small-scale receivers, a sort of poor-man's radio telescope, backed up by a distributed botnet to provide the computational power necessary to separate signal from noise. As far as I knew, the guy never found any signal out there. Just plenty of noise. Cassie, who could never resist a chance to cast humanity as the bad guys, asked him if he thought an extraterrestrial species would treat us as an inferior civilization. Treat us the way the Europeans had treated the Indians. Conquest and slavery. Guns, germs, steel.

The SETI man had said he was more afraid that an extraterrestrial species would be nothing like us, that they would be so alien that they wouldn't recognize that we were intelligent at all. What if they were so different from us that they didn't acknowledge anything here worth talking to? Or even capable of talking? Ants are pretty good engineers. We don't go around trying to converse with them.

Some of us pour lighter fluid on their nests and drop a match in when we're pissed off.

I recalled the exchange between Cassie and the SETI scientist while I walked along the side of the road, and I counted three more ravens descending and then flying away.

Something is dead. Land and investigate. No, nothing here that resembles food. Classification: unknown. Move on.

The creature's spindly limbs were broken in places and the head was split open. That's where the grey and gold liquid was flowing from, although the flow had slowed to a trickle. It was all over the road by the time I got there. The smell lingered over the body, but it was overpowering when I got to within a couple of steps away. It smelled like burned sugar mixed with isopropyl alcohol. My stomach tried to send back my lunch. I choked it back down. I pulled away from the smell and from the taste of bile in my mouth, suddenly aware of the isolation of the desert road. No one had driven by. I couldn't remember the last time I passed a car.

I scanned the empty sky, trying to decide. Call someone? I knew biologists, ecologists. The SETI professor finished his research and headed back to Florida, but Cassie would have his number. Wait for someone to show up? Load the body into the back of the truck? Or just drive away? I wondered if I could be arrested, or maybe just locked up for knowing too much. What would Cassie say? Just another human fuck-up. Welcome to Earth, here's a truck to run you over.

I didn't stop to consider what the creature was doing here. I'd have plenty of time for that later.

Ravens were circling, waiting for their chance to investigate. I took a few steps backward toward the truck, still undecided.

A raven flying above the road flickered out of existence, and then reappeared. I didn't have the luxury of questioning whether my eyes were playing tricks on me. I was holding a simpler answer in my hand. Something in the sky, bending the light. An invisibility cloak.

I ran for the truck and got it started. It stalled out. Dead. Then my muscles stiffened and froze up.

I'm on my back in a room wallpapered with reflective foil that bends light depending on the angle from which you look at it, and I feel the flesh of my left arm burning away slowly as the creature with the spindly limbs and gold-flecked skin listens to me screaming.

The pain stops, but I don't bother looking at my arm. I know it's still there, the flesh smooth and unblemished.

She's doing it to me with telepathy. That means she can do it over and over again, as many times as she wants. She starts on my right leg.

Cassie won the argument with the SETI scientist. The extraterrestrials are not so different from us. Their children still like to play in boxes. And their mothers still rage at the loss of a child.

Rick Silva

AFTERWORD

Traditional legends are very often cautionary tales. As children, the tale of the Three Little Pigs teaches us the value of keeping our homes well-prepared for disaster, while Red Riding Hood warns of the perils of talking to strangers. Many of the urban myths that get passed around the internet, or told in amid sessions of late-night drinking in college dormitories are simply the old warnings reinvented.

The cardboard box legend, sometimes reinvented as a leaf-pile, is a commonly-told driving horror story, and it serves as a reminder of unintended consequences. The driver, distracted, angry, or just in the mood for fun, swerves his vehicle into the cardboard box or pile of leaves in the road instead of away from it, killing the child who had been innocently playing inside. This legend frightens us not only because of the gruesome tragedy involved, but because, for many of us, it's all too easy to think of some circumstance when we might have steered the car toward the box, and toward whatever unintended consequences awaited.

END OF LIFE
By Richard Lee Byers

One man was young and skinny, and the other, middle-aged and fat. But their briefcases and dark suits, worn despite the blazing sun, made them look alike. So did their toothy smiles.

Joey thought, *Missionaries. Or salesmen.* He took a breath to send them on to bother the neighbors, and then they showed him their IDs. They were from the Surgeon General's Office.

"Hello, young man," the fat one said.

"Hi," Joey answered. He'd just turned fourteen, and didn't really like it when adults still called him "young man" or "son." But he also figured it wouldn't do any good to get an attitude about it.

"I'm Mr. Baker," the fat man said, "and this is Mr. Sloane. Does Mary Wilson live here?"

"Yes." She was Joey's grandma, and having medical people come to see her scared him a little. "Does she have some kind of problem?"

The smiles stretched wider. "Not at all!" said Mr. Baker. "Not at all! We'd just like to ask her a few questions."

"It's a kind of survey," murmured Mr. Sloane.

Joey hesitated. He was supposed to look after Grandma while Mom and Dad were at work. But if these guys were from the government, and the Federal government at that… "All right. But please don't wear her out, okay? She was in the hospital just last month."

As he let them in, he noticed that despite the black coats and summer heat, they didn't smell like sweat (or anything else). He guessed they must have a car with air-conditioning parked nearby, even though he hadn't spotted it out front.

Her swollen feet propped up and her gray aluminum walker standing beside her easy chair, Grandma was in the Florida room watching Judge Judy. She muted the show and smiled when she saw she had company.

Mr. Baker reintroduced himself and his partner and said they hoped she wouldn't mind answering a few questions. She said she'd be happy to—it was nice to have visitors—and sent Joey to the kitchen for iced tea.

By the time he came back with the tray, Mr. Sloane and Mr. Baker were perched rather stiffly on the edge of the couch. Mr. Baker had a ballpoint in his pale, hairless hand and a clipboard in his lap.

"As you may have heard," said Mr. Baker, in a way that made it obvious he'd recited the exact same words many times before, "the President's health-care initiative encompasses a number of new programs, including one commonly called end-of-life counseling."

"Hey!" Joey said. "She's not at the end of her life." It was true as far as he was concerned, and he didn't want anybody upsetting her by suggesting any different.

"No," Grandma said, "I certainly am not."

"I'm sure you're not," Mr. Baker said. "But you fit the demographics, and this is the pilot study. It will teach us how to set up the service so as to provide the greatest possible benefit. So, if you're simply willing to complete the survey, your cooperation could help many of your fellow seniors."

Grandma shrugged. "All right, then. When you put it that way."

"But if you don't like it," Joey said, "or you get tired…"

"All she has to do is say so," said Mr. Baker, "and we'll stop immediately. That tea looks very refreshing. May I have some?"

Joey handed him a glass. He set it on the coffee table untasted. Mr. Sloane did the same with his.

"Now, then," Mr. Baker said, "can you imagine a set of circumstances in which you would not want your life prolonged by artificial means? Like, for example, a respirator?"

Grandma hesitated. "Well, maybe. If I was in a coma and would never wake up."

Mr. Baker blacked in a circle on his paperwork. "Can you imagine a situation where you might take advantage of the option to use artificial means to bring your life to a close?"

"Absolutely not," Grandma said.

"I assume you're aware," Mr. Baker said, "that people in the final phase of a terminal illness sometimes suffer severely, and their doctors are unable to alleviate the pain. You're probably aware, too, that those last few months can place a significant strain on families, both emotionally and financially."

"I do know that," Grandma said. "I've lived through it. But killing yourself, or having somebody else do it for you, is against the Bible."

Mr. Baker blacked in another circle. "I understand, and I hope you realize that nothing I ask or say during the interview is meant to challenge or disparage your beliefs. I'm simply collecting information. Now, we've established that you would never ask a government agency to help you complete life at a time of your own choosing. But please, for purposes of the study, just imagine that you feel differently. Would you prefer to perform the actual act of termination yourself, or have someone perform it for you?"

Grandma snorted. "It's all so different from anything I'd really do that it's hard to pick."

"Just try. Please."

"All right. I guess I'd want some handsome young doctor to help me." She gave Joey a wink that made him feel a little better. Maybe this creepy shit bothered him more than it did her.

"And would you prefer an injection," Mr. Baker continued, "or an odorless, colorless gas? Both would be quick and painless."

"The gas, I guess. I never did like needles."

"Good. Thank you so much! That finishes the hard part. I promise, the rest will be less personal, and less potentially unpleasant. Mr. Sloane is simply going to show you some colors, patterns, shapes, and images that could be used to create the décor of a medical facility. We'd like you to tell us which ones seem calming and restful."

"All right," Grandma smiled. "I expect I will like this part better."

Mr. Sloane stood up and moved over beside Grandma's chair. He opened his briefcase and took out two square pieces of cloth, one gray and one orange.

"Which one do you prefer?" Mr. Baker asked.

Joey shook his head. One moment, they were asking her about assisted suicide, the next, they were making her look at carpet samples. It had started out weird and gotten weirder.

But it did seem that, like Mr. Baker had promised, the part that might have upset Grandma was over. In fact, the parade of bits of cloth and colored pieces of cardboard was boring enough to make Joey fidget. His eyes wandered to the glowering people on the silent TV, and he wondered what they were mad about. Unpaid rent, maybe. Watching with Grandma, he'd learned that half of Judge Judy's cases were arguments between landlords and tenants.

Grandma gasped. Joey turned in her direction.

"Which one are you reacting to?" Mr. Baker asked.

Grandma pointed to the oval piece of cardboard in Mr. Sloane's left hand. "That one. It…reminds me of Warren's eyes. Warren was my husband."

And he'd had blue eyes. Joey got up, walked over, looked at the cardboard, and saw red and yellow spatters on a tan background. It looked more like puke than anything else, and made him feel vaguely sick to his stomach.

He guessed Grandma was actually thinking about his grandfather just because she missed him. She was still getting over his death, even though she did her best to act cheerful when other people were around.

"I see," said Mr. Baker. Mr. Sloane set that particular piece of cardboard on the armrest of her chair, then brought out two more pieces of cloth.

After a couple more minutes, Grandma gave a little jerk. It made the loose flesh under her chin wobble.

"Now what are you reacting to?" Mr. Baker asked.

"That one." When she pointed, her hand trembled. "It's like the floor of the club where my friends and I went dancing when I lived in Miami."

Joey peered at the card. Seven-sided and irregular, charcoal gray with white lines zigzagging through it, it was as indefinably ugly as the one that reminded him of vomit. He couldn't imagine anyone putting the pattern on a dance floor.

"How does it make you feel?" Mr. Baker asked.

Grandma hesitated. "Good, I suppose. Those are good memories." She smiled a strange, bleak smile Joey had never seen before. "But I won't be doing any more dancing, will I?"

"Grandma," Joey said, "I think you should stop."

"I promise, we're almost done," Mr. Baker said.

"It's making her feel bad," Joey said.

Mr. Baker kept his eyes on Grandma. "If we don't complete the protocol," he said, "we can't use any of the information. It would be a shame if the time you've already given went to waste."

"Yes," Grandma said. "I'm fine, Joey. It's just that when you're old, and sick..."

Everyone waited, but she didn't finish her thought. Mr. Sloane laid the charcoal card on the armrest.

After that, it went all right for a while, until Joey could see that Mr. Sloane's briefcase was almost empty. He started to relax, and then the skinny man brought out a trapezoidal piece of copper with ovals etched into the surface.

Grandma sobbed.

"What's wrong?" Joey asked.

"It's everyone," she quavered, sounding twice as old as she had before. "Everyone who's gone. Warren, and my friend Alice, and my parents and grandparents that you never knew."

"It's just circles!" Joey said. "There aren't any faces or anything!"

She kept crying. He reached to push the copper sheet away from her. As he did, he got a second look at it and the ugly pieces of cardboard, too, still balanced on the arm of the chair.

Suddenly he felt more alone and unhappy than ever in his life, a rush of emotion that hit him like a punch. No one cared about him, and no one ever would. Nothing good would ever happen to him, and it was his own fault. Because he was a loser. Nothing. A worthless piece of....

Tears running down his face, he sucked in a breath and fought to stop the racing thoughts and the feelings that came with them. Because they weren't *true*. He had a family who loved him, and friends, and a plan for the future. He was going into the Army, and that would pay for college.

When the hurtful thoughts finally did stop, he had his back against the wall and snot hanging out of his nose. For a moment, there was no room in his head for anything but relief. Then he heard the *smack-smack-smack!*

Grandma was beating herself in the face with her heel of her hand.

He scrambled around her chair and grabbed her wrists. She struggled and nearly broke free, so wild that it made her strong despite old age, diabetes, and a bad heart.

He remembered the men from the Surgeon General's Office, and turned his head to find them. Mr. Baker had gotten up from the couch. Mr. Sloane was stuffing pieces of cloth and cardboard back into his briefcase.

"Help her!" Joey said.

"I'm sorry," Mr. Baker said, "we can't."

"You did this to her!" Joey said. Grandma thrashed.

"No," Mr. Baker said. "I believe she's having a seizure."

"Will you at least hold onto her while I call 911?"

"All right," Mr. Baker said. He came around the coffee table and gingerly took hold of Grandma's arms. Joey let go and scrambled into the kitchen.

As he picked up the wall phone, he heard the smacking start again. Mr. Baker had let go, too, as soon as Joey left the room.

Joey went stiff and cold with anger. He didn't know how, but Mr. Baker and Mr. Sloane had done this to Grandma, the same way they'd made Joey hate himself for a second. And now they didn't even care.

But they might be the only ones who could fix it. He hung up the receiver and opened a drawer.

Mr. Baker and Mr. Sloane froze when they saw the Beretta. Joey told himself they were right to be scared. His father had taught him to shoot, and he'd gotten better in JROTC. He could do whatever he needed to.

He swallowed, but still found it hard to talk loud enough for anyone else to hear. "Help her."

"We can't," Mr. Baker said. "Honestly,"

"I'm going to shoot one of you, and then see if the other one still says the same thing."

"Please," said Mr. Baker, "I know you're upset, but this isn't accomplishing anything. You need to restrain Mrs. Wilson like you did before. Otherwise, she could have a heart attack, or damage her eyes."

The maddening *smack-smack-smack* made it feel like he was right.

But Joey kept the gun raised. In fact, he aimed it right at Mr. Sloane, who, with his wide eyes, looked more scared than his partner.

"I'll give you to three," Joey said. "One."

"All right!" yelped Mr. Sloane. "It's possible I can help her. I have something in my briefcase."

It occurred to Joey that the something might be another gun. But he probably would have spotted it when the briefcase was all but empty before. "Okay," he said, "get it."

Then he realized he was looking too hard at Mr. Sloane, and only Mr. Sloane. He shot a panicky glance at Mr. Baker, but the fat man wasn't doing anything. He was still just standing in front of the couch with his open hands raised to chest level.

Mr. Sloane got down on one knee and rooted in his bag. He pulled out pieces of cardboard and cloth and tossed them onto the floor. A skinny red triangle was almost painfully bright.

"Hurry up!" Joey said.

"I know it's here somewhere." Mr. Sloane took out more stuff, including the card that looked like puke. Joey's stomach churned.

"Two," Joey said. He shot another glance at Mr. Baker. Who still wasn't moving.

"I swear it's here!" Mr. Sloane babbled. He tossed out more crap, including the copper trapezoid.

Joey had brains enough not to look at it straight on. But that meant he had to look somewhere else instead. At a round blue piece of cloth with a shape like a green eye staring out of the center.

And then he hated himself again. This time the feeling was so strong that he couldn't even think about whether it made any sense. He jammed the Beretta under his chin and pulled the trigger.

He didn't hear the bang. The world seemed to jump, and then he was lying on his back. He was cold, and everything was shadowy.

The smacking had stopped. Straining, he just barely managed to turn his head. Grandma slumped motionless in her chair.

"He really would have shot me!" said Mr. Sloane.

"But you handled it," said Mr. Baker. "Well done."

"If we had armor, or our own weapons--"

"We can't risk them falling into enemy hands."

"And if they kill one of us, and perform an autopsy, *that's* not going to warn them that we're here?"

Mr. Baker shrugged, "I didn't make the rules or the plan. But I think it's a good one, and worth the risks. Once we find the right combination of triggers, they'll kill themselves by the millions and never know why."

Mr. Sloane grimaced, "I suppose you're right."

"You know I am. And now we should go. The neighbors may have heard the shot."

"Just give me a minute. The child agitated me. I need to eat."

Mr. Sloane's body swelled and squirmed into something as lumpy as a sack of potatoes. Stretching, his fingers slithered across the floor. Little round mouths opened in the tips, and then they crawled on toward the hole in Joey's neck.

Richard Lee Byers

AFTERWORD

We live in a time when people craft urban legends for propaganda purposes. In 2009, opponents of healthcare reform spread stories to convince voters that changes to the existing system would result in rationed care and even euthanasia. One such story claims that every old person should expect a visit from bureaucrats intent on providing "end-of-life counseling." I took the notion and ran with it to create the yarn you just read.

Teacups and Saucers
Ramsey Lundock

"The real reason you were transferred is not because you were a disappointment. It is because you have potential," the steel haired Colonel said, "Enough potential that we decided to tell you the truth."

"Sir, I have already seen the flying saucer and studied some of its components," Army Captain Richard Williams responded.

"And I said I'd tell you the truth."

Captain Williams' head was spinning. Only eight months ago, he had been assigned to study a captured alien spacecraft at the Area 51 base in Nevada. He hadn't been given a chance to examine the craft up close, but his passing views of the saucer and his detailed study of some engine components had fascinated him beyond words. Then it all seemed to end.

He had been transferred to Raven Rock in Pennsylvania. Also known as the Underground Pentagon, urban legend held that Raven Rock would have become the new military command headquarters in the event of a nuclear strike on Washington. But with the end of the Cold War and even the most advanced rouge nations lacking ICBM, all Captain Williams had to look forward to was a long dull career changing backup batteries on the facility's numerous broadcast towers. Now a mysterious Colonel Jonathan Grieger was telling him things were only beginning as the elevator descended into the heart of Raven Rock.

Captain Williams had by no means avoided hardship in his career, but his face was pale and smooth compared to the Colonel Grieger. His hazel eyes were wide with confusion under a mass of disheveled brown hair. It didn't help that the Colonel stared straight into his soul, with eyes as blue and deep as the sea.

"Do you remember what you said in your last update to the project head down there?" Colonel Grieger asked.

Captain Williams remembered too well. One thoughtless comment had ended his time working with alien artifacts. "I said that the device didn't appear to work within the bounds of known science, sir."

"I don't want what you said in your report, after you had time to think." The Colonel glared at him, "I want what you muttered, disgusted, in your superior's office."

Captain Williams grimaced; it was bad enough that he had said it once. "I said: According to the laws of science the accursed thing shouldn't work."

"Thank you. I need you to be honest with me and everyone else on this project." Colonel Grieger smiled, "When we recruit people, they have become so indoctrinated to lie and keep secrets that we have trouble getting them to trust their coworkers."

"Sir, I have accepted that withholding facts from the public, as well as the elected government, and embezzling tax dollars are necessary evils." Williams was pleased to be ahead of the Colonel's expectations for once, "And I manage to function in a military research unit."

"Even the Pentagon doesn't know what I'm about to show you."

"How is it possible to hide secrets from the Military inside one of our own bases, sir?" Captain Williams asked. "What if a General comes in and demands to see what's behind this or that door?"

"We used to have to have to hide things from inspecting Generals, so back in the Seventies, we had a new sub-basement dug that even the most classified documents don't show."

"I thought the Alternate National Military Command and Control Center Improvement Program was canceled in 1979."

"You can get an amazing amount of work done in two years; especially when you have the right…'advantages.' Even with the sub-basement, when the VP was staying here after the terrorist attacks we had a couple of close calls; but we managed to get through."

The elevator stopped and the doors opened on to that forgotten sub-basement. Colonel Grieger stepped out into the corridor lit by a strip of overhead fluorescent lights. The walls and ceiling were curved, like the inside of a pipe, but the floor was level. Captain Williams followed him through a maze of identical corridors.

Teacups and Saucers

"Would you like to see the vessel recovered from Roswell in the Forties?"

"Sir, at Area 51…"

"You have a mock up we use to keep the military inspectors off our back. My question stands, Captain," the Colonel snapped.

"Yes sir."

Colonel Grieger stopped at one of the unmarked doors along the hall. Inside the cavernous room behind the door was a disk of over fifty foot radius with a burnished silver color. A section of the hull was folded down, forming a ramp into a dark interior. It was identical to the one Williams had seen in Nevada and he said as much.

"Did you ever see the inside of your copy?"

"No sir."

"You can dispense with the 'Sir' down here," Grieger said. "Climb inside this one."

Captain Williams did so. He was expecting the well upholstered, diminutive chairs; the gleaming metal levers and even the brightly colored crystals glowing on the walls, ceiling, and work stations. He could accept the ornate carvings covering every surface and purple carpet concealing the floor. It looked as he had expected, except for one detail.

"Sir," the Captain stammered, "It's made of wood, sir."

"The entire thing is carved from one ageless oak tree." Colonel Grieger glowed with satisfaction, "We counted the rings in the ceiling and came up with seventeen hundred and thirty-nine."

"The color of these controls is the same as the engine pieces I was shown. Or were the drive components and schematics all faked as well?"

"The diagrams are fiction, but some of the pieces you were given are from this craft and some we manufactured. Did you ever detect the difference?"

Captain Williams choked on his tongue, "I, I sometimes felt that the supposed piston rod was of coarser manufacture than the ring it slipped though. I had theorized that it was a jury-rigged field repair to replace a worn out component. Was the rod one of your pieces?"

"Very good. You're more promising than I realized."

"It's an odd alloy. Unnervingly equal molar quantities of copper, gold, mercury, and silver." Williams knelt to examine an ornate metal carving affixed to the wall just above the carpet, "I never could explain its weight, magnetic, or electric qualities from its composition."

"The alloy is called orichalcum."

Williams jumped up and bashed his head on the low ceiling. He ducked and rubbed the sore spot, "The ancient astronaut theory is correct?"

"Why do you say that?"

"Well, orichalcum, it's a term from, you know. Ancient astronauts must have tried to teach humans their science, but we weren't ready to learn so we misunderstood and turned it into, well you know or you wouldn't use the term 'orichalcum.'" Like many teenagers Williams had read some books of urban myths when he was in high school. He had forgotten most of those rumors and lies, and he certainly never expected to hear a self respecting scientist use the term 'orichalcum.'

"This is the first bit of the truth I'm giving you. Don't reject it." Colonel Grieger's eyed him, "Where is orichalcum used?"

"In primitive chemistry."

"No. Do you want the truth? Then quit making excuses." Grieger repeated, "Where is orichalcum used?"

"In alchemy, Colonel. But that's as much magic as science."

"It is a great deal more magic than science."

"Then why use that name?"

"Because, that's what it is. Would you like to see the craft's pilot?"

The question took the Captain off guard. It was several heartbeats before the meaning finally forced its way into his convulsing brain and he could answer.

"Yes." Then, rather than 'Sir,' he added, "Please."

Colonel Grieger again led him through the labyrinth; navigating the identical unmarked intersections without any hesitation. He stopped at another nondescript door and knocked.

"Coming," answered a high pitched female voice that reminded Captain Williams of wind chimes.

The door opened revealing a woman about four and a half feet tall. She didn't appear stunted or immature however; she had the complexion and proportions of a Grecian marble statue, except for her ears which rose several inches to a point. Her long, blond hair waved as she moved, like a field of ripe wheat rolling in the wind. She wore a simple green dress, accenting her emerald eyes.

Grieger gave a hint of a bow, "Excuse us, Miss Celest. This is the new man you've heard about. I brought him to meet you."

"Please come in. There is no need to apologize. I get so few visitors down here in this dungeon." She took Williams by the hand and led him to a simplistic but comfortable wooden chair. "You sit down and rest. I'll go make some tea and open a tin of biscuits."

Colonel Grieger seated himself across the dark wood table from the Captain, "Do you have those biscuits with the chocolate on one side?"

Celest turned to him and put her hands on her hourglass hips, "You're the one in charge of the supplies down here, Johnny. You probably know what's in my cupboard better than I do."

"You needn't get all fourteen of them, six will be enough for the three of us."

Celest laughed and sauntered out of the room. Williams' eyes followed her out. The goofed up smile on his face betrayed his opinion of Celest.

"Go ahead, enjoy her company, but realize that she flirts with everyone like that. It doesn't matter who it is; she grows strong in the presence of love, joy, and general good cheer," Colonel Grieger warned.

"I never imagined aliens would look like her,"

"She's not an alien."

"I won't believe you if you say she's human."

"She's not."

"Well, that kind of covers everything, unless you're trying to convince me she's some kind of sprite."

"I told you: You have to accept the truth on your own."

Just then Celest returned with a silver tea service. Six cookies were arranged in a flower petal pattern on the tray, alternating between having their chocolate side up and down. She set the tea service on the table, then chose a chair and positioned it half way between the two men.

Williams watched her every movement with curiosity, compassion and delight. Lust, which always clouded his thinking around beautiful women, was still present but contained and unobtrusive.

Celest poured the steaming amber liquid into porcelain cups painted with different combinations of festive colors, "Please Johnny, don't take my comments the wrong way. It's literally a life saver having an enclave who believes in me with such dedication." Her eyes unfocused in memory, "In old times we would come from Home and play with humans. They would come dance with us in our circles on our holidays and chase us through the woods in the liveliest of games."

Celest giggled at some memory she decided not to share, then sighed and continued, "But people couldn't understand us, and 'They' did nothing to help matters. People labeled us as 'evil' or delusions, and didn't want to play anymore. So we spend more and more time at Home."

Captain Williams took advantage of the melancholy pause, "Where's home? What planet?"

Celest gave him the most endearing look of confusion, "Planet?"

Colonel Grieger cleared his throat, "Not another planet. The answer is a popular cultural motif, and also not a bad Broadway song."

Celest giggled again. Her voice was harmonic in regular conversation, but when she sang it was enthralling, "Somewhere over the rainbow…"

When Celest finished the final chorus, Captain Williams found he was giving a standing ovation and wiping his eyes on his uniform's sleeve. He dropped back down into his seat, his face flushed with blood, and took a sip of his tea. In a futile attempt to change the subject he commented, "You come from a beautiful home. The large trees you live in and play around…You never described your home did you?"

"Not in words," Celest smiled.

"But during your song I saw…it must be telepathy." The Captain sat back, disappearing deeper and deeper into his own thoughts, leaving Celest to turn her wily charms to the silver haired Colonel.

The Greek Olympia, Norse Asgard, and even on occasion the Christian Heaven, all had their entrances depicted as across the rainbow. The stories must be confused references to alien ships, perhaps with light refracting off of them. But why would Celest continue the symbolism? Unless…

But what about the real aliens? Were they driving the elves and spirits away? Were aliens the 'They'? Declaring their dominance by placing crop circles where fairy rings once stood. After all, fairy rings and crop circles both appear overnight and are associated with strange lights. As fairy circles became less common, crops circles became…

When the officers left their hostess and stepped back into the hall, Captain Williams tried to regain a military demeanor.

"She really treats everyone like that?"

"Well," Colonel Grieger stifled a smile, "I like to think it's personal with me, since I pulled her from the Roswell wreckage."

"I don't believe you. The math doesn't work. Approximately twenty years old to be in the military then add about sixty years since then." Williams spoke in a matter of fact tone, "That makes eighty minimum, and you are not eighty."

"Don't I look all of my ninety years?"

"A well persevered sixty five maybe, but not any older."

"Fifty years ago we came close to one of the goals of alchemy."

"Lead to gold?"

"Oh, we have that one figured out. How do you think we support Celest? What I tested forty years ago we named Ambrosia One Half."

"Ambrosia, food of the gods?"

"One Half. Aging slowed by half, wound recovery doubled." Grieger bragged, "I think we've distilled down to 51/64ths now. You want a taste? You could easily add one-hundred years to your life. But I have to warn you, only your first dose works. Our head Alchemist is older than me, but refuses to touch the stuff. He says he'll find the formula for true immortality any day now."

"Why don't you release the formula? Think of the contribution to society."

"Sure, Ambrosia would help the population crisis. 'Okay, everybody can live forever, but you can't have sex.' You know how long that would last."

Captain Williams nodded, the Colonel was right, "I was told that one of the alie...fairyfolk" the word still stuck in his throat, "did survive the crash, but died of some strange disease after a few years."

"It wasn't a disease; Celest was mentally suffocated in the laboratory environment. The head physician pronounced her dead, but I had begun to suspect her true nature."

"So what happened?"

Grieger cleared his throat, "Well, first I tried to kiss her awake."

"Who wouldn't?"

"True, but then I gathered up the six most idealistic people on the base and we stood around the body clapping and chanting softly 'I believe in fairies.' We never informed the commander of our success. That was the beginning of our arcane conspiracy."

"How many people know about it now?"

"You make eighteen."

"Colonel Grieger, why keep it such a secret? Even more than the normal secrets. Couldn't America benefit from the controlled use of magic?"

"At first, I didn't want to deal with the fallout of sending the U.S.S.R. the way of Atlantis." Grieger hesitated, "I'll show you the other reason."

Once more they wandered through the sprawling dungeon under Raven Rock. As confused as Captain Williams was, the Colonel could have lead him back to Celest's door. The door they stopped at looked no different from any of the others. But this time there was a small room behind the door. On the far wall was a cast iron door fastened with a pad lock.

"We captured this 'guest' in the Okefenokee Swamp, while we were looking for Ponce De Leon's Fountain of Youth, but she is identical to the bodies found in the second New Mexico ship in '47."

"Ah, yes. The urban legend that two ships were recovered by the military after they had suffered a midair collision. I never got anyone to confirm or deny that one officially."

"It was no collision," Grieger stated as he worked the pad lock. "They shot each other down."

Of course! The fairies and aliens fighting for dominance over the world; the elves with magic, and the aliens with technology. Williams tried to imagine the spectacular battle that must have occurred, but his mind was still wondering why an alien had been wandering around in the wetlands.

The Colonel opened the door revealing a room split by an iron grate. On the other side of the bars, a small woman beautiful enough to have been Celest's sister, sat on a prison cot. Williams stared; she looked no more like an alien than he did.

"Now I'll show you what this changeling really looks like." The Colonel grabbed the cord of a bell fastened to the wall.

"No, please!" the woman shrieked.

"Wait!" Captain Williams tried to stop him.

Colonel Grieger shook the cord and the clear notes resounded in the confined room. Williams watched in horror as the woman sank to the floor. Her flesh rippled and swirled over her body, changing hue. When the ringing stopped, what Williams had learned to call a 'Grey' knelt hunched over in the cell. Indeed its skin was gray and bald; the hands elongated; and the head and eyes disproportionately large.

"Look well at this Dark Elf." Grieger's voice boomed, "She and her kind are the opposite of our previous hostess. They live off of negative emotions: suffering, fear, hate, apprehension. To maintain their health they promote these wherever they can. If we announced their existence to the world we would create enough chaos for them to feast and grow strong."

"Of course, the terror of the abduction experiences… But why did the bell force this transformation? Bells are used to ward off evil spirits, not little green men." Captain Richard Williams' mouth stopped as the truth forced itself into his mind, and he believed.

Ramsey Lundock

AFTERWORD

Raven Rock is real. Everything written here except for the secret sub basement is real or rumored to be true. But there really was Alternate National Military Command and Control Center Improvement Program started in 1977 that was 'canceled' after two years. The 1947 Roswell crash site, Area 51 and the related stories should be well known to alien enthusiasts. Ambrosia and orichalcum are actual alchemy terms. The Fountain of Youth was said to lie in Florida; the Okefenokee Swamp is as probable a location as anyplace else. Crop circles are a debunked urban myth. Pranksters have come forward to take credit for the crop circles, but I included them because of the nice parallel to fairy-rings.

This story was inspired by the crop circles back before they were debunked. I had the realization that writing inscrutable patterns in living crops was much more in character for fairies than for extraterrestrials. Once I started thinking of Greys as demons instead of aliens, it was a little scary how easily the facts fit together for this story.

GLOOMY SUNDAY
Eddy Webb

The last time Jeanette asked me for a favor, I ended up in jail for a week. The time before that, I got two broken ribs. So when my cell phone rang and I saw her name on the screen, I knew I should have just let it go to voice mail, or thrown it against the wall and moved to Tijuana. But as usual I didn't have enough cash to go across the street, let alone across the continent, and every time Jeanette needs a favor, I'm able to cover the rent for another month or two. And I usually get lunch out of the deal.

That's why I was sitting on a rainy Saturday at a table in a trendy café, where the entire menu was in some language I didn't recognize (French or something) and the coffee cost more than my shirt. Pouring in some whiskey from my flask made it feel cheaper, and made me feel more human.

She finally showed up, half an hour late as usual. She smirked at me over her trim sunglasses while I nearly choked on my third impromptu Irish cappuccino. Sure, we broke up five years ago, but she still knows how to get my motor running, even wearing the standard Fed business suit (with skirt) and sunglasses. Maybe that's why I continue to put up with her shit.

"Good to see you again, Michael," she said as she sat down next to me, casually tossing her sunglasses on the table.

"It's always good to come home and find your lapdog panting, isn't it?" Yeah, it was a dick thing to say, but Jeanette and I have history from back when we were both in the Army, so she lets me get away with it most of the time. Besides, she left me first. Said she had her career to look after.

She chuckled and crossed her legs, and I was glad that the table stopped me from staring at them. The waiter came over and took her order, which she rattled off in some language I still didn't recognize (maybe it was Italian). Bitch. When the waiter nodded and scuttled off, she turned to me. "I have a job for you."

"No you don't. Kimera has a job for a down-on-his-luck snoop who's used to seeing weird shit." I started pulling out my three-year old brick of a laptop as she rolled her eyes at my hard-boiled colloquialisms. "Let's just cut to the chase, Nette."

That's how things were between us. She worked for a special, quiet branch of the Department of Homeland Security, code-named Lacuna. (Yeah, I had to look it up, too.) Both Jeanette and I ran into some officially deniable problems back when she was Lieutenant Jeanette Frasier and I was Sergeant Michael Callaghan. Something about some experimental genetic technology that wasn't created on this planet. Turns out that the extraterrestrial find belonged to a General Richard Kimera who was running the afore-mentioned division of Homeland Security, and he tried to tell us that we didn't see what we saw. I might have implied something about his mother's occupation and the nature of his conception during that conversation.

Anyhow, long story short, Kimera got a stick up his ass about it, so Jeanette got a transfer to Lacuna and I got a dishonorable discharge. But every once in a while Kimera needed something done, something nice and deniable, so they sent my ex to soften me up. After I got out of jail or the hospital, there's a stack of non-sequential bills waiting to keep me company before the next time they called.

I still called her "Nette," though, because I knew it irritated her. Or at least, it was supposed to. This time she glanced down at her mug and looked sheepish. "Actually, Kimera doesn't know about this, and I'd like to keep things that way."

Luckily, I'm such a suave motherfucker that I didn't spill my coffee all over my laptop. I just managed to get it all over my lap instead. After a few seconds of the "Fuck Fuck My Nuts Are Burning" dance, I looked over at her as I pressed a wad of napkins into my lap. "Why? What's going on?"

"Does it matter? I'll pay twice your usual fee. I just need you to look at something for me."

My genitalia seemed to have settled into a nice first-degree burn, so I threw the wad onto her half of the table and continued waiting for the

GLOOMY SUNDAY

laptop to boot up. "Fine, okay. Give me a second, and start shooting me the details."

"Actually, it's easier to show you. Are you capable of walking?" she asked, glancing down at the wad of coffee and paper in front of her.

Sunday is gloomy, my hours are slumberless

I don't care if you're a cop, a private detective, or a soldier; it's still tough looking at a dead body. Mind you, this one wasn't so bad...looked like the guy passed away in his chair, probably helped by the empty water glass and aspirin bottle lying on the floor next to his table.

Dearest, the shadows I live with are numberless

The apartment of Mr. John Reese (now deceased) wasn't much to look at, but it was clean; cleaner than mine, at any rate. It was an open floor plan, with a small counter separating the kitchen from the living room/dining room area and a short hallway leading back to what were probably the bedroom and bathroom. The guy looked like a geek with money: multiple game consoles and DVDs stacked up next to a wide-screen plasma television with surround-sound speakers playing some old jazz tune, but for furniture he only had one massive easy chair and a couple of tables covered in remotes and controllers. I took a slug of whiskey from my flask as I walked around the place, taking it all in.

Little white flowers will never awaken you

"Do you have to drink all the time?" Jeanette asked as she stood in the doorway.

"It helps me think." I bent over to pick up the bottle of Aspirin, where it had rolled under the table.

Something bounced off my head. I glanced up to see a pair of plastic gloves lying in front of me. "You don't think," she said. "Put those on before you touch anything."

"I was going to," I whined.

Not where the black coaches, sorrow has taken you

I grabbed the gloves on my second attempt and managed to keep my hands from shaking long enough to tug them on. I finished picking up the aspirin bottle and looked at it. Scraps of the foil seal and stray wisps of cotton were all that was inside. "Looks like a new bottle. Did he own a gun?"

"Why?"

"Men usually use guns to kill themselves, and women tend to use drugs. So either he didn't own a gun, or he was a big girl. Did you know this guy?"

"Yeah. I slept with him."

My head jerked up and slammed into the coffee table.

Angels have no thoughts of ever returning you

I rubbed my head as I straightened up to look at her. "Seriously?"

"Just once. More importantly, though, he works for Lacuna. Well, used to work for Lacuna."

I poked around the sound system and tried not to think about Jeanette and Reese. He had an iPod hooked up, and it was playing a song named "Gloomy Sunday," though both the artist and the album were listed as "<Unknown>." I pushed the pause button.

Wouldn't they be angry if I...

The music stopped. Good. The damned song was starting to depress me. "I'm betting your boyfriend here wasn't a field agent. Why isn't Kimera looking into this?" I asked.

"Kimera asked me to look into it for him. When I reported in, he told me that it was probably suicide, and that I should go ahead and start cleaning the area. But something doesn't sit right with me, so I wanted another set of eyes helping me before I started tossing his apartment and destroying evidence." She shrugged. "Even if those eyes are drunk."

I quickly slipped the flask back into my back pocket and tried to look sheepish while I continued to look around the corpse's man cave. I moved aside a Playstation 3 and found a stack of open envelopes and papers. I pulled them out and glanced at the first few sheets. Most of them seemed to be medical bills, but his insurance was really good — everything was one-hundred percent covered. "Looks like he went to the doctor a lot. Maybe he just got sick."

"He was diagnosed with cancer a few years ago. He went to a lot of specialists to deal with it."

I waved the pages at her. "Lacuna paid?"

"Of course, in exchange for Kimera getting copies of all his medical records."

"How nice of him. So maybe this guy found out he was terminal and decided to off himself. Listen to some sad music, take a lot of Aspirin, and call it quits."

She shook her head. "That doesn't add up, Michael. He wasn't acting depressed at all. Besides, Kimera would have noticed that earlier."

I started flipping through the sheets before one caught my eye. It was a report from John's doctor, probably opened in the past day or two. "Holy fuck."

She finally left the doorway and walked behind me to look over my shoulder. "What did you find?"

I showed her the report from a Dr. Andres Whelan. "John Reese's cancer had gone into full remission. He was going to live."

The address on Whelan's report led to a tiny little office in a stupidly expensive building in the same part of town as the stupidly expensive café. It seemed like every place I went to in this case was trying to make me feel inadequate. I offered Jeanette a chance to give me a ride over, but she said she had to finish cleaning up the scene, so she gave me a small wad of bills and told me to get a cab over while she did whatever it is that people do when they make corpses disappear. I must have missed that course during my training as an MP.

The cabbie stopped abusing me after I paid twice what the fare was worth. I made my way to the third floor, weaving through enough hardwood railings and potted plants to make a small rainforest, until I found Whelan's tasteful little bronze plaque smirking at me: Andres Whelan, MD, PhD, Dr. of Oncology. I pushed through into an empty waiting room with a closed frosted glass panel next to a small desk bell. Before I could even put my hand over the bell, the glass slid open. "Can I help you?"

The middle-aged receptionist was pretty enough, but had that tired look of someone who actually busted their ass dealing with sick people all day instead of yapping on the phone. I put on my nicest smile, and hoped it wasn't too worn out. "Hi. Sergeant Michael Callaghan, CID." I flashed her my old ID card and slapped it closed before she could get too close of a look at it. "I'd like a look at John Reese's medical records, please."

Her smile never slipped, but I could see a stubbornness settle in around her eyes. "I'm sorry, sir, but we can't share medical records unless the person in question…"

I leaned on the counter, putting my face closer to hers. "Look, I…"

At that point, the door to the waiting room opened, and a small man in a black trench coat came in, shaking out his umbrella. "Sorry, Betty, but lunch ended up being longer than I expected." He spoke with some European accent I couldn't place. "Everyone seems to forget how to drive in the rain."

"That's okay, Dr. Whelan," Betty the receptionist said. "Your two o'clock had to reschedule anyhow."

He draped his coat over his arm before turning to me. "I'm sorry, I thought you were my appointment, Mister…?"

"Callaghan. Sergeant Callaghan, CID. I was just asking your lovely assistant about one of your patients. John Reese."

He looked confused for a moment. "Excuse me… CID?"

"Criminal Investigation Command. We still call it 'CID' from back in the days of the Great War. I'm a cop for the US Army." Well, former cop for the US Army. Close enough.

"Ah yes. Mr. Reese did mention that he did some government work, but wouldn't elaborate. What about him?"

"He's dead, Dr. Whelan."

His eyes went wide. "I… I'm sorry to hear that. How did he die?"

"It appears to be a suicide. I'm trying to determine if he had any reason to do that."

"I don't…" He looked to the door he just walked in, and then sighed. "Technically, I can't discuss my patients…"

"Former patient," I corrected.

"… but I don't believe John would have minded me telling you. His cancer was in remission, and recently I told him that the chance of it returning is now less than five percent."

"So he knew that he wasn't going to die from cancer?"

"Quite the contrary, he seemed very pleased when I told him."

I could feel my hands starting to shake, so I put them into the pockets of my jeans. "Well, some people get weird when they find out that they're going to live. Maybe he was more afraid to live than to die."

Whelan shook his head. "I'm not a psychologist, but that's unlikely. He worked for years on his diet and exercise to fight the cancer. He is an inspirational figure," the doctor paused. "Was, I suppose. How did he die?"

"Right now, it's looking like an aspirin overdose."

He nodded, and looked at the floor. Christ. I find the one specialist with a soul in the entire city, and I just told him his favorite patient offed himself. I started to ask something else when he spoke again. "It might be due to the abnormality I found."

"Abnormality?" I could feel my tongue turning to dust in my mouth. God, I needed a drink.

"The remission was quite sudden, and I was checking for any indication that it might come back, even considering potential genetic conditions. When I compared his latest tests with his original tests, I found…"

"… a base-pair transition indicating a genetic mutation that didn't previously exist," I finished, only half paying attention to what he said.

"Y…yes. How did you know?"

I had to get out of there. "Thanks, doc. You've been very helpful." I bolted through the door and down the stairs before they could ask me any more questions.

When I got to the street I called Jeanette. "What is it?" she said.

"You bitch. You told me that Kimera had that machine decommissioned, that he wasn't using it to experiment on people anymore. You lied to me."

"Michael, what are you talking about?"

"The alien machine you and I found in the Army, the one Kimera drummed us out over."

"Drummed you out over, you mean."

"Shut up, Nette. He told us that it was a device to force genetic mutations in people by creating base-pair transitions that would normally take thousands of generations to develop."

"How does this relate to me supposedly lying to you?"

"Your John Reese had a similar transition, but it wasn't in an earlier scan. It's too much of a coincidence that Kimera had a machine that created genetic mutations and also employs a now dead government agent that mysteriously has a sudden genetic mutation, don't you think?"

There was silence on the other end. "Michael… I didn't lie to you. The machine was destroyed. I saw it with my own eyes, years ago."

Jeanette sat next to me on the threadbare orange couch I saved from a street corner a few years back. It was evening, and she had changed into snug jeans and a worn T-shirt for Fort Campbell, KY. "When I started sanitizing the apartment, I didn't find anything unusual. His iPod was set on shuffle, so it couldn't have been intentional that he was listening to that particular song…"

She kept rattling off information at me, but I wasn't listening. For all I know, it was all bullshit, one huge cover-up to protect her boss's ass. But why go through all the song and dance for me?

"Why even bring me into this?" I asked her.

She stopped her recital and looked at me. "I told you why. I needed your help."

"No you didn't. You could have figured this out without me. What's the real reason?"

"I…" She closed her mouth, then opened it again. "I just… needed to."

"Bullshit!" I snarled as I turned on her. "For years, the closest you've come to giving a shit about me is making sure that I get a head start before Lacuna tries to fuck me over. You only call when you need something. You called, so you need something. What *is* it?" I hoped my eyes blazed fiercely or something.

She shook her head. "I don't know. I got the call from Lacuna about the clean-up. They put me on hold to look up some information, and while I was waiting I got the idea that I needed to call you in."

"Just like that."

"Just like that, Michael." She looked at me. "You don't think… that I care about you or something, do you?"

Yes. Yes, I want to think that. I want you to tell me that everything that happened was a huge mistake, and then you would jump into my bed and make love to me while we listen to "Patience" on the stereo. Even now, whenever I think about her, I think of that song.

That song…

I got off the couch and walked quickly into the kitchen, grabbing a glass and some random bottles to make something alcoholic to hammer my brain into shape. "You said that the iPod was on shuffle in Reese's apartment."

"Yeah. Not a huge surprise, since he often listened to music at work."

I drank whatever was in the glass. Apparently it was a whiskey sour without much sour. "Does he normally listen to Billie Holiday?"

"Who?"

"Jazz singer in the 40s and 50s." I hurried over to my already-on laptop and started typing into the search bar.

Gloomy Sunday

"I guess so," she said. "He's always listening to weird stuff."

I found the site I was looking for, and pointed at the screen. "This look familiar?"

She leaned over and looked at the website I had summoned, casually putting a hand on my shoulder. I tried to ignore her warmth as she read what was on the screen.

Sunday is gloomy,
My hours are slumberless
Dearest the shadows
I live with are numberless
Little white flowers
Will never awaken you
Not where the black coaches
Sorrow has taken you
Angels have no thoughts
Of ever returning you
Wouldn't they be angry
If I thought of joining you?

"That's the song that was playing in the apartment."

I nodded and took another swig from my drink. "It's called 'Gloomy Sunday,' also known as the Hungarian suicide song. A bunch of people killed themselves when the song was released, including the composer himself. Billie Holiday did a version in 1941 that ended up being banned by the BBC and in the US."

I clicked on the play button on the website, and Billie Holiday's voice crackled through my laptop's old speakers. "That doesn't sound like what we heard at the apartment," Jeanette said matter-of-factly.

I turned it back off. "It was probably a new cover or something. There's actually a few different versions of the song around. The Billie Holiday one is the most famous, even though there weren't many deaths attributed to that particular rendition."

Jeanette crossed her arms and looked down at me. "Are you trying to tell me that a *song* killed Reese?"

"I'm just saying that it's a strange coincidence that such a technologically-oriented guy would choose an obscure cover of a seventy-five year old song to kill himself to, especially after being given news that he was cancer-free."

She started to respond when her cell phone rang. Her ring tone was an instrumental version of the first few measures of "Patience." She quickly ripped the phone out of her pocket and opened it. "Hello? *Hello?*" She clicked the phone closed a little more forcefully than she needed to. "Wrong number...all I heard was someone's stereo," she muttered.

"I like the ring tone," I smirked.

She had the decency to blush. "Shut up," she whispered. She walked over to me and took the whiskey-with-not-much-sour out of my hand, setting it deliberately next to the laptop. "I don't want to talk anymore."

"You don't want to talk about the dead guy you slept with anymore? I thought that was the whole reason for us getting together."

She carefully took my hand, and pulled me out of the office chair. "Maybe not the entire reason."

Jeanette took me back to my squalid bedroom, and deliberately closed the door. I still didn't entirely believe what was going on until she pushed me onto the bed and started pulling off her shirt.

When I woke, I was sitting up, and I could hear music in the other room. I was having trouble remembering what happened last night, but I'm pretty sure I would have recalled being tied naked to a chair next to a case of whiskey within my limited reach.

I'm also pretty sure I would have remembered inviting General Kimera to the party.

"No offense, Jeanette, but you look like hell the next morning," I rasped. I tried to pull on the ropes binding my chest and biceps. Nothing.

Kimera laughed and sat on the edge of my bed, just out of reach. He was middle-aged, around forty or fifty or so, with short, steel-gray hair. He was wearing a black shirt, black slacks, and black gloves—typical gear for a military guy doing things that the military doesn't want other people knowing about. The solid green eyes were a new addition.

"Don't you ever get tired of being clever, Callaghan?" He asked.

I reached down and grabbed a bottle, setting it in my lap. "Not really. It's the little things in life that keep you going. Nice eyes, by the way."

He smiled, but his lips seemed to stretch a little too far. "Thank you. I thought you should get a look at the real me before you died."

"What am I going to die of? Sexual exhaustion? Homoeroticism? Why are you here, anyway, and where's Jeanette?"

Kimera ignored my questions and stood up, starting to pace the room. "When my people landed on this pathetic rock a century ago, we had already determined that our goals would not be served by open revelation, or by any short-term action. We live much longer than humans, so we had time. It was decided that some of us would merge our genetic properties with that of humans, in order to act as well-placed spies for the coming years."

I wanted to ignore his Saturday afternoon sci-fi movie monologue, but something about what he said clicked in my head.

"Kimera...chimera...a mythological monster made up of parts."

The monster chuckled. "See? There you go, being clever again."

I threw the bottle at him. I don't think I really expected anything to happen, but I never liked Kimera when I thought he was a human, and I liked him even less as an alien monster, so really I just wanted to throw shit at him. Either way, he ducked the bottle easily, which shattered against the wall.

"I wouldn't do that, Callaghan. You'll need those soon."

"That's true. But with this many bottles, odds are, one of them will hit you."

"Not for that." He motioned to the door of the bedroom, which was open. "Do you hear that?"

I tried to listen to the faint music, and my blood went cold. It was "Gloomy Sunday," the version from Reese's apartment.

"You see, Callaghan, after we first landed around Hungary, our plan wasn't to wipe out humanity. That's wasteful and pointless. How much better is it to convert everyone here to serve our purpose?" He walked over to the wall and ran his finger through the dripping whiskey. "So we started injecting our genes into humans, using the genetic enhancer that you and your charming little girlfriend unfortunately discovered some years back. But I'm getting ahead of myself." He stuck the finger in his mouth, and grimaced. "Terrible."

I tried to struggle against the ropes again, but it was getting harder to care about my situation. I picked up another bottle and opened it. "Assuming I buy all this, why start dealing with all this now? Jeanette told me the device was destroyed."

He shook his head at me. "All in due time. One of the downsides of combining human genetics with our own is that we made you susceptible to our weaknesses, including vulnerability to sonic attacks. When a disturbingly perceptive songwriter found out about this unfortunate problem and decided to take advantage of it, his song ended up causing the most evolved of our minions to commit suicide."

"So there's something in your genes that lets sound take control of you?"

"A specific structure of sounds, but yes. What's worse, the song ended up being obscenely popular. It took a while to get a version out that was safe to us but popular enough to replace the more dangerous version. Since then, we've had a number of agents in the music industry."

"But I repeat, the machine's destroyed. Your plan's done."

"Is it?" He sat back down on the bed, and patted it affectionately. "We realized that we needed a new way to get our genetic material into humans, and it was decided to let humans do it themselves. Through sexual fluids."

I choked on my whiskey, and nearly spit it all over me. "What?"

Kimera leaned back on the bed. "By the time you found our machine, it was already obsolete. Oh, I put on a good show for people, to make them think that the machine was important, but humans had already been spreading our genetic instructions between themselves for years.

"When I got copies of Reese's medical records and realized that his doctor had stumbled upon the unique genetic markers that our instructions possess, we decided it was time to move to our final phase. I was asked to quietly get rid of the loose ends, so I pulled the more… effective…version of 'Gloomy Sunday' out of storage, along with a few other sonic commands, and started spreading a more aggressive version of our organic evolution technology among those who might know too much. Reese was only the first."

"You're talking about me and Jeanette."

"Of course, although she's actually a part of my plan. If it's any consolation, she has no idea she's been programmed to respond to a variety of musical cues."

The hold music. The ring tone. Oh, Jeanette.

Kimera stood up. "And now, that leaves you. Since you were never part of Lacuna, I had to find a way to infect you. The murder of Reese allowed me to kill two very annoying birds with one stone. After your night of passionate lovemaking, you should be pliable to sonic instruction."

He pulled a small remote from a pocket and pushed a button a few times, and the music swelled in volume. I suddenly felt like there was no point in resisting, no point in struggling against the inevitable. Kimera walked behind me and loosened the ropes around my chest. I could see that he was wearing some kind of earplug that emitted a faint static. For a second I thought maybe I should resist, but he walked away again, and the weight of the depression crushed my chest again.

Kimera stood in the doorway again. "Soon, you'll want to do something—anything—to end the emptiness you feel. And naturally, you'll do what you always do when you can't handle something." He motioned to the case of whiskey. "You'll be dead from alcohol poisoning by the end of the day."

It took every ounce of energy to speak. "Jeanette... she knows. She'll stop you."

Kimera reached into another pocket and threw a photo on the bed. It was a picture of Jeanette. She had a gun in her hand, and her brains were splattered all over the floor. "It would seem that the disgust from sleeping with her alcoholic ex-boyfriend drove her to end it all. So sad. She had such a promising career ahead of her." He smiled at me.

"You won't get away with this," I said. But it was just a sentence, something you say when someone has gotten away with something.

Kimera walked out.

I looked over at the photo. Jeanette. I'm sorry. I'm so, so sorry.

Angels have no thoughts
Of ever returning you
Wouldn't they be angry
If I thought of joining you?

I put the bottle to my lips, and started to drink.

Eddy Webb

AFTERWORD

The song "Gloomy Sunday" is real. It was composed by a Hungarian pianist named Rezso Seress in 1933, and was dubbed the "Hungarian suicide song" in the United States due to rumors of the song causing hundreds of suicides, including that of the composer himself.

I like the idea of this and other, less specific urban legends of certain sounds being able to manipulate human behavior, and I wanted to write a story around it. I've also had this scene between an ex-Army detective and his currently-employed ex-girlfriend in a café in my head for a while now. Songs and music often tie into my own memories, and these characters clearly had a lot of history between them, so I stitched the two ideas together, and "Gloomy Sunday" was the result. I love the image of how much music is a part of our mental makeup, and it was great fun to mix the two sides of musical resonance in our lives—both the song you fall in love to and the song you kill yourself to.

Mastihooba
Joshua Palmatier

"Jake's missing."

Cold sank into Devon's chest on hearing his ex-wife's voice over the phone, stretched thin with concern. His fingers tightened and a single, inexplicable thought flared across his mind: *Mastihooba*.

He drew in a ragged breath, forced himself to be rational. He hadn't thought about Mastihooba since the disappearances had died down fifteen years ago, since Mary had threatened to have him evaluated. He'd carefully stored all of the news clippings of missing persons in a cardboard box and hidden it in their basement; although he hadn't stopped scanning the paper. Nothing of significance had happened in the last fifteen years. It couldn't be Mastihooba.

Except...

He shivered, swallowed. "What do you mean he's missing?"

"He was supposed to meet me for lunch downtown today. We set it up days ago. I tried his cell phone when he didn't show, but he's not answering."

"Did you try his friends?"

"They said he went out with them last night to the bars and stayed out late." Disapproval crept into her voice. "Bill said he left Jake and Seth at the Rathskeller. I haven't been able to reach Seth."

The cold clamminess of his skin hadn't gone away, but Devon heard himself say, "They're college students, Mary. He's probably passed out at a friend's house somewhere and hasn't woken up yet."

He listened to Mary breathing, could picture her, eyes closed, lips pressed tight together as she tried to calm herself.

"He would have called to tell me." Her voice was cold and angry.

The same anger that had seeped into their marriage the last few years before the divorce, when his obsession with the stars and his job at the observatory had finally taken its toll. "It's not like him. Find him, Devon."

She hung up before he could respond. He closed his cell phone and leaned back in his chair in his office, staring at the pictures of astronomical nebulae, galaxy formations, and star charts, not seeing them. Instead, he saw darkened tunnels, smelled raw sewage and the damp concrete of a drainage tunnel.

He shuddered, popped open the phone and speed-dialed Jake. When it clicked him to voicemail he snapped the phone shut and stood, agitated. He paced his office, listened to the sounds of his two colleagues in the outer depths of the building, scrubbed at the clammy sensation that clung to his arms, then leaned against his desk with both hands. Drawing in a deep breath, he closed his eyes and bowed his head.

He'd told Mary that Jake was probably sleeping off a rough night, but he knew better. He *knew*.

"Mastihooba," he muttered to himself.

He stood, snatched up his jacket from the stand by the door, and headed toward his car.

He knew where he could find Jake, if he was still alive.

He'd been there once before, thirty-five years ago.

"Cole, wait up!"

Twelve-year-old Devon spat a curse as the limb of the tree his best friend Cole had just passed snapped back into his face. Thrusting it out of the way with a burst of anger, he caught a flash of Cole's bright red shirt through the dense growth near the edge of the Chenango River, followed by the flare of sunlight off the water beyond. He stepped forward, the ground sloping sharply toward the riverbed, fingers still clutching the offending tree branch, and slipped.

He landed hard on his ass, his hand ripping leaves from the branch as it wrenched his arm around. Pain spiked in his shoulder, but he caught himself. Letting go of the branch, he inspected the burning scrapes.

Then stilled.

The entire section of woods had gone preternaturally quiet. No twitter of birds or rustle of wind in the leaves. No rush of water from the river, or rumble of cars on Front Street. Sounds he *should* be able to hear.

Sounds he couldn't.

The eerie silence broke with a grating voice, mumbling words he didn't understand. Devon's breath hissed out between his teeth. His muscles locked. Even though he could feel mud seeping through his jeans, he didn't move.

Mastihooba.

He saw him out of the corner of his eye.

He looked like an old man: thin, scraggly beard, face wrinkled, smeared with streaks of dirt, eyes caked with grit. A beat up fedora sat atop stringy hair. The brown suit he wore, with elbow patches and a light tan shirt underneath, torn in a half dozen places, clashed with the surrounding trees.

Devon's father claimed he was a vagrant, a crazy drunk, derision in his voice. His older brother claimed he was the bogeyman, that he'd steal Devon from his room if he didn't do what his brother wanted. Devon was old enough to scoff at his brother now, but not certain enough to keep terror from trembling in his arms.

He watched as Mastihooba stomped down through the trees twenty paces away, toward the river, muttering the same long unintelligible phrase over and over. Then he reached the river and passed from sight. Devon heard splashing, then silence.

With a gasp, sound returned: wind, water, cars, and birds.

Devon sucked in a gulp of air, only then realizing he hadn't been breathing.

"Come on, Devon! Or I'll leave you behind!"

Cole.

Devon lurched to his feet and broke through the last of the undergrowth, emerging on the edge of the river. He scanned for Mastihooba but didn't see the old man anywhere. Cole was already halfway to the confluence of the Chenango and the Susquehanna, where the concrete flood wall that protected the city began.

"Cole!" he shouted, terror in his voice. "Wait!"

He tore down the edge of the river as fast as the rock and mud-strewn bank would let him, clutching the weeds and grass and scrub trees for support. "Mastihooba," he gasped, the name catching in his throat as a foot slipped and sank into ankle-deep water.

"What?" Cole had halted and half-turned. His blond hair burned in the sunlight, his face set in an irritated frown.

Devon sloshed onto firmer ground at the base of the flood wall, his sneaker squishing. He came to a halt behind Cole.

"Masti – hooba," he wheezed. "I saw Masti – hooba."

Cole snorted, "That old geezer? What did he do, mumble at you?"

"No, he...he..." Devon swallowed and leaned against the flood wall, half bent over. Tremors still shook his arms, from the silence of the wood, from his dash down the river's edge. He couldn't seem to catch his breath.

"He's a bum," Cole said, waving his hand as he headed farther downstream, balancing on the water-worn rocks as he moved toward the underside of the Clinton Street Bridge. "My mom says he's been here forever, since she was a kid. And to leave him alone. He stinks, so why would I mess with him anyway? Now come on!"

Devon straightened and scanned the bank behind him, the pain in his chest easing, but he didn't see Mastihooba anywhere.

Where had he gone? There wasn't anywhere on this side of the bank he could have hidden.

When he turned back, Cole's slim frame slid into the shadow beneath the bridge. He rushed to catch up.

They worked their way along the bank, stopping to toss rocks at the fish they could see beneath the clear water of the river farther out. Ducks shied away at their approach, quacking fitfully, a few taking flight and gliding across the river to the far side. But Cole wasn't distracted for long, his excitement growing as they neared the underside of the Main Street bridge.

When they stepped into its shadow, Devon shivered. He could hear cars crossing the span above with a low rumble like thunder. Farther downstream, a few kids splashed in the water, screaming with laughter, parents on the steps of Confluence Park behind them. An older couple sat on a bench, feeding bread to the ducks. The scene shone bright and sharp in the sunlight, the sounds muted by distance. Beneath it all lay a steady, nearly imperceptible thrumming, like the hum of power lines on a hot summer afternoon.

"Look," Cole said. He climbed up from the wide bank beneath the bridge and pointed to the gaping mouth of the drainage pipe that jutted out from the flood wall. Nearly four feet in diameter, the pipe was usually covered with a heavy metal grate, but the grate was missing.

To one side of the hole, someone had painted an array of five asterisk-like stars, large and small, in a pattern like a comma.

"Tom said the grate broke loose during the last storm," Cole crowed. He stared into the black depths of the pipe, then turned with a sly grin. "I want to see what's in there."

"Cole, no," Devon said, the shiver that had coursed through his skin returning, but Cole didn't hear him. He heaved himself up onto the lip of the pipe, grunted as he rolled into the opening.

Crouched down, he stared into the darkness a moment, then stretched out an arm toward Devon. "Come on."

"It's dangerous. That's why there's a grate on it normally."

Cole rolled his eyes. "How dangerous can it be? It's for rain water. Does it look like it's going to storm today? Now *come on*."

Cole's voice had lowered with impatience, had taken on a darker tone, enough to move Devon up to the edge of the pipe. But staring up into Cole's face, he hesitated.

He could hear the people at the park, the water slapping against the bridge supports behind him, the roar of a truck trundling by overhead. He could feel the unearthly thrum, tickling his skin.

Cole sighed. "We won't go far, just enough to see what's inside. Are you coming?"

Cole's derision made Devon wince. Feeling sick, he reached up. Cole grabbed his hand and hauled him up over the lip.

"*...number you have reached is unavailable. Please leave your name....*"

Devon swore and slammed the phone shut, then opened it again and dialed Jake's number, but got kicked to voicemail immediately. He tossed the phone into the passenger seat of his car, then changed lanes. As he did, a violent gust of wind rocked the car, the trees to either side of the parkway thrashing. He glanced into the rearview mirror.

The entire horizon behind glowered with black clouds. He caught a flicker of lightning before turning his attention back to the road ahead. He was nearing downtown.

Ten minutes later, he stepped from his car, tucked his cell phone into his front pocket, a small Maglite into the other, and glared up into the darkening sky, the scent of the storm strong. People on the street hustled for shelter as gusts tore past them, setting loose clothes flapping and blowing litter down the sidewalks. He'd parked as close as he could to the confluence, but the brick and concrete buildings still obscured the rivers. Devon retrieved an umbrella from the trunk and opened it as the first fat drops of rain speckled the dirt on his car, then hesitated.

Reaching into the trunk again, he grabbed a tire iron and tucked it under his arm.

Moving with purpose, he cut down State Street, turned right onto Main, and then left into Confluence Park near the bridge. The storm broke when he reached the water, rain sheeting down, thundering on his umbrella. The surface of the Chenango and Susquehanna Rivers roiled. Lightning flared, followed instantly by thunder. Devon paused a moment at the crux of land near the confluence to watch the raging water, already beginning to edge up the banks. Energy spat in the air, from the storm, from the turbulent waters, but also from the ground itself. He could feel it thrumming through his feet, prickling against his skin. Storm energy, but something else as well, something deep and primal. A force that radiated from beneath the two rivers.

He shuddered, remembering the thrum he'd felt at age twelve.

He spun from the torrent of water and rain toward the walk that ran along the banks, paved in the thirty-five years since he'd been here last. He sucked in a harsh breath, tasted the slickness of the rain, the taint of ozone from the lightning. Wind tore at his umbrella as he moved toward the underside of the bridge, down the tiered stairs of granite to the path now half-submerged in the storm's runoff. The wind turned cold as he slid beneath the protection of the bridge. Shivering, he collapsed the umbrella and set it aside, then worked his way deeper beneath the bridge, using the occasional flashes of lightning to guide him. He didn't even know if the pipe was still here. The bridge had undergone reconstruction in the past ten years, the drainage systems updated and redesigned after the disastrous flood of 2006. He hadn't paid attention to the changes, had never expected to be back here again, and even if it were here the grate would have been replaced....

He gasped and nearly stumbled backwards off the sculpted steps of the walkway into the swollen river when lightning flared and the empty, black hole at the end of the pipe blazed out of the darkness ahead. Water sluiced from the pipe in an arching stream.

But something was different.

Juggling the tire iron, he dug the Maglite out of his pocket and pointed it at the pipe.

A giant metal cap covered the opening, hinged at the top. The cap was open because of the storm, water spilling out of the pipe's mouth in a growing flood, but it was rigged to close as soon as the rain stopped and the water receded.

Climbing up to the pipe, so close he felt the spray of the water gushing from the opening, Devon scanned the interior with the flashlight. Nothing but darkness.

His hands were trembling. Not from the cold, or the rainwater. He tried to make them stop, swallowed down nausea, but tasted bile at the back of his throat. His heart thudded hard in his chest and his breathing escalated.

He didn't want to be here, didn't *need* to be here. Jake was fine. He'd gone out with Seth and Bill and the others, drunk too much, and was probably waking up right now on someone's couch where he'd crashed for the night. Mary was worried over nothing. It hadn't even been twenty-four hours since Bill had seen him last. Not even the police would be worried yet. He should wait, at least until tomorrow. Then, if they hadn't heard from Jake, he and Mary could report it.

He stepped back from the pipe, his heart already calming, even as guilt settled over him like a shroud.

But as he turned, he caught something out of the corner of his eye in a flare of lightning.

He spun, slipped on the wet stone, caught himself as cold clutched at his throat. The Maglite swept across the end of the pipe, juddering erratically.

Then settled. He stilled, breath held.

His indrawn breath rushed out in a ragged sigh and he closed his eyes.

Stars. Painted next to the pipe in the shape of a distorted comma.

Devon held perfectly still for a long moment, the storm raging around him. Then he opened his eyes and straightened. He no longer shook—with fear or cold—although his skin still felt clammy, slick with rain, sweat, and memory. When he stepped forward to the edge of the pipe, he moved without hesitation. Maglite held in his mouth, he shoved forward into the frigid water pouring from the opening, his entire body getting soaked. With a grunt and heave, made awkward by the tire iron, he hauled himself up and into the pipe.

It was harder than he thought it would be; the pipe felt tighter and more constraining than he remembered. But it had been thirty-five years.

And he didn't have Cole helping him.

Both Devon and Cole stumbled and fell, silt and pebbles from the run-off—still damp with rain from the previous storm—gouging into Devon's hands. Cole laughed, the sound echoing, then scrambled to his feet and headed deeper into the pipe.

Devon wiped the mud from his hands on his pants and followed. The metal of the pipe was smooth, and the mud in the center of the drain thickened the deeper they went. Debris began to appear—the twisted and bent remains of an umbrella, a Coke bottle, water-logged cardboard boxes—the items harder and harder to identify as the light from the entrance diminished, even as his eyes adjusted.

"Disgusting!" Cole barked, groaning and turning a wrinkled nose toward Devon as he pointed toward the carcass of a cat, half-eaten, with fur so matted it was nearly unidentifiable. Cole picked his way past it with a shudder and a distorted, "Ugh!"

Devon gagged as he approached. He slipped as he inched around it, his foot kicking the corpse. Maggots writhed at the disturbance and Devon cried out, stumbling into Cole who caught him with a snort.

When Devon's heart had stopped thundering in his chest, he shoved Cole away and spat, "That's far enough, Cole. It's just a stupid pipe."

Cole's snicker vanished, his face blank. "We've barely gone twenty feet. We can't back out now."

"There's nothing to see down here! It's just mud and garbage, and we won't be able to see anything if we…."

Devon broke off and sucked in a harsh breath, one arm reaching out to clutch a handful of Cole's shirt.

The world had gone silent.

"What is it?"

"Shut up," Devon whispered.

They both stared at the entrance. Devon's heart began to race as water splashed and the mumbling began. Inexplicably, he thought of the painted stars.

Mastihooba

Mastihooba's silhouette appeared at the end of the pipe.

The old man's grated mumbling halted. In the tense silence that followed, the dampness of the pipe settled across Devon's skin like a blanket, chill and visceral. It held the reek of the dead cat, the slime of the silt beneath his feet, and tasted of wet metal and rain.

Behind him, Cole muttered, "Shit."

Mastihooba roared, the sound crashing down the pipe. Devon's heart stuttered, and he felt Cole flinch backwards, his shirt ripping from Devon's grasp. For a single, eternal moment, Mastihooba's silhouette shifted from an old man's hat-topped torso to something else, something horrifying and indescribable.

Then Mastihooba leaped into the pipe, moving unlike any man Devon had ever seen, crouched forward onto all fours, shoulders pressed low and close to the bottom of the pipe, back curved up. Devon didn't have time to make sense of it because Cole suddenly screamed, "Run!" the sound pummeling Devon's ears. His friend spun, tearing down deeper into the pipe. Devon cried out and dove into the darkness after him. His heart thundered in his chest, his feet slid in the slick filth, and everything vanished in the sudden convergence of pitch black.

"Cole!"

"I can't see anything!"

"Keep going! He's following us!"

His voice thudded against the walls, tinged with panic. Behind, he heard Mastihooba scrabble toward them, the sounds no longer like footfalls, more like the scraping of metal against metal. The screech tore at Devon's nerves and he clamped his teeth together, breath harsh through his nose. Reaching forward into the darkness, his hand brushed Cole's back and his friend screamed.

And slammed into a wall, Devon crashing into him a half-breath later.

"It's a dead end!" Cole gasped, his voice escalating upwards. Devon felt him scrambling against the concrete at their backs and he reached out in the other direction, expecting to touch the edge of the pipe, but there was nothing there.

"Cole, the pipe turns!"

"What?" But Cole didn't wait for him to repeat himself, fumbling past him in the darkness. Devon glanced behind. Mastihooba skittered toward them, so close his body blocked out the sunlit entrance, so close

Devon could smell him; rotten cloth, rank sweat, and the faint hint of cinnamon.

Devon swallowed against the lump clogging his throat and dodged right. He heard Cole whimpering ahead of him. They were in concrete drainage channels now, the walls vertical, the floor sloped toward the center and the pipe behind. He careened from one wall to the next, then settled on the left wall, used it for support, hand scraping against the concrete. The scent of sweat and cinnamon grew, overpowered the reek of garbage and silt and dampness. His breath came in hitches and a stitch pierced his side. He stumbled over something, felt despair rising, tears leaking from his eyes.

And then he saw sunlight streaming down from overhead. "Cole! I see sunlight. It's another tunnel." He heard Cole halt, turn toward him. "Over here!"

Devon stepped into the new tunnel, Cole scrambling in behind him.

And then something heavy hit Devon from behind, shoved him forward so hard he gasped. The bottom of the concrete tunnel slammed into him and he skidded through the filth, coming to rest beneath the sunlight. When he looked up, face caked with mud, he could see the light filtering in through a sewer grate from a gutter on the street above. Beneath the grate, the same comma-shaped asterisks were painted on the wall.

He drew breath to cry for help, but Cole's foot stomped onto his back and all of the air gushed form his lungs. Cole staggered, thudded into the opposite wall and collapsed to the floor, rolled onto his back.

Then Mastihooba loomed over them, a vague shadow in the half-light, a scraggly-bearded man in a fedora, but something else as well, something blurred and green-black, glistening with ridges and steeped in the dense scent of cinnamon, so overpowering Devon choked on it as he drew in a new breath to scream.

Cole screamed for him, the sound shattering the stillness.

Mastihooba reached for Cole, one hand holding his friend to the ground, the other latching onto his face, the palm settling over his nose and mouth, muffling the scream. Long fingers—too long, too jointed—reached up and over his friend's head, one at each temple, the elongated thumb curving around his chin. Cole kicked, lashed out with his hands, fingers clawing at Mastihooba's extended arms, his body contorting beneath him, screams trying to break free from the palm pressed against his nose and mouth.

Then Cole fell silent.

Devon coughed harshly, air scraping in and out of his lungs.

Mastihooba held still, Cole's arms and legs falling limp around him…and then he turned toward Devon.

Devon heaved backwards, back slamming against the wall, hands scrabbling in the mud as he tried to push himself upright.

Mastihooba's hand lifted from Cole's face, a thin trail of snot and blood dangling down from it. Blood snaked out of Cole's nose and mouth, leaked from his ear. Where Mastihooba's fingers had settled and pressed against Cole's face, the skin was burned.

Mastihooba pointed towards him with the strange fingers, his old man's face and beard contorted and out of shape, like rumpled clothing. He uttered a grating, hissing rasp of unintelligible sound.

Then he leaped, the hand that held Cole's body to the ground snaking around and clutching Devon by the chest, lifting him up and thudding him hard into the wall of the tunnel near the stars. The other hand closed in on his mouth and he screamed so hard something in his throat tore. The hand clamped down over his face, covered his eyes. Fingers slid up through his hair, thumb along his jaw, then pressed down hard into his skin. Something bit deep, a slivering spike of pain at the side of his neck, two more at his temples, and his skin caught fire, burning as if he'd rubbed stinging nettles across his entire face. His breath seared his lungs, and against the confining blackness of Mastihooba's hand he saw Cole's body, saw the trail of snot and blood dangling down from Mastihooba's hand as it lifted, and something inside of Devon broke.

He went limp, didn't struggle against the pressure against his skin, didn't fight to take a breath.

And the moment he broke, the blackness before his eyes flared with light. White light, flooded with images, with colors, with blurs of sound and smells, passing too swiftly to catch, too jumbled to understand. He didn't struggle against them, simply let them flow, felt his chest aching for air, felt his arms and legs tingling with numbness.

Then the pressure of Mastihooba's hand against his chest released.

He slumped to the wet, muddy ground, sprawled there as the white light receded, replaced by a blackness deeper than night. In the emptiness of that darkness blossomed five stars in the distorted shape of a comma, some burning brighter than others, all fierce, tantalizing, wistful.

Mastihooba's hand withdrew from his face, and with that withdrawal, with Devon's hungry indrawn breath, the stars faded, the darkness complete.

He woke to someone shouting, "Over here!" followed by the crunch of gravel and the clatter of stones. He lifted his head, opened his eyes, and through the throbbing haze of a headache, winced at the sunlight and the shadowy figures approaching along the riverbank. His head and arms dangled from the end of the pipe, his thoughts thick with the heavy pounding of blood, his arms numb. He screamed when someone lifted him from the pipe and laid him down on the stones of the bank, heard someone swear, someone else yelling for help. More stones rattled against each other, followed by the dull echo of someone shouting from inside the pipe, someone muttering with horror, "He's dead."

A woman leaned over him, brushed his hair back from his forehead, then gasped. Fingers touched his temples, traced a line along his jaw where he knew there were burn marks. He could feel the tightness of his skin there.

Then the woman leaned forward and said in a hard voice, "Who did this to you?"

Devon tried to speak, choked on the rawness in this throat, but managed to murmur, "Masti – hooba."

Devon aimed his flashlight at the five stars painted on the wall of the tunnel, rainwater pouring down from the storm drain above. He touched his temples, where the burn marks had faded over time. He'd told them that Mastihooba had killed Cole, had burned him. He'd told them everything. They'd searched the drainage system, rounded up all of the vagrants, but they hadn't found Mastihooba. Devon had told them that it wasn't a man, but no one believed him. All that had changed after the initial anger and frenzy of hate was that the grate on the pipe had been replaced.

Devon had become obsessed with stars.

Five years later, he'd noticed a missing persons report in the paper. A young woman who'd vanished along the riverbank near the park. They'd assumed she'd fallen in and drowned. He'd watched the papers closely after that, kept track of the attacks. Sporadic enough to go unnoticed, unless you were looking.

Devon turned and stared down into the darkness of the tunnel. He hefted the tire iron.

"Where are you, you bastard? Where have you taken my son?"

He hadn't seen any sign of Jake or Seth since he'd entered, but the ankle-deep-and-rising water from the storm would have washed any signs of them out to the river.

Devon stepped around the water pouring down from the drain and slogged forward, until two other tunnels met up with his at right angles. He stared down both passages. If Jake was down here, he could be anywhere. Mastihooba could have brought him through any of the drainage pipes, anywhere in the city.

"Shit," Devon swore, and leaned forward against the damp wall.

A weight shifted in his pocket.

His cell.

He lurched back and dug it out. The signal was weak, but he flipped it open and dialed Jake's number without thinking. When it immediately clicked to voice mail, he realized his mistake: Jake's cell was dead or off.

But not Seth's.

Shivering at the cold water swirling around his feet, he dialed Seth, then held the phone against his leg to muffle the sound and listened.

Faintly, he heard a phone ringing, some kind of rock song.

He dodged down the right tunnel, the light from the Maglite skittering erratically across the concrete walls of the tunnel. Thirty paces down, it caught the edges of a set of five stars painted along the wall and Devon cried out in triumph, even as he heard the phone click over to voicemail. He hit redial, heard it connect.

And tripped over something submerged beneath the water, crashing to his knees and then face first into the water. The cell jounced from his hand and the tire iron slid from beneath his arm, but he clutched the Maglite tight, surging upwards and spluttering into the near darkness. Twisting, he aimed the light into the water.

Seth's water-chilled face stared back.

He gave an inarticulate cry, backed into the wall behind him. He couldn't breathe, his mind a white sheet of nothingness as the thought that he could find Jake like this shuddered through his body. Then he choked, raised a trembling hand to wipe the water from his face, and forced himself to lean forward, to look at Seth's face more closely.

His eyes and mouth were open, his skin pale in the light, blonde hair waving in the rushing currents. No blood, but there were burn marks on his temples and along his chin.

"Cole," he muttered, then winced at his mistake.

Sitting back, he realized that Seth's phone was still ringing.

He stood, edged forward, retrieved his own phone and the tire iron from beneath the water, then followed the tinny sound of rock music.

It sat just inside a branch from the main tunnel, one not part of the drainage system. It had been dug out of the earth, the opening sliced through the concrete wall at waist height, well above the rushing water. No water drained from the hole, and when Devon pointed the flashlight into the opening he found the walls shored up with some kind of metal he didn't recognize, black with something embedded in it that glittered like stars in the light.

Devon hefted himself up into the opening. The ceiling was half the height of the tunnel, forcing him to hunch his back to proceed. He felt a familiar prickling of energy against his skin, increasing as he moved forward, the hairs on his arms and neck stirring even though they'd been plastered to his skin by the rain. The passage sloped down deep, then leveled off before rising again, a few fist-sized holes branching away to either side; a drainage system, in case the water rose high enough to enter the new tunnel.

Then the passage ended, opening up into a huge, low-ceilinged chamber, completely enclosed in the black-starred metal. In the center sat a triangular object, filling most of the space, held off the floor by old stacked tires. Panels on the object lay open and what looked like the inside of an engine were exposed, the parts strangely shaped, the circuitry laid out in bizarre patterns. Jutting out of the engine at odd angles were various recognizable electronic devices—cell phones, a camera, the exposed innards of a laptop, various parts of car engines, and what appeared to be a coffeemaker—all lit by an ethereal blue-white glow emanating from the foreign parts of the engine. Thousands of other devices were strewn about the chamber, piled in the corners, shattered or dismembered, including a gutted washing machine, three televisions, and boomboxes dating back to the 80s.

What caught Devon's attention, what tore through his chest with a lance of pain, was Jake, his body slumped against one wall, head hanging limp over his chest.

"No!" he choked, the sound dense and unrecognizable in the chamber. Images of blood flared through his mind as he staggered across the chamber and knelt before his son's body. He reached forward and tilted his son's head back. Burns marred his son's temple and chin, and blood threaded down from his nose and ears.

Devon's chest clenched and bitter grief and acrid despair welled upwards, growing even as his lungs constricted. It seized his throat and choked off his breath, prickling his skin.

Then Jake moaned and stirred.

Devon's muscles locked in shock, broken when Jake's eyes fluttered. Devon seized him by the shoulders, drew him close to his chest, hard enough that Jake began struggling. When Devon released him, tears coursing down his cheeks, the bitter constriction in his chest had eased.

Jake blinked at him blearily, "What...?"

"I thought he'd gotten you. I thought he'd gotten you, just like he got Cole. And Seth."

Jake frowned in confusion...and then sudden horror filled his face. He lurched back, out of Devon's grip, tried to stand, his legs and arms too weak to support him. "Seth! He killed Seth!"

"I know." Devon grabbed him, slung one arm over his shoulder, lifted him up off the floor, gasping at how heavy he'd become. Jake wasn't the boy he pictured in his memory any longer. He'd grown, bulked out during his years in college. "We have to get you out of here."

Jake shuddered, one hand rising to touch the burn marks. "He attacked us on the street, dragged us both down here, but he didn't find what he wanted from Seth. He found something inside me though, inside my head. Something to do with stars..." Jake shuddered again, "Who is he, Dad? *What* is he?"

"He's Mastihooba," Devon said. He shoved the tire iron into his son's hands, took the Maglite himself. Lurching, he half-dragged, half-led his son toward the entrance. "He's the bogeyman."

They were five feet from the passage when Mastihooba slid from it. Devon felt Jake start in his grip, jerk backwards. Devon gasped, then gagged on the intense scent of cinnamon. Every terrifying moment of the scramble through the tunnels thirty-five years before flooded through Devon's body, tingling in his arms and shoulders, seizing in his chest. He stared at the figure before him, the twelve-year-old boy inside screaming.

But Mastihooba had changed over the years. He no longer appeared as an old man in a brown suit, although vestiges of that remained. Patches of the green-black skin he'd caught glimpses of as a boy had torn through the façade beneath the fedora. Ridges of the same skin ran down the old man's arms and legs. One of the old man's bleary, encrusted eyes had been torn away, replaced by a thin sliver of yellow and black that slid to white as the creature paused and stared at them. This was not the Mastihooba of Devon's childhood.

And yet it was. Devon could see it beneath the layers, an amalgam of ordinary and alien.

Mastihooba roared and with one blindingly fast step forward, he grabbed Devon by the shirt and heaved him upwards, scraping skin from Devon's chest and knocking Jake back down to the floor, the tire iron flying. Jake scrambled backwards on his ass, legs kicking, face blazing with terror, and Devon yelled, "Run!" even as Mastihooba's other hand closed down upon his face.

Mastihooba's elongated fingers snaked up into Devon's hair and around his chin. The palm cut off Devon's breath, his sight. White blossomed in the darkness, flashing with images, with blurs of colors, with scenes that passed too quickly for Devon to comprehend. Cole had died because he'd fought the images, had struggled; Devon had survived because he'd relaxed and let them flow.

Devon forced himself to relax. The sickening cascade of motion continued for a single heartbeat....

And then paused.

Through the terror, through the thunder of blood pounding in his ears and the seething burn across his face, Devon sensed recognition: Mastihooba had been waiting for him, had thought he'd returned when he smelled Jake on the street above, the scent so close, but not the same.

Devon sensed something else, a well of emotion he couldn't fathom; loneliness, despair, frustration, rage.

Before he could reach out to touch the blackness of the emotions, the blur of images resumed, flickered through images of Devon's life, moments from childhood: parks, bikes, boats, fishing, the river, then skimming ahead, past the horror of Cole's death, through high school, prom, the first fumbling moments with Mary in college.

Then the visions slowed, even as he sensed growing excitement from Mastihooba. All of Devon's life accomplishments—graduation, marriage, the birth of Jake—all of that fell away. Mastihooba focused on Devon's studies, on nebulae and planets, galaxies and solar systems, pulsars and quarks and solar flares. The focus shifted to visions of the sky, stars against the darkness, constellations and star charts, and the hours and hours Devon had spent viewing images through telescopes around the world.

Until he found what he was looking for, what he'd been looking for all along: five stars, some brighter than others. But these weren't in the shape of a comma, not at first. The image of the five stars held for a long moment, blazing, gaining dimension on Devon's mind, as if he were standing in space, seeing them with his own eyes instead of through the two-dimensional lens of a telescope. The image deepened... and then it shifted, the skyscape moving subtly, almost imperceptibly, with thousands upon thousands of years of galactic shift, thousands upon thousands of years that Devon felt emanating from this creature. Years that it had lived here on Earth, stranded by its limited escape pod, hibernating for hundreds of years on end, emerging to search for what it needed to repair its ship, for the maps it needed to find its way back, hibernating again....

The five stars shifted enough to form the shape of a comma.

Mastihooba dropped him and roared in triumph, the sound rebounding throughout the chamber. Devon barely heard it, gasping in air, trying to pull back from the blackness of Mastihooba's pain. So many years lost and marooned after the accident that destroyed his ship. So many years searching for a way to repair the escape pod with such limited technology. Devon staggered under the enormity of it all, under the creature's patience, of his efforts to transform himself so that he would fit into a race he didn't understand, using a language he could not master.

But now he could go home.

Devon heaved in another breath and rolled to his side, still clutching the flashlight, fighting back the blackness. Mastihooba sprinted toward his vessel, slammed down panels, the black-starred metal molding itself to the contours of the repairs within, melding the mismatched technologies to the ship. As he watched, the last tattered vestiges of the old man in the fedora shimmered and vanished, Mastihooba's true shape emerging with all of its green-black ridges, varied joints, and yellow-slitted eyes. Jake skittered away from it as it worked, edged around to Devon's side, began to pull Devon to his feet, but paused.

Mastihooba had spun back toward them, skin bathed in the blue-white light of the ship as it powered up. It regarded them silently, its expression impossible to read....

And then it turned away, a portal irising open in the craft. It vanished inside, the portal hissing shut.

"Let's get out of here," Devon said, then coughed, the stench of cinnamon already fading.

"Right," Jake agreed.

They staggered to the passageway, Jake ahead, as a high-pitched whine began in the chamber behind them. The strange energy Devon had felt above escalated sharply, building in sudden surges, like waves. Hairs prickled on his skin as they spilled out into the main drainage system, Jake yelling in shock when he found Seth's body. Devon grabbed his son and pulled him away with a shouted, "Come on!" Then they ran, slogging through the water, now knee-high, pushed by the current.

The energy spiked a moment before they fell from the end of the pipe onto the banks of the Chenango River, the storm still raging, the water of the river high enough to reach their calves. Staggering along the flood wall, they moved toward Confluence Park.

They emerged from beneath the bridge into the sheeting rain, climbed up the bank and collapsed to the grass of the park. Rolling onto his back, Devon grabbed his son's shoulder, to reassure himself that Jake was there.

And from the raging confluence of the two rivers, Mastihooba's triangular ship burst forth in a froth of white spume. Lightning crackled, highlighting its dark contours for a brief moment...and then it was gone.

Gasping, Devon lay back against the grass, let the rain wash across his face, staring at the lightning-flicker of storm clouds above, thinking of Cole, of Seth, of Jake and Mastihooba. Beside him, he heard Jake gasping as well.

Then Jake asked, "What do we do now?"

Devon considered for a long moment, letting his pulse die down, the ache in his chest relax.

"We contact the police about Seth," he said. "And then, like Mastihooba, we go home."

Mastihooba

AFTERWORD

"Mastihooba" is based on a local urban legend of Binghamton, NY, about a man named Masty Huba, a personifaction of the bogeyman, used to scare children into behaving. I learned of the legend through my partner, whose parents and grandparents would often tell him that "Masty Huba will get you!" when he was younger. I extrapolated from his description of Masty Huba for this story.

Apparently, this legend is based on an actual man who would make the rounds of the local bars, getting "free" drinks for work (such as shoveling snow, etc.) that he would never actually do. Thus you can find a sketch of Masty Huba on the wall as a warning at many of the local bars.

I am Sorry for Talking So Rarely to Strangers

Alma Alexander

Bess Bennett was two days shy of her sixth birthday when the body was discovered just outside the abandoned Government storage bunkers on the outskirts of Sunnyvale. She never saw the actual corpse, but her father, Burt, was one of those who buried it quietly and without fuss where it was found, hoping to scotch the inevitable rumors before things got out of hand.

It was a vain hope, in a township which seemed to run on high-octane gossip fuel for sustenance. The body had been buried for less than twenty four hours before the first wave of whispers rolled over Sunnyvale, and Mary, Bess's mother, confronted Burt when he came home from work on the eve of Bess's birthday.

"Annie Coutts says she *saw* the monster," Mary said, piling Burt's dinner into a chipped plate and taking it over to where he waited at the kitchen table. "She says it was all gray, and it was some eight feet tall! And it had *wings*! And you never said anything!"

"Annie Coutts could not have seen it to begin with," Burt grumbled, "but trust her to lay it on with a trowel even sight unseen."

"That's unkind," Mary said.

"True, though," Burt said, speaking with his mouth full. "Annie's the first port of call when you want something spread about in the community as fast as you possibly can. Especially if you insist that it's a secret. And anyway, the thing was hardly eight feet tall."

"But there *was* something! And it had wings?"

"I didn't say that," Burt said, swallowing, his voice chagrinned.

"You didn't say *not*," Mary said.

"A big monster with wings?" Bess said, curious and vaguely alarmed.

Mary threw a disapproving glance at Burt as though it was all his fault, and went over to put a reassuring arm around her daughter's shoulders.

"Nothing for you to worry about, honey," she said soothingly. "Now come on, let's wash up, it's bedtime for you and it's a big day tomorrow!"

Bess settled into bed happily enough, accepted a goodnight kiss, and snuggled back against her pillow. Mary left, leaving a small nightlight on and closing the door behind her. But Bess was not sleepy, and although she lay for a long time with her eyes obediently closed nothing seemed to happen, except that she kept on thinking of great gray bug-eyed monsters with enormous wings—it was the last vivid image that had been planted in her head before bedtime and it refused to go away.

When she finally gave up and sighed, opening her eyes as she sat up in bed, her gaze fell upon the goldfish bowl on the dresser where Winkle-fish lived out his days, darting from one glass wall to another ducking a frond of plastic greenery in the midst of the bowl. But Winkle-fish was not darting tonight. In fact, Winkle-fish was not moving at all. He was floating on the surface of the water, belly up.

Bess cried, a little, and then she decided that, like everything that died, Winkle-fish needed to be buried, and it needed to be done immediately. It was her birthday the next day—not too far away now—and she didn't want to start off the day with a fish funeral; besides, she was starting to feel distinctly queasy about going back to sleep now, knowingly sharing her bedroom with something dead. After she had thought about all this for a few moments, things just seemed to settle into an inevitability.

Bess slipped out of bed, thrust her feet into pink slippers, took her broken music box from the back of her closet, and stood on tip-toe to scrabble in the fishbowl for Winkle's cold clammy little body. She let him drop into the box, and then, pausing, said the Lord's Prayer over him because it seemed to be the right thing to do. Then she closed the box on the dead fish, and very carefully padded downstairs and then out into the back yard through the kitchen door, collecting one of her mother's large serving spoons on the way.

As a digging implement, the serving spoon was a little less than completely efficient. But for a six-year-old's strength and hand size it worked as well as could be expected. Bess crouched on the edge of her mother's prize flower bed and scooped out a hole big enough for the burial box with great dedication and concentration. Once she had achieved the required depth, she reverently placed the casket into the hole and let her hand rest gently on the lid for a moment.

"Good-bye, Winkle," she said. "You were a good fish."

It wasn't until she had piled the earth back over the box and patted the resulting small mound down with the serving spoon that she looked up and saw the monster.

The one which was supposed to be dead.

Bess stood up, very carefully, without taking her eyes off the creature. She was only six (it was after midnight, after all, and she *was* six) and she had very little ability to judge size; all she was certain of is that it was, for her, huge; taller than her father. It stood on two thin, almost spindly, legs which seemed wholly inadequate to support a bulbous body and what Bess at first thought was a rich cloak but realized, instead, that it was a pair of great folded wings. The creature's head was strange—most of it seemed to be occupied by a pair of enormous jeweled eyes the color of Mary Bennett's grandmother's antique ruby brooch, the one which Bess loved because of the way red light broke and fractured in its depths when it was turned against sunlight in the window, and the rest of the head narrowed down from a broad forehead to almost a point where the creature's mouth ought to have been. It looked as though it had another pair of tiny arms there which moved restlessly while its ruby gaze rested on Bess.

Do not be afraid.

The thought was in Bess's head, clear, calm, as though a gentle woman's voice had whispered it into her ear.

"I'm not," she said, and, oddly, was speaking the truth. The creature was strange, to be sure, but even after building up the image of the 'monster' in her mind while she had been lying awake in her bed there was little about it that she found actively frightening now that it actually stood before her. She wasn't scared at all. She was, rather, fascinated. "Who are you?" she asked.

I am a stranger, the creature thought at her.

I Am Sorry for Talking so Rarely to Strangers

"Mama told me never to talk to strangers," Bess said, sounding ambivalent.

She meant the ones who mean you harm. I do not. I come from very far away, and I am lost, and alone. I need your help. Will you help me?

"Sure," Bess said. "What do I have to do?"

Will you save my children?

This sounded serious. Bess squirmed a little. "I'm only six," she said.

That is why you are the only one who will listen. They killed my mate, my love, and they buried him in a shallow grave—he died badly, and he didn't go into the light, and he and I will never meet again. But he left me with the children…and I have to try and save the children. Because I also will die soon—too soon, because I cannot give them shelter and nurture and sustenance. If I tried to speak to one of your elders… they would kill me on sight, just like they killed my mate, and they would destroy my children before they are even born…

"I'll help," Bess said. She didn't understand all the big words, words like 'nurture' and 'sustenance', but they had been planted into her mind with a meaning and she was aware of what she was promising to do; that seeing to the welfare of this creature's young would become her duty, and her responsibility.

The creature bowed its head, as though in thanks.

Then listen closely, because there is not much time. I will give you the cocoons; my children still lie sleeping in silk. You need to put them somewhere dark, and quiet, and warm—some place where they will not be discovered. And then, when it's time, you need to help them when they are ready to wake.

"How will I know when they are ready?"

Their silk is pale, like the light of your moon. When it changes, you will know. Remember these… The creature suddenly straightened and spread its wings. Bess stared, rapt in enchantment, the wings were huge, and soft, and subtle patterns of black and silver wove in them until they shimmered in the night. They were magic, real magic, it was the gift of the Universe to Bess Bennett on her birthday, and she drank it all in.

"May I touch them?" she asked diffidently, reaching out a small hand.

Don't, for they are delicate and will tear if you press too hard, the creature said in a gentle voice. *But remember their color, and their softness, for this is what my children will look like, when they are born. And remember, these are far too fragile for the light of your day. The heat of the sun will shred them, and my children will fall and die. They must be born into the night, their wings touched by nothing but moonlight. Take care of my children, human child.*

"I will," Bess said. "I promise. I'll keep them safe."

Then I give them to your keeping, the creature said.

It reached down to where its bulbous belly hung over its thin legs, and seemed to find a fine seam in the skin, opening the sac up like a ripe fruit. Five small pale silk-wrapped cocoons lay within. Bess instinctively made a hammock from her nightgown, and the mother creature gathered each cocoon carefully into a hand with only four long fingers and deposited them, one by one, into the place Bess had made for them.

The creature leaned over, bringing its head closer to the cocoons, and passed its mouth parts over each one in turn, as though she were kissing them goodbye. Bess caught a strange but not unpleasant scent, a little dusty, like petunias in full bloom. Then the creature straightened again and stepped back.

Farewell, human child. I owe you a great debt. And those who have what lies between us this night…can never be strangers.

It seemed to close some inner eyelid over the ruby eyes, then, because they faded away into nothing and then the entire creature seemed to vanish, as though it had been only a ghost.

Bess made her careful way back into the house, and then, grabbing the big flashlight that lived in the kitchen with one hand and holding her nightgown gathered up over the precious cargo in the other, crept down into the basement, being extra careful to avoid the steps she knew creaked when trod on. The basement had seemed to be a good idea for hiding the cocoons, but as she looked around in the flickering shadows that the thin beam of the flashlight cast none of it seemed to be good enough. Wherever she looked it was some place or some tool that she knew would get used more quickly than she needed it to be moved, and lead to the discovery of the cocoons.

Her searching eyes finally fell on the wooden chest tucked away under the stair.

Her older sister's hope chest. Abby was thirteen years old; the girls in their circles married young, to be sure, but even given that, Abby's hope chest was at least three or four years from being disturbed. Mary Bennett always talked about airing out the stuff in it but she never did it, and only opened it up to place some other small item into it, laying it away against the day of Abby's eventual marriage.

That would do.

Bess placed the flashlight on the edge of the stair just above the chest and heaved the heavy lid open with one small hand. Embroidered things lay in careful layers within, covered with tissue paper; Bess lifted one corner of the layered contents carefully, trying to disturb it as little as possible, and gently laid the five silk-wrapped cocoons, one beside the other, on the bottom of the chest, letting the embroidered tablecloths and napkins and the lace collars fall back into place above them.

"Sleep well," she said, her small face very serious, and then she closed the chest over its treasure, took up the flashlight again, crept carefully up the creaky stairs and then back into bed where, finally, sleep came.

They found the second creature, Bess's own 'monster' from the night garden, in the morning, not too far from the Bennetts' house. Bess actually caught a glimpse of it herself this time and she had cried when she did, and they whisked her away and fussed over her, and called her a poor dear, and told her what a great pity it was that it all had to happen on her birthday. But only Bess knew why she was crying; it was not that she had been frightened or that she recoiled in horror. It was the anguish of seeing the magnificent stranger of the night before, the one of the midnight-and-moonlight wings and ruby eyes, shriveled into a gray shapeless pile on the ground, the wings broken and graceless around her. The sun had touched her—Bess had heard her say as much, that sunlight was lethal for her kind—but now that she knew that her children were safe she was happy to let it burn her, to go into the light, lost and alone as she was, the last of her kind.

They left Bess alone at the kitchen table long enough for her to find some wax crayons and a piece of paper, and she drew a yellow sun with a smile on its face but with frowning eyebrows above its round empty eyes, hanging over a house with an open door, and huge flowers which grew way taller than the house itself was. And she wrote, in childish capitals, on the top of the drawing: I AM SORRY FOR TALKING SO RARELY TO STRANGERS. And then hesitated, but came to a decision and signed it: FROM BESS.

"Honey!" her mother had exclaimed in consternation when she had come back into the kitchen and leaned over Bess's shoulder to inspect her handiwork. "Whatever do you mean? You know I told you never to talk to strangers, how dangerous it is! Who's been talking to you…?"

"Nobody, Mama," Bess said. "Nobody at all…"

The piece of paper with her artwork on it was whisked away, with more remonstrances about the danger of strangers engaging little girls in conversation; Bess herself said nothing more about it. But she would sneak into the basement every so often after everyone else in the house was asleep, and check on the five pale cocoons sleeping under the layers of her sister's future. For a long time they lay there unchanging, pale and quiet, waiting.

The months slipped by, one by one, like pearls on a string. Bess turned seven. And then eight. And then one day, in her eighth summer, she crept into the basement to check on her charges and discovered that one of them had…changed.

It was now the color of midnight, shot through with silver, and it was warm to the touch.

Bess took it carefully out of the hope chest, and cranked open the small basement window, laying the changed cocoon on the sill so that it was touched by night air and the pale sweet light of a waxing moon. And then sat back on her heels, enraptured, watching as the silk cocoon cracked slowly open and then as something unfolded, emerging from its confinement, stretching out wings dark as night until they stopped glistening slightly in the moonlight and became all shadow and power and then the new-born creature launched itself from the windowsill and through the open window, out into the summer night. Bess poked her head out of the window, watching the spread of dark wings briefly silhouetted against the pale moon, and then the creature vanished from her sight, disappearing somewhere into myth and legend. Somewhere, perhaps, where it would show itself to another little girl some strange and enchanted night.

The second cocoon hatched almost a year after that, and the third, nearly sixteen months later. The fourth followed almost precipitately, only three months after the third.

And then Abby announced her engagement.

It took Bess a moment to get past the first pulse of excitement of being asked to be her sister's bridesmaid to realize what this meant. The hope chest from the basement had finally become something that mattered, something that Mary Bennett was already making noises about having to haul up from the basement and sort through the contents and air everything out and have it all ready for when Abby would take it away to her own home.

The fifth cocoon. The fifth cocoon was still in there.

Bess crept down to the basement that night, more carefully than ever, but the silk was still pale under the flashlight beam. She hesitated, deeply torn. Abby's wedding was still a good six months away, Mary might take her time about airing out the hope chest, the fifth cocoon could hatch any day, any minute, and this might still very well be the only real safe place for it until it did. But what if she bet on all of this and the odds were against her? What if the fifth cocoon chose the very moment that Mary lifted the embroidered sheets off of it to split open and release the winged creature that it sheltered?

What would be better? Leave well enough alone, keep the system that had worked for years, or move the cocoon…somewhere else… somewhere that would be less under the public eye.

"Oh, *Abby*," Bess whispered, frustrated. "Couldn't you have waited another year…?"

In the end, she was too scared to leave the cocoon where it was. She gathered it up, carried it up to her own bedroom and buried it underneath an old quilt at the back of her closet.

She checked it every night for a week after that, obsessively, hoping that it would change, that it would be ready…but it stayed pale, stayed dormant. And then, somehow, she *forgot* about it. She met Abby's fiancé's niece, the other bridesmaid, a girl only a year older than herself, and the two of them unexpectedly hit it off; they spent a lot of time together, giggling over town gossip that still filtered down regularly from Annie Coutts, sharing books and magazines and photographs of movie stars and dreams of a future when they themselves would be brides and some other young girl would pace solemnly down the aisle before them to the place where a young man—a young man whose face was still a rosy blur for both of them—would wait to take their own hands and slip a ring on their finger.

Bess did remember the cocoon when the hope chest was finally brought up the basement stairs and thrown open, and the women of the family—Mary Bennett, her sisters, Abby's two grandmothers—all gathered to cluck and coo and fuss over the contents. Bess wondered for a heart stopping moment if the cocoons had actually left any visible trace—or even a remnant of that strange dusty scent of petunias in full bloom which she still somehow vividly remembered from the night that she turned six years old. But apparently there was nothing incriminating there, or at least if there was it was entirely overshadowed by the wedding fever.

She checked the cocoon again on the night that the hope chest was broken open. She peered at it with her flashlight. Was it turning darker? She couldn't really tell. Perhaps it was only hours away from hatching. Perhaps she needed to wait for it. She curled up on the quilt beside it and stared at it, quiescent in the circle of her flashlight's beam, willing it to crack, to change, to release its creature and release Bess herself from a promise made all those years ago to a stranger in the night.

She did not realize that she had fallen asleep there on the quilt, her cocoon uncovered, until she was woken by her mother's scream.

Bess roused, suddenly and sharply awake, and stared in consternation at the midnight-black cocoon which was rocking gently back and forth… and her mother standing with both hands pressed against her mouth, her eyes wide with horror.

"What is that thing? What *is* it?"

"Mama," Bess said quickly, scrambling to her feet, "Mama, it's okay…it's okay…it's…I promised…Mama, it's not bad, it's not evil, it's just strange, and I promised…"

The cocoon cracked gently across the middle. Bess turned to stare at it in anguish. They had never made the mistake before, the creatures—they had always hatched at night, always, flown away into moonlight and shadow—but it was morning, full morning, and the room was flooded with sunlight.

"Oh, no," she whispered, heartbroken, knowing there was nothing she could do; that there was nothing that she knew how to do.

The cocoon split a little wider, and then rocked violently and split all the way. The winged creature that lurched out from it looked like it was confused and in pain; it stumbled forward, its wet wings still glistening, straight into the path of the sun.

The wings sizzled softly. The creature uttered a high agonized keening noise. Bess stepped forward, awkward, at a loss.

"It's all right," she crooned, "it's all right, you're okay, get back into the shadow, you'll be okay until the night comes, come back…"

She had reached out a hand to the creature when she suddenly felt an arm snake around her middle and felt herself being yanked back away from it.

"Get back! It could be dangerous. It's the same sort of abomination that we killed out on the commons. Where did you *get* this thing? Get back. I'll deal with it…"

That was her father, brought up here by her mother's screams. Bess fought him, flailing against his grip. But then he passed her on into Mary's hands, and if anything Mary's were the more vice-like on her arms while she struggled to get free.

"Don't hurt it! It won't harm you! Stay away from it! Get back into the shadow! Oh, please, get away from the sun…"

But the window was open, and the creature smelled the free air. Still keening in pain it hopped unsteadily onto the windowsill, turned to look back into the room with its ruby eyes, and then launched.

It did not get far.

They all rushed to the window, to watch, and they all saw it fly into the sun, like a moth into the candle flame, and they saw its wings shrivel in the harsh light and shred like an illusion…and then they saw it fall.

Or at least they knew that it fell. Bess herself was weeping wildly, her vision blurred with helpless, scalding tears, and she could have sworn to seeing nothing at all beyond the creature's turning to look into the room—not one of the others had ever done that before—and then leap to its doom, knowing, perhaps, that its doom among men would be far worse than this sacrificial flight into the bright heart of a star whose harsh light was too heavy for its gentle soul and fragile body. Bess did not see it fall, did not see it actually hit the ground; she *felt* it, as though she herself was the one plummeting towards the earth, smashing against it, her wings dust and ashes around her, her corpse burned gray like her father's and her mother's had been.

"What are you crying for? It was a *monster*," Bess's father said, possibly in an attempt at awkward comfort. "It's just as well that it came to a good end…"

"It was…a stranger," Bess managed to get out, through choked sobs. And then she finally tore herself free from her parents' hands and fled down the stairs and out of the house and into the woods where she could be alone with her hopeless, heartbroken grief.

Nothing more was said about the winged creature's last flight, and it was the last that Sunnyvale saw of its kind. Abby got married as planned, and in due time Bess herself walked down the aisle, just as she and her fellow bridesmaid had once dreamed; she and her new husband settled into a small bungalow not too far away from her parents and from Abby, and raised four children there.

Bess was fifty-four years old when her mother died. Her father had passed away some four years before. Abby had just become a grandmother for the second time, and was kept busy by the demands of her daughter and the new baby. It fell to Bess to go through their mother's papers and put everything in order so that the house could be emptied out and put on the market. Mary Bennett had never been a very tidy woman, and her filing system, if it could be called that, had been wildly erratic; sometimes four different copies of the same document would surface in four different places, often highly inappropriate, and other times a single copy of an important document would turn up missing only to be found hours later at the bottom of a box filled with old letters and fading family photographs.

It was these boxes that were fatal because it was impossible not to get sidetracked when one of them turned up and hours would slip by imperceptibly as old photos with illegible and mysterious annotations on the back were scrutinized for clues as to the identity of the people in the picture, or a letter would be picked up at random and then it would be discovered to be so interesting that Bess would find herself pawing through the box for others which linked to it, to learn the whole of a tantalizingly unfinished story.

It was at the bottom of one of these boxes that she found, carefully folded, a faded piece of paper which bore a faded child's drawing on it.

A drawing of a house, and some enormous flowers, and a frowny-smiley sun whose rays looked oddly like fronds, and the writing at the top: I AM SORRY FOR TALKING SO RARELY TO STRANGERS. FROM BESS.

"She kept it," Bess said out loud, although there was nobody at all with her in the old house at the time. "Mama *kept* it."

She tried to wrap her head around this, to find a reason that she could give for her mother's so carefully stowing away that piece of childish art, that one out of dozens, maybe hundreds, of crayon drawings that the girls had both done and with which the refrigerator had been wallpapered for all the years of their growing up. None of them had survived. But this one, Mary Bennett had kept. The one that had disturbed her so much when she had first seen it. The one that, although she had it safely put away, had not stopped her from screaming when she had come upon her child sleeping next to a monster's cocoon—talking, once again, to strangers.

Mary had never spoken again of that incident, never mentioned it to Bess in all the years that had followed that tragic morning. But there had been times when the air had been strained between her and Burt, as though they had been arguing about something which had no rational answer. It was only now, as an adult with the perspective to bring to bear upon it, that Bess realized this.

She wondered which of her parents had defended the monsters, and which had defended Sunnyvale's right to destroy them. She wondered if there had ever been a touch of empathy that had found a place in Mary's own heart...the knowledge and understanding, however indirect, of one mother's act by another mother, no matter how different their children might look to outsiders. Whether Mary had ever wondered, however briefly, if that other mother had left her unborn children with the warning not to talk to strangers.

"Well, Mama," Bess said softly, staring at the faded streaks of crayon. "Wherever you are. I hope that you and she met. I hope you finally understood. I hope...you were not too scared to talk to a stranger. For once."

They were gone, the moth-people, those who had been born and had taken wing from the basement of this old house. They were long gone, and there had been no sign of them since they had launched themselves from the windowsill into the bright moonlight. They were gone, into absence, and silence.

But now, sitting on the floor of her mother's house in the gathering twilight with the family papers in untidy heaps around her and a child's reaching for understanding and a tenuous bond with the numinous and the enchanted trembling in her hand, Bess could swear that she could hear them; that the night air around her was suddenly alive with the soft whisper of moths' wings.

AFTERWORD

The urban legend being followed here is the Mothman.

The visions of the Mothman as reported in various sightings do have variations, but on the whole are remarkably internally consistent, enough for there to be a basis for assuming in this story that the creature is a physical reality. And if it was a living alien presence, it would have a mind and spirit, and motivation—its own genetic imperatives of self-preservation.

And it stands to reason, alas, that the only human being with the imagination and the compassion to talk to it, to give it sympathy and give it aid, would be a young child. Adult humans are hardened to fear the unknown, to shoot first and to ask questions afterwards—if at all.

If we all talked to strangers more often?...we might discover that the stranger is us.

Dead Letter Drop

Pete Kempshall

Elsa picked her way down the street, arms wrapped tightly around her chest. She kept her eyes on the ground, partly so she wouldn't attract attention, partly for fear of turning her ankle on the rubble. The Tiergarten had suffered some of the worst shelling in the city. Gangs of trummerfrauen like herself had worked for weeks removing shattered bricks, blasted concrete and twisted wire but it would be months before the district was cleared. Accidents were all too common, especially if your mind was on something else. And everyone's mind was something else.

She'd never become used to the persistent growling in her stomach. It was true, things had improved with the arrival of the Americans: they did their best to provide rations for as many of the survivors as they could. But with refugees continuing to flow into the city, food was running out faster than it was being brought in.

Skirting a shell hole, she saw a bird out of the corner of her eye. A crow, and a big one too. It swooped and landed on a burned-out roof, eyed her glassily. Elsa considered stooping for a half-brick, trying to bring the bird down, but knew deep down she'd be too weak to hit it.

She hadn't had meat in so long…She remembered just after the surrender, a group of men had found a horse that had been killed in the fighting. They'd stripped it to the bone, arms red to the elbows as they tore at it with axes, saws, fingers. If you wanted to eat, you took your opportunities where you found them.

There were always black marketeers, of course, but even their supplies were limited, and snapped up all too quickly by the small minority willing to pay through the nose for them.

Today Elsa could finally join that minority.

She'd been digging through the wreckage on her last shift, her sore, callused fingers scrabbling to load chunks of masonry into a barrow. Shifting a lump of stone the size of her head, she'd spotted it, just sitting there, waiting. A camera case, battered but obviously intact.

Buried treasure.

Elsa had flicked her eyes from side to side, terrified that someone else might have seen it too. A camera, undamaged, could get twenty-five cigarettes at the exchange near the Brandenburger Tor and twenty-five cigarettes could get you…more food than she had now, that was for sure. People had killed for far less. She had seen them do it.

Fortunately the other women in the kolonne had so far been too busy with their own labours to notice the change in Elsa's posture, the stiffening in her shoulders and her furtive glances. Quickly she had stashed the case in her barrow and covered it with bricks.

When the shift had finally ended, every minute crawling like a gut-shot soldier, Elsa had retrieved her booty and slipped away as quickly as she could without attracting attention. Her small, precious bundle she held in place under her coat, ostensibly hugging herself for warmth.

She stopped now and glanced around. She was far enough away from the others to look and see exactly what she'd found. Cautiously she padded towards the shadows between two structures that had once been buildings but now struggled to meet the definition in any recognisable way. She hesitated, still nervous about dark, confined spaces but equally fearful of examining her prize in the open. Making a decision, and still scanning the street warily, she vanished into the gloom.

Once she was far enough into the alley, she crouched and withdrew the hard leather case from her clothes. Tingling with anticipation, she popped the lid.

It was Leica, almost new and, she was elated to see, completely intact. GIs loved that kind of thing, it'd get a good price. Satisfied, she snapped the lid back on and stood up.

"Hello."

She spun around, almost dropped the camera. A man stood between her and the road. Quickly Elsa snatched up a stone. There was only one reason why a man would follow a woman into an alley, the same reason a knot of Russian soldiers would follow a woman into a bombed-out church. Since the Soviets had given way to the Americans, such attacks had dwindled in frequency, but that didn't mean it couldn't happen to her again.

"Get away from me," she spat.

"I'm sorry? I don't...I just need some help. Please."

The man stepped forward. Elsa stepped back, praying she didn't lose her footing on the loose bricks.

Closer up, Elsa could see the man was in his sixties at the very least, although the effects of malnutrition made him appear still more wizened. His dark suit was ragged around the cuffs and ankles, torn at one shoulder and discoloured with fine grey dust, and his shoes proclaimed him to have walked no small distance through the city's devastation. Quite how he'd managed that without toppling into a shell crater, Elsa had no idea, for on the bridge of his nose sat a pair of glasses, their lenses painted black. His right hand gripped a thin, battered cane, with which he cautiously prodded the ground in front of him.

"Please, I heard your feet on the rubble and I came to find you. I need your help."

"I'm warning you," Elsa breathed.

"Please, fraulein. It was hard enough for me to find my way around the streets before all this." He gestured vaguely with his cane and chuckled wryly, seemingly oblivious to the tension in Elsa's voice. "Now there are no streets and I'm afraid I'm quite lost."

"I can't help you," Elsa said. "I have to be somewhere."

"I have something, you see," the blind man continued, regardless. He reached into his pocket.

"Don't," Elsa said, raising her rock. The man seemed not to hear, and pulled out his hand. In it he held a crumpled off-white rectangle. A letter.

"It is for a friend of mine, she lives near Moritzplatz."

"This is the Tiergarten," Elsa said.

"Ach." The man slumped on his cane. "I shall be in my grave before I can deliver this wretched thing." He raised his head, and it felt to Elsa as if the dead eyes beneath his glasses were focusing directly on her face. "I have no right to ask you this, fraulein..."

"You want me to deliver it."

"You would be doing me a great kindness."

"I can't. Moritzplatz is out of my way, and I have to be somewhere. Now please...."

"I am sure my friend will reward you," the man said. "She has certain contacts, people that provide her with items of value."

Elsa lowered her rock a fraction. She'd heard rumours of a black marketeer in Moritzplatz who had access to regular supplies of fresh food, but the exact location was a closely guarded secret. A trip across town could be perilous, the streets still weren't entirely safe...but to learn where the food was coming in, wasn't that worth the risk? Yes, she could barter the Leica and eat tonight, but do a favour for these people, get in with them, and she could eat regularly.

"It is important that your friend read this letter?"

"It is vital."

"Drop it on the ground and back away."

"Thank you, fraulein." The man's mouth broke into a smile, revealing teeth like mouldered gravestones. For an unpleasant second Elsa was put in mind of a crack she had seen opened in the street by the Russian artillery, the hole deep enough to expose the U-Bahn platform beneath. A fetid stench had risen from it, of stagnant water, of sewage and of far, far worse, and despite herself she imagined the same odour on the stranger's breath.

He opened his fingers and let the envelope flutter to the fractured pavement. Slowly, he stepped backwards.

"Please," he reiterated. "It is most urgent. The address is on the envelope."

Once she was sure the man was far enough back, Elsa crouched slowly and retrieved the letter. "I shall deliver it for you."

"God bless you, child." He was clear of the alley now, still stepping backwards, one tentative foot after the other. Finally he turned, started to walk. Hesitated. "Fraulein?"

"Yes?"

"A final favour?"

"Yes?"

"Could you direct me towards Budapester Strasse? I need to get home."

"Left," Elsa called. "Keep walking and ask again when you reach the end of the street."

"Thank you again, fraulein."

She watched him for a minute or two, shuffling slowly down the road. Then putting the camera case inside her coat and the letter in a pocket, she turned away.

Dead Letter Drop

* * *

She had barely reached the end of the road before having second thoughts. She was still carrying the camera she'd hoped to exchange at the Brandenburger Tor and every second it was in her possession was a second it could be stolen by another desperate, starving citizen. She was only a few minutes away from her original destination, it made sense to stop there and swap the Leica first, didn't it?

But what if the letter was truly as urgent as the blind man had said? What if every minute she delayed made a difference? If she got there too late, angered the blind man's friend, what possibility there was of a reward would disappear like smoke in the wind. Besides, if the Moritzplatz contact really was a black marketeer, Elsa could just swap the camera there, right at the source of the food.

On the other hand, she could just open the letter…a quick look wouldn't hurt, and it'd help her choose what to do.

As she mulled the possibility, she realised she'd reached a junction. Turn one way for the Brandenburger Tor, the other for Moritzplatz. Dipping her fingers into her pocket, she felt the crumpled envelope, heavier to her mind than the camera she had hidden under her coat.

She chose hope.

She'd wasted her time. Her time, her energy, and her chance of eating before sunset. After weeks of Allied bombardment, the streets around Moritzplatz were a succession of rubble piles and craters, peaks and troughs of destruction. On the point of tears, she checked the address on the envelope again. There was no doubt this was the right street, but with the exception of two burned-out shells at the far end, the entire road had been bombed flat.

She slumped against what remained of a wall, eyes hot. The brickwork still bore one of the slogans the Party had daubed around the city to galvanise resistance before the Russians came: "Victory or Siberia." Drained of hope and energy, Elsa entertained the irrational thought that Siberia might not have been so bad, compared to this. Dying there in the snow, dying here in the dirt, what was the difference? At least the cold would make it quick.

Something clattered in the distance. She lifted her head wearily, and was surprised to see a flicker of movement near the crumbling structures at the end of the road. No matter what the buildings down there looked like, someone had just slipped inside one of them.

Hauling herself up, Elsa trudged the length of the street until she was standing in front of the houses. From a distance they'd looked uninhabitable, but up close she could see the ground floor of one of them was virtually intact. The whole upper storey had come down, turning the floors of the bedrooms above into a roof for the rooms below, but there was no doubt it could provide shelter. She didn't need to look at the envelope again to know.

This was the house.

Dimly it made sense to her. If you were going to run a secret black market outlet, you'd choose somewhere most people would overlook. She approached the door, knocked as loudly as her debilitated body would allow.

When a minute passed with no response, she knocked again. Again, no answer.

She pulled out the letter. There was nothing to stop her slipping it through the door, going on her way. Except that while she'd done the blind man a kindness, the harsh truth was that no one survived in Berlin by being kind. Like a fool, she'd foregone a certain meal on the vague promise of better, and she was damned if she was walking away with nothing now.

Except she didn't have nothing. She had the letter. If it contained information that could lead her to one of the black market contacts… well the day wouldn't be a total loss.

She turned from the front door, strangely embarrassed in case someone inside should be watching, should see this breach of trust. And slipping her finger under the flap, she tore open the envelope.

Shakily she removed a single sheet of paper, folded sharply down the middle. Her numbed fingers were fighting to open it out when she spotted something, just for a second. There, right across the street.

Someone had slipped out of sight behind a collapsed wall. Someone with darkly painted glasses and a cane.

Her mind stuttered over the sight, starvation-sluggish. How could he be here so quickly, at the very place he'd been so utterly unable to locate before?

Unless he wasn't….

As realization hit her like a speeding truck, her eyes fell to the words in the letter:

Dead Letter Drop

This is the last one for today.

The air shifted behind her. Elsa barely had time to turn and see the woman in the doorway before the coal shovel descended and smashed her into darkness.

Elsa opened her eyes to candlelight, a futile flickering attempt to hold back the shadows. She shivered violently from the cold and the sudden movement brought with it the realisation that she was both restrained and naked. She had been placed on a table and someone had passed ropes under it, looping them back over her neck, upper and lower arms, and lower legs. She was utterly helpless.

A flash-flood of icy panic engulfed her, sweeping her back to a night in a razed church, Russian soldiers finding her alone...

"What are your orders?"

Elsa twisted her head, left, then right, heedless of the rope chafing her neck. On the edge of her vision she could see the woman who'd hit her, her haggard, lined face expressionless in the gloom.

"Who are you?" Elsa asked, the words barely escaping her dry lips. "What do you want?"

"What are your orders?"

"Please. Why are you-?"

"What are your orders?"

"I don't know what you-"

The woman stepped forward from the darkness, the movement so fast that Elsa barely had time to flinch before a heavy weight crashed down on her hand, pulverising the bones between her wrist and fingers.

Elsa howled in unrestrained agony, her body arching, straining against her bonds. The pain continued to stab up her arm after all the air was gone from her lungs, and she sucked in another breath, expelling it in a second anguished shriek. And another. And another.

At last her screams became sobs, great heaves that tore through her chest. She opened her eyes, and through vision blurred with tears saw the woman looking down on her. As Elsa had done many times on her shifts with the trummerfrauen, the woman was holding a large, blunt-headed hammer.

"Why?" Elsa whimpered.

Her captor walked slowly round the table, stopping by Elsa's feet. "What are your orders?"

"I don't know...I don't know what you...."

The hammer shattered her ankle and a small portion of her lower leg, the skin exploding in a shower of blood and bone. Elsa screamed again and again and again, at last embracing the merciful blackness that rushed at her.

As she passed out, a small voice demanded, "What are your orders?"

A cool palm rested on her forehead, scant distraction from the pain pulsing up her limbs. Elsa cracked open eyes crusted with tears. In the murky light the newcomer looked tired, eyes sunk deep under a ragged fringe of blond hair. A swathe of scar tissue—burns—covered his face on one side, puckered and sore-looking. The opposite side of his face, where hair could still grow, proclaimed days without the attention of a razor, creating a strange half-beard.

Seeing Elsa was awake, the man smiled and for the briefest of moments Elsa was sure she saw kindness in his face.

"Puh...please," she whispered.

"We just want information," he said... and the moment was gone.

"Don't...understand..."

The man sighed. "We know about you. We know about all of you. We just need to know what you're planning."

"Not planning...anything."

The man stepped away, scraped a chair along the floor and dropped into it. His face was now inches from hers. She could smell his breath, the sour reek of the starved, of a body consuming itself to survive.

"Plainly, you don't believe me, but I tell you again: we know." The chair creaked as he shifted position. "We know, Elsa, that you are not from Earth."

"You're mad," Elsa rasped.

"Come now, with everything the world has seen in the last few years, the insanity, the hysteria, the death...it's not so ridiculous."

"Please," Elsa said, straining to make eye contact, to make a connection. "Please, you're wrong. I'm from Dresden, I came here after...."

"Yes, yes, you came to Berlin with all the other refugees from the east. And that's the thing, isn't it? All those people missing, displaced. Who'll notice a few extras amongst them?"

"I don't know what...."

"It's the perfect opportunity to slip in unnoticed, to join society. To infiltrate, wait for the right time to strike against a civilisation already on its knees."

"You...."

"Please, Elsa, stop. You're part of an advance guard, an army from another world sent to invade us. The man you met in the Tiergarten, he cannot see as you or I can see, but he can tell when he meets one of your kind."

"You're crazy," Elsa said wide-eyed. "Starving...delirious. I'm as human as you are."

"Tell me your orders. Tell me how you plan to strike against us."

"I can't tell you what I don't know!"

The chair scraped again and the half-bearded man stood. Elsa lost sight of him as he walked into the gloom.

"Please!" she called. "Please, let me go! I need a doctor! Please! Don't hurt me!"

The dark congealed into a shape. Part of it shone dully in the diffused light.

"Oh no. Oh God, please no! Please, don't-"

The hammer destroyed her other leg, splintering the kneecap and bending the joint back against itself. Elsa shrieked, writhed in excruciating torment. She was still screaming when her other knee went.

Then deep inside her, something cracked...and the walls came down.

She remembered. She remembered the briefings, the rooms filled with warriors, senso-net headsets loading mission parameters directly into their brains. She remembered the psycho-conditioning, rank after rank of blocks and barriers behind which to hide her true nature, an assumed personality so thoroughly embedded, and a cover so deep that she wouldn't even be aware she was playing a part.

She remembered changing.

Her screams became roars. She thrashed against her ropes, the force of her spasms enough to shift the heavy table beneath her.

It started beneath the skin, her joints cracking, loud, like small arms fire. Bones attenuated and twisted, broke and reknitted. Muscles pulsed and flexed, growing, shrinking; organs contracted, repositioned, ceased to exist.

The ropes holding her down snapped one after the other, unable to contain the sudden, brutal rewriting of DNA. Elsa rolled to the floor, her body melting here, solidifying there. Spines punched through her epidermis bristling up her arms and shoulders, across her back. Her skin greyed like corpse-flesh, her breasts stretched and flattened into a solid, well-muscled torso. Her nose collapsed, drawn back into the skull until only two puckered holes remained beneath eyes that burned with pure hatred. Atop her head, her hair thinned, receded, vanished.

She bellowed at the pain, no less intense than that from the hammer blows but so, so different: not the pain of imminent death, but of rebirth.

Until, finally, silence.

Slowly, the creature that was Elsa tried to stand, but for all the physical changes it had experienced its legs were still ruined. It looked up at the half-bearded human. He must have known the damage would take more to heal than a simple body morph.

He'd done this before, to others of her kind.

"Now, shall we try again?" the man asked. "What are your orders?"

The Elsa-thing spat at him weakly, the speckles of saliva falling well short. "Enjoy your little victory," it wheezed. "I'll not help you."

The man reached across to the creature and stroked its true visage, its flat, alien geometry. "I think you will. One way or another, I think you'll prove to be most useful."

He couldn't believe his luck. The man selling food just off Moritzplatz was supposed to be hard to find, but all it had taken for Horst to locate him was to follow a shifty looking co-worker from Gitschiner Strasse. Simple.

Horst had been hoarding items to trade for some days, and so he had plenty to barter for a decent meal, but he hadn't expected this. He'd almost fainted with glee when the dealer informed him he had just taken delivery of a consignment of fresh meat.

Horst didn't ask what kind of meat it was and he didn't care. He was so happy just to have it that he'd have skipped home, if such behaviour wouldn't have marked him out as someone worth robbing.

That thought made Horst cling all the more tightly to the brown paper parcel he'd tucked under his coat. No, he thought, he'd be fine. Luck was on his side today and it'd hold until he got home. Ten minutes and he'd be safe. An hour and he'd be fed.

He was so distracted by conflicting thoughts of roast meat and lurking brigands that before he could stop himself he'd clattered into an old man who'd stepped around the corner in front of him. The stranger staggered backwards, bracing himself against the wall with one hand.

"I'm so terribly sorry," Horst spluttered. "I beg your pardon."

"Please, think nothing of it, mein herr," the man replied, straightening his dark glasses and poking the ground in front of him with his cane. "I wonder, though, could you please help me?"

PETE KEMPSHALL

AFTERWORD

A blind man who roamed the streets of post-war Berlin, persuading trusting young women to deliver letters for him, letters that marked their bearers out as fresh meat for black market abattoirs…Some even said that he didn't prey exclusively on women, that it was easier still to lure away hungry children. The Allied troops that occupied the city didn't really believe the story was true, of course. But the horrors they'd seen in the bombed-out capital—the rapes, the murders, the breaking down of humans to their basest instincts for survival—meant there was always an element of doubt.

It was the perfect legend: creepy, disturbing and, better yet, little-known, because I could just imagine our poor, suffering editor opening my email and finding another spin on someone waking up in a bath full of ice, sans kidneys…

It was also an ideal tale for working in some alien involvement. Of course, the easiest, most obvious kind of story to write would be one where the off-worlders were themselves responsible for the urban legend: "Oh, the Loch Ness Monster was controlled by aliens all along!" (Actually, that does sound familiar…). No, I wanted my ETs involved, but not pulling the strings. This legend gave me the chance to make my aliens victims.

Throw in the idea of an invasion masking an invasion, and an homage to Marathon Man's "Is it safe?" scene and I had my story.

And not a stolen kidney in sight.

IT CAME FROM THE BACKSEAT
Eric R. Lowther

Mary sent up a prayer to her divine namesake and gripped the steering wheel as the gas station's lights came into view. The red light on the Buick's fuel gauge had stopped blinking and was now a steady, ominous glow staining half the dashboard. "Come on, baby, come on…" Mary breathed softly, performing it like a mantra until a bell chimed, the urgent plea for fuel punctuating the muttered encouragements.

Her husband, Bob, had used her car the night before and had neglected to fill it up, and in her usual morning haste Mary herself hadn't wanted to stop. This never happened when the call center where she worked had their offices downtown. This would be the third time since the company had moved to the business park outside town that she'd fueled her car with prayer, curses and sheer force of will to reach a gas station before being stranded on the dark, lonely stretch of road.

"Just get to the pumps and I'll fill you up with the good stuff," Mary said. The warning claxon sounded again, manifesting itself as a steady drone as the car started chugging and wheezing with perhaps a quarter-mile to go. Mary's cooing turned urgent as the engine let out a final sputter then died. She picked up her mantra at a feverish speed, the words tumbling faster as the car lost its momentum. She punched the button for her emergency flashers as the car's speed dropped from fifty to forty then prayed as it dropped from forty to thirty, prayed harder as it slowed to twenty with perhaps another fifty yards left to the station's entrance, then screamed in frustration as it rolled to a stop some twenty yards shy of her goal.

Mary slapped the steering wheel repeatedly, stopping only when her palms stung, then got out of the car. She left the driver's door open and braced her shoulder against the doorframe but the best she could manage was to rock the car on its tires. After a moment she threw her elbows onto the roof and dropped her face into her hands to muffle a string of obscenities. Just then a light, rhythmic slapping sound came to her. She looked to the station and saw a man jogging towards her.

"Need help, ma'am?" he asked as he neared. He was young, perhaps in his late twenties. She couldn't tell much more since he was backlit by the gas station's lights, but he'd have to be better at pushing than she was.

"Yes...yes, I do," Mary said as he slowed to a walk.

"Out of gas?" he asked.

"Uh, yeah," Mary said. Even her tongue-biting wasn't enough to remove all traces of the acerbic from her tone. The young man looked at her sheepishly and grinned.

"I'm Ted, and I ask stupid questions," he said.

Mary immediately felt like a heel. "I'm Mary. Nice to meet you, I only wish it were under better circumstances."

"We'd better get you off the road before a truck comes along," he said as he took up a position at the back of the car. "Hop in. Without power steering you're gonna have to use both arms to wrestle the thing. You ready?" Ted asked. Mary got in the car, closed the door and rolled down the window.

"Okay," Mary called out. After a moment the car started rolling slowly, picking up speed with every few feet. As they neared the drive Mary grabbed onto the wheel with both hands and started turning then watched Ted in the rearview mirror as she coasted to a stop in front of one of the pumps.

Now that she could see her Good Samaritan, she grimaced. He was indeed a young man, but one dressed in dirty, faded jeans and a stained T-shirt. His face hadn't seen a razor in days, the blondish stubble mixing with multiple facial piercings and a few swipes of grime. Everything about him except his benevolence rankled on her middle-aged sensibilities. She'd trained dozens of his kind as telemarketers and they'd rarely lasted more than a month. She took up her purse and climbed out just as Ted came around the car.

"You made it after all," Ted said. She returned his smile with a completely fake one and pulled a ten dollar bill from her wallet.

"Thank you so much. I don't know what I would've done without you," she said, holding the money out to him.

"I can't take that ma'am, really," Ted said with his hand in a stop gesture. "But I wouldn't say no to a ride. My car broke down a few miles back," Ted said.

"I didn't see any cars on the side of the road," Mary said.

"Oh, great! The bastards probably towed it. So, do you think you can give me a ride?" Ted asked. Mary put her free hand back into her purse and came out with another ten.

"I really can't, but take this. That should just about cover a cab," Mary said.

"Cabs don't come out this far," Ted said. He gave Mary his best and most pitiful eyes but she wasn't biting. After a moment Ted sighed and took the cash. "Thanks, Mary."

"Thank you, Ted," Mary said. They stood looking at each other until Ted realized Mary was waiting for him to walk away. Ted shook his head and chuckled low in his throat then walked towards the station.

"Shame that a nice young man like that doesn't show any pride in his appearance," a voice from the other side of the pump said. Mary peered around it to see a short, wizened old man pumping gas into his Cadillac. "In my day, when a service station actually gave you *service*, even the young men that pumped the gas had more pride in their appearance than that." Mary smiled at him and dipped her credit card into the pump's computer.

"I guess every generation has their rebellions," Mary said as she pulled the nozzle from the pump and shoved it into her car.

"I suppose you're right, but it's a sad state of affairs all the same," the old man said then turned back to his own fueling.

While the pump worked and the dollars ticked by, Mary daydreamed about what she would do to her husband once she got home. She was in the middle of beating him with a frying pan when she felt something cold pouring over her hand. She looked down to find gasoline rolling from the fuel door as the pump ignored its safety system, overflowing liquid gold over her hand, her car and down to the concrete below.

She let out a rough cry of disgust and jammed it back into the pump. "Shit!" The gas was evaporating rapidly from her skin, leaving behind its sickly-sweet, cloying odor. She cursed again then stomped across the lot towards the station's convenience store.

Much to her surprise the station's restroom was cleaner than the average public bathroom, though the cleanliness of the facilities had done little to stem her anger at her husband for running her out of fuel, at her job for moving so far from the city and at the pump for failing in its sacred duty to pump gas *into* the vehicle. She couldn't do much about the pump and could do even less about work. That meant Bob would suffer the full brunt of her anger. Mary pulled her cell phone from her purse as she got into the car, slamming the door behind her so hard that the whole vehicle seemed to shake. She patted the steering wheel apologetically then started the car.

Mary pressed Bob's speed dial and was rewarded with a series of high-pitched tones. She looked at the screen in time to see the words "low battery" before it issued a plaintive beep and went dark. Cursing softly, she dropped the phone onto the passenger seat then hit the button to roll up the window, dropped the car into gear and rammed her foot down. The car's traction control kicked in before she could express her anger with the squeal of burning rubber, but the high-pitched chirp from the tires suddenly grabbing the pavement felt good as the car rocketed out of the parking lot and onto the highway as a horn blared behind her.

Mary checked the rearview mirror to see a car so close that its headlights were lost behind her own trunk. Only when it fell back several yards did she realize she'd almost caused an accident. She held up her hand and waved in the wash of the following car's headlights, the universal symbol for *sorry, I was an ass, my fault* and hoped the driver could see the silhouette of her apology.

She had another fifteen miles of featureless, ill-lit road to follow; plenty of time to rehearse exactly what she would say to her husband. She was trying out one such tirade when the trailing vehicle's lights suddenly went from dim to bright and quickly drew closer. "Jesus! What the hell?" Mary said as she flipped the lever on the mirror to deflect the light towards the ceiling. She dropped her foot onto the accelerator out of instinct and the Buick responded instantly, the needle on the speedometer climbing rapidly from sixty-five to seventy-five. The headlights behind her fell back a bit and dropped to their dim setting as

Mary split her attention between the road ahead and behind.

"Okay fella, you had your little revenge, now knock it off," Mary said into the mirror. As if in response the car's lights clicked back to their bright setting and again drew close. Mary checked the mirror again and tightened her grip on the wheel. "I said I was sorry, asshole!" Mary screamed at the growing lights.

This time the car moved to within just a few feet and added several menacing horn blows. Again, Mary hit the accelerator and traded nervous glances ahead and behind as the Buick climbed past eighty. Her pursuer fell back though kept his lights on their bright setting, matching her speed. Mary was sweating now as she guided her car along the road, the break-neck speed and the tenacity of her pursuer rattling her. She thought of trying the phone again, to see if it had just enough power to eke out one last call to the highway patrol but she was afraid to take her eyes off the road. If he didn't drop back soon she would be forced to keep up this pace all the way into the city.

They drove this way for less than a minute before the other car pulled close again, lights beaming and horn blaring. Mary screamed in frustration, kept screaming as she floored the accelerator and the speedometer's needle buried itself past the one-hundred mile an hour mark. Her tail dropped back only a little but his horn kept blaring. Now the driver was flashing his lights, alternating from bright to low to completely off and then back again. Mary flicked a glance into the mirror to see ghosts of flashing red and blue lights coming from somewhere behind the trailing car.

"Oh thank God!" Mary said. She settled her eyes forward in time to see another pair of eyes near the edge of the road some fifty yards ahead and closing fast. "Just stay there, Mr. Deer…" Mary begged as she took her foot off the gas. Spooked by the approaching lights and her pursuer's blasting horn, the deer had other ideas. It vaulted onto the road then froze as if it were posing for the cover of a hunting magazine, the Buick's lights freezing it in place. Mary stomped hard on her brake pedal and braced for the impact.

The deer practically exploded before her, showering the front end of the Buick with its gore. The airbag blasted from the steering wheel, slamming Mary's face as hard as any prize fighter's fist ever could. Her nose immediately released a torrent of blood and pain across her face but she managed to keep her foot on the brake pedal. The Buick lurched to and fro then turned nearly broadside in the road and slid another twenty yards or so before finally coming to rest beneath one of the few pole-mounted lights to be had before the road reached closer to the city.

Mary sat for a moment with her head against the headrest, listening to the hiss and crackle of escaping coolant and watching flashes of red and blue light reflect off the plumes of steam bursting from her ruined car before turning her head to the right to look out the passenger window. The car that had been following her sat at an angle in the road about fifteen feet from her, beside a large black SUV with its emergency lights cleverly embedded into the dashboard so as not to be noticed by the casual observer. A tall, broad man dressed in a dark suit got out of the SUV and moved rapidly toward her car. Her smile faded when she saw what could only be a pistol in his hands.

Mary fumbled at her seat belt and after several attempts released the catch. Suddenly, the car door jerked open. A dirty hand reached across her, grabbed her right arm and violently twisted her from the car. Mary screamed and struggled as she fell to her knees but the hand wouldn't release her. "Mary! Get up! Get away from the car!" Ted said. Mary screamed when she realized who her attacker was and renewed her struggles.

"No! Get away from me! Help!" Mary screamed.

"Mary, you're in danger! Get away from the car!" Ted said.

"No!" Mary repeated. Summoning all her strength, she stood and pushed Ted's chest with her free hand. His grip broke and he stumbled back a few feet as Mary's body fell back against her car. "Get the hell away from me!" Mary screamed. Ted took a step toward her then stopped. His eyes were wide and he spread his hands in a non-threatening gesture.

"Mary... you don't understand. You have to get away from the car *now*," Ted said. He extended a hand but his eyes were no longer on her, rather they were focused at a point to her immediate right into her open car door. "Mary, you have to get away from the car," Ted said again.

Shaking with fear, pain and adrenaline, Mary risked a quick glance where Ted's eyes led her. Something green and alive like an octopus's tentacle was coming out of the car. It hung there for a moment as long strands of thick, opaque liquid slid from it to sizzle against the highway, the blacktop melting under it as if it were butter. A second then a third tentacle joined the first and the trio slowly wriggled along the top of the door frame towards her.

Mary opened her mouth to scream but her voice was cut off as Ted lunged for her, grabbed her blouse in both hands and threw her towards the rear of the car. One of the tentacles shot out, its tip just brushing against the side of her neck as she half-flew, half-stumbled along the length of the Buick. Pain like she'd never experienced it, a mixture of burning and electrical jolts, ran through her body. She hit the ground again just past the trunk and rolled a few feet. Ted was standing over her a breath later, dragging her towards the black SUV.

"Simon! Light him up," Ted said. Mary's vision was blurry but she looked up to see the other man nod and advance on her car. Ted propped Mary against the front of the SUV and stood beside her, supporting her so she wouldn't fall.

"Karrack," Simon said, addressing the thing in the ruined Buick, "you've got a choice... you can surrender or I can fry you." Several more tentacles were visible now, wrapping themselves around the door frame and tensing like steel cables under a load. The driver's seat ripped free of its mount with a steel-on-steel shriek and exploded out the open door to allow the creature's bulk to move from the back seat and through the driver's door. Mary tried to scream, but the pain of the creature's touch had rendered her nearly mute and only a pained whimper escaped her throat.

The thing Simon called "Karrack" had a tall, humanoid-shaped body. Fine scales covered its entire green-black and impossibly-muscled body. Long, black talons capped each of its fingers and toes. It flexed them warningly at Simon who paid them no mind. Simon's attention, as well as Mary's and Ted's, was on the thing's head. It looked as if someone had mounted a large squid on the creature's otherwise humanoid neck. A mass of tentacles of varying lengths writhed and wriggled from the thick, fleshy folds around its mouth, hanging down around its shoulders and chest as if they had minds of their own. It regarded Simon for a moment before the tentacles spread out and to the sides to reveal a large maw lined with dozens of glinting, shark-like teeth.

"Don't do it..." Simon warned as he leveled his weapon. The creature hissed at Simon, took a threatening step forward and leaned towards him. A glob of the caustic fluid spewed out from its terrible mouth but Simon was ready for it, ducking and leaning to his left, the viscous fluid shooting over his right shoulder as Simon fired his weapon. Mary had expected a booming report but instead heard the hiss of compressed air and the soft sound of glass breaking against the door of her car.

"What the… hell is going on?" Mary asked Ted in a harsh croak. She clung to him with one hand to keep from falling over and had her other pressed against her burning neck. "What is that thing?" she asked. Ted gently moved her hand from his arm to the hood of the SUV.

"Wait here. If something goes wrong, get in the truck and drive to the gas station. Other agents will track you there and help you," Ted said as he moved around her to the passenger side of the SUV, returning a moment later with a wicked-looking pump shotgun. "Simon! Back off! He's not gonna go quiet!" Ted racked the slide.

Simon dropped into a crouch that allowed him a more steady aim for another shot but before he could touch off another round the beast aped Simon's posture and dropped to the ground itself. But it hadn't crouched so much as *shrank*, its heft and bulk physically turning in on itself, making itself shorter yet much longer.

"He's morphing!" Simon said. The creature no longer resembled anything humanoid and was now more like a massive snake, an impossibly long boa constrictor with green-black scales and thin, probing tentacles protruding from the length of its serpentine form. The street light mounted high above them had provided more than sufficient light for Simon and Ted to acquire their target. With its metamorphosis complete, the serpent had slid quickly and soundlessly under the Buick just in time to avoid the shot from Simon's weapon. The liquid-filled, impact-injected vial smashed against the asphalt just inches from the retreating snake, spilling its amber liquid payload uselessly on the highway. "I've only got one round left!" Simon said.

"Save it for a clear shot," Ted said as he stepped towards the Buick and brought the shotgun around. The two stood stock-still, waiting for the snake to appear from beneath the car. Mary pushed herself away from the SUV's grill though left a hand on its hood. Her neck was hurting less now but her legs still felt soft and rubbery.

"What the hell is going on?" Mary's voice had regained some of its strength as well, at least enough for her to generate a demanding tone to the two men.

"Get in the truck..." Ted started to say. The sudden, wispy sound of scales grinding against the asphalt cut off his words and a flash of movement beneath the Buick's muffler caught his eye. He dropped his right foot back to brace himself and fired the shotgun at the ground beneath the muffler. Mary cried out at the sudden, thunderous sound and fell back against the support of the SUV's front end as the tightly-patterned buckshot carved a chunk out of the asphalt beneath the Buick's back end. Ted and Simon thought the blast had completely missed the thing, but only for a fraction of a second. The Buick trembled, squeaking as it rocked on its springs for several seconds before first the front end and then the back rose several feet off the ground in turn.

"Fall back," Ted called as he chambered another round then followed his own advice. Simon scuttled back a few feet as the Buick suddenly lurched skyward, rolled over in mid air and came down with a jarring crash onto its roof. Simon and Ted both threw up a hand to ward off the exploding chunks of safety glass from their eyes, missing the sight that Mary alone was left to witness.

The snake that was Karrack slithered onto the car's exposed undercarriage, his serpent's form bubbling and pulsing. By the time the tip of his tail was off the road, a beautiful and buxom woman stood on her overturned car. Her scarlet hair picked up every trace of the light, making it seem like it was living flame and further contrasting against her pale grey flesh. She opened her eyes to reveal white orbs with black centers and no pupils to speak of. She smiled, her impossibly white teeth gleaming in her grey face conveying nothing but horror to Mary.

Simon and Ted looked up at Karrack's new and terrible visage in unison as Karrack spread his horrible, taloned and perfectly-sculpted hands wide then leaned forward. Great wings like those of a bat sprouted from his shoulders in an explosion of poisonous blood.

"Where the hell did he get that one from? What is it, a succubus? He can't do that. That's not even a real creature," Simon said. Ted stared hard at Karrack. The alien's powers of transformation were far beyond what he and Simon had ever thought possible.

"Close, Simon," Karrack said. The voice was sweet and perfectly pitched though lacked any suggestion of warmth. "But you can do better than that."

"Karrack... look, drop the demon act and we can all go home, okay?" Ted said. He wanted to raise the shotgun, but Karrack's voice in this form seemed unnaturally soothing as if it sapped the will to fight from him.

"Demon? That would be so pedestrian, wouldn't it?" Karrack said.

"Banshee?" Mary's voice asked from behind them. Karrack smiled at the completion of their ghoulish round of charades then opened his form's perfectly shaped mouth. A guttural yet incredibly high-pitched keening became the only sound the assembled humans could hear. Mary dropped to the ground, covered her ears with her hands and leaned against the truck's still-warm grill. She was screaming at the assault on her nerves and ears, but even her voice was lost in the din of the creature's cry.

Simon tried to call out over the shrieking thing then shoved the gas-charged pistol under his arm and fumbled a pair of earplugs into his ears as he ran towards Ted. He could feel the intensity of the creature's wailing as a palpable sonic wave as he neared, the shotgun making Ted Karrack's target of choice.

Ted had dropped to his knees at almost the same time as Mary, the sonic wave powerful enough to tousle his hair as if it were a strong breeze. Simon winced, as much at the onslaught of sound seeping around his earplugs as in seeing the rivulets of blood that ran from between the fingers of Ted's left hand as it tried to protect his ear. Simon held out the plugs but instead of taking them Ted used his bloody hand to point to the Buick.

Simon spun just as the Karrack banshee leaped into the air. Simon grabbed Ted, stood and then tried to drag him to his feet. Karrack's ululating screech stopped as instantly as it'd started, the sudden absence of sound nearly as deafening as the cry itself had been. The banshee fell upon them from several feet up, striking the two humans and dropping them to the ground.

His body shifted and changed as he stood glaring down at them, changing from deadly, beautiful woman to the squid-faced abomination as they tried to regain their senses on the cold pavement at his feet. Ted's shotgun blast had opened a ragged, fist-sized wound on Karrack's serpent form that equated to the upper right side of the alien's humanoid chest but he ignored the pain. The adrenaline contained in even one of them would be more than enough to heal his wounds.

Karrack was on them before either could fumble their weapons into play. He kicked each of them where they lay, delighting for a moment in their muffled cries of pain when the talons on his toes speared their skin before retrieving Simon's air pistol from where it'd fallen. He held it over Simon and crushed it to shards of plastic and aluminum, his tentacles grouping into a grotesque, cartoon-character smile around his horrible mouth as the shards of the weapon rained down on Simon's head.

The pistol was by far the less-lethal of the humans' weapons, but the chemical compound contained in the projectile would've not only caused the alien great pain but would've also weakened him enough to be unable to change his shape. The scrape of metal on asphalt turned Karrack's head towards Ted. Ted was still on the ground but his fingers had found the shotgun where it lay a few feet away and was dragging the weapon towards him. Karrack spit another glob and Ted jerked his hand back in time to avoid the worst of it. The shotgun's receiver took the brunt of the attack though, and within seconds was reduced to a blob of useless metal. Ted turned towards Mary.

"Get in the truck! Get out of here!" Ted said. Mary looked at him uncomprehendingly and was galvanized into motion only when Karrack turned his tentacle-moustache towards her. She kept her back to the SUV's nose and slid along it without taking her eyes off the alien.

Karrack wrapped a taloned hand around each of their necks, holding the men there in the road on their knees. "You are pathetic excuses for warriors," Karrack said. Blinding light suddenly burst into being on the road ahead, causing alien and humans alike to squint as the SUV's engine roared to life. But instead of backing away from the scene Mary rocketed forward, the screech of rubber rivaling Karrack's earlier sonic barrage. Mary gripped the wheel in both hands and leaned back in the driver's seat as the SUV chewed up the few dozen feet between it and the monster.

Karrack released Ted and Simon out of violent reflex, the suddenness of the act throwing them from the path of the careening truck. He bent at the knees and tried to leap, hoping to land on the vehicle's hood, but disoriented by the sudden light he'd misjudged both the vehicle's speed and nearness. Karrack's feet were less than a foot off the ground when the two-tons of rolling steel collided with him, the truck's high profile and tall tires ensuring that what little vertical distance he gained wouldn't save his torso from taking the brunt of the assault.

The SUV's decorative plastic grill shattered and the hood crumpled like paper as the vehicle impacted with the thickly-muscled alien, but behind that plastic façade and sheet-metal hood was nothing less than solid Detroit steel. Mary's scream took up where Karrack's howl left off. The alien was firmly embedded in the SUV's front-end now, his clawed fingers digging deep furrows in the hood as it struggled to pull itself onto it.

Panic kept Mary's foot on the accelerator. She'd expected to run the creature down, not to turn him into a hood ornament. She lifted her eyes from the writhing mass of tentacles in time to see her battered Buick looming ahead. Karrack didn't have time to scream as Mary rammed the truck into her car, trapping Karrack between the two, but Mary was doing enough of that for the both of them. The second airbag of the evening blasted into Mary's face. She was still screaming when Ted came to the driver's door and pulled it open.

"Mary? Are you okay?" Ted asked. Mary slowly turned her bloody face from the steering wheel, swallowed several gulps of air but didn't try to raise her head.

"I... am... *not*... okay!" Her voice was thick and nasally as it echoed through what could only be a broken nose.

"Ted...we've got company," Simon said as he trotted past them, straightening his dark suit and tie as he went. "I'll handle the locals. There's another dart gun under the seat," he called over his shoulder. Ted could see the pulsing, colored lights coming down the highway; a single patrol car. He and Mary hadn't passed a car coming in either direction in their mad dash down the highway. Like as not, it was only a state trooper making an accidental discovery of them while out for his evening rounds.

"The police... I need to talk to them... need to file a report," Mary said. Her voice was almost as hollow as Karrack's had been.

"Mary, you're in shock. You need to stay here and get your head together," Ted said. He managed to get one of his hands away from her and reached down beneath her seat for the back-up air pistol. "Can you do that for me, Mary? Can you stay right here and wait for me? You're safe now, he can't hurt you. You did a really brave thing and now it's our turn, okay?"

Mary looked at him for a moment longer then let her eyes close, "I just want to go home."

"And you will, real soon," Ted promised. He closed the door and moved around the front of the truck. He took a moment to examine the tangle of steel, blood, plastic, bone and aluminum that had once been two separate vehicles and a very nasty extraterrestrial being. Now it was difficult to tell where any one of them began or ended. To Ted's surprise, Karrack lifted his head. One of his eyes was swollen shut and the other had green blood the viscosity of puss oozing from under the lower lid.

"You were... lucky, *human*," Karrack said with a special disgust on the last word and bringing more green blood to his lips. His tentacles lay spread across the hood, twitching. His blood, like the milky stuff seeping from his tentacles, was pitting and burning through the SUV's black lacquer paint job wherever it fell.

"One of us had to be," Ted said. He cocked his head at his crushed adversary and smiled. "Though I have to admit, the banshee was a nice touch. Want to tell me how you pulled it off? You know you want to, you arrogant prick."

Inside the SUV, Mary lifted her head and watched Ted and the creature. She couldn't hear what they said through the SUV's thick body and the rushing of blood in her ears. Ted was right; she was in shock. There was a logical explanation for all this. She leaned her elbows on the wheel and brought a hand up to her neck to cradle the burn the beast's tentacle had given her. The only thing she knew was that none of this would've happened if Bob hadn't run her car out of gas. She seized on the thought, focused on it. He was *so* going to pay for this. Outside, Ted slowly raised his weapon and trained it on the alien.

"Just so you know... when they lay you to rest on this planet the ceremony is full of beautiful flowers, soft music... all very quiet; very, very quiet. Nobody is going to sing your songs... nobody is going to recount your battles. And you know what happens after that? They don't burn you so your spirit goes on to The War. They *bury* you in a *box*," Ted said.

Karrack's eyes narrowed until it seemed he was able to see the dart waiting for him at the bottom of the pistol's barrel. He opened his mouth but only managed to release a river of caustic blood down his chest. Ted fired the weapon, the soft hiss of air sending the dart the few feet from the barrel.

Mary let out a cry of surprise as the dart seemed to bloom from

Karrack's neck, the scene all the more eerie for its silence, but what happened next took her voice away. The alien's body started to pulse and shift like it had done before. But this time when the transformation was finished instead of an impossibly huge snake or some other, unimaginable abomination, it was something vaguely familiar; the old man from the gas station.

She gagged at what she could see of his wrecked body and at the now-red blood that seeped and oozed from his nose, mouth, even his ears. The old man stared at her for a long moment before his head finally slumped onto the hood.

Ted took a deep breath then exhaled with his whole body, shaking out his arms and shoulders before he came back and opened Mary's door, leaned his arms against the roof and looked back towards the rear of the SUV. Simon had flagged the trooper down a good twenty yards from them, far enough to keep the cop from seeing much and hearing even less. Dealing with the locals was Simon's forte, and Ted was glad to let him handle it. If he knew Simon, he was showing the cop his National Security Agency identification and was calling the scene a terrorist investigation. Ted poked his head into the SUV and gave Mary a soft smile.

"I know it's been a really strange night, and I know you have a lot of questions that I either can't or won't answer," Ted said. Mary stared at him, dumbfounded. When she finally did open her mouth to speak, Ted stopped her with a look. "You can tell them whatever story you want. You can even tell them the truth; how a seven-foot-tall alien with green skin and tentacles attacked you, how you had to run it down and then it turned into a naked, little old man. Best case, they assume you have a concussion and are delirious. Worst case, they think you've went around the bend and you end up under psychiatric observation."

"But I..." Mary said. Ted hit her with the look again and she fell silent.

"Simon and I are government agents. We were tracking the alien using the cover story that the guy he looks like now was a big-time arms dealer trafficking to terrorists. We'd tracked him to the gas station but he'd spotted us and hid out in your car when you went inside. Of course, you wouldn't know any of that. Your part of the story picks up where I was chasing you, trying to get you to stop. I followed you in his car, the one he abandoned, and kept trying to flag you down to get you to stop. That's partly true, at least. He would've had you within a mile of the station except that every time he poked his head up I could see his silhouette and hit my lights and horn so you'd look up and he'd have to duck down. By then you were going too fast for him to attack you without risking killing himself in a crash," Ted said.

"Is that how it happened?" Mary asked with as much sarcasm in her tone as she could muster.

"If you're smart, yeah, that's how it happened. You're really pretty lucky though, you know?" Ted said. Mary looked down the hood and chuckled.

"*Lucky*? Just how the hell do you figure that?" Mary asked. Her tone was dead-pan now, the events of the evening having sapped what energy and emotion she'd had.

"They want our adrenaline. Human adrenaline feels like cocaine, heroin, your first kiss and your greatest and best orgasm all rolled into one to them, not to mention the fact that it heals their wounds and allows them a greater ability to shape-shift and for longer periods. The old man he was masquerading as was named Harold Chalmers. This one, Karrack..." Ted said with a sideways nod to the alien, "He's done this same thing three times before. After he killed Harold and took his identity, he went to Harold's home, invited all of his children and grandchildren for a big dinner. Then he killed every one of them; eighteen men, women and children, a couple of infants. He was so full of adrenaline we didn't know how we were going to bring him down. But he slipped up with killing off the whole of the Chalmers clan and we were able to track him when he ran in Harold's form. If he would've killed you, he would've assumed your form, went to your home and would've done the same to your family that he did to the Chalmers."

Sirens were sounding in the distance, their wailing coming closer with each second. Mary had thought up a surprisingly high number of near-medieval punishments for her husband's thoughtlessness, but none of them had involved being brutally murdered by a homicidal alien drunk on adrenalin, though she was afraid if she dwelled on it too long the thought may become appealing after the events of the evening.

"I can't believe that... it's insane..." Mary said.

"Weren't you just here a few minutes ago? Does that acid burn on your neck feel like it was all a dream?" Ted asked. His expression softened a bit just then. "I wanted to tell you the *real* story, so you wouldn't think you were going crazy; that it wasn't real. Again, what you tell them is up to you, but I'd go with the comparatively tame version of the story if I were you."

"Are there more like… like *it*?" Mary asked. Ted sighed again and his face seemed to become drawn and somehow older in the space of her question.

"Yeah, yeah there are. I don't think too many, but yeah, I think there are more of them. But as long as we have people like you around, I don't think they'll get too far," Ted said with a wink. An ambulance arrived followed only seconds later by two more patrol cars. Ted watched the paramedics approach the truck with a wheeled gurney between them. "It's probably best that you not talk to anyone tonight regardless of the story you're going to tell. After Simon and I deal with the mess, we'll come around the hospital and talk some more, okay?"

Mary nodded at him wearily then he stepped back to allow the paramedics' access.

"Holy shit!" one of them said under his breath at the sight of the dead man between the two vehicles. "Barry! We need a meat wagon out here! It's an ugly one!" the paramedic said into his shoulder-mounted radio.

"Belay that," Ted told him. "There's a special wagon coming for him. You just worry about your patient and I'll worry about the little old dead man, okay?" The paramedic caught the hard look in Ted's eyes, shrugged and helped his partner situate Mary on the gurney. "You boys take good care of her," Ted said as they wheeled Mary towards the waiting ambulance. She managed to crane her head for a last look at Ted and he gave her a smile and wave.

Simon was surrounded by several state troopers, his cell phone still at his ear. After a moment he handed the phone to one of the troopers, the captain if his clean white shirt was any indication, and Ted knew his and Simon's boss was telling the patrol captain exactly who was in charge here. Ted turned and went back to Karrack's borrowed form and pushed his head to the side. It lolled back like the dead meat it was, exposing the corpse's neck.

"Sorry, Simon, but you got the last one, and he's just got too much of the good stuff to waste. And you know how much I hate waste," Ted said.

His cheeks puffed out slowly, the skin and muscle beneath shifting their shape and form. "You just couldn't stick with the plan, could you, Karrack? You never did have any patience."

Ted visibly shivered as his tentacles grew out of his face then latched onto Karrack's cooling flesh, their tips making sucking sounds as they drew the adrenaline from the corpse. "Thank you, brother," Ted said. His smile was ringed by more small, flesh-colored tentacles sprouting from around his lips. "I only hope this will give me the strength to help your mate through her grieving…"

Eric R. Lowther

AFTERWORD

I chose the urban legend of the "Killer in the Backseat," that tried-and-true campfire tale, because it speaks to our collective fear of being attacked somewhere we feel we should be completely safe; our cars. We do things in them we would do in our own homes, though we give little consideration to the fact that so many others can see us. When we come home at night we rarely go through the place, checking every closet and room for danger before settling in to rule our castles, and we tend to apply this same level of inferred privacy to our cars.

After a long day, our first place of refuge is usually our cars. We get in and settle back in our seats, tune the radio to our favorite station or our iPods to our favorite playlist and start our own little decompression rituals. We don't think that danger could be lurking for us in our personal safe haven because we don't *want* to believe something would violate the sanctity of that haven. You never know what could lurk among the petrified French fries, discarded water bottles, overdue library books and forgotten movie rentals. When was the last time you checked *your* backseat before you got in your own personal Fortress of Solitude? Well, perhaps it's time you start…

BIOGRAPHIES

ALMA ALEXANDER is a fantasy novelist who writes for both adults (*The Secrets of Jin Shei, The Hidden Queen, Changer of Days*) and for YA audiences (the *Worldweavers* trilogy, *Gift of the Unmage, Spellspam, Cybermage*). Her work has been translated into 14 languages worldwide, including Turkish, Hebrew, Lithuanian and Catalan. She lives in the Pacific Northwest with her husband, two cats, and assorted visiting wildlife. Visit her online at www.AlmaAlexander.com, or drop in on her blog at anghara.livejournal.com.

RICHARD LEE BYERS is the author of over thirty fantasy and horror novels, including several set in the Forgotten Realms universe. His recent titles include *Dissolution, The Rage, The Rite, The Ruin, Unclean, Undead, Unholy*, and *The Captive Flame*. His short fiction has appeared in numerous magazines and anthologies.

Born and raised in Columbus, Ohio, Richard holds an M.A. in Psychology. He worked in an inpatient psychiatric facility for a number of years, then left the mental health field to become a writer. He currently lives in the Tampa Bay area, the setting for much of his horror fiction, and spends his free time fencing, shooting pool, and playing poker.

Visit him online at richardleebyers.com

The eldest child of an existentialist librarian and a teacher/child-care specialist, NATHAN CROWDER had always tended towards the literary. Lurid ghost stories and big books chock full of pictures from classic horror movies captured his imagination early on, and nothing was ever quite the same again. Inspired by Edgar Allan Poe, he wanted to be a writer from as far back as the age of 10. This career dream was later replaced by chef, paleontologist, teacher, and any number of things, but he was drawn back to writing again and again.

Due largely to his love of movies, his first serious writing was screenplays, of which he's written five over the past several years. He has also written eight novels, including the super-hero tales *Chanson Noir* and *Cobalt City Blues*. His short fiction has appeared in such places as Thuglit.com, *Byzarium, Crossed Genres, Absent Willow Review*, and WilyWriters.com, and his story *"None Left Behind"* won the Hauntings competition at the prestigious Hugo House in 2007.

Nathan currently lives in the Bohemian wilds of north Seattle, where micro-brew beer flows like water and everyone wears ironic t-shirts and goatees—even the women. Nathan lives alone with his cat, Shiva, who is currently managing his career in exchange for fresh kibble.

IVAN EWERT is an author, artist, layout designer, podcaster and full-time layabout. He lives with his lovely southern wife in a tiny slice of northern Illinois which is bursting with stories about devil-worshipping dairy farmers, cornerless Tindalosian houses, possessed locker rooms, suburban mountain lions, hitchhiking murder spirits and the unwary ghosts of children trapped forever in subterranean ice houses.

Despite this embarrassment of local riches, he remains more attracted to learning new legends that frightened children from further afield—especially those Southern gothic delights that routinely terrified his in-laws. When not otherwise engaged, he knocks about at ivanewert.com on a slightly less than regular basis and is a more regular (monthly) contributor to the online magazine, *The Edge of Propinquity*. Ivan's work has previously appeared in the magazine *Alimentum: the Literature of Food,* online at *The Suicide Tourist,* and most recently in *Grants Pass:* a post-apocalyptic anthology from Morrigan Books.

ROBERT FARNSWORTH was born and raised on the southern coast of Connecticut and now lives in sunny Central Florida with his wife and three cats. For his day job, he works for a major software company, where he travels around teaching IT professionals how to use his company's software. Bob started writing when friends in the Role Playing Gamers Association (RPGA) talked him into trying his hand at writing role playing events for the Gen Con gaming convention. Discovering that writing could be fun, he was hooked on telling stories and never looked back. Since then, Bob has written over thirty role playing adventures for a wide assortment of game systems. His role playing adventures have employed undead creatures, giant robots, evil wizards, dragons, gunslingers, Japanese Samurai, fairy creatures, lycanthropes, and most recently witch hunters in colonial America. Tired of being limited by other people's rules, Bob has decided to switch over to writing fiction where he can make up the rules as he goes along.

In his spare time, Bob enjoys reading and collecting science fiction and fantasy books, role playing, traveling (for fun) and practicing Anasura Yoga to relieve stress and to keep fit.

A relative newcomer to the world of published fiction, CAROLE JOHNSTONE was first featured in *Black Static Magazine* in early 2008. Since then she has sold numerous short stories to magazines and anthologies in both the US and the UK, including PS Publishing, *Black Static*, Eneit Press and Morrigan Books. Her first novella, *Frenzy*, was published by Eternal Press in August 2009. Originally from Lanarkshire, Scotland, Carole now lives in north Essex with her fiancé, Iain. They are in the process of looking for a cat. Preferably a cantankerous one. Her website can be found at www.carolejohnstone.com

ROSEMARY JONES has written two novels for Wizards of the Coast: *City of the Dead* and *Crypt of the Moaning Diamond*. Her short fiction has appeared in the anthologies *Hitting the Skids in Pixeltown*, *Realms of Dragons II*, and *Realms of the Dead*, among others. When not meeting her fellow Seattle authors for coffee, she collects books and listens to her favorite baseball teams lose enough games to keep them out of the World Series. More about her writing can be found at www.rosemaryjones.com.

PETE KEMPSHALL has had endless trouble finding people to mind his kids since that time he unthinkingly phoned home with a sore throat and asked the sitter if she could check on the children. Most of his day is spent working for magazines, but despite the lack of dependable childcare to free up his time, he still manages to squeeze in some fiction writing. To date he has penned several short stories for Morrigan Books, plus a novella and a number of shorts for Big Finish's Doctor Who and Bernice Summerfield ranges. He is also the co-editor of the Australian short fiction anthology *Scenes from the Second Storey*, available late 2010. Pete lives in Perth, Western Australia and tries to keep people up to date with his writing at tyrannyoftheblankpage.blogspot.com.

Perth-based writer MARTIN LIVINGS has had over fifty short stories published in a variety of magazines and anthologies. His short works have been listed in the Recommended Reading list in *Year's Best Fantasy and Horror*, and had stories in *The Year's Best Australian SF & Fantasy*,

Volume Two and the 2006 and 2008 editions of *Australian Dark Fantasy & Horror*.

His first novel, *Carnies*, was published in Australia by Hachette Livre in 2006, and was nominated for both the Aurealis and Ditmar awards. It's currently available for purchase through Martin's website www.martinlivings.com

ERIC R. LOWTHER is an author living in northeastern Ohio. He is hoping that either this writing thing takes off or the zombie apocalypse occurs so that his life's knowledge won't be wasted. He also believes that everyone has a story to tell and so encourages you to get off your arse and tell it. His previous work can be found in the magazines *Blood Blade & Thruster #3*, *Night to Dawn #13*, *Necrotic Tissue #3* (2008) and *#9* (2009) and coming soon to *All Hallows* (late 2009). He also appears in the anthologies *Dark Distortions I*, *Magazine of the Dead*, *Theaker's Quartely #19* (2007) & *#26* (2008), *A Collection of Unknown Horrors*, and the *Bump in the Night* anthology from Drollerie Press. He has also appeared as a Guest Author for the *Edge of Propinquity* fiction website (archived, December 2008) and will be coming soon to the *Red Blood, Black Sky* anthology from Another Sky Press (2009).

RAMSEY LUNDOCK graduated as Valedictorian from North Marion High School in 1997. His first article "Marybelle for Arrivers," appeared in *Polyhedron Magazine* in 1999, published by the gone but not forgotten TSR. In college he was involved in the Role Playing Gamer's Association, eventually becoming the Campaign Director for Living Verge. He studied abroad for one year at Kansai Gaikokugo Diagaku (Kansai Foreign Language University) in Osaka, Japan. This would turn out to be one of the pivotal events in his life.

He graduated from the University of Florida in 2002, with degrees in Physics and Japanese, and went to work on his parents' longhorn cattle and thoroughbred horse farm. On June 7th 2003, he had the incomparable thrill of watching their horse Supervisor run in the Belmont Stakes. During the Fall of 2004 he had a different kind of adventure as 3 hurricanes struck central Florida. He worked on the farm and wrote freelance, but he could not forget about Japan, and the need to return burned in his blood. He found his way back to Japan by spending a year as a graduate student in physics at the University of Florida, then transferring to the Astronomical Institute at Tohoku University. In 2008 he successfully defended his Master's thesis in Japanese. His first scientific paper appeared in Astronomy & Astrophysics in 2009. He is currently pursuing his PhD at Tohoku University.

JONATHAN MCKINNEY lives in Winchester, Kentucky with his wife Charla and their three children. He enjoys PC gaming, reading, and playing Hold'em. "Shiny Eyes" is Jonathan's first published fiction story. He currently writes articles and reviews for Examiner.com and has become serious about writing since he received *The Writer's Market* from his wife on his birthday.

SHANNON PAGE was born on Halloween night and spent her early years on a commune in northern California's backwoods. A childhood without television gave her a great love of books and the worlds she found in them. She wrote her first book, an adventure story starring her cat, at the age of seven. Sadly, that work is currently out of print, but her short fiction can be found in *Clarkesworld*, *Fantasy*, and *Interzone* (with Jay Lake), *Black Static*, and a handful of independent press anthologies; a nonfiction article will appear soon on Tor.com. Shannon is a longtime practitioner of Ashtanga yoga, has no tattoos, and lives deep in the San Francisco fog with eighteen orchids and an awful lot of books.

JOSHUA PALMATIER is a fantasy writer with a doctorate in Mathematics. Born in north-central Pennsylvania, he currently lives in Binghamton, NY, working as a professor of Mathematics at SUNY—College at Oneonta. His *Throne of Amenkor* trilogy, comprising *The Skewed Throne*, *The Cracked Throne*, and *The Vacant Throne*, is now complete and available from DAW Books wherever fine books are sold. The most common word used to describe his books is "gritty." He is hard at work on the start of two additional series. You can find out more about Joshua Palmatier at his website www.joshuapalmatier.com, or follow him on Facebook or LiveJournal (jpsorrow). He has not yet succumbed to Twitter.

JENNIFER PELLAND lives outside Boston with an Andy, three cats, and an impractical amount of books. Her collection *Unwelcome Bodies* was released by Apex in 2008, and includes her Nebula-nominated story, *Captive Girl*. She's also a novice belly dancer, an occasional radio theater voice artist, and, of course, a wage slave. To see her full list of publications, go to www.jenniferpelland.com.

A Californian expatriate, ERIK SCOTT DE BIE is a twenty-something speculative fiction writer currently living and writing in Seattle, Washington, along with his wife Shelley and three irrepressible cats: Apollo, Athena, and Artemis. His hobbies include reading, RPGs, fencing, rock music and, of course, herding three irrepressible cats around the house. When possible, he avoids alien abduction but always leaves out milk and cookies.

To date, he has published three sword and sorcery novels—*Ghostwalker*, *Depths of Madness*, and *Downshadow*—and a number of short stories and RPG design material. Catch up with him at eriksdb.livejournal.com, on Myspace, or on Facebook.

RICK SILVA grew up in Boston, Massachusetts, attended Cornell University, and currently teaches chemistry at a high school on Cape Cod. Rick has been involved in writing and small press publishing since his college days. Along with his wife, Gynn, Rick is a partner in Dandelion Studios, a small press comic book company. Rick co-writes the Dandelion Studios comics *Zephyr & Reginald: Minions for Hire*, *Stone, Kaeli & Rebecca*, and *Perils of Picorna*. He publishes his own zine, *Caravan*, and he is one of the featured contributors for the fiction webzine *The Edge of Propinquity*. He is a frequent attendee at gaming, SF, anime, and comic conventions in the northeast, and he still manages to find time to host the occasional D&D game at home. Rick and his wife recently traveled to China to complete the adoption of their son, who is now adjusting to his role as apprentice geek in his new home on Cape Cod.

JEFF SOESBE lives in Northern California, where he writes software by day and stories by night. His stories have sold to *Weird Tales*, *DayBreak Magazine*, *Flash Fiction Online*, and *Byzarium*. He is a graduate of the Viable Paradise Writing Workshop.

BEV VINCENT's most recent book, *The Stephen King Illustrated Companion*, won the London Book Festival award for non-fiction and was nominated for a 2010 Edgar Award. His first book, *The Road to the Dark Tower*, was nominated for a Bram Stoker Award. He is a contributing editor with Cemetery Dance magazine and has published over fifty short stories. His book reviews can be found at Onyx Reviews and he writes a monthly rumination on writing for *Storytellers Unplugged*. He lives in Texas and avoids looking in mirrors, although he has long suspected that if he could somehow make himself invisible and stand between two parallel mirrors he could see infinity. His web site is www.bevvincent.com.

EDDY WEBB (with a "y", thank you) is a game designer, writer, and developer working for CCP North America/White Wolf Publishing. He has been writing and designing games for money since 2002, but he's been doing it on his own time for over 25 years. Other people seem to like his work, as he has won an award and been nominated for a bunch more. He lives a sitcom life in Atlanta, Georgia with his wife, roommate, a cat, and a pug dog that thinks he's a cat. He has also have been known to swear. Sometimes, he swears a lot. You can find some of his fiction (and his swearing) at his personal blog on LiveJournal—eddyfate.livejournal.com.

COVER ARTIST

ALINA PETE was born and raised in Saskatoon, Saskatchewan, and is a proud member of Little Pine First Nation, a Cree Indian reservation in central Saskatchewan. She is the author and artist for two online webcomics, *Weregeek* and *Moosehead Stew*. She has published two collections of her comics and does freelance illustration on the side.

Over the years, Alina has lived in Alberta, Fiji, Arizona and China. She has applied her talents as a web designer, costume artist, art gallery director, graphic artist, and digital effects artist on various projects. Her talents can be viewed in such projects as *Wapos Bay* (a Gemini-Award-winning children's animated show for Canadian television), and online at www.weregeek.com.

EDITOR

JENNIFER BROZEK is a freelance author for many RPG companies including Margaret Weis Productions, Rogue Games and Catalyst Game Labs. Her contributions to RPG sourcebooks include *Dragonlance*, *Colonial Gothic*, *Shadowrun*, *Serenity* and *White Wolf SAS*. Author of *In a Gilded Light* (Dark Quest Books, 6/2010), she is published in several anthologies, is the creator and editor of the semi-prozine, *The Edge of Propinquity*, and is a submissions editor for the Apex Book Company. When she is not writing her heart out, she is gallivanting around the Pacific Northwest in its wonderfully mercurial weather. Jennifer is a member of Broad Universe, SFWA and HWA. Learn more about her, her projects and her publications at jennifer-brozek.livejournal.com.

Evil lives in the hills of Kentucky, as black as coal and buried just as deep

"A delightful romp through the back-woods of hillbilly horror."
—Scott Nicholson, author of *Scattered Ashes*

In the black heart of coal country, malevolent spirits and unearthly creatures slip from the shadows into the minds and hearts of men. Young women, twisted by pain, call for love and revenge by the light of the moon. A dead dog by the side of the road is more than it seems. In Harlan County, Kentucky, the supernatural and the mundane mingle in the depths of the earth, filling the mines with powerful forces that draw people down and corrupt from within.

HARLAN COUNTY HORRORS

Available at ApexBookCompany.com or fine stores everywhere

So much of our reality is determined by what we believe, and it can so easily become…undone.

Featuring:
Jay Lake
Catherynne M. Valente
Brian Keene
Tom Piccirilli
Ekaterina Sedia
Gary A. Braunbeck
Wrath James White
Jennifer Pelland
Lavie Tidhar
Alethea Kontis
Linda D. Addison
Nick Mamatas
Mary Robinette Kowal
Lucy A. Snyder
and many others...

The destructiveness of passion, both earthly and supernatural, makes cities bleed and souls burn across worlds, through endless time. Experience the spiritual side of the zombie apocalypse in "The Days of Flaming Motorcycles" and transcend both hell and nirvana in "Zen and the Art of Gordon Dratch's Damnation." Look into "The Mad Eyes of the Heron King" to find the beautiful brutality written in the moment of epiphany or "Go and Tell it On the Mountain," where Jesus Christ awaits your last plea to enter heaven—if there is a heaven to enter when all is said and done.

Horror's top authors and promising newcomers whisper tales that creep through the mists at night to rattle your soul. Step beyond salvation and damnation with thirty stories and poems that reveal the darkness beneath belief. Place your faith in that darkness; it's always there, just beyond the light.

DARK FAITH

Available at ApexBookCompany.com or fine stores everywhere

"THESE VOICES DESERVE TO BE HEARD."
– FREDERIK POHL

THE APEX BOOK OF WORLD SF
EDITED BY LAVIE TIDHAR

"THESE VOICES DESERVE TO BE HEARD" – FREDERIK POHL

FEATURING WORLD FANTASY AWARD WINNERS
S.P. SOMTOW & ZORAN ŽIVKOVIĆ
AND STORIES BY: MELANIE FAZI • JAMIL NASIR • ALIETTE DE BODARD
JETSE DE VRIES • ANIL MENON • KAARON WARREN AND OTHERS

Among the spirits, technology, and deep recesses of the human mind, stories abound. Kites sail to the stars, technology transcends physics, and wheels cry out in the night. Memories come and go like fading echoes and a train carries its passengers through more than simple space and time. Dark and bright, beautiful and haunting, the stories herein represent speculative fiction from a sampling of the finest authors from around the world.

"This literary window into the international world of imaginative fiction, the first in a new series, is sure to appeal to adventurous sf fans and readers of fiction in translation."
– *Library Journal*, August 2009

"The great thing about Tidhar's collection is that it is full of such masterpieces."
– 42SciFi-Fantasy.com

AVAILABLE AT YOUR LOCAL BOOKSTORE OR FAVORITE ONLINE SHOPS.
FOR MORE INFORMATION OR TO ORDER DIRECT VISIT APEXBOOKCOMPANY.COM

LaVergne, TN USA
29 March 2010

177455LV00002B/3/P